MODERN HUMANITIES RESEARCH ASSOCIATION
NEW TRANSLATIONS
VOLUME 3
General Editor
ALISON FINCH

Germanic Editor
RITCHIE ROBERTSON

Wilhelm Raabe

GERMAN MOONLIGHT

HÖXTER AND CORVEY

AT THE SIGN OF THE WILD MAN

Translated by
Alison E. Martin, Erich Lehmann and
Michael Ritterson

Edited by Florian Krobb

Wilhelm Raabe

GERMAN MOONLIGHT

HÖXTER AND CORVEY

AT THE SIGN OF THE WILD MAN

Translated by
Alison E. Martin, Erich Lehmann and
Michael Ritterson

Edited by Florian Krobb

MODERN HUMANITIES RESEARCH ASSOCIATION
2012

Published by

The Modern Humanities Research Association,
1 Carlton House Terrace
London SW1Y 5AF

First published 2012

ISBN 978-1-907322-54-9

Copies may be ordered from www.translations.mhra.org.uk

The cover shows two ink drawings by Wilhelm Raabe: 'Landscape with Rocks' (dated 2 November 1873) and 'Scene with Soldiers and a Monk' (dated 13 April 1874). Cf. the catalogue of Raabe's graphic œuvre: Wilhelm Raabe, *Das zeichnerische Werk*, ed. by Gabriele Henkel (Hildesheim: Olms, 2010), p. 200 (no 104) and p. 335 (no 501).

Reproduced by kind permission of the Städtisches Museum Braunschweig; Depositar Referat Wissenschaft und Stadtarchiv.

CONTENTS

Introduction

I

Wilhelm Raabe is one of the main representatives of a movement in German literary history conventionally designated as Realism. Their activity broadly lasted for the second half of the nineteenth century. The qualifiers that the label 'Realism' has received help to define the character of this period in German literature that sits between the eras of Classicism, Romanticism and politically engaged writing in the run-up to the revolution of 1848–49 on the one hand, and the onset of radical modernism in the last decade of the nineteenth century on the other. The label 'Bürgerlicher Realismus' [Bourgeois or Middle-Class Realism] highlights the social situatedness as well as the scope and thematics of this literary current, namely its aim to deal with concerns, preoccupations, self-imaginings, social interaction, politics and morals of the group that became the dominant cultural, economic and political force during the period in question. The label 'Poetischer Realismus' [Poetic Realism] captures the authors' intent to achieve their aims with aesthetic means that, while portraying a recognizably real world inhabited by familiar characters with plausible stories, still elevated their readers beyond the trivial and mundane. The various authors associated with the movement developed different models of achieving their realist goals – some adopted the paradigm of the educational novel, dominant since Goethe's *Wilhelm Meister* novels (1795/96 and 1821), to show a protagonist's journey towards fruitful integration into, and assimilation of the values of, their middle-class community; some set their stories in the world of industry and commerce to paint pictures of perseverance and productivity; some turned to historical subject matter with a view to strengthening their readers' sense of fitting into a historical continuum that bestows identity on the individual and the community he or she is part of; some chose to portray smaller communities and village life as a microcosm of society as a whole; some tuned into the conversations, distractions and idiosyncrasies of metropolitan society in a Berlin that was on the verge of rapid expansion. While their predecessors had expressed their ideas in drama and poetry as well as prose, narrative fiction now became the genre of choice to capture the realities and satisfy the expectations of the readership that this literature was intended for and consumed by.

Wilhelm Raabe's works show traits of all of the above trends. Some of his narratives contain elements of the developmental novel; there are pieces set in all strata of Berlin society; about a third of his works are historical texts; a majority of both his historical and contemporary works describe provincial, small-town or rural communities. He avoids, though, large or panoramic designs, most of his narratives concentrate on groups of only a few people instead, who are often thrown together by unusual circumstances. One of the aspects that make Raabe unique in the chorus of German Bourgeois Realism is a convoluted, deliberately dense style that constantly gives out confusing, even misleading signals. More often than not human catastrophes lie hidden under a façade of normality, respectability and ordinariness, and the narrators' signals allow readers to uncover the true stories and their meaning only when they pick up on certain clues and search below the surface. Raabe's narrative technique often profoundly undermines the principles of coherence, linearity and suspense, and increasingly withholds any sense of narrative authority as voices contradict each other until doubt is cast over the veracity of any number of versions of the same events. His texts are also distinguished by a liberal use of allusions to generate meaning, by direct or concealed quotations, snippets of public discourse derived from the media or simply from a conversation overheard on the street or at the inn. These features may make his narratives seem somewhat awkward in the eyes of an audience looking for easily digestible reading matter. They account for the fact that, one or two best- and long-sellers aside mainly from his more conventional earlier production, Raabe's work did not enjoy much commercial success during his lifetime; they also explain why only few of his major intriguing works have been translated into English. For a number of decades now, however, critics have come to appreciate Raabe's idiosyncrasies; they have highlighted the author's perceptive and clear-sighted engagement with the society he inhabited, and they have understood some of the features that prevented greater popular acclaim during his lifetime as precisely those traits of his art that capture a modern condition of insecurity, bewilderment and lack of simple orientation. Raabe's experiments with narrative form and technique have earned him a reputation for being one of the outstanding representatives of his time, though not in an obvious, manifest sense.

Raabe's unique and distinctive voice emerged in the mid- to late 1860s, a decade that he spent in Stuttgart in southwestern Germany, at the time one of the leading cultural centres in German lands. The three narratives assembled in the present volume all stem from the period shortly after his relocation to Braunschweig, the capital of the duchy of the same name, a medium-sized cultural backwater at the time, but the centre of his native region. He had returned there on the eve of the outbreak of the Franco-Prussian War in July 1870. Even though this move was probably motivated by private reasons, maybe even the realization that he did not fit as well as he had hoped into the industrious yet cosy atmosphere of the sunny and fertile southwest, there is poignant symbolism in this return to Braunschweig. There, for the rest of his life, he occupied a slightly remote vantage point that allowed him to observe the wider world even more intensely. The backwater of familiarity, ordinariness and belonging sharpened his senses to detect the exemplary in the insignificant, it honed his ability to capture the essence of human behaviour in poignant detail, and it whetted his appetite to confront his contemporaries with uncomfortable truths about themselves and their pettiness.

While all three narratives assembled here were written in the early to mid-1870s and clearly address issues very much of this period immediately after German unification, they still afford a representative insight into Raabe's production by encompassing a psychologically intriguing miniature, a historical narrative from one of Germany's most troubled times located off the flashpoints of history yet at an unlikely crossroads of world affairs, and the travesty of a genre piece from contemporary Germany that links the remotest corner of Raabe's native region to global developments and dispels all assumptions that private idylls could provide sanctuary in troubled times. None of the texts are in any way uplifting; on the contrary – they offer quite disturbing glimpses of human nature and the state of the world.

Wilhelm Raabe was born on 8 September 1831 in Eschershausen, near Holzminden on the River Weser, in the western ward of the Duchy of Braunschweig where his father worked as an actuary in the district administration. Soon after Wilhelm's birth, the father was seconded to the magistrate court in Holzminden itself where Wilhelm Raabe began his schooling. In 1842 the family moved again, this time to nearby Stadtoldendorf. When the father died three years later, at the age of only forty-four, his widow moved to Wolfenbüttel with her three children where an assembly of relations could offer some support for the family bereft of its bread-winner. Raabe attended the local municipal grammar school where two of his uncles worked as teachers, and it amounted to something of a disaster that he failed to achieve his school-leaving certificate (*Abitur*) and had to start adult life without the qualification that would have set him up for a career in the civil service – as would have been expected of the offspring of one of the duchy's clans of public servants. For the next four years Raabe learned the book-trade in nearby Magdeburg, and the almost limitless supply of all kind of reading matter during this phase might explain the vast but rather random and unsystematic literary knowledge evident in his own writings. After another spell in Wolfenbüttel where he probably made a second (unsuccessful) attempt at the *Abitur*, he moved to Berlin in 1854 to attend, as an occasional student, lectures in Philosophy, History, Literature and Geography at the University. Towards the end of this time, after four semesters of more unsystematic education, yet attending lectures by some of the intellectual heavyweights of the time, his first novel, *Die Chronik der Sperlingsgasse* [The Chronicle of Sparrow Alley] was completed, and it appeared in 1856 to considerable critical acclaim, even though it became a commercial success only much later. He returned to Wolfenbüttel and continued to write and publish: after the encouraging reception of his first novel, he was now determined to pursue a career as a professional author.

During this phase (in 1859, to be precise) he embarked on the only longer journey of his life, a kind of middle-class version of the grand tour, a trip that took him to Leipzig, Dresden, Prague and Vienna, and back via Munich and down the Rhine. The aim was not only to visit the main urban centres of German-speaking Europe and introduce himself to authors, publishers and editors of periodicals that might, in the future, print his works, but also to sample the great works of European art and see the remnants of European culture in Italy. However, his aim to continue his journey across the Alps was prevented by the Austro-Italian War. Around that time he also joined the Deutscher Nationalverein and attended its national congresses in Coburg (1860) and Heidelberg (1861). The primary aim of this newly-founded political party was to promote German unification in a truly constitutional and liberal state and to end the fragmentation into thirty-nine independent kingdoms, duchies, principalities and free cities that was blamed for the stagnation and much of the democratic deficit that had marred German history throughout the nineteenth century so far. The act of joining this association and contributing actively to its goals attests to Raabe's political consciousness – and explains some of the disillusionment apparent in his works after the goal of unification was achieved, but the spirit of national revival was lost quite quickly.

In 1862, Raabe married Berta Leiste, member of one of Braunschweig's leading legal families, and soon set up house in Stuttgart in the south-west German duchy of Württemberg. Stuttgart at that time was one of the major cultural centres in the German Federation, home to several publishing houses, periodicals, social and political circles and leading intellectual figures; and it was distinguished by a generally open and liberal atmosphere. Here, in a decade of breathtaking productivity,

Raabe's most pronounced literary development occurred. While the works at the beginning of this period still rely on rather conventional literary techniques to appeal to an audience that wanted to be entertained, moved and uplifted, his offerings from the latter half of the 1860s onward demonstrate the unique and unconventional idiom that distinguishes his entire later production. On the eve of the Franco-Prussian War that sealed the process of German unification which had gathered momentum since the Dano-German conflict of 1864, in the midst of the mobilization of German troops, Raabe moved his family (two daughters had been born during the Stuttgart period, two more daughters were born in the early Braunschweig years) back to the capital city of his native duchy, at the time a medium-sized provincial backwater of a place. Here he remained until his death on 15 November 1910.

Raabe's œuvre comprises over sixty narrative texts, ranging in size from a few dozen pages (like *German Moonlight*) to several hundred. Many of his mature works from the Braunschweig period are of a medium length (some 200 pages when originally published in the nineteenth century; in modern type-face normally just under one hundred pages in length) and defy genre designation. They are too short and concentrated to qualify as novels, yet they are too meandering and lacking in distinctive compositorial clarity to be classified as novellas. Raabe stopped writing in 1898; only one narrative was begun in the last twelve years of his life but never completed. In some of his later narratives like *Im alten Eisen* (Any Old Iron, 1887) and *Die Akten des Vogelsangs* (The Birdsong Papers, 1896) the story is partly or completely set in Berlin; in the main, though, Raabe took his inspiration from and set his plots in his own home region, namely the duchy of Braunschweig that was nestled between the kingdom of Hanover in the north, the kingdom of Prussia in the east and various Thuringian, Hessian and Westphalian lands to the south and west, and stretched like a narrow band from the River Weser to the Harz Mountains. While *German Moonlight* is unique in that it is set on an island in the North Sea, the other two narratives of this volume are located in exactly this inconspicuous region in the geographical heart of northern Germany, yet strangely removed from the metropolises where history was made and modern culture flourished. Raabe's writing seems to confirm the common conviction that, compared to contemporary Russian, French and British literature, German writing of the second half of the nineteenth century is distinctly provincial and epitomized by a marked lack of concern for seminal tendencies like industrialization, urbanization, the emergence of a metropolitan culture with all its distractions and deviations, and the globalizing trends of the age. And while it is true that his literary creations lack the air of the wide world, of fashion and urbanity, that they lack the social differentiation and pulsation of crowds, it is not true to say that they lack relevance for his age or, indeed, for posterity. He simply finds this relevance in quieter, remoter places and in rather unspectacular events.

Raabe's withdrawal into Germany at its most provincial amounted to an immersion into Germany at its most typical, at its barest, most unadulterated and most inconspicuous – that is where he found his stories of a universal, and that means a deeply human and humane interest. The position of detachment from the excitement and excitedness of metropolitan culture, for him, was the most conducive vantage point for the writer as observer; non-involvement in the seminal developments of his age facilitated the recording of them in disguised, distorted and condensed form. Raabe's writings, particularly the masterpieces of his Braunschweig period, are keenly topical, albeit not in an obvious way; they deal with the world and the most pertinent and pressing topics of the age, yet in a provincial, quaint guise. With thoroughly ironic intent he called a representative collection of his narratives from the 1870s *Krähenfelder Geschichten* (3 vols, 1879) [Stories from the Crows' Field]. This relates to an unremarkable suburb of Braunschweig, a congenial environment for a writer whose own name also derives from that of a species of black bird (and who had used the Latin for raven, Corvinus, as a pseudonym for his first few publications). Two of the three narratives assembled in this volume were contained in that raven's collection of stories from the crows' field.

II

More often than not, Wilhelm Raabe created audible narrator figures, narrators who refuse to hide behind their objects and characters, narrators who refer to themselves in the first person (mostly plural) and who interact with their readers. These narrators introduce themselves as guides to the events, in the case of *At the Sign of The Wild Man* quite literally, in that this story's narrator takes his readers by the hand and leads them verbally out of the storm and into the shelter of the pharmacy that provides the title for the narrative (*Zum wilden Mann*). These narrators also have a distinctive voice. The first-person narrator in *German Moonlight*, himself a participant in the story, uses the detached, slightly formal, always polite register that his profession as a magistrate has trained him to employ; the narrative voice of the historical novella *Höxter and Corvey* is characterized by the stylistic flavour of the early-modern period in which the story is set, a language strewn with Latin and French expressions, redundant forms of place names, an occasionally cumbersome syntax with long-winded sentences and flowery epithets, and other mannerisms. The narrator of *At the Sign of The Wild Man* creates an intimacy commensurate with the cosiness of the pharmacy's parlour where old friends meet to celebrate an anniversary. But in all three instances, this first impression of the narrating voice is deceptive: the façade of formality in *German Moonlight* conceals a realization that the encounter relayed holds a disturbing mirror to the first-person narrator; the antiquated and clumsy historicizing style of *Höxter and Corvey* suggests that the events chronicled are far removed from contemporary concerns and told purely out of antiquarian interest – an impression that is cunningly misleading; and the comforting and quaint mood that the narrator of *At the Sign of The Wild Man* employs lulls his readers into a false sense of security that is completely shattered during the course of the story.

The narrators' mode of telling their stories may be unreliable and deceptive; the content of their narration is not. All of them manage to create the illusion that what they have to relate has really happened. In *Höxter and Corvey* the language of the sources that Raabe used to provide factual accuracy and historical flavour, is clearly audible in the fictitious narrative, thus creating a sense of authenticity. In *At the Sign of The Wild Man* the intimacy creates a closeness between the narrative voice, the characters and the readers who also escaped the storm to tell each other, and hear, of certain events from the past. In *German Moonlight* the narrator is presented as participant, even catalyst of the action and himself functions as an authenticator of an internal narrative that is ostensibly told to him. All three texts are thus different and intriguing from a narratological point of view. In the context of nineteenth-century German literature, with its tendency to employ unobtrusive, hardly noticeable narrators who discretely exert their authority so that an impression of completeness and persuasiveness ensues, Raabe's technique of obvious narration appears as somewhat experimental, unorthodox and deliberately challenging. Raabe moves the question of narration per se centre-stage; by drawing attention to the fact that all representation is mediated, he questions the illusion of reality created in fiction and the claim to veracity implicit in conventional authorial narration. He does so not only through the visibility of the narrators of his stories as a whole; he also uses further narrators inside all of the pieces to a greater or lesser degree who all send out signals that may indeed differ from the stance of the overall narrative voice and, in the case of *At the Sign of The Wild Man*, even contradict the latter. Consequently, through the multiplicity of voices, the readers are called upon to decipher for themselves much of the meaning of the information on and evaluation of events provided by the various parties – if it can be deciphered at all. In *German Moonlight*, the protagonist of the internal story, narrated by an acquaintance of the text's first person narrator, appears like an alternative incarnation of the original narrator; the latter's differing experience of an essentially similar career and position in life sheds a sceptical light on the self-assuredness of the former – raising the question of whether the detached and ostensibly objective voice the reader hears is nothing but a mask. In *Höxter and Corvey* there is a tendency to make light of sinister goings-on; but jokiness turns on itself when a whim deteriorates into sinister action. In *At the Sign of The Wild Man* the overbearing narrative voice of the opening soon disappears behind the voices of the narrators of the internal stories with their conflicting perspectives on essentially the same events, refusing to provide orientation when it is needed most.

Conflicting versions and contradictory signals from unreliable narrative voices create tensions and fluidity of meaning; they also convey profound epistemological doubts about appearances, preconceptions and assumptions. These techniques challenge readers, they demand their participation and engagement; they refuse to rely on an affective reaction to the characters or on the suction of excitement exerted by suspenseful events. In *Höxter and Corvey* the narrative technique is characterized not so much by perspectivization and multivalence, but by the breathlessness with which the narration leaps from location to location in the closest proximity and in the shortest period of time, creating an almost filmic quality of simultaneity. Threads are intertwined, events proceed in different strands and erupt when these converge – a formal reflection of a muddled world that has confused its inhabitants' sense of propriety and morality; but also an expression of the realization that linear, chronological narration falls short of capturing the complexities of the reality it claims to represent.

In all three texts, the plot is compressed into a very brief time span. In *German Moonlight* the action as such consists of a short night-time stroll on a northern German holiday island during which the narrator's companion explains the predicament in which the former has found him. The action of *Höxter and Corvey* stretches over no more than twenty-four hours of conflict and strife between the 1st and 2nd of December 1673. The first two thirds of *At the Sign of The Wild Man* are devoted to one evening of story-telling and reminiscing in the apothecary shop; the final third expands over a number of weeks, but very little actually happens even then, only that clandestine clues about the meaning of it all are placed in a multitude of conversations between various major and minor characters, and almost imperceptibly the atmosphere turns from jovial and warmhearted to chillingly desperate. In all three narratives, place is also quite restricted: The action of *German Moonlight* covers a short walk across the dunes on the North Sea island; the historical novella is set in the narrow city walls of the municipality of Höxter with only a short glance at the monastery of Corvey a few miles away; the apothecary's shop forms the focus of the last of the three narratives, only occasionally other localities in the remote Harz community come into view, but these places are not described in any detail.

However, all three narratives manage to widen their spatial and historical scope decisively by way of allusions and internal narratives rendered by one or several of the characters involved. *German Moonlight* references the events of 1848/49 as the starting point of the condition that the narrator's acquaintance complains of; *Höxter and Corvey* recalls names and events from the days of the Romans' unsuccessful incursions into the Germanic lands east of the Rhine which brought them as far as the Weser and eventually led them to suffer a decisive defeat close to the remote parts of Germany where the story is set. Other events, mostly from recent history, i.e. from the time of the Thirty Years War (1618–1648) and its aftermath, are constantly alluded to by several of the story's characters and by the narrator. In *At the Sign of The Wild Man*, a pre-history is unravelled that, according to a letter written during that period, took place in the 1830s, while the events themselves are set thirty-one years later, in the 1860s. When, at the outset, the narrator mentions Germany's political development since the Congress of Vienna in 1815 down to the proclamation of the German Empire in January 1871, he extends the time frame explicitly to the time of writing. The most important extension of the spatial perspective in this story, though, is represented by one of its central characters, in fact one could call him the antagonist, who is introduced as a returnee from Brazil.

In all three works the milestones of Germany's history that culminated in 1871 are referenced in a deliberate and manifest way, anchoring all three of them, even the one set two hundred years earlier, in contemporary German history. All three stories signal that one of their prominent themes is Germany past and present, and even if the story is set in the past, the historical experience is narrated for the benefit of the present and claims relevance for the contemporary situation. The reference point in all three stories, the big caesura that motivates the look back to the immediate past or to a time long ago that could, however, offer a mirror to the present, is the establishment of the German Empire. Contrary to the prevalent *Zeitgeist* in the 1870s, though, Raabe does not praise the establishment of a united empire as some kind of destiny fulfilled, he does not join in the jubilant chorus that set the tone in the new empire. Instead, his three stories cast a critical eye over the new social and political realities, he sounds a note of caution vis-à-vis the exuberance and hubris that accompanied this historical achievement. Not all promises were fulfilled, Raabe maintains, not all wounds healed and obstacles overcome, and there are signs that his fellow Germans use the new-found unity to obscure sinister, egotistical and divisive traits. These realizations determine much of the tone of the three selected texts, and it is not least the tangible disillusionment and the subtle contrariness to prevalent currents that give these stories their appeal.

III

The short narrative *Deutscher Mondschein* [*German Moonlight*] was written between 24 March and 8 April 1872 in response to a publisher's request for a contribution to complement three other narratives destined for publication in one volume. The idea for this particular story was conceived in October 1864 upon Raabe's return from a summer vacation to places on the Baltic and North Seas. In August 1867 he then spent several weeks on the German North Sea island of Sylt, the location where the narrative was eventually to be set. *Deutscher Mondschein* first appeared in the magazine *Über Land und Meer*, vol. 29, no 7 (1873); later it was integrated into a collection of four narratives under the title *Deutscher Mondschein* (Stuttgart: Hallberger, 1875), and eventually it was included in vol. 2 of Raabe's *Gesammelte Erzählungen* (three editions, Berlin: Janke, 1896, 1901, 1907).

The premise of the story is simple. While on a stroll through the dunes of the North Sea island of Sylt, a nameless first-person narrator comes across a man who is obviously in distress and rushes to his assistance. This other man tells the former aspects of his life's story in a bid to explain the strange condition he found him in. The two men involved, the narrator and his strange holiday acquaintance, Löhnefinke, show uncanny similarities: both are of a similar (middle) age, both have wives and families, both work in their respective German states' legal systems in positions of authority: Löhnefinke is identified as a Prussian *Kreisrichter* [magistrate]; the narrator seems to occupy a comparable position in a neighbouring jurisdiction, perhaps Raabe's own duchy of Braunschweig. In fact, on recognizing the other man as a fellow professional in the legal system, and recalling that they had corresponded about a certain case in the past, the narrator pays tribute to his new acquaintance's professionalism. In their professional environment as the highest legal authority of a district, as householders and family men, both characters fulfil roles as pillars of their communities. They also epitomize the spirit of their age: they are members of the academically trained professional middle classes, engaged in maintaining law, order and stability, beacons of respectability, exemplars of the very fabric that they themselves believed held German society together. Significantly, the case that is cited as having crossed both their desks, concerning a vagrant, illustrates that part of their job is to shield society against outsiders. Raabe obviously had a case in mind that crossed inner-German borders as they existed in Germany before 1871, and the case also suggests that, in spite of different rulers, different names and different laws, the inhabitants of all the German states shared a desire for stability, for a well-organized, functioning community. The two protagonists are the type of person who had campaigned for German unification and to whose acclaim German unification was brought about by Bismarck. They are representative of German society and of Germany's consensus about its political destiny. Pertinently, Raabe lets Löhnefinke exclaim on his political convictions: 'I naturally voted with the majority' (p. 13)

But while the first-person narrator's life is apparently untroubled by any unusual afflictions, his acquaintance and fellow professional Löhnefinke suffers from the condition of 'lunacy' in the literal sense: the moon forces him, he protests, to become driven and irrational, a condition that manifests itself in sleeplessness, restlessness and the writing of poetry. While the description of this ailment clearly serves satirical purposes, the striking resemblance between the two holiday acquaintances suggests a more profound reading of the configuration: The story seems to be about different sides to the same personality – with an uncanny, uncontrollable, erratic, pathological side externalized and projected onto the *Doppelgänger*. The exaltation is indeed framed as a psychological condition; somnambulism and sleepwalking can, in the vernacular, be described as 'mondsüchtig' [Lat. lunaticus, literally 'addicted to the moon']. The condition was known since the eighteenth century as 'Mondsucht' [lunaticus morbus]. In the story, the unlikely manifestation of this condition, the compulsive composition of poetry, might seem harmless enough; the symptom of restlessness during moonlit nights does not seem to be uncommon or particularly worrying. Löhnefinke's predicament only becomes a 'deviation' in so far as societal norms are concerned, as internalized expectations and his perceived inability to fulfil them force him to lead a life of duplicity – conformist in the eyes of the outside world, successful according to normal middle-class standards as exemplified by the narrator, yet driven, torn and tormented by the poetic urges during moonlit nights. Clearly, the moonlight is a metaphor for uncontrollable forces, drives, urges and predispositions at work in any human (hence attributed to the moon's power), for an irrational side in every personality. Poetry, then, is a metaphor for any form of expression, any release of this dark side of human nature.

The condition of deficiency and fanciful desire is, in this story, projected onto the course of German history during the period designated in the references to the protagonist's youth, to writers and historical events that influenced his life. Significantly, the first symptoms of the condition are said to have shown in 1848, in the context of the bourgeois revolution against German disunity and bondage. Thereby Raabe exposes 'lunacy' as a quintessentially German condition, a condition of constant illusion, of unrealistic aspiration, inflated desire and fanciful dreaming. Written just after the establishment of the German Empire in 1871, and set immediately before it, Raabe's story offers a pathology of the German designs on statehood and unity as driven by an unachievable desire to reconcile the poetic and the prosaic dimensions of their collective (and individual) psyches. Löhnefinke's references to his ancestors, all of them civil servants, and their prosaic outlooks on life, points to a severe deficit of 'poetic' inclination as an endemic condition amongst the middle classes that considered themselves to be the backbone of the emergent nation. In Löhnefinke and others of his generation of 1848 who were enchanted by high hopes and idealism for a united and democratic Germany, the dormant idealistic side erupts now because of the accumulated and unreleased surplus of emotion and sentimentality, and turns into the opposite, but equally pathological extreme. Writing from the vantage point of hindsight, Raabe seems to warn against an over-investment of hope and idealism in the unification; he seems to warn against an irrationality of expectations projected onto the unified empire. He diagnoses the Germans as split internally (not politically along party or regional lines, but psychologically) into the straight and the enchanted types, and thus suggests that the nation is not at ease with itself until the tensions are resolved between the two extreme symptoms of the same collective identity that condition and enhance each other.

The text is highly satirical and remains ambivalent throughout. In spite of the politico-historical subtexts discussed above, it can still be read as a case study in lunacy and the dilettantish cures against somnambulism prescribed by contemporary medicine. It derives a considerable satirical edge from the apparent discrepancy between Löhnefinke's civic status and his being reduced to a nervous wreck by a bit of moonlight. The conclusion of the story focuses on the narrator; his act of committing his encounter to paper could be, and has been, read as a form of therapy; and the gesture of giving to his son (who as a student of mathematics might be seen as destined for an uninspired, unromantic, unenchanted life) the works of one Jean Paul Friedrich Richter (1763–1825), a romantic writer of meandering narratives, could signal his resolve to introduce his own offspring to the uncanny complementary 'Other'. Since Jean Paul was less of a rapturous, idealistic Romantic than a keen and often satirical observer of the idiosyncrasies of human nature, this very conclusion could also imply the attempt to arm his progeny against the temptations of getting lost in fantasy, of surrendering to the irrational side of nationalism. The evocation of Jean Paul at the very end is not only a tribute to one of Raabe's favourite authors, but also a definition of the role of literature in a modern society not to fan the flames of enthusiasm and intoxication, but to hold a mirror to society, to expose its foolishness and self-deception in a bid to increase self-awareness and perspective. The evocation of Jean Paul stands in contrast to the earlier reference to Heinrich Clauren (1771–1854), a prolific writer of sentimental, romantic fiction. In Raabe's story, Clauren is assigned to the female sphere and acknowledged as reading matter to suit the female imagination; thus a clear demarcation between the sphere of the private (marked as female) and the public (marked as male) is drawn which in Löhnefinke has become blurred. Interestingly, another German writer of the Romantic period, Wilhelm Hauff (1802–1827), published a satire of Clauren in 1826 that he entitled *Der Mann im Mond* (the image of the man in the moon, in German, denoting something like the product of an excited imagination).

Löhnefinke's condition is thus somewhat belittled and ridiculed. In particular, the manifestation of his condition, writing poetry, cannot be taken seriously as casting doubt over the whole edifice of bourgeois stability and respectability. And yet, Löhnefinke's condition is the German condition, and an inclination towards the irrational and unrealistic of an entire nation might be considered more severely than a personal idiosyncrasy. Löhnefinke makes manifest the German tension between an unremarkable, well-functioning, efficient workaday incarnation and an enchanted undercurrent that erupts when uncontained. But over and above defining and satirizing the German condition as one of unresolved tension between enthusiastic enchantment and boring yet reassuring mediocrity, *German Moonlight* defines the modern individual as subject to the same contradictions. The fact that Raabe describes the two different dimensions of German identity and of every individual as manifestations of essentially the same source betrays a keenly modern, psychological sense of the personal constitution of the individual, it demonstrates how close together normality and aberration live, and how fragile the surface of respectability and stability actually is. By conveying the insight that a constant dissatisfaction and almost pathological condition is typical of a modern existence between prosaic necessities and suppressed desires, an existence of permanent non-fulfilment, the text can be seen as a precursor to literary modernism which addressed similar issues. As social satire on German collective mentalities, however, the text firmly remains within the confines of nineteenth-century Bourgeois Realism.

IV

Plans for *Höxter and Corvey*, as Raabe's diaries confirm, date from late October 1872 to January 1874; the execution lasted until the middle of April 1874. The narrative was serialized in the April and May 1875 issues of *Westermann's Illustrirte Deutsche Monatshefte*. Raabe then included the piece in his collection of shorter stories *Krähenfelder Geschichten*, vol. 1 (Braunschweig: Westermann, 1879) and later in the third volume of his *Gesammelte Erzählungen*. The story is loosely based on a conflict between the municipality of Höxter and its new ruler, the prince-bishop of Münster Christoph Bernhard von Galen, in 1670–1674, a conflict known as the 'Bierkrieg' [Beer War]. Grievances between the (traditionally Protestant) town and the absolutist prince-bishop who was embarking, with counter-reformatory zeal, on the re-catholization of this newly-won strategic city, erupted in a dispute over brewing rights and proceeds. Höxter invoked the assistance of their traditional ally, the Protestant duke of Braunschweig, while Bernhard von Galen received military support from the troops of the French king Louis XIV who was, at the time, engaged in a war against the Netherlands in which the ruler of Münster served as an ally. Louis XIV's so-called Dutch War, of which the events in Höxter chronicled in Raabe's narrative are but an insignificant side-show, are themselves an echo of the great Thirty Years War (1618–1648) which had devastated German lands down to the remotest corner. The fact that, in Höxter, confessional quarrels are at the core of the *Bierkrieg*, with Protestants defending their inherited rights against the centralizing measures and strict enforcement of authority that formed part of Galen's absolutist reign, designates the local case as a reflection of larger conflicts fought along confessional lines. The suffering that the foreign and domestic armies traversing the land during the Thirty Years War had inflicted on the population are constantly evoked by the older characters in the story; the history of perpetual conflict and the physical exhaustion and moral confusion this generated form the background to the mood of suspicion and confusion described in the story. The former masters of the abbey of Corvey, the Benedictine monks, whose decision in 1661 to elect Christoph Bernhard von Galen their prince-abbot had brought the municipality under his rule in the first place, are charged with enforcing the authority of the prince after the withdrawal of the French troops. Formerly the centre of a tiny, yet independent German principality in its own right, the monastery now seems little more than a retirement home for old warriors who are just as exhausted from decades of warfare as their subjects in the nearby city. These political relationships are clearly foregrounded as a mirror of, and an explanation for, the confusion of minds that led to a violent eruption during the night described in the narrative.

Raabe learned of these events from a contemporary publication, Heinrich Kampschulte's *Chronik der Stadt Höxter* (Höxter 1871), which also allowed him to quote from pamphlets and treatises published by all sides in the conflict. He does so liberally, using names and titles for his characters as he found them in his source, and borrowing snippets from the polemics of the time for their dialogue. However, in one important respect he veered from the historical case – he makes the conflict about the Jewish levy instead of beer-brewing privileges. The right to raise special taxes from the Jewish population as a condition for permitting their residence inside the city walls was a source of income and a test case of local autonomy. Furthermore, Raabe invents a trigger that sets off the action: an old Jewish woman brings back from a funeral a bundle which the townspeople believe to contain a rich inheritance and which thus incites their greed and leads to the eruption of pent-up frustration. This allows the author to provide his readers with an insight into the psychological genesis of anti-Semitism, a groundless mass hysteria with catastrophic consequences that unites the warring parties within the community, Protestants and Catholics, against the most vulnerable minority in their midst. The fact that the ensuing pogrom must be understood as the rather pathetic insurgency of a community that felt helpless and exploited to the point of exhaustion does not serve as an exculpation; it does, however, direct the readers' attention to the deeper roots of violence against powerless victims.

Deep division at every level, utter bewilderment as to their destiny, powerlessness and suffering – this is the state of the locals in the small municipality of Höxter. The causes for this picture are identified clearly; references to atrocities committed by German war lords and by their foreign allies from Sweden, France and elsewhere during the Thirty Years War and beyond puncture the narrative; these atrocities are part of collective experiences and individual memories of all characters in the story regardless of their religion and political affiliation. The fact that the person charged with maintaining law and order in the community feels the effect of a humiliation that consisted in the stealing of his drum is not inserted to belittle this very experience, but to draw attention to the realization that trauma is relative, that all dents to one's pride have lasting effects; trauma and the various possible reactions to humiliation are perpetuated through the generations and might surface after a long interlude. This very period of German history, the climactic end of one and a half centuries of confessional division, was marred by internal strife that set neighbour against neighbour, ruler against subject and communities against each other.

A story about the detrimental effects of territorial fragmentation in Germany must have had enormous resonance in the early 1870s. The mention of the French occupiers would have recalled experiences of helplessness against Napoleon's might at the very beginning of the century. Hence, the narrative could have served as a reminder of the disunity that had been overcome by the creation of a united empire in January 1871; the narrative could thus have fulfilled an affirmative function by vindicating the path of recent German history. However, to join in a celebration of German unity with the help of a reminder of the bad old times that are, finally, left behind, seems to have been far from Raabe's mind. He rather suggests parallels between then and now, and the acknowledgement that there are still internal conflicts in unified Germany does not sit very comfortably with the prevalent triumphalism of the early years of the new *Reich*, the era commonly known as the *Gründerzeit*. Indeed, he encourages his readers to relate the events of some two hundred years ago to the very present, not so much where details are concerned, but with regard to the mentalities that perpetuate hatred. In the story, the French have just withdrawn, and, paradoxically, both their presence with all the hardship that the occupation by foreign troops entailed, and their absence, the power vacuum that neither the civic guards nor the force of the nearby monastery are able to fill, are blamed for the lawlessness that ensues. In the early 1870s, the French had just been defeated and the German Empire was made possible by rallying support in all of Germany behind the victorious Prussians. The question is raised why a foreign 'Other' always needs to be blamed for the twists and turns of German affairs, and why Germans are so reluctant to take their own destiny into their own hands.

Both in the historical example and the contemporary parallel, there is an implied message that, now the French cannot serve as scapegoats for a deficient condition any more, other scapegoats will be found to serve as pretext for a convenient evasion of responsibility. Indeed, during the time of writing the trend of blaming Jewish citizens for some detrimental effects that the foundation bubble had generated, namely the overheating of investment activity that led to a stock market crash in 1873, became visible. In identifying in his narrative a Protestant pastor as a particularly narrow-minded and vindictive figure guilty of shirking responsibility and shifting it onto others, Raabe may be pointing the finger at the Prussian court preacher Adolf Stoecker, who soon after 1871 started his agitation against the Jewish minority. At the same time, the cohabitation of a Protestant majority and a Catholic minority within the new state also experienced first frictions that would lead to decisive measures to be taken against certain freedoms enjoyed by the empire's Catholics. Indeed, one of the perceived and real obstacles to a unification of the minds was the cultural division, since the age of confessionalism portrayed in Raabe's text, between the Protestant north of Germany and the Catholic south. Exclusion of the dominant Catholic power, Austria, from the German equation in the Austro-Prussian War of 1866 paved the way for a political solution, but turned the Catholics of the empire into a minority. The anti-Catholic campaign pursued by Bismarck after unification, known as *Kulturkampf*, aimed at curtailing Catholic independence in, for example, the running of schools and charitable establishments, at weakening their allegiance toward the supranational power that was the Roman Church, and exerting much firmer state control. The historical situation highlights similar tendencies the other way around and on a much smaller scale, with the Catholic ruler's attempt to erode Protestant privilege and inherited autonomy. By thus reversing the relationship, Raabe warns against the arrogance of the victorious, the self-deluding fallacy that history has declared a winner – history knows no absolutes, creates no finality. All parties are in it together and depend on one another, and it requires courage and determination to step up to defend the human dignity of all.

In his story, Raabe creates sympathetic and strong characters that command his readers' admiration on all sides of the manifold divides. These are rather unlikely types like the old veteran brother Heinrich von Herstelle with his big Hussite sword (itself a symbol of division and strife), and Kröppel-Leah, the ancient matriarch of the Jewish community and bearer of the contentious bundle. These members of an older generation are distinguished by their historical experience that, in the Catholic brother's case, prompt them to step up in defence of basic human decency and, in the old Jewish woman's case, by an endurance and resilience that commands the readers' respect. From the younger generation, these two protagonists are joined by an expelled Protestant student who, in the eyes of his uncle, the aforementioned bigoted pastor, is a failure. With his Horace edition that serves as pillow, as a source of entertainment and as a weapon he joins in the efforts to protect the Jewish inhabitants from the enraged multi-confessional mob. Clearly, personal traits like courage, resolve and integrity, and a cheerful, unprejudiced sense of justice are credited with the potential to provide the solution to the turmoil of minds and morals. This sentiment is embodied by the young scholar's irreverent use of Horace's poetry, but also by the Roman satirist's clear-sighted exposure of human folly, ambition and ignorance itself. Interestingly, just as *German Moonlight* ends with the evocation of Jean Paul, this story also ends with the mentioning of the name of a man of letters, the enlightened aesthetician Alexander Gottlieb Baumgarten, thus, again, identifying a clear-sighted and enlightened stance towards life as an alternative.

Within all of the hardship and aggression and frustration, the desperate hopelessness of the endless cycles of abuse and violence staged in the story, one note of sentimentality is sounded. This concerns a brief moment of intimacy of sorts between the two female members of the Jewish community and two Christian boys two generations apart. The moment of tenderness between the irreverent relegated student Lambert Tewes and the young Jewish girl Simeath seems to mirror, or reenact under reversed auspices, the tender moment experienced by her grandmother – the victim of the current events – and the young horseman Just von Burlebecke two generations earlier. The token of that encounter, completely worthless in material terms, forms the main content of the knapsack the old woman brings home from burying her relative, not untold riches as the Gentile community wants to believe. This, a memento of human compassion and decency, forms the key symbol of the story. The intricate narrative design and vivid characters command aesthetic attraction; and its firm warning against anti-Semitism or any other form of discrimination and violence is its moral message.

V

A dysentery infection suffered by his daughter Margarethe forced Raabe, at the time in July 1873 on a summer holiday in the Harz Mountains, to attend a pharmacy named Zum wilden Mann on an almost daily basis. It is believed that his observation of the customers, their anxious wait for the apothecary to prepare the prescription, their worries not only about the state of their loved ones at home, but also about their own ability to pay, galvanized the idea of creating a story set in an apothecary's office. And while the plot of the finalized narrative *At the Sign of The Wild Man* does not foreground the woes and concerns of the customers of such a rural establishment, they certainly lend an atmospheric backdrop that also helps to give contour to the story's protagonist as a member of this community. Raabe conceived the plot in late July and early August of that year and finished the manuscript by the end of September. It was first serialized in *Westermann's Illustrirte Deutsche Monatshefte* in 1874, and later included in vol. 1 of his *Krähenfelder Geschichten*. Originally, friends and critics deemed this story to be far too bleak and disturbing to win Raabe any new friends, and it alienated old ones like the novelist Wilhelm Jensen. Asked for a contribution to mark the two-thousandth number of *Reclams Universalbibliothek* in 1884, he chose this very story almost as if to express his disregard for public tastes. Thereby, he clearly signalled that he considered this narrative one of his best and that it would have a role to fulfil in this, Germany's most popular series of cheap and canonical texts. Raabe thus espouses a critical and subversive rather than an affirmative sense of representativeness. The interest that this particular narrative has enjoyed amongst scholars in recent years is testimony to its continued appeal as one of the most puzzling and multi-layered narratives of Bourgeois Realism in Germany.

The narrative about the apothecary and its inhabitants has two distinct halves. In the first section, a community is described that is at ease with itself and contentedly celebrates its self-contained existence; in the second section, their peace is disrupted and eventually destroyed. The horrible point that Raabe reveals as the story unfolds is that the very person who is credited with having enabled the creation of this little idyll is the same who eventually brings it down. The community concerned, gathering in the apothecary's parlour, represents the middle-class dignitaries of the rural community, pastor, doctor, forestry inspector and, at its heart, the pharmacist Kristeller himself and his sister. As their comfortable circle is threatened, so is middle-class respectability as a whole, and with it the foundations of the society that has campaigned for German unification and now feels that it can reap the rewards of its efforts. This wider meaning of the story is introduced from the outset when, through the insertion of a narrator's voice, an allegorical reading of the events that are to follow is suggested. By insinuating that the narrator guides himself and his readers from the exposure to the hostile elements into the shelter and sanctuary of the shop as his readers have followed him through the various stages of German history of the nineteenth century under the umbrella of the empire, Raabe proposes the equation of the apothecary's shop with the newly-founded German Empire, and of its well-settled, contented and jolly inhabitants with German society as a whole. The pharmacist's recollection of how a stranger bequeathed him the means to establish himself sets the scene for a second half when the rug is pulled from under their feet and the unravelling of their life's achievements unfolds before their eyes. Reading the story as an allegory of the self-delusion of the *Gründer* generation, the generation that has experienced and participated in the struggle for German unification, allows readers to understand Raabe's aims. He intends to shatter their sense of security and expose their complacency. The benevolent gift had only been a loan, as the new German empire is a loan from posterity, and the creditor has appeared to claim his dues. The chilling story about the inhabitants of a remote apothecary's shop turns out to be a stinging political intervention.

The figure of the returnee, the conveyor of Raabe's messages, is initially introduced in quite a misleading, confusing way. Raabe gives him the characteristics of a jovial, jolly elderly blow-in who wins over the local community with his enthusiasm and his exotic tales, and only gradually hints at his sinister characteristics. He uses the description of this intruder to highlight several severe problems that, in his view, riddled the new German Empire; and by making him a figure of the past, he also hints at continuities between the old, deficient conditions and the situation in the new empire, thus undermining the assumption that now, post-unification, the problems of the past have been left behind and the wounds healed. But not only is this figure of the former emigrant a vessel for Raabe's social criticism, he also functions as a catalyst that brings out traits in the local community that have, hitherto, lain hidden under a surface of routine and contentment.

In the second half of the narrative, the returnee from Brazil called Agostin Agonista is described as an emigration agent, praising the opportunities of his adopted homeland, encouraging his new acquaintances to seek their fortune on foreign shores, tricking locals into agreements that they soon regret. While he is never actually shown to employ dodgy methods, the reactions of locals, their distress on the morning after, their shame at their own greedy gullibility, suggests that Agonista's powers of persuasion might have contained a rather sinister note, that he might have talked his victims into emigration agreements under duress or false pretences. This whole motif taps into an ongoing discussion in Germany about emigration in general and to Brazil in particular.

Without this being mentioned, Agostin Agonista is modelled after one of the most notorious emigration agents in German history who was active in the 1820s shortly after the establishment of the Brazilian Empire in 1822. Two features that are also visible in the fictitious character distinguished this historical figure: (a) His boastful manner, claiming to be the confidant of the young Empress of Brazil, a Habsburg princess and daughter of the last emperor of the Holy Roman Empire. This agent liberally used his military rank and noble title, awarded by Russia, calling himself chevalier and Ritter Major von Schäffer. (b) His methods of promoting emigration to Brazil were perceived as severely despicable, he is reported to have put on spectacular shows where alcohol flowed liberally, to have offered huge rewards and not to have fulfilled all the promises by which he lured vulnerable victims, mostly members of an impoverished under-class, to sign his contracts. He became the focal point for public anger at the fact that emigrants were forced to live in Brazil under intolerable conditions, having, to afford the crossing, given away any claim to financial and personal self-determination for a disproportionate length of time. He is also known to have bought petty criminals free from prisons in Bremen, Hamburg and elsewhere and inscribed them in the Brazilian army. Of course Germany had no penal colonies at the time, so to sell petty criminals to overseas potentates to serve in their armies, often against their own populations, might have been some authorities' way of ridding their jurisdictions of undesired elements. This Ritter von Schäffer was, and herein lies a nice punch line, a trained pharmacist.

Raabe treats the problem of emigration, and the success of exploitative methods of recruiting immigrants to overseas destinations, as a symptom of the victimization of vulnerable citizens, vulnerable because they were bereft of viable alternatives. He considered this kind of social injustice and exploitation one of the worst of all the curses that marred German society throughout the entire nineteenth century. Delegations were sent to Brazil to investigate reports of intolerable conditions there, for example the allegation that Protestant emigrants could not legally get married in a Catholic state that did not have provisions for civil marriages, and were thus forced to live in sin. As late as 1859 the Prussian government saw fit to issue a decree banning the activity of all Brazilian recruitment agents. The fact that European emigrants were forced to exist in Brazil in a kind of bondage known as white slavery, indebted to their agents, deprived of free movement until their debts were paid, serves as a reminder of the conditions under the *ancien régime* before serfdom was abolished in Germany and equality before the rule of law became the guiding principle of social organization. Agonista's description of his duties as police colonel in the service of the emperor of Brazil, mowing down the multi-coloured riff-raff in the streets, paints the picture of a police state that deprives its citizens of basic human rights. This stands in stark contrast to the propaganda of the 1820s and 1830s, the early days of the Brazilian Empire, when the constitutionality and liberal spirit of this newly independent former Portuguese colony were praised in the brochures distributed by agents like Schäffer. While parallels might exist between the establishment of Brazil and that of the German Empire, since in both cases the aim of national self-determination under a constitutional monarchy was claimed to have been achieved, Raabe warns against believing in propaganda or falling into the trap of self-congratulatory complacency that ignores the problems and injustices behind the propaganda. He encourages his readers to reassess the alleged achievements of their own nation in the light of the realization that, in the parallel case of Brazil, the political structures of the old régime, i.e. Portuguese colonial rule, have apparently not changed at all. By analogy, he asks the same question of the German Empire, namely if conditions here have really changed after its creation.

The returnee also serves as the embodiment of a harsh and exploitative global capitalism when he suggests that, with Kristeller's chemical expertise, they could produce in Brazil the commodity meat extract, a product that Justus Liebig had patented not long ago, and rival his success. When he fails to win his old friend's assent to becoming his business partner, he tries to extort from him the recipe for the apothecary's own invention, a bitter schnapps that bears Kristeller's name. This episode serves as a reminder that the global economic scene of the latter third of the nineteenth century became increasingly marked by an extreme capitalism that used immoral means in its pursuit of profit. Raabe's message is contained in the fact that this capitalist mentality is reimported into the rural community contaminating and undermining a healthy social fabric; as his Harz village serves as a microcosm for the German Empire at large, his warning extends to unscrupulous capitalist tendencies emerging in the Germany of the *Gründer*.

Behind these very concrete critical references to the realities of the day there are additional layers of meaning hidden in the story. The reason why the returnee had left his homeland thirty years ago is revealed as his inability to cope with the inherited profession of executioner. His moral scruples and decisive action of making a clean break with the past could have provided the basis for a story of a truly new beginning. However, hints are given to suggest that during his long journey to his final destination, he had entered into a pact with the devil on board the Haitian ship, explaining his miraculous cure from the wounds incurred in the naval battle. This pact, it is hinted, is responsible for his heartless and ruthless career that led him through a number of new South American states to his present position. Suggestions about his youthful appearance and his fear of Christmas underline this rather spooky strand. Suspicions that the rock formation known as Blood Rock, where Kristeller and Agonista had originally met, might have been an old pagan sacrificial site, cannot be dismissed; the feeling lingers, too, that something far more sinister than either of the two former friends' recollections reveal might have happened at this mysterious place, maybe that an abortion had been performed on Kristeller's bride who did not live to see and enjoy the benefit of the inexplicable bequest.

Further layers of meaning intersect in the figure of the Brazilian. The title of the story and name of the apothecary shop is obviously an allusion to a figure from the folklore of the Harz mountains, but there is also a suggestion that the Agonista figure might be associated with the mythological Wild Man that early explorers believed they had found in foreign parts. Since early modern times, the idea of the Wild Man, living outside civilization, helped to imagine earlier stages in the development of the human race, stages closer to the state of animal than present-day Europeans. Allusions to the scientific practice of classification of species transport such considerations into the age of modern biologist discourse which imposed on human races a hierarchical taxonomy of both physical and, by extension, civilizatory development. This association poses very fundamental questions both regarding the nature of 'civilization' and the definition of 'humanity' – can the representative of all social ills, and at the same time of the pinnacle of economic progress epitomized by global trade and the invention of meat extract, lay claim to either humanity or civilization? Have the achievements of the civilizatory process, the summit of which the Germans of the new *Reich* believed they had climbed, tipped over into its opposite; i.e. have the protagonists of progress and of economic globalization regressed into barbarians again? But even if his readers are willing to follow this premise, does the model of the old apothecary sitting under the reproduction of Dürer's allegory of *Melancholia*, stoically suffering the extinction of his life's attainments, truly point to an alternative way of life amidst all the uncertainty, loss and strife encapsulated by the other scenes decorating his walls, from famous rulers to tragic lovers and (again) references to the dashed hopes of 1848?

VI

Only about ten of Raabe's over sixty prose works are available in English translations; amongst these are the two novels *Der Hungerpastor* [*The Hunger-Pastor*, 1864] and *Abu Telfan oder Die Heimkehr vom Mondgebirge* [*Abu Telfan; or, The Return from the Mountains of the Moon*, 1867] which marked the transition, during Raabe's Stuttgart phase, between his sentimental juvenile works and the mature and intriguing production of his last three decades of productivity. These two works were translated during the 1880s and were deemed to be good examples of the new trends in German literature at the time. *The Hunger-Pastor* constituted one of Raabe's greatest and most enduring successes, but in making his antagonist Jewish – or rather a renegade who betrays his Jewish heritage just as he deceives his non-Jewish contemporaries – this book later earned him a reputation as anti-Semitic. *Abu Telfan* with its multiplicity of characters, its intertwining stories and its vivid depiction of life in a typical German residence might have seemed more current and accessible to English readers both from a compositional and from a thematical point of view than many others of Raabe's works, his debut and most successful product on the German book market, *Die Chronik der Sperlingsgasse*, included. The translations *Black Galley* [orig. *Die schwarze Galeere*, 1861] and *Elsa of the Forest* [orig. *Else von der Tanne*, 1865] came out in the 1930s and 1970s respectively; their choice still represents a relatively conventional taste and does not yet take account of the re-evaluation of Raabe's oeuvre that was underway since the late 1960s and 1970s. In recent decades, however, translators have turned to some of Raabe's complex masterpieces, the satirical *Celtic Bones*, the historical novella *St. Thomas* – in some respects foreshadowing the historical narration of *Höxter and Corvey* – , the disturbing story of crime detection and deceptive posturing *Stopfkuchen* [*Tubby Schaumann*]; and most recently Michael Ritterson has published a highly acclaimed English version of Raabe's last historical, and arguably narratologically most intriguing novel, *Das Odfeld* [*The Odin Field*, 2001]. The present selection thus fills a gap; the three stories from Raabe's early Braunschweig period present partly bitter, partly melancholic, always haunting vivisections of the German psyche and of German society; they expose prejudice, hatred and violence, international capitalism and its exploitative practices, social injustice and ill-founded complacency both in the individual and in the collective that is German society in the first decade after unification. All three works show the individual as exposed, victimized, subject to psychological, historical and economic forces beyond their own control, but also afford glimpses of an alternative, at a possible uncorrupted way of reacting to the hurt inflicted by fellow humans, to the randomness of history, to the general feeling of vulnerability and contingence. The reactions to this realization of utter exposedness vary: active, humane, defiant and unpretentious compassion in *Höxter and Corvey* as the only way to maintain some level of integrity in barbarous historical circumstances; melancholy resignation and moral integrity in the honouring of old obligations in *At the Sign of The Wild Man*. The most poignant reaction, though, to the uncanny depth of human nature illustrated in *German Moonlight*, consists of the purchase of a good book – and here, surely, Raabe makes a point on his own behalf.

Raabe's narratives require some work on the part of the reader, their messages and the aesthetic pleasure they can provide are not glaringly obvious. The English translations with their tendency of simplifying by disentangling Raabe's syntax and by avoiding his practice of naming the same things in several different (dialectal, Latinate, mocking) ways, of using more common English expressions for some dated or very quaint German words that Raabe uses and for which there are no equally strange equivalents, might even make the appreciation of his works a little bit easier in English. It is the aim of any translation to win new readers for the author and the work selected. This edition would achieve its goal if it could encourage readers to (re)visit some other of the author's texts as well, be it in English or in the original German version. The themes of the selected pieces – psychological uncertainty and self-doubt; painful historical experience and the genesis of a pogrom (with a sympathy and understanding displayed for the Jewish victims that clearly dispel any accusation against the author as an anti-Semite); international capitalism spilling from the colonial world into the remote and presumably self-contained domestic realm – have universal appeal and at the same time shed light on the very specific conditions and concerns of Germany after her nineteenth-century unification. It would thus be especially pleasing if the present edition would find entry into courses of comparative literatures, and that the availability of translation could contribute to securing Raabe a place, albeit a small one, in libraries and on German curricula of educational establishments in the English-speaking world.

Foreign-language terms and other expressions, names, and dates used by Raabe marked with an asterisk (*) in the text are glossed in the *Explanatory Notes* section.

German Moonlight

German Moonlight

Let us speak calmly and without any commotion. I am, even by German standards, an exceptionally unemotional person and I know how to keep my emotions in check. Besides that, I am a lawyer, the husband of my wife and the father of my sons. Neither upon the blooming of the elderflowers, nor of the hollyhocks, sunflowers or asters do I feel myself subject to sentimental or romantic emotions. I do not keep a journal, but several years' worth of appointment books firmly maintain their place, well-ordered, in my library. Having said all this, let me state that in 1867 I was on the island of Sylt on doctor's orders, on account of the sea air and salt water, and that there I made an acquaintance – a most extraordinary acquaintance.

Obviously I cannot dwell on correcting or confirming what is often felt and more often depicted and circulated in letters or print with a written account of my own experiences and emotions. The crashing waves, sand-rye and lyme grass, gulls in flight, and, above all, the westerly wind left a pleasant, refreshing impression on anyone who needed to wash off the sweat and dust of German bureaucracy. They did not fail to have the same effect on me, all the more so since the exertions which preceded this refreshment were not slight.

I was staying on the border of the two villages of Tinnum and Westerland and therefore had to walk for at least a half an hour to get to the beach and the hallowed salt water. A route no shorter led from there to the estimable man who every midday, for a fair price, restored us from the inside out. As a German civil servant accustomed to frugality, I make absolutely no claims to creature comforts, much less to luxury. Since I had brought seven of my twenty-one pipes with me, I could even have set myself up comfortably in one of the island's prehistoric burial mounds.

Good – I was staying with a baker who fuelled his oven with driftwood purchased at beach auctions, which is to say, with the beams and rafters and timber of ships run aground. I helped him now and then to split this wood, which made me feel pleasantly inspired – at home, I devote myself to this work more for health reasons.

Typically, I saw and split my firewood in my leisure hours; here I spent my time skylarking or studying several treatises – deliberately packed for my sojourn – about the *Brunswick Succession. During business hours, I went strolling on the beach.

Stays like this at seaside resorts make everything become drawn out. At home I stroll every day and in all weathers along the ramparts in my administrative city, which are well-suited to such walks. On Sylt,

I dined, took an hour-long nap on a dune, and then walked along the beach heading directly north, sometimes all the way to the *Red Cliff, but normally just to the bathing huts of Wenningstedt.

Since the sea, like a *washerwoman of both genders, can keep nothing to itself, but rather casts it all back out, these walks were never without their charm; although I am a man of prose, I can turn a dead seal lying on its back over onto its belly with a certain melancholy and still have my own thoughts on the matter.

Good – or rather this time: better! – for about three weeks I had been on this island, which stretches from south to north, or vice versa, when I made the acquaintance mentioned at the beginning of my account.

It was nearly evening. The sun had gone down and I was returning on this day from the Red Cliff, and not a little tired, because the low tide had, to the best of its abilities, rendered the path on the beach traversable for all those patients with abdominal ailments on Sylt. If one took ten steps on fairly compacted sand, one sank still deeper during the next two hundred. And I would, in fact, gladly recommend to a poet as lyric or epic subject matter my reader's wife, daughter, cousin, or beloved, who would have glided gracefully over this path, so uncommonly beneficial to the health, if I knew of such a poet, apart from the district judge Löhnefinke, amongst my colleagues and other friends and enemies.

I said the sun had gone down, but let me correct myself. It was just setting as I arrived at the dunes south of Wenningstedt, across from the island's ancient, crater-like earthworks. A fishing boat from Blankenese or Cuxhaven disappeared with the sun in the fog of the horizon, and a turbid grey grew out of the green of the water, so pleasing to the eye. The reddish-yellow colouring of the sand mounds to the left of the healthful but arduous path vanished, and the grey colour won the upper hand on the left as on the right. The dune grass began to lisp in the cool wind. Evening had fallen, and there was every indication that it would soon be night.

Stumbling and bathed in sweat despite the coolness of the evening, I accelerated my pace in anticipation of my evening pipe, when the unexpected happened and I made the acquaintance of my colleague Löhnefinke.

Everyone familiar with the western shore of the island of Sylt also knows how steeply the dunes fall off towards the sandy path along the sea, and at one of the steepest points, my colleague landed on top of me and threw me into a state of astonishment for the rest of my journey on this earth. May the dear reader allow me to continue my account with customary calm and without commotion.

I found myself, as I said, across from the ancient earthworks, and the sun had taken its leave five minutes prior, when suddenly, at the top of the dune to my left, approximately seventy feet over my head, a person appeared who frantically headed for the slope in a desperate sprint, threw his arms up towards the evening sky, then cowered and all of a sudden, to my hair-raising horror – slid – slipped – shot – down the sharp, almost vertical hill!

Before the cry of partial terror and total surprise that I let out had died away, the man was already sitting at the foot of the dune in the soft sand between a washed-up, half-splintered barrel and a ship's lantern, looking at me as I hastened to him, his mouth drawn, his face pale with fright, and yet apparently grinning. He shouted, cried, or rather wailed:

'He – she – is after me! I beg your pardon, kind sir, but who can keep his nerve?'

'Who? What? Who is after you?' I cried, peering up at the grey wall of the dune without seeing anything threatening. Nothing showed itself that could account for the reckless slide of the portly and well-dressed individual still sitting in the sand before me, nor for his unbounded dismay.

'Who is after you? Nobody, it appears to me! Out with it! Who's hunting you? What drives you to make such leaps? I don't see the slightest thing up there!'

'Yes, yes! He – she – the moon – *Luna – Selene! No, no, not Luna and Selene, but rather she, the moon, the loathsome German moon! Just now, she's coming up over the tidal flats and in a few minutes she will be there over the dunes, after me! And not a roof, not a screen to be found – not even an umbrella – and the next *bathing machine to duck under is a quarter-hour off! She will be the death of me!'

Normally I carry an umbrella with me and had one then as well; the stranger, however, in his state of distress, had not noticed it, and before I offered it to the fool, I naturally considered the situation.

It was clear to me, legally speaking, that I had a lunatic before me, and quickly composing myself, I considered the proper approach to take with him under such circumstances. Should I abandon this man to his fate, since I could not change his peculiar delusions, and leave it to his guards to catch him? Or should I enter into conversation with him, at the risk of getting mixed up in unpleasant quarrels, in order to get closer to the root of his condition?

As a person, I would have preferred the former, but as a lawyer, as a criminologist, the latter attracted me. I yielded to the temptation and continued the conversation.

'My dear sir', I said, 'If you believe yourself to be safe from your – enemy – under an umbrella, I will gladly lend my services. Take my arm.'

I had already opened the silk canopy, and the lunatic had himself already leapt to his feet with a cry of joy.

'Oh sir, the heavens have led me to you!'

He took my arm and said, doffing his hat:

'Permit me to introduce myself. My name is Löhnefinke – Royal Prussian District Judge of Gross-Fauhlenberge, in the Province – '

Immediately, I jumped to one side in complete amazement:

'My dear sir, that is impossible!'

'Sir?'

'You? You, the gentleman who attempts to escape the rising of the moon and leaps headlong at the risk of breaking your neck to avoid it, District Judge Löhnefinke from Gross-Fauhlenberge? Impossible, it is completely impossible that you are District Judge Löhnefinke.'

'But I am, I am! If you want to call it a pleasure, it is entirely mine, and I am the aforementioned.'

With much effort, I regained my composure and said to myself: Now there is no doubt that he is a lunatic with some very eccentric notions. The unfortunate man not only believes the moon to be his enemy, but he also clearly believes himself to be someone else.

'Yes, my name is Löhnefinke, and I would consider it an honour if you, my worthy sir, would now acquaint me with yours.'

How could I avoid this? I introduced myself and gave my name and title. At once, the lunatic again doffed his hat, grasped my hand, shook it cordially, and exclaimed:

'Oh, my dear colleague, see how destiny brings people together! Truly, I would never have imagined this encounter even fifteen minutes ago. My goodness, we have been best acquaintances for quite a while. Don't you remember? Did we not in the case of Johann Peter Müller, the imposter gypsy chief from Langensalza, exchange files and correspond with each other? Isn't that so, you remember? Oh, I am so pleased.'

Was this a dream or was it reality? Was this person insane or was I?

The case had indeed developed in that manner, and I instantly remembered very clearly the details of my correspondence with the Prussian District Court in Gross-Fauhlenberge. And my strange companion (we were already striding along together) did not in the least limit himself to ascertaining and verifying this fact; no, he immersed himself instantly in the minutiae of the case in question, orally presented all of his concerns which he had previously mentioned in our written correspondence, and – I replied to him as if there were no longer any doubt in my mind that he was the Royal Prussian magistrate in question and his name was really Löhnefinke. The full moon meanwhile had indeed ascended on the eastern horizon and shone on our heads; my companion was not concerned. As we continued arm in arm along the beach at Westerland, we were more and more engrossed in our learned profession and let the moon shine as she pleased. We had nearly reached the men's bathhouse and were approaching the stairs which led from the beach to the top of the dune when my colleague, who, despite his initial outburst, had by this stage proved himself to be a clear-headed, sharp-witted lawyer, suddenly halted in the sand, looked around, became ghostly pale as he peered up at the sky, and moaned:

'O ye gods, we're in the midst of it!'

There was no doubt about it: we were in the midst of it; this mania once more seized my hapless companion. Enraged and terrified, he pulled the opened umbrella tightly down over his hat, and I – I could not do anything but hold him, District Judge Löhnefinke, more firmly by the elbow and urgently coax the angrily squirming and floundering man:

'But my dear sir, I beg you. Compose yourself! Compose yourself! This is madness! What has this innocuous illuminative creation done to harm you? Or how have you transgressed? Use your reason, satisfy yourself of this: the harmless sphere has not the slightest intention of falling on our heads.'

'Oh my head! My head!' moaned the district judge, holding the body part in question with both hands.

'There now, come on, friend, no one is chasing you, no one is driving you. What an utterly insane fixation! But please do not be offended!'

'No one? No one?' groaned Löhnefinke.

'No one! Now, let's go up there; in the pavilion we can find more people – company, some fortifying beverage, and certainly a kerosene lamp, against which your enemy surely stands no chance.'

'Kerosene!' murmured Löhnefinke, seizing and clinging to the word like a criminal before the High Court to his plea for: Mercy!

'Listen, there is even music still coming from the pavilion. How would you feel if we go and sit down a while to share a glass of grog there, and – '

'– wait for the moon to go down?! Oh yes, that's right!'

'But that would keep us there rather a long while. The moon does not set until past a quarter to seven in the morning, but another consolation is rising before us. Look there. There are dark clouds out over the water – we can wait until a cloud has drawn in front of the moon.'

'Yes, yes, agreed! Only too gladly! Done! Colleague, I place myself under your guardianship. We will enter the building, wait until a cloud drifts in front of that grinning monster, and meanwhile, we'll have some grog!' exclaimed the excited Prussian civil servant. So we climbed the steep stairs, reached the top – without any broken necks – and continued through the dune grass towards the pavilion, which was packed full with guests and blaring music.

However, at the moment we crossed the threshold of the wooden rotunda, the music of the brass band suddenly stopped. The musicians packed away their instruments, or simply tucked them under their arms. They drank their free glass of schnapps at the bar and departed, and the majority of the audience strangely followed close on their heels without first having recovered from savouring the music. Only a few groups of sensible men lingered over their drinks.

A rather strong wind was blowing across the North Sea now. The waves crashed more loudly and were topped with whiter, more ruffled crests. The warming, invigorating drink which we had ordered before we settled down must certainly have had a beneficial effect on our mental state and put us at ease.

Now we sat, and while a lively group at the next table merrily chatted with one another, I beheld my new acquaintance better by the lamplight, certainly not furtively, and my amazement grew under the scrutiny.

District Judge Löhnefinke from Gross-Fauhlenberge was a man of about fifty, portly, as I have said, but otherwise without any outward peculiarities. A wide chin, a short-cropped, grey-flecked head of hair, the beard of a Prussian civil servant, and two shrewd grey eyes that fixed sharply on every person upon whom they were cast. His eyes gave me no reason to think he was a candidate for a mental asylum and yet – I could not take it any more! Laying my hand upon his arm and leaning close to him, I said:

'Please do not take offence, dear Löhnefinke, but at this moment I can no longer believe it.'

'What do you not believe?'

'Your behaviour a short time ago. Well, your breakneck flight over the dune, that reckless tumble in Wenningstedt, your – in short, your hatred of the moon, colleague.'

Immediately, an extraordinary change came over the entire presence of the man sitting next to me. Löhnefinke ducked once again and, as he had seized my umbrella earlier, he now seized the glass that stood before him, poured the hot, steaming mixture down his throat and whispered through clenched teeth:

'What I say is true! I hate the moon; she is my mortal enemy and against her I am defeated, just as she is defeated by the lamp overhead there.'

I signalled to the waitress, who understood my gesture and set a second steaming glass before him.

'Thanks!' said the district judge. 'And thanks to you also; for had I not run into you and your umbrella a little while ago, I truly don't know what would have become of me on that moonlit beach.'

'Colleague', I said, 'I am a quiet man and have served in office for years to the satisfaction of my associates and superior officers. I have the state medal at home in a drawer and have never made unlawful use of a secret entrusted to me. Would you be terribly offended if I ask you to share with me how you came into conflict with the innocent satellite of our sinful earth?'

'I would not be offended at all', said my colleague. 'On the contrary, I feel the intense need from time to time to vent my hatred and rage, as well as express my bitterest trepidation and anxiety, to a sensitive soul. Order another glass of grog for yourself and listen. Afterwards you may judge, and I will rely on your decision all the more because I've already learned from our official correspondence that you are a skilled lawyer.'

'At your service', I said in utter suspense and looked him in the eye now as I had not looked into my bride's eyes twenty-five years before. He sipped again at his steaming drink and then he began and made his confession.

'First', he said, 'I must note that my doctor sent me here to the seaside at the prompting of my wife, because of my condition, so she says – because of my nerves, so he says. For years, the man who has known me from my youth and who grew up with me has laughed about my condition; he only began to think the matter suspicious through the suggestions of my wife. All of a sudden, he decided that it was high time to do something about the deplorable situation, and – here I am and I go dutifully into the water daily, as you learned tonight, without the least improvement up to now. But let me get to the point: In short, I am paying for the sins of my youth.'

'Aha!' I murmured. However, my colleague, quickly sensing my thoughts, shook his head emphatically and sighed:

'Oh no, no! Alas, how happy I would consider myself if that were the case! It is precisely my misfortune that this disturbance is caused by just the opposite of what you are thinking. I assure you that neither wine nor women affected me that way during my youth. I have been all too upstanding and I regret it today in sorrow, pain and in a bathing suit from Sylt. Oh, if only I had run riot in the days of my youth! If only I had given free rein to my imagination at the appropriate time and assumed the risk of being thrown and breaking my neck. Colleague, colleague, it is suppressed poetry that makes me insane – insane far after the fortieth year of life. The German moonlight retaliates against me and I doubt that any *waters, sour or bitter, will help.'

'The German moonlight?'

'Yes, yes and six times yes! The leering moon drives me out of my mind; me, the Royal Prussian District Judge Friedrich Wilhelm Löhnefinke of Gross-Fauhlenberge. And I pay not only my own debt, but I also pay the debts of innumerable generations of my ancestors to that shining monster. Oh colleague, I feel very unfortunate at times!'

'Colleague, you are in any case a very interesting person. In keenest suspense, I beg you for a more precise explanation.'

'Which I will give you. My father was a royal official, like my grandfather, and it would be ridiculous of me to doubt that my great-grandfather had also been a royal official, on a provincial level, of course, like all of us. My mother was a German woman and likewise my grandmother, and of course my great-grandmother no less than they. They, too, were all descendants of families of royal provincial officials. Of poetry they knew nothing and they only paid attention to the moon to the extent that she was so kind as to inform them of when to have their hair cut or be bled. Oh, they simply left it up to me to pay for their negligence! – My mother read *Clauren, my grandmother read the Bible and the hymnal, and my great-grandmother probably could not read at all. My forefathers read and wrote their records, read the official gazette and perhaps also the newspaper, and I was their worthy descendant until quite recently. Then came the year 1848 and the moon rose upon me.'

'Aha!' I exclaimed; but the District Judge again shook his head and said:

'Oh no, no and twelve times no! *You are still as mistaken as you were before. Do you know what the word *'old-liberal' means?'

I nodded with the energy of a *Chinese pagoda.

'So you will grant me that an old-liberal is far from likely to hate the moon and take to his heels at the sight of the moon?'

It would have been foolish of me not to concede this point and I did so, but at the same time offered a counter-question:

'How old were you in March of '48?'

'I had just reached the age of a Prussian *court intern.'

'Bravo! Please, go on.'

'In March, the moon came over the rooftops and shone into my room in Berlin. I rubbed my eyes because I didn't believe them. I still did not have the slightest notion of how dangerous this damsel was, but in the following year, 1849, I received more than a mere notion. Returning hot-headed from an impassioned public assembly, I fell asleep with this very head lying on the windowsill and the malicious orb shining on me for several hours.'

'And?'

'And the following morning not only did I have a headache, but also a downright disgust of many things and people whom I had held in high regard, esteem and admiration. Poetry manifested itself to me – and – colleague, do you know what it means when life's poetry manifests itself to a Royal Prussian court intern?'

'Fortunately not; you will recall that our correspondence with each other had to do with our respective district boundaries.'

'That is true. I didn't know either, but I know what I speak of now! Peacefully and soundly, you dream all night of the legal code and the district law, and you awake and seek to recall the contents of your dreams. You succeed only too well, and the misery begins. You look from your pillow over to your library and suddenly you are seized by the desire, which you can scarcely overcome, to jump up, to grasp all the rubbish in your arms, and – and – and – things – do unspeakable things with it. But you restrain yourself, because it occurs to you how much money you have invested in this mess of papers – and luckily for your future career you restrain yourself and move on to prepare your coffee. While doing so, you are seized with staggering force by the thought that you are still an under-compensated employee of the state; and not only does your blood begin to boil, but so does your coffee, so you cool the one and you don't pour the other down the drain, but rather down your throat. You have lost some illusions and acquired some new ones; you see, there you have the first effects of our enemy, the moon! Yes, you create strange illusions, and what is strangest, you don't hold it against yourself at all. Afterwards, you go to work at the office, meet your supervisor along the way, greet him most civilly, and suddenly a different dream occurs to you! You remember what you dreamt as you lay with your head in the open window and the moon shining upon it. You stand there and follow the man with your gaze; and now, entirely the fault of the German moon, you are struck by the thought that you, for your part, have read more than your ancestors: not just the newspaper, but newspapers; also *Schiller and Goethe, Voltaire and Rousseau, Börne and Stahl, Ranke and Raumer, and an incommensurable assortment of the latest poets of the most liberal type. You remember something that you sang at the university during *Kommersch, and the gentle, lovely moon, that perhaps hangs over you just now as a slender crescent in the light blue of the morning sky, puckers her mouth derisively – and waxes – waxes – waxes from new to full, while you go about your official business day to day, week to week. You feel boundlessly uneasy, you find yourself unspeakably stupid, silly and vulgar, and you perform your work stupidly – an occupation that suits you well. Then you go home and happen to observe your receding hairline in the mirror, and if at the same time you should discover a grey hair in your beard, that suits your good friend the moon very nicely, too; for she can grasp you more tightly and lead you around more easily by it than by any other means. The next time you sit alone by the window at night, she takes you by this hair. You long for a bosom, a tender, sensitive bosom on which you can pour out all your despair, to which you can tell all your grief, with which you can share your vexation and discontent. You dream while awake, and the moon mocks you more harshly than ever – '

'Stop a moment, Löhnefinke!' I exclaimed, clutching my head with both hands. 'Must someone else always come and lay out for us, clearly and objectively, his most personal circumstances, past, present and future? Colleague, you are entirely correct; excited, like you, I follow your explanation! Do continue – the moon is truly a monster!'

'She is, and above all, this German moon! There she comes over the roof again, and you lay your head on your shoulder and blink, stupid and disconcerted, at her broad grimace. And suddenly, a field of tall wheat sways before your eyes, the nightingale or some other bird chirps in the bushes, the pond twinkles, the brook murmurs, and you, colleague, begin to murmur likewise. What do you murmur? Naturally, some melodious name ending in E or A – Klothilde, Josephine, Maria, Amalia – how should I know? No matter! It is all over – she has you; she has you hand and foot, this treacherous, deceitful sneak, the moon, the German moooon! You feel in the mood to call her your friend, to stretch your arms out to her, to shed a tear for her, and without a doubt you make an utter fool of yourself.'

'Yes!' I said, and nothing more. But my colleague kept silent in deep melancholic thought for a good while, then gave a start and continued:

'I was a delegate to parliament during the deadlock over military reform, when His Majesty gave our prime minister the famous symbolic staff; I naturally voted with the majority and now – now, in the year '67 – I have written a sonnet – think of that, a sonnet! – a sonnet praising the honourable prime minister, and have had it printed in the classified section of the *Nationalzeitung*. Do you understand me and my attitude towards the moon? The German moon?'

'Perfectly!' I said, after some consideration.

'Then I can and will be brief. One knows – and the moon is aware of this – a tolerably melodious name ending in E or A, and naturally one knows the bearer of the name – or one searches quickly for such a name and its bearer; and that the moon readily assists in finding it and her, is self-evident. In such cases, no matchmaker offers her hand more promptly or skilfully. Oh, she shines her light on the lyric poet with whom we suddenly feel ourselves more than familiar. Oh, she illuminates the page upon which we are courting the muse. Oh, she sneers down at us when we wait for her at the exit of a ballroom, theatre or concert hall. Oh, oh, oh, she accompanies us home, if our sweetheart's mother had no objection to our escorting her there. Oh, oh, oh, oh, who knows better than she how to light the way home for a man, the ass? It hardly matters, but it's a question worth asking, whether she is at fault if, one beautiful morning, the old man, her father, consents and says "Yes!" Are you also married, colleague?'

The question was thrust upon me so abruptly that it almost knocked me from my seat, and I had to collect myself for a moment before I could answer in the affirmative.

'Well! Then we won't waste another word on this subject! Look, there she is and she's looking in the window – the clouds with which you consoled me a little while ago are also powerless against her. The distant meadows are bathed in the light – oh, how beautiful, how wonderful! Dearest colleague, how charming the world is – how magnificent in war and peace! Poetry rains down from above and springs up from below. Listen – listen to the music of the eternal sea. The waves dance an immortal dance in the German moonlight, why shouldn't we dance along with them? My soul is a drop in the harmonious flow of the world, a glistening, light-filled drop. Colleague, let's escape into the fair countryside; it is a sin to sit in this airless chamber while earth and water lie so extraordinarily lovely in the German moonlight outside the pavilion; come, drink up, let's – '

'You're not afraid any more?'

'What should I fear? Dearest, good friend, that's just it! She triumphs over us all and in her light we win all of our victories.'

'Even the *Battle of Königgrätz?'

'That one, too, whatever objections one may have to it. And future great and memorable victories as well! Ah – what air, what light! Please, let's climb the dune one more time to cast one more glance at the divine sea.'

'And after that, standing in the moonlight, will you relate further how your life unfolded?'

'Gladly, with pleasure, immediately, although in my opinion that's actually not necessary anymore. You see, my good fellow, it is a fact as terrible as it is comforting – the moon now and then overpowers the Royal Prussian Judicial Officer Löhnefinke, and the latter has, in the end, not the slightest objection to the intoxication and giddiness forced upon him. Yes, I also found a German girl in the German moonlight; I was betrothed to the same girl with the consent of her parents and subsequently married her. To this day, I am in undisputed possession – with the addition of an eighteen-year-old daughter – and perhaps later I can introduce you to both ladies.'

'So, you're not really walking around alone – you haven't been left here on your own on Sylt?'

'By no means. I live with my wife and child there in Westerland and have come here to the baths under their supervision. What did you imagine?'

'Excuse my foolish question, colleague. This is such a wonderful evening, such a pleasant encounter and such an utterly interesting conversation, that everything is to be excused.'

'Let me reassure you: we understand each other perfectly. Unbeknownst to you, I have been observing you day after day; as a person you caught my eye, and I immediately recognized the lawyer in you, and it was not without intent and complete justification that fate sent me tumbling into your arms just now. It was necessary for us to have this discussion this evening; it is all part of the treatment and also, in great measure, an effect of the salt water. But the moon – I must repeatedly draw your attention to this glorious moon. Yes, I am in her thrall and shall have to remain so until death releases me. Colleague, by means of her and abetted by the present times and world conditions, I have become – the poet in my family. Grasp that completely and understand me completely, both in my disposition at our encounter on the beach and in my present state of mind.'

Löhnefinke, the poet of his family! I took several steps back. Although the madman stood before me as clearly as the island of Sylt lay in the German moonlight, the word still caught me off guard. It was like the boom of the cannon that startles you even though you watched through the field-glass as the gunner lighted the fuse.

'I, the inheritor of such endless prose', continued my colleague, 'I am overcome by my enemy, enslaved to her whenever she peeks above the horizon, despite all my kicking and clawing. I am an idealist in politics, a poet in the management of my budget. I see the time coming when I will record my account book in hexameters and *ottava rima. I am wild about the sentiments and congeniality in the events of the hour, and – colleague, colleague! – I am not understood by my women – my ladies do not comprehend me. That is what has shattered my nerves and brought me here to Westerland under their – my ladies' – direction. Now let us go home if you don't mind; it is growing quite cool.'

He had taken me by the arm – very gently, and we strolled arm in arm over the moonlit moorland of Sylt. Never in my life had I walked side by side with such a poetic Prussian district judge. He, this exalted colleague, declaimed more and more loudly. He showed an astonishingly broad familiarity with German and foreign verse. Poems to the moon alternated with hymns to freedom and battle songs against all possible and impossible enemies. Tropical landscapes and impressionistic images mixed with fragmentary stanzas of familiar and unfamiliar romances and ballads of all sorts of historical and fictitious content. Löhnefinke was superb, and his enemy, the moon, could truly be pleased with him; but more than one of his or my superiors would have been caused not only moral, but even physical discomfort by him in this condition. In the distance, to the north, the flashing beam of the Kampen lighthouse winked like the eye of a cynic making his surroundings aware of something exceptionally funny. The sheep on the moor, whose ropes, or tethers, we stumbled over, stood up, looked at us in awe and gazed after us with astonishment.

Thus we came ever closer to the village of Westerland; however, before we reached it, we were hailed and – in the loveliest of ways, judging by the outward appearance and tone – brought back from this moonlit dream- and sleepwalk into reality. Luckily, both of us were standing firmly on the ground, and so could not fall to earth when the spell was broken.

As if formed out of the rays of the moon, the uncommonly dainty, graceful form of a girl stood before us on a swell of ground, and the most charming face of a girl, pretty as in a fairytale, was turned towards us in the moonlight. I cannot say that the district judge Löhnefinke of Gross-

Fauhlenberge had a most charming face, though he did possess an honest, and to a certain extent, jovial visage, and the 'enthusiasm' of the last hours had enhanced it still more: so much the more intensely did I have to wonder at the expression with which he regarded his sweet daughter. Instead of becoming even more serene and happy, all his features suddenly went slack, then drew together into a tangle of troubled wrinkles.

'Is that finally you, Papa? Well, I must say!' called the elfin grace as she approached us.

'Yes, I am finally here,' grumbled the colleague, 'and here – '

He did not finish, because the young lady sharply cut him off.

'We have been waiting ages for you, Papa, and Mama is very angry with you!'

'Oh? Hm!' grumbled the colleague, and I also said 'Hm!' in the depths of my heart.

'Come, Helene, let us go home together', said the father of the lovely child, soothingly. But the elf in the moonlight only replied more sharply:

'I thank you, Papa; but I will go with Mama. Here she comes now, and she will tell you how she has been waiting for you. Mama, here is Papa at last!'

Ah, he really was here, Löhnefinke the father, and he quoted no more German or foreign poets at this moment. Indeed, through the German moonlight, Mama approached, and in fact rather briskly and energetically. I would gladly have bid farewell and taken my leave before she reached us, but my colleague grasped my arm with the grip of a dragoon and whispered:

'Oh, I must introduce you, friend. Where are you going? Oh, colleague, allow me to introduce you to my wife.'

What could I do but express the greatest desire to make his wife's acquaintance?

Advancing between the houses at the edge of the village of Westerland, the worthy woman had now reached us and taken the arm of her daughter. Of course, she completely ignored me at first and devoted herself solely to family matters.

'So, finally, Löhnefinke?! Your old, accustomed inconsiderateness! Let me tell you, Löhnefinke – '

'But dear Johanna, look here! My friend and correspondent here – allow me to – '

Thus one is not infrequently thrust like a paravent between a draft of air and the recliner of a rheumatism patient. The introduction was accomplished, and with my innate bonhomie I assumed the role assigned to me. After several courteous exchanges, we four walked together towards the humble, huddled, friendly Frisian cottages; and if up to now I had been in the dark regarding one final aspect of my colleague's state of mind, it became completely clear to me along this short walk.

Oh, how the moon, the German moon laughed down on the two women and the Royal Prussian district judge! Oh, she knows how to avenge herself, the German moon! She has her means, knows her means, and knows how to use her means. My friend Löhnefinke is absolutely correct: It is miserable having to inherit the legacy of generations, of centuries, without first being permitted to make use of the legal provisions of *beneficium inventarium*. It is a terrible thing, first to disregard that pale, waxing and waning companion, then to scorn her, and finally to be subjected – and to submit, with little resistance – to her influence!

One must be a man – a German man and government official – to experience complete and utter dread. Frau Johanna and Fräulein Helene Löhnefinke, without ever having paid heed to the moon's claims upon this man, had placed themselves entirely on the side of the moon and were likewise taking vengeance on the one who had spurned her. It could not be foreseen how far they could yet bring down their husband and father – low enough they had brought him already.

Late that evening, as I sat in my room at the baker's again, I smoked a half dozen pipefuls over the events and experiences of the day and, around midnight, came to the conclusion that I should give my son, then studying mathematics at Göttingen, a copy of *Jean Paul Friedrich Richter's complete works for his next birthday.

17

Höxter and Corvey

Höxter and Corvey

I

We have always liked to provide our readers with the correct time of day, but this has never been made so hard for us as this time. In the town of *Höxter, the clocks of all the churches were in a muddle. St. Peter and St. Kilian showed a wrong time, St. Nicholas rang incorrectly, and at the *Brothers the mechanism had come to a complete standstill. Only at the monastery of *Corvey, a quarter of an hour downstream, was the clock still working fairly well, and someone had been found to keep it going and to wind it at the right time. On the tower of the abbey, it struck four o'clock in the afternoon.

So much for the time of day. Concerning the time more generally, it was the first of December in the year 1673. We are beginning our story on the twenty-third of November in 1873, so just about 200 years have passed since that winter day. Bricklayers, carpenters, joiners, locksmiths, glaziers and, above all, clockmakers have been at work, have rebuilt the walls, righted the posts, hung the doors, installed new windows, and have seen to it that the church clocks show the right time again. It had taken much work and great patience – woe to anyone who wantonly offers his hand to once more knock down the walls, take down the roofs and demolish the doors and windowpanes. Today's readers are reminded that the rebuilding, the setting up and filling out, in addition to all else, costs a lot of money.

It was a wintry day, damp and cold. Heavy rain and snow clouds were rolling up over the wooded slopes of the *Solling. The swollen River Weser, always hasty and too much in a hurry, swirled its yellow floods in seemingly pulp-like eddies from the mountains between Fürstenberg and Godelheim and Meigadessen, churned through the bare willow bushes and the withered reeds on her banks, and was highly annoyed at any obstacle that stood in her way.

Such an obstacle she found beneath the walls of the town of Höxter, because there she encountered not only ice-breaking boulders but also the remnants of the piers where peoples had crossed the river since time immemorial; but as so often before, she did not find the bridge itself. Fiercely, she roiled and boiled up around the broken supports, but there was also something like a cry of triumph in its uproar:

21

'Ho ho, the work of humans! The foolishness of humans! Ho ho, over it and onward, toward the ocean, taking along what can be grabbed! The same game we've played for thousands of years – triumph!'

The yellow waves of the Weser had a right to roar and sneer. They had borne the bridges of *Drusus and Tiberius, of King Chlotar and of Charlemagne, on their shoulders at this place – nearly each century, half a dozen times, a new bridge had been built here for war and peace – triumph! Where were the beams and planks of the last one floating now? It had been built nearly three years ago, and the day before yesterday *Monsieur de Fougerais, the French commander of Höxter, had ordered it demolished before departing in the wake of his field-marshal, *Monsieur de Turenne.

The day before yesterday, Monsieur de Fougerais had followed the marshal and had marched off toward Wesel. His Princely Grace, *Christoph Bernhard von Galen, Bishop of Münster and Administrator of Corvey, Lord of Stromberg Castle and Bordelohe, had played the *French card against the Emperor and the Republic of Holland. And the French had settled in, according to the Germans' wishes. As a result, as we have mentioned, the clocks on the church towers from Rhine to Weser had become muddled once again, and showed the wrong time or had stopped altogether. As far as the bells of Westphalia were concerned, quite a number of them had been taken along by the French allies of the honourable prince-bishop, to be recast into gun barrels and used in the *Wars of Reunion, the seizure of Strasbourg and the *Wars of the Spanish Succession.

More about this later. The abbey tells us the right time; Christoph Bernhard has seen to it. It is four o'clock in the afternoon, and we are standing on the right bank of the river, facing the demolished bridge. We are waiting for the ferry, which has been operating since the departure of the wild, invited-uninvited guests and allies.

We are waiting for several people who will arrive to cross over to *Huxar – and they do indeed arrive, one after the other.

The first is a monk from the abbey, who under the dark clouds strides from the guard tower across the field toward the Weser. It is Brother Henricus, formerly in the secular world a *Herr von Herstelle. Eight days ago, his prior, Nicolaus, formerly in the secular world a Herr von Zitzewitz, had sent him with a letter to the steward of the Duke of Braunschweig at the magistrate's office in *Wickensen, and he had carried the letter there and has strange things to tell.

Instead of the steward, he had found *His Serene Highness Duke Rudolf August himself, in high good humor despite the recent events and the French hubbub on the left bank of the Weser. The Duke had opened the well-sealed letter of the Prior of Corvey, and another dispatch – written and addressed in French – had fallen out. His Serene Highness read this first: a third of it accompanied by frowns, the rest with some laughter and derision.

'You carry weighty matters around in Germanic lands, without knowing it', the Duke had said. '*Inasmuch as in the year seventy-one We have brought Our town of Braunschweig, which is finally loyal again, to do Our bidding – this with God's help and Our dear cousin's aid, with the force of arms and with persuasion – We thank the Bishop of Münster, the Prior, Chancellors and Councillors of Corvey, and also Marshal von Turenne for extending their greeting to Us. Furthermore, as is only right and proper, We are aware of our duty and oath to the Emperor and his rule. As far as Marshal Turenne is concerned, We wish him a safe journey to Wesel. At the moment, We have no message for you, reverend brother, except that you are welcome to remain our dear guest for as long as it pleases you; and also, according to your pleasure, to take a look around the area. However, since the abbey and the royal headquarters at Höxter have sent us in your person a man who did not always wear a monk's garb but formerly also arms and helmet, We trust that at home you will praise us *in re militari* and will recommend us to the powers in Huxar and Corvey to the best of your knowledge.' –

Since in fact Brother Henricus, in addition to his dispatch, had also willingly accepted an oral commission to look around the area to the right of the Weser, he made use of the duke's invitation. He looked around, and now he was coming back after having looked around – which gives us the opportunity to take a closer look at him.

There he stood leaning on his staff, in the field next to the grumpy river, waiting patiently until it would please the ferryman on the Höxter side to fetch him over. And despite his clerical garb, he indeed looked like a man who was well able to give his superiors a report on the military measures and preparations of His Ducal Highness at Wickensen, and a competent and professional report at that. Brother Henricus von Herstelle wore his Benedictine habit with great dignity, but even someone completely without preconceptions would not find it hard to believe that this broad chest and those solid shoulders had once borne iron armour without any discomfort. That the wrinkled but still vigorous fist had once enclosed something other than a harmless staff of hawthorn, that too could not be doubted by any attentive observer. Brother Henricus faced the wintry day with his hood thrown back and freely offering his shaved crown to the wind, some isolated snowflakes and the sharp showers of a fine rain. A wreath of gray, somewhat bristly hair surrounded the round, well-formed head, and a scar on the brow spoke of other and fiercer encounters than with his brothers in God and Jesus Christ during vigils and sacred offices. Squire Heinrich von Herstelle was now an old man, but young and hale on his legs. Even when he sneezed or cleared his throat, it sounded forceful and virile, and you could not blame Father Adelhardus, the abbey's cellarer, formerly a *Herr von Bruch, if he preferred the friendship and good fellowship of this particular venerable Brother to that of any other within the walls of the abbey.

'I can well imagine what happened to the bridge', said Brother Henricus, shaking his head. 'Still, it is an annoyance!' he added, shading his eyes and looking out for the ferry. He had to wait some more, for the ferryman over in Höxter was in no hurry on account of just one passenger. He was lying lazily on his bench beside the arch of the gateway to the bridge, and he too was waiting, namely for more than one person to gather over on the Braunschweig side.

Finally the second passenger arrived. It was a tiny old woman who came hobbling along on the towpath from *Lüchtringen, panting under a heavy bundle – an old Jewess named Kröppel-Leah, well known to the rabble at Huxar but held in high regard by those of her faith; tired from walking, tired from age, battered by the war, yet looking defiant from beneath her pack despite her age and fatigue.

With deep curtsies and respectful bows, the old woman approached the grizzled Benedictine monk. He nodded to her, raised his hand in greeting, and said:

'May the God of Abraham unbutton the ears of that rascal over there. Come closer, woman; throw down your bundle and sit down. Just for the two of us, that lackadaisical fellow is not going to move yet.'

'I thank you, kind and reverend sir', replied the old woman. 'Old bones, tired feet, a heavy heart – I can wait patiently.'

'So can I!' said the monk and then, with a glance at the remnants of the bridge piers standing out from the eddies of the river, he asked: 'Do you perhaps know, mother, what exactly happened here? Even if one has one's own ideas, one likes to hear the report of another. When I left Corvey, I was still able to walk across the Weser without getting my feet wet.'

The old woman shook her head:

'I cannot tell you, reverend sir. In the year seventy, on the seventeenth of January, the river did it itself. Earlier, in forty-six, it was *Master of the Ordinance Wrangel; before that it was the work of *Kasper Pflugk and the members of the *League – and still earlier *Christian von Braunschweig, whom they called The Mad Duke. In between, always the river itself. But who did it this time?'

Brother Henricus gave a faint smile.

"What you are rattling off there, woman, is correct; I can vouch for it *in persona*. But where are you coming from?'

'From *Gronau in the Principality of Hildesheim. The son of my sister died there. He was the last male family member. I watched him die, and I am carrying the inheritance with me to Höxter.'

'Hmm!' muttered Brother Henricus, looking at the bundle on which the woman huddled and from which she glanced at him askance, unvertainly.

II

'For a monk and an old woman I won't give the rope a single pull', growled Hans Vogedes, the ferryman, as he sprawled on his bench from his left onto his right side; and the city-guards posted there beneath the arch laughed in unison and completely agreed with him.

It was a unique company of guardsmen. Its composition mirrored the utter confusion of the town. There were two infantrists from Münster-Corvey, shouldering their muskets. A shoemaker, a carpenter and two tailors from the predominantly Lutheran part of the population, who had been called up by the town council, had armed themselves rather strangely with helmets and armour from the times of the League and the Swedes. They were leaning martially on their spears and poles. But the commander of this group, Corporal Berthold Polhenne, had been supplied from its midst by the Catholic citizenry with the assistance of the abbey and the friars of the town itself: the discipline he kept and the authority he could claim thus left much to be desired.

Trodden down by the heavy boot of Herr de Turenne, sucked dry with contributions by Herr von Fougerais, tormented by the French occupation in their houses and streets into the utmost misery and rage – unruly subjects of His Grace the Bishop of Münster, hungry citizens of the good 'municipality of Höxter' – in short, poor, needy, tormented, confused German folk, grown up from the ruins of the religious wars, like the sprouts around a felled tree – things were bad in Höxter after the noble French allies had marched off! - - -

Over on the right bank of the Weser, the monk stood motionless, leaning on his staff, and Kröppel-Leah sat on the bundle with her nephew's inheritance. They were quietly waiting for fate to send them the third man, for whom Hans Vogedes might be willing to move, and this third man now really did appear. He came through the low fields and commons meadows from the village of Boffzen – old like the other two, tall, skinny, in a black cassock and cape, hurrying briskly along with wide-legged strides – Reverend Helmrich Vollbort, the pastor of the Lutheran Church of St. Kilian in Höxter. It seemed to him a good idea to get home soon, since the weather was not improving and it was getting steadily darker. Whether the pastor had any other reasons for his haste we might find out later. For now, as the imposing figure of the Benedictine monk at the crossing came into his view, he moderated his steps, but only for the briefest time, then strode on even more energetically, nodding silently in greeting as he approached.

Brother Henricus acknowledged the salutation politely; the Jewess rose laboriously from her seat and curtsied. It was a curious group that had to wait for the ferry from Höxter on the yellow, rancorous, rapid floods, under the stormy dark sky. The monk from Corvey was the first to find the silence awkward and thus also the first to open his mouth. This was, indeed, two hundred years ago, but Brother Heinrich von Herstelle, too, began with a comment about the weather, and it had the same effect as it does today.

'It is a rough day', replied the Reverend Helmrich Vollbort, the pastor of St. Kilian, looking across to the town and the demolished bridge. 'A day or evening well suited to time and place.'

'Truly spoken, Herr Pastor', said the monk. 'Although I have been away from home, I appreciate any remark designed to compare the *tempora et mores* of today.'

The old Jewess, who had hunkered down on her bundle again, covered her face with her right hand, sighed heavily and furtively nodded also.

'You weren't in the abbey when the French left, Father?' asked the pastor.

'I was carrying a letter to Duke Rudolfus Augustus – and I found him with his troops at Wickensen – I found him there with his troops in the Solling forest.'

'Did you indeed!' murmured the preacher of St. Kilian, pricking up his ears. 'Did the authorities at Corvey expect that? Has the French Holofer – '

He broke off and concluded – now sighing heavily himself: 'It does not matter, we are most certainly in distress. The Lord's will be done, now and for evermore.'

'Amen!' said Brother Henricus. –

The ferry was still taking its time, but a conversation had now started on the right bank of the Weser, the monk politely raising questions and the Lutheran minister replying equally politely, though in a much gloomier and somewhat annoyed tone. Both learned much from each other that they must have found worth knowing. Brother Henricus in particular now learned exactly the manner in which the Höxter bridge had come to float downstream this time and how the houses over there had once again lost walls or roofs, abandoned to every gust of rain or storm. The old Jewess was monotonously mumbling her prayers, the dirty river was swirling sullenly, and at the bridge tower in Huxar, Hans Vogedes was finally preparing to get under way. The strange guard company at the gate had become enlarged by an additional person of similar oddity, and it was he who was prodding the lazy boatman to do his duty.

He had come down the road, his hands in his pockets, his hat pressed on his curly head at an angle, dressed in a well-worn scholar's gown, a short clay pipe, filled but not burning, in his mouth, and his sole possession in this merry world, the *Poemata* of *Quintus Horatius Flaccus in a well-thumbed pigskin volume in his pack, and – his own version of the Roman poet between his teeth:

> '*Now reigns in my heart in flickering flames
> The Thracian Chloe with laughter and games.
> She sings, strums her lute, her playing is fine,
> To double her life I will give up mine.'

Since we shall be further concerned with this young man, we shall immediately reveal his name, say who he was and how things were going with him.

His name was Lambertus Tewes and he was the nephew of the Reverend Helmrich Vollbort, the preacher at St. Kilian. Regarding his trade, a week ago he had unfortunately been expelled as a student of jurisprudence from the famous university, the *Julia Carolina at Helmstedt. His age was nineteen years, maybe a half more. Otherwise he was probably the only person today in the town of Höxter on the Weser who was in a happy, benign and carefree mood and who, of course, behaved accordingly. He went up to the guard company, all of whom were smoking, to ask for a light. He had no pressing obligations and was pleased when anywhere, for example here, room was made for him on the bench.

'Sit down, comrade, if you have nothing better to do', called one member of the Lutheran guard who had been at school with him at Höxter. 'But if you want to cross the Weser, Hans Vogedes will take you right away and even without charge, that is, for a Latin piece from your book of solace while he unties the boat. Agreed, is it a deal?'

'Agreed? All right!' laughed the wayward fellow from Helmstedt. 'Indeed you escaped the clutches of Mother Philosophy before she managed to pour you into her Greek and Roman cauldron. Either way, you would not have been that splendid an addition to the learned Höxterian sauerkraut dish.'

'Corporal Polhenne, he starts to make trouble the moment he arrives. We know your kind of talk, you turncoat.'

'Be quiet there! Master Lambert, keep your mouth shut; and you, cobbler Kappes, your trap! Apart from that, I too wouldn't mind hearing a piece from that old heathen!' muttered Corporal Polhenne.

'Do you like the old heathen that well, Corporal?'

'There is no one here who can compete with you in that respect. Latin is becoming rarer and rarer in this world. Jesus, if I think of my youth and how they used to throw it at us from the pulpits!'

'*O nata mecum consule Manlio*', hummed the student, but immediately broke off, so as not to cast his pearls before swine. 'Forget about the Latin, Polhenne –

> *Corvinus adjures us
> Never ceasing to think,
> Let's open the barrel
> And have us a drink.
> As Socrates teaches
> So drink too as he
> Thus teaches old Cato
> The way we should be.

Tell me boys, what's there to drink on the banks of the yellow Tiber – I mean the yellow Weser? What did that false Carthaginian, that grim fiend Hannibal, leave for your and my thirst?'

'If you mean that Fougerais, Master – There! There it flows!' shouted the guard company at the gateway in Huxar furiously, with one voice, pointing to the river.

'This barrel won't run out so easily, Doctor!' muttered one of the Münsterian musketeers over his shoulder; but the student shuddered:

'Brr! ... He finally marched off after his master Turenne – *ultimo scabies*, may they all get the itch! By the immortal gods, gentlemen, in this case even the most kindhearted Teuton may find the day too grey to quote Horace. Give me a light for my pipe.'

He lighted his pipe, and at the same moment there came a hoarse cry from the other side of the river and a man in black waved his white handkerchief through the evening dusk. Herr Lambert Tewes, blessed with eyes like a falcon's, said:

'I looked for him at home, so as to tell him once more of my plight. But my *chère tante*, before slamming the door in my face and bolting it, informed me that my uncle was not at home, that he had gone across the Weser to his colleague in Boffzen. And here now is this excellent man – *avunculus divinus ac singularis* – and a monk and an old woman to boot! Get going, ferryman, and fetch me my uncle; I need him more desperately than you can imagine, gentlemen and dearest friends.'

'I have been telling you for some time that you should get started, Hans', one of the spear carriers added. 'And now it's our pastor who has finally lost his patience.'

That did it. The ferryman rose, stretched himself, yawned, stepped into his vessel and took hold of the rope. His place on the bench, as we have said, was taken by the student.

It was heavy work for the boatman against the powerful swollen winter currents, across to the other bank. The guards watched him with comfortably lazy interest. Herr Lambert Tewes blew smoke from his short clay pipe and hummed:

> '*Serenely take whate'er you may,
> The world much like a river glides,
> Which gently in its bed today
> Toward Etruscan waters slides;
> But next day stormily rebels,
> Beyond the muddy banks it swells,
> Moves bulky stones and heavy rocks,
> Doth even sturdy trees uproot,
> It swallows shepherds and their flocks
> And gobbles up their huts to boot;
> When Jupiter lets his anger roll
> And sends dark clouds down from the pole.'

III

Just as the student had fitted the ode of his Roman poet to his patron Maecenas to his taste, the ferry reached the far bank of the Weser. Politely raising his cap and with a bow, Hans Vogedes invited the Lutheran clergyman to get in. He also acknowledged the monk from Corvey, although with much more formality. As far as the old Jewess was concerned, he was already about to embark on his journey back without taking her along to Höxter. However, the monk saw to it that she got a seat in the boat for her money, and the preacher of St. Kilian too had moved to make room for her bundle.

Now the ferry was floated back toward the town. The two clerical gentlemen sat quietly; the Jewess, crouching down, did likewise. The crude ferryman, while carrying on with his admittedly heavy work, was constantly cursing under his breath and from time to time glanced furtively at the sack containing the inheritance of Kröppel-Leah. Midstream, the monk asked:

'How are things going with you, ferryman – at home – since the foreign folk have taken their leave?'

'The devil has kept his headquarters here, Father', came the reply. 'In Corvey there was great rejoicing – they probably kept the food warm for you too. Höxter is hungry and chewing on its rage. You'll find few houses there where the wind is not whistling through the walls. *Sacré*, as those French dogs say, what do I care. At least I don't have to provide for wife and children. If he'd offered a bit more, I would have marched off with Fougerais too.'

Brother Henricus sighed; Pastor Helmrich Vollbort also sighed and pounded with his fist against the gunwale of the clumsy craft.

Then the pastor said:

'The fellow is speaking the truth, Father, as I stated it earlier. It looks bad in the poor town; may the Lord preserve us from further harm.'

The wild river was writhing under the boat like a vicious animal.

'The world is like the river', the pastor continued. 'It is covered with wreckage, but the Lord yet walks on the waters. In the end He'll prevail.'

'Amen!' replied Brother Henricus, and then no more was said until the boat reached the bank beneath the ruined town wall of Höxter. At the same moment the student jumped up from his bench towards the ferry, politely doffed his hat, extended his hand to the guardian of St. Kilian's as he was getting out, and said:

'Reverend uncle, sir, just a little while ago I had the honour of trying to call on you at your domicile. My aunt has directed me here *ab ostio *ad Ostiam,* from the door – which unfortunately she shut in my face – to Ostia, I mean the harbour. My respectful greetings, uncle.'

'And I have nothing further to say to you, sir! Why do you constantly bother me?' –

'Out with you, crone! Be off! Pay up and be gone, you witch!' yelled the ferryman at the Jewess.

'God of Abraham, right away, good sir!' cried the old woman. 'Have mercy, don't get angry – here, here!'

With a trembling hand, she passed the poor pennies and stumbled and fell as she climbed out of the boat with her bundle. The members of the guard company all laughed at the old woman.

From the monk the boatman took the fare without further comment, but the two warriors from Münster and the citizen-corporal Polhenne took off their hats. With a silent greeting to all and a nod to those of his faith, Brother Henricus stepped through the gateway ahead of the others.

For the fun of it, one of the guards, a tailor, prodded Kröppel-Leah to make her hobble faster. It was she after whom the ferryman now looked the most thoughtfully, and he took a few from the crowd that had assembled at the ferry landing aside for a whispered conversation.

After the rude and curt rebuff from his venerable relative, the student, Master Lambert Tewes, had put his hat back on; but as a stout fellow who knew how to handle the Philistines, he did not give up so easily. If earlier he had sung of the Etruscan Sea, he now transferred to other waters, reached in his back pocket for his Horace to make sure that this comforting volume was still present, and hummed for his peevish uncle Helmrich of St. Kilian's what once had been warbled to *Aelius Lamia:

'*Musis amicus, tristiam et metus
Tradam protervis in mare Creticum
Portare ventis – ,

However, he sang it in a very unique translation:

'The wind blows t'ward the Cretan Sea
And with it flee
Annoyance and rage!
The poet's mightily amused
That sages scratch their heads confused.'

It would break my heart, Reverend uncle, if as your wife's nephew I should so lightly let you go on your way ill disposed, without first having clasped your knee once more. It is true, they expelled me, but – '

'And I and my wife have done the same!' shouted the pastor, angrily. 'Sir, stop bothering me. I and my family have nothing more to do with you.'

The preacher walked faster, but the nephew stubbornly kept by his side.

'By the gods of your hearth, uncle – '

Again he was not able to finish. The stern old gentleman stood suddenly still and exclaimed:

'What more do you want, Monsieur, after I have told you so clearly my opinion? Is this a time for tomfoolery? Look around, is this a sight to rattle off your Horace? Look into my heart – in God's house the aliens have stabled their horses; in my church they held their bacchanalia! And you cry *Evoë, Evoë, and you praise *Bacchus and Venus who – look into your own heart: Do the Germanic people, those poor and miserable people – without houses or roofs here and elsewhere – wish and crave to hear the Roman poet's lewd rhymes in their aching ears? Look around you, fellow, and let me go on my way. What good would it do you if you came home with me? There too you would find a wrecked abode and a cold hearth.'

The clerical gentleman had swept his hand in an arc, and what this hand, this skinny, bony hand pointed to, gave much reason indeed for despair.

Since the year *1618, the town of Höxter had experienced storm after storm. It has not been chronicled yet how many times this place, the ferry landing and bridge at this important crossing between East and West, had been assailed by sword and fire. But the ruins, the wasted sites, the shabbiness of the few human habitations that had been rebuilt, and these in their state of most recent destruction, bore witness to it. The town of Huxar was lying in December's grey evening light like a rotting corpse, and the old black churches jutted out like a skeleton from the decomposing flesh of the town. And the lane was full of crushed straw, of debris, of ashes and wreckage, and in other ways, too, the army of His Most Christian Majesty had left a great stench. The student held his nose, shifted his hat from one ear to the other, and nodded:

'By God, it's a misery!'

Indeed that was what it was. Nevertheless, though, his frivolity was too much in his blood. And so Herr Lambert quoted again, albeit with a most sorrowful mien:

> '*To whom should our people groan,
> The country's downfall to bemoan,
> Whom will Zeus as avenger send,

To whom give arms us to defend?
Conceal your light, down to us fly,
Apollo hear my anguished cry –

The ode is entitled, "Ad Augustum Caesarem", uncle.'

'Ye shall call on the Lord; His name is Sabaoth! Emanuel is His holy name', said the pastor. He raised his hand menacingly and walked on. This time the student and nephew let him go and stood still. He watched him go and then once more looked around in Höxter.

IV

'So we have troubled our cousins and gentle relatives in vain!' said the citizen and wayward son of the venerable and enlightened *alma mater Julia Carolina. 'They have always accused me of being too softhearted, but this time I really did not lack stubbornness. I did and tried as much as my late parents could possibly ask for. Anyone else would have lost his patience and shown the door to dear aunt and uncle long ago. Only a good-natured fellow like me submits to being kicked out three times without summoning the devil. All infernal spirits, deliver me from my soft heart!'

He thoughtfully scratched his curly head, although only ten minutes ago he had reviled any sage doing the same. Then he reached into his back pocket once more, but this time too found little there except the favourite of *Maecenas, the lover of Glycene, the friend of Varus – the merry old jester, Horatius Flaccus. Thus he stood as night was falling in this German winter, when suddenly the white Benedictine monk passed him once more. The friar had tried to pay a quick visit to the priest whom His Princely Highness Bishop Bernhard von Galen had installed as the pastor to the Catholic community of Höxter, but had not found him at home. He had then followed him to the house of burgomaster Thönis Merz and exchanged some words with him there. Now he was on his way to the Corvey Gate.

'Salve Domine', said the student amiably, and startled the monk from what seemed to be rather disturbing thoughts. But he too bowed amiably and was about to pass the young scholar. But that was not so easy. Herr Lambert Tewes fell right into step with him and continued the conversation.

'You are on your way home, Reverend Father?'

'After a long, arduous journey through the wicked world, I am returning home to my cell.'

'And so you don't even know how well off you are, Father?'

Despite his low spirits, the old man had to smile and, slowing his pace, he asked:

'In this nasty weather, you are not yet going home, learned Herr Studiosus?'

'How I wish I could!' sighed the student. 'But have you, Father, ever had an uncle and aunt? Oh Holy Kilianus, into what hands has your house passed! I had so definitely counted on an evening meal there and a sack of straw under the protection of your instruments of torture! Reverend Sir, when they chased me out of Helmstedt, I left them my debts, and took with me from their library this son of the gods in pigskin. Him I will now have to take in this lovely weather as pillow for the night at the wrecked hearth of one of these Höxterian ruins. But what do you think, Father, of buying it from me for a cheap price? If *Phoebus had not long ago turned his back on this vile corner of the earth, I would gladly offer you this volume for closer inspection. It is an excellent edition – *Amstelodami, ex officina Henrici et Theodori Boom – with a frontispicium by the famous painter and engraver *Romeyn de Hooghe; how about it?'

'I was a horseman in my youth and as the noble knight Heinrich von Herstelle I unfortunately left all the Latin I had learned in the bushes', replied the monk. 'I thank you kindly, my dear young friend, and commend you to the protection of the Almighty. But besides, we have a massive and excellent library and if I brought this kind of thing back from my travels, they would make great fun of me.'

'You don't say', mumbled the student. 'I'll be polite and believe it. So – have a pleasant night, Father!'

The monk bowed once more and left. But the student from Helmstedt stayed and called out, when Brother Henricus seemed out of earshot:

'So, turned down once more! It may pay to load your musket or your blunderbuss! Blast! *Palsambleu! Mille millions tonnerres! No German curse is adequate to comfort a person in my situation. There goes that Holy Joe and in his habit he takes my warm seat in the abbey's kitchen with him, but – these are the times we live in, such are our times! That's the way they all are – no matter whether decked out as Catholic or Lutheran. Oh you *fleshpots of the alma mater Julia! Oh you long bench in my Helmstedt cellar! – And to such a *Bœotian I offered my laureate for the price of a supper?! Shame on you, Lambertus, and repent! By the immortals, I'll really have to spend the night in the ruins left by Quartermaster von Wrangel. Blessed be his memory! Blessed be his passing through here on his march to the Allgäu to attack Bregenz. Blessed be his cannons and bombards from anno forty-six! It is enough to tempt you to cheer even *Tilly and

Marshal von Gleen and the year thirty-four! What would someone like me do today without the ruins from the bloodbath of Höxter?!' –

True enough, but who else in this night had quiet, warm quarters and a secure and comfortable pillow and bedcover in Huxar on the Weser? No one really. With the exception of healthy children, nobody got a sound sleep. It was, after all, the week after the great flood. And just as Noah's family soon expressed their discomfort in their devastated world with discord and mockery, so also the citizenry of Höxter had already begun to quarrel and to get into each other's hair.

Both Catholics and Lutherans had endured a lot from the foreign occupation, from Mylords Turenne and Fougerais. Now the French were gone, but the poison in hearts and heads had remained. Everyone was searching for someone on whom he could spill his bile, preferably with impunity. And if you looked at it in the right light, there was nobody who could have arrogated to himself the role of guardian of these boiling passions and the job of putting a lid on them. Everyone was partisan. Herr Christoph Bernhard, the bishop of Münster, could have had the upper hand. But he was at war with the *United Dutch Estates, cared very little for the Empire, expected no favours from Duke Rudolfus Augustus at Wickensen, and knew in addition that the majority of citizens in his 'good municipal town' of Höxter was also looking toward Wickensen, although for a very different reason than the bishop.

'Someone run to the mayor!' tends to be the motto in a well-organized community. But unfortunately, this too was of little use at the present juncture. The mayor of Höxter, Herr Thönis Merz, was partisan like everybody else. In order to get him and his 'poor good town' under the thumb of the abbey and the bishop, the Catholic side had borne down hard on him with chicanery and even violence. His reports and written complaints to his protector in Wickensen bore loud testimony to this.

How long ago, for example, was it that they had sent him, the right noble mayor, and his honourable council on a sparrow hunt? Was that not chicanery that Corvey had required of the good and glorious town Höxter, as if it was the meanest peasant village, to deliver to the abbey their share of sparrow heads, tally them and pile them up?!

Per vulnera Christi, the town had cried for help from Duke Rudolfus Augustus, and Brother Henricus could report what His Ducal Highness thought of the matter.

One can, indeed, read on many a page that has come down to us, yellow and musty, how bishop and duke scuffled with each other across the Weser by letter and recently even with several companies of foot soldiers and imposing troops of horsemen deployed by the ruler of Braunschweig.

'The good and ancient town of Höxar, which for the sake of its freedom and its holy religion hath lost lives, property and blood, is now treated like the meanest village. Its keys have been taken, and its proper right to maintain its own executioner has been abrogated. Even the *levy on the Jews, which the town had had both before and after the year of the Lord 1624, hath been revoked so that at this time a horde of Jews all live there in handsome houses, carry out their usury, and yet give nothing to the town!'

Thus screamed the Lutheran citizenry. –

'We shall teach you to brazenly spread such provocative words!' grumbled the Catholic part of the population. And from Corvey, His Episcopal Grace could be heard:

'To date We have treated you unruly and refractory people of Huxar with singular restraint and clemency. We have only acted within Our rights as your governor. How do your attempts to disguise the hostile Braunschweigian incursion accord with that?

'Were Mayor Johann Wildenhorer's grain stores not confiscated just three years ago, when the Lord Abbot Arnold Zeiten was already dead, because *sixteen* years ago, in his capacity as mayor, he had petitioned the aforesaid Lord Abbot's Princely Grace for certain municipal rights?' came the word from the town hall.

'And who was responsible', came the word in reply, 'when he and twenty of his men were stationed in your town, for taking by force Our Captain Meyer's set of drums, with which his drummer was charged to beat the daily reveille, watch and retreat, and removing them to Braunschweig's armoury beneath the town hall?'

'Are you not in this matter, effectively, *judex, pars et advocatus* in one?' screamed the town.

'By no means! We, Christoph Bernhard, Bishop of Münster and Administrator of Corvey, are by divine right the legal and anointed sovereign of your godless and rebellious town', came the resounding reply.

'Hmm, your Honour', the written answer, addressed 'To the Bishop of Münster', came back from the opposite bank of the Weser. 'Without wanting to call into question Your Grace's undisputed and exalted title and rights, We have nevertheless, as hereditary Protector in the interests of Our Princely House, to see to it that the poor town in its desperate straits does not, as it were, sink into ruin in front of Our eyes. Signed: Rudolfus Augustus.'

In good time after this goodneighbourly epistolary exchange – Herr von Turenne had moved into Höxter. This was the clearest answer to the Duke's letter that Herr Christoph Bernhard von Galen could devise; that his good neighbour in Wickensen had immediately understood it will become clear to us when the old horseman Heinrich von Herstelle reports what he saw on his journey.

As far as the Jewish community was concerned, about whose abolished levy the citizenry of Höxter also was so enraged, it wisely kept as quiet as possible, without that doing it much good, as we shall see betimes. – –

And now, on the day before the return of Brother Henricus, Herr von Fougerais had marched off toward Wesel, had left the prince-bishop of Münster's good town and had – not without good reasons – pulled down the bridge that led across to the right bank of the Weser. Christoph Bernhard, with his forces, was far away opposing the Dutch; for the time being, Höxter and Corvey were left to themselves – and the mood was as wild and desolate as the state of the houses and streets.

The student who had been expelled from Helmstedt and who – or so he said – was about to look for quarters for the night in some ruin of previous wealth, might perhaps, under the circumstances, find there the quietest and most comfortable place in all of Huxar. By now night had fallen completely; it was much too dark to get out the Horace and, by inserting his index finger among the pages, to pick out a prophecy from him the way one used to do this from Vergil. Herr Lambert, therefore, simply went like every other human being where fate took him; and until now it had led him through the wicked world, if not always comfortably then always quite enjoyably.

V

All of us in this wretched world are like children who are being taught to write and whose hand is guided by the schoolmaster. At this point we would love to follow Brother Henricus; however, we have been tapped on the shoulder and pointed in another direction.

Like the other two who had crossed the wild river with her, Kröppel-Leah had gone home. And just as the pastor of Saint Kilian found his wife at the warm stove behind the door that had been bolted against his nephew, and just as the monk of Corvey found his cell, so did the old woman find her home in order – in as good an order as the times would permit. Fifty men of a French regiment of musketeers had been quartered in her house and had made themselves comfortable there during her absence. The front door had been half torn from its hinges and most of the windowpanes had been demolished. All utensils had been knocked to pieces. The walls had been soiled and blackened by smoke, and they had been befouled with names and disgusting drawings. Not all the foreign guests had known how to write, but they all had understood how to draw – and how! …

The fifty French warriors had had the house to themselves. But as soon as they had departed with Monsieur de Fougerais, someone had turned up, someone who stood there for a while, numb, with folded hands and suppressed sobs at the sight of the devastation until she broke out into loud weeping. That someone was a young girl of fourteen years, the old woman's last granddaughter. Neither abbey nor town cared where the child had hidden herself during those last wild weeks, though we do. Now she was home again and was crying over the ruins of her grandmother's house just as loudly and bitterly as once did the prophet Jeremiah over the ruins of the great city of Jerusalem.

But the child had taken hold of herself. She was, after all, a descendant of that bravest of all peoples which – even more stubbornly than the German people – on the ashes of every conflagration of its fortunes had known how to reattach itself with the fibres of its roots. Before anything else, the child had fetched a small lamp from the house of fellow Jews who had charitably taken her in, and with its help had started her heavy labour. The young Jewish girl had cleaned the house!

With the little lamp in her poor, tiny, trembling hand, she searched the devastated house from cellar to attic, and often she moaned and called to the God of her people, when she found that once again a cleverly and securely arranged hiding place had been discovered and emptied by the soldiery of Marshal de Turenne, who in such matters were even cleverer and who had thoroughly studied this subject. And the child had been all alone in her misery. No one in Höxter had bothered when the glow of the little lamp had flickered in one or another of the dark window openings. A fellow Jew, Master Samuel, had lent her the lamp and his wife, Siphra, had added a basket with a loaf of dark bread, a poor knife without a handle, an earthen pitcher and a pot in a wire mesh.

'If we could, Simeath, we would fill your pockets with gold and silver, have you led by a flock of billy and nanny goats, and followed by a wagon filled with flower and honey and oil and spices, but we cannot', they had said in Master Samuel's house.

'There, let me at least give you a broom, it is probably our poorest but all the others we need ourselves', Frau Siphra had added. And so the child had left with many thanks and flowing tears of gratitude, and she had been able to cope on her own until her grandmother came home – despite King Louis, the Bishop of Münster, the Maréchal de Turenne and the Commandante de Fougerais.

In the upper story of the house, on the courtyard side, there was a narrow dark chamber in which the sergeant had taken up his quarters with the stout woman from Troyes in Champagne whom he kept as his companion, and which therefore had not suffered quite as much as the other rooms. In this chamber, the bed was still standing as well as a table of which only one leg had been knocked off. Two or three stools on which it was still possible to sit had also escaped the merry high jinks of the departing army. It looked bad enough even here, on the floor, in the corners and on the walls, and a horrified Simeath immediately threw the bedding into the courtyard. But there was the broom and her diligent, hard little hands! By midnight the room had been swept, the table secured and a bundle of straw that had been left behind in the street dragged up into the bedstead of Mademoiselle Génévion. At a quarter past midnight, Simeath was lying on this straw and was sleeping in expectation of her grandmother's homecoming.

We shall not describe how the girl woke – perhaps from a happy dream! – how she sat up, bewildered, as she returned to consciousness, and looked at the hideousness all around her, and how she passed the day until dusk set in again. We saw the grandmother with her bundle hobbling toward her abode, pursued by the mockery and the dirty looks of the guardsmen at the ferry. We picture in our imagination how she stood in front of the house and gazed up at the broken windows, how she then stepped over the demolished threshold through the doorless entrance and how her granddaughter, screaming and with outstretched arms, ran toward her and pointed:

'Look, look! ... All gone, nothing whole – everything filthy and horrible – everything ruined and destroyed by those bad, horrid men!'

Afterwards, the old woman had bent her head and recited a saying of her forefathers. After that, the girl had led the old woman up the stairs to the little room that she had cleaned. And now night has fallen again. The little lamp borrowed from Master Samuel and his good wife Siphra is burning on the table which Simeath had so artfully restored to its upright position. Grandmother and granddaughter are sitting across from each other. The bundle with the inheritance from Gronau in the Principality of Hildesheim lies beneath the table. –

'My dear child, how often have the enemy or bad people of the town pulled down this house since I have drawn breath! Anyone who has lived as long as I, who has seen Crazy Christian and Tilly, Herr von Gleen and the *Duchess of Hessen, Field-Marshal Holzappel and Wrangel and so many less important commanders ride by or suffered to be kicked aside, someone like that does not care much about Messieurs de Turenne and de Fougerais! I only see once more what I have already seen a dozen times. It is a time in which a person accepts the worst as normal. Don't cry, dear heart, you are young and may yet live to see a purer, better time!'

In this way Kröppel-Leah had comforted her granddaughter. Meanwhile, the Pastor of Saint Kilian's had wished his nephew a good night in the manner which we know; meanwhile, the student had offered his solace in misery, his Horace, to Brother Henricus to buy or trade for a supper and a place for the night; meanwhile, at a site which we now enter for the first time – there was talk of the old Jewess's inheritance.

Near the Corvey Gate, in a tavern with a sign showing a man carrying his head under his arm, in the ale-house named after St. Vitus, there was talk of Kröppel-Leah's bundle.

The student, Herr Lambert Tewes, had three times groped his way into the demolished walls where urban comfort had resided in an earlier time, and had three times felt about for the remnants of the hearths.

'Brr!' he had groaned each time, and he did not make a fourth attempt to find a place for the night in Höxter among the ruins of the Thirty Years War.

'*Basolamano, messieurs, most honourable sirs', he said politely on entering the pot-house of St. Vitus at the gate on the Corvey road. This was received with joyful shouts and loud bellowing.

Except for Corporal Polhenne, all were again present, and a few others of their ilk to boot. A pretty bunch, most of them already half drunk and ready for any devilment and mischief! There was also his classmate Wigand Säuberlich, who had not been of much help to the scholars of Höxter in their learned work. And Säuberlich was the first to step up to him with his foaming pitcher of beer, grab the student by the collar and yell:

'There he is! Where have you been, fellow? For the last hour we have been yearning for you like an old maid for the groom. Hurrah, the stove is hot and the roast ready! Serve up, good fellows; out with knife and fork! You are coming with us, Lambert, aren't you?'

'Where to, *Signor Strillone?'

'No foreign languages now, old fellow! We won't stand for it. You'll go with us wherever we lead you.'

'Bad weather out there – '

'But good enough to make a merry night of it in Höxar! The whole honourable and cheerful gathering is coming along, man for man.'

'But first I'd like to know what's going on, friends.'

'Hunger and rage, doctor!' retorted a voice from the crowd. 'All that the French have left us.'

'And a wretched thirst to boot!'

'Yes, you know how to booze, but this is the end of the barrel, and nothing more's to be had in Höxter! That's just why we want to get the keys to the cellar. The Lutherans fall upon the Catholics, and conversely. And you surely won't mind, Lambert, if we also visit your uncle in his bewilderment.'

'*Scabies capiat – the devil take my uncle!' shouted the student; but now Hans Vogedes took him by the arm and whispered something to him which, so he thought, would triumphantly overcome his last hesitation and doubt.

'And afterwards, or in between, we'll go after the Jews! Eh? What do you say?'

The student took a long look at the tempter, and then said:

'You must be from *Merxhausen, ferryman!' At which it was as if the general cudgeling of the Jews had already begun here and now in St. Vitus's pub. To completely understand the student's reply and the anger of that worthy fellow Hans Vogedes, though, a short explanation of the term is required.

Namely, when the foul fiend, the tempter, led Jesus to the pinnacle of the Temple, he said to him – according to a tradition that has been preserved along the Weser – 'If you fall on your knees and worship me, all of this shall be yours – except for Merxhausen and Sievershausen – those two villages I reserve for myself.' –

'You are not from Sievershausen there in the Solling woods, Tewes', said the boatman Hans with raised fist. 'But neither did they kick you out of Helmstedt because you are so very respectable. You inflated windbag, you blockhead, are you going to affront a decent fellow here and at this hour? Mind your Latin skull, you learned moocher!'

Master Lambert looked the furious fellow over once more from head to toe; then, unconcerned, he took a step closer to the table, seized the first pitcher that came to hand, lifted it to his mouth, and leisurely let its contents run down his gullet. He sighed, banged the empty vessel down on the board, and recited with much pathos:

> '*I hated you since time began,
> Just as the wolf is loathed by lamb.
> Think of the rope around your neck
> Which with deep streaks it will bedeck;
> And on your leg with bells a ring,
> Monsieur, what an unpleasant thing!

Is that the path on which you want to take me with you?'

'By God's thunder!' screamed the ferryman, foaming at the mouth and rushing at the student; but Wigand Säuberlich threw himself in the way and caught his arm:

'Stop, stop! That's what his book says!'

'Is this what the book says? Is this what the book says?' shouted the rest of the crowd. 'Let's see it, Lambert must prove it, that this is what's printed about Hans!'

'It's in my book, gentlemen!' laughed the Helmstedt student, 'just keep him away for a moment longer; I'll proceed to prove the truth. And then give each of us a saber – I'm not willing to match fists with him!'

He had taken out his Horace and now read with the greatest pathos:

> 'Lupis et agnis quanta sortito obtigit
> Tecum mihi discordia est
> Ibericis peruste funibus latus
> Et crura dura compede!'

'The deuce!' groaned the whole praiseworthy company, scratching their heads. 'Give up, Hans Vogedes, you cannot get the better of that. That's the language in which they pronounce judgment and the law. That damned foreign Latin tongue is enough to spoil one's fun from the start. It puts before your eyes the green table with its drapery of graybeards and the slavering snouts of council, judge and advocate! Well now, who comes with me to have some fun?'

Despite the 'damned foreign Latin tongue', they all went – except the student. He, however, first made a little speech:

'Did I run away from the august Mother Julia, the divine Carolina, to throw longing glances at an old Jewess and her pack?! *Apage, apage – leave me alone. In other words, gentlemen, what do I care! Do what you want, but leave me out of it. In the meantime, I'll look after the house here and will keep the bench warm for you.'

More grumbling ran through the vile circle, but Lambert did not let that bother him. He merrily joined the row of those still seated at the upper end of the table next to the stove, swinging one leg over the bench.

'Dearest of brothers, just think it over once more', Wigand Säuberlich encouraged him.

'Dearest of brothers, that's what I am doing. But see, brother dear, who would preserve the history of your glorious, heroic deeds if in all the confusion one of your cudgels bashed in my brains?'

'Well then, without you! Onwards, brothers! *En avant, as that dog the Commandante de Fougerais shouted when marching off. In these times, everyone must decide for himself. That's just what our fathers taught us!'

'By the immortal gods, that's true!' shouted the student; but after the mob had stormed out, he jumped up from the bench and onto the table and exulted:

'Höxter and Corvey!'

That's what they shout in the bowling alley when all the skittles fall. –

VI

'That'll be a nice brawl! Well, landlord, are you for abbey or town?'

'They should both drop dead! But first come down from the table and don't break my dishes; they are the last that the French left in one piece.'

'That indeed calls for prudence, old man', said the student, and he followed the glum request of the tavern keeper. He climbed down from the board, stretched this way and that, lay down on the long bench, pulled the smoldering lamp closer, and placed the Horace under his head as a pillow. Then he also folded his hands under his head and watched drowsily and without interest as the landlord, softly humming to himself, cleared away the glasses and pitchers and from time to time stepped to the low window or outside the door of his pot-house where he listened into the night for the noises of his amiable patrons. From the depths of the house came the muted sound of a whimpering infant and, in between, the singing voice of the landlady of St. Vitus. The wind could also be heard and from time to time the downpour of a rain shower. With all these sounds, and after the mental and physical exertions of the day, Herr Lambert Tewes gently dozed off and for half an hour slept better than perhaps any other person in Höxter.

But after half an hour he woke up with a start and stared angrily about him, and not without reason.

The alarm bells had not yet been ruined in Höxter; they were sounding alarm at St. Kilian and at St. Nicholas!

'*What din assaults this quiet hearth?
Don't punch a hole in our fair earth!

Hallo, the battle has started! Vivat, Höxter and Corvey! Höxter and Corvey!' shouted the student jubilantly. As for us – we stop up both our ears and embark on the way by which earlier the good monk Heinrich von Herstelle had gone home. –

Today a good road lined with lovely chestnut trees leads from the town to the abbey, and we know from more than one cloudless summer day how to appreciate their shade. In those days the path, eaten bare by the war, stretched along the Weser, and only here and there a stubborn willow stalk rose ghostlike from the low bushes of the bank. The night and the winter weather had the path to themselves. Brother Henricus pulled the hood over his head and did not look left or right. He tripped too often even for his patience on the rough ground that had been ripped by horses and carts.

'Praised be the Lord', he groaned when he finally stood in front of the gate of Corvey and felt for the porter's bell. But his patience was about to be tried even more. He might as well have come to the castle of Princess Sleeping Beauty.

He rang the bell, and he rang in vain.

They were all asleep: from the prior, Niklas von Zitzewitz, down to the brother porter. Not a ray of light fell from any window. Even if Father Adelhardus, the cellarer, still had light, that for now was no help to Brother Henricus because the cell of the pater cellarer faced to the east toward the river, and the tired traveler arrived at the gate from the west.

'All ye saints', moaned Brother Henricus after ten minutes of ceaseless knocking, calling and ringing. 'What did the evil one mix into their nightcap?' Once more he laid hold of the bell, and never had he pulled the same in the church tower so fervently for evensong or mass.

'At last!' he called grimly when the window next to the portal opened and the porter asked who was seeking entrance. –

The answer was given and Brother Henricus admitted. In earlier times he would now have grabbed the gatekeeper by the throat; as an old man and humble, gentle disciple of St. Benedictus, he contented himself with the gruff question:

'Do tell me what has happened here that at this early hour of the evening the whole abbey is down like a nest of hamsters in January?'

'Rich living and jubilation, Reverend Sir', replied the drowsy porter, who was hardly able to keep on his feet and yawned between every two words. 'An open house – since your departure – for weeks on end – the

French generals by night and day! – Oh, we have proved ourselves to be good hosts, Brother – as was only fitting, Brother – and the French gentlemen were very satisfied with us. We sent a good aroma of us away with them.'

'Hmm, hmm, indeed', growled Brother Heinrich von Herstelle. 'And in the meantime the likes of us had to tramp about in the Solling woods and make do with the cold food and the watery beer of the surly people of Braunschweig! Aye, aye, but I bring news from the journey – important tidings! Are none of the fathers still awake, that they may relieve me of my news and free me of the responsibility?'

'Not one! We are all in bed, worn out – unless – perhaps the Reverend Father Adelhard – '

'Aha!' muttered Brother Henricus. 'Say no more, my son. I thank you for having opened the gate for me; now lie down again, and may Saint Benedictus send you a salutary and pious dream.'

'The same to you, Brother', replied the porter and withdrew to his cell. Brother Henricus had no trouble finding the way by himself.

He groped along the passageways and cells, and behind many an oaken door he heard the sonorous snoring of the brothers and fathers in the Lord.

'They sleep like angels', muttered Brother Henricus, but then rather ominously added: 'Well, well!'

Thus he arrived at the door of the abbey's steward, Adelhardus von Bruch, and knocked.

'*Domi!*' came the response in a deep bass voice – *domi*, which means: 'I am at home! I'm in here!'

'Thanks be to God', murmured Brother Heinrich and entered with the salutation prescribed in the Rule of St. Benedict. But one who did not chant the appropriate responses was Father Adelhardus. Indeed he was inside and was sitting bulkily in a comfortable chair at an oaken table. And if what was spread out in front of him was the last remnant of the French feast, they must have had a grand time of it at Corvey; still, quite a bit had been left over.

A dish with a boiled ham, half of it unfortunately already devoured! A dish with the skeleton of a turkey! A loaf of bread the size of half a cart wheel and a number of earthen jugs and glass bottles next to a tankard which just by itself – that is through its appearance alone – gave pleasure to the eye, whatever its contents might be!

'*Non confido oculis meis*, I don't trust my eyes!' cried Father Adelhardus, his speech a bit thick. 'Is it you, my son Heinrich?'

'It is, and I like what I see', replied the fine old horseman and good brother of Corvey, Heinrich von Herstelle.

'*Cor meum prae gaudio exsultat*, my heart jumps with joy. Do you want me to get up, my son, to embrace you? *Desiste*, refrain from it – better you sit down because I know that you were sent on an arduous journey *ad paganos*, to the heathens – into the deserts, *per deserta ac solitudines*. I greatly missed you, my son, during the recent tribulations.'

Brother Henricus stood his staff in a corner and looked across the table, smiling happily, benevolently and comfortably at the steward in the Lord's vineyard.

'I have traveled and I have seen. I have returned with news from the desert and the wild forest. Do you want to wake the prior, Father, so that I can report what I have seen and found out?'

'*Non sum hebes nec stupidus*, only if I was an ass or a fool. Sit down, my dear son, and for now tell me what you saw – tomorrow is soon enough for the others.'

'But the prior enjoined me on his soul to appear before him immediately on my return, be it day or night.'

'All right!' retorted Father Adelhard and rose laboriously, supporting himself with both of his soft and broad hands on the armrests of his chair. 'He also likes to irritate us as often as possible; let's annoy him in return! Come with me, my son Heinrich, I'll wake him for you.' –

And they certainly did wake him, the prior of Corvey, Herr Nikolaus von Zitzewitz, and he received their fervour as it deserved.

The cellarer went into his room after having first poked Brother Henricus slyly with his elbow. Brother Henricus waited outside the door, but he did not have to wait long.

'His Reverence sends his regards, my son, and gives you his blessing –'

'And?'

'He nearly threw the first thing at my head that came to hand under his bedstead. Tomorrow at an appropriate time, he will talk to you and hear what you have to say, my son. Is it now your wish that we also betake ourselves to Brother von dem Felde, Father Florentius, the subprior?'

'I think we'll leave it at this', Brother Henricus suggested somewhat dolefully and irritably.

'Or to Father Metternich, our good provost Ferdinandus?'

Brother Henricus only shook his head.

'Then you had better come back with me. I am the only one in the abbey who will still get you a supper and something to drink!'

In a gesture of familiarity, Father Adelhardus put his arm into that of his aged son: 'As I told you, we could have saved ourselves the trouble', he said once they were back in his chamber sitting in front of the ham and the turkey. Brother Henricus took a long, long draft – sighing again but this time quite comfortably – and only then pushed the aforementioned tankard toward his best friend in Corvey, for refilling from one of the monstrous gray stone jugs with the abbey's coat of arms painted on it in blue.

VII

That the walls were still standing in Corvey, and the doors were not taken off their hinges or knocked in, we know. In that regard, the abbey fared better than the town. But otherwise, conditions at the good Benedictines, too, left much to be desired after the departure of the august Allies.

Pater Adelhardus now gave Brother Henricus a detailed report about this.

'I advise you, my son', he said, 'to make the most of the bones. I fought a hard battle until I had them safely here in my cell. *O gula, gula hominum!* Alas, the gluttony of people! There was not one, not a single one of the brotherhood, who did not begrudge me the slim morsels. But they'll pay for it at the next brewing. *Cellarius sum*, I am the cellarer! Take my advice and make do with the ham bone. I went to work on the turkey, but only because getting hold of it caused me the most anxiety and trouble. Truly, they all puffed up their own combs and went after me with ferocious gobbling, *sed palmam reportavi*, I won the victor's crown!'

'Are things really that bad here, Father Adelhard?'

'Woui, *mon fils*. Until they drive new cattle for slaughter to us from the upper villages, hunger will indeed be our best spice at Corvey. I don't even want to think of the poultry house. Make the most of the ham, Heinrich, my son. Tomorrow the motto will be buckwheat, and buckwheat it will also be the day after tomorrow. Buckwheat, buckwheat, a healthy supplement. But I love you, Henricus, and I am not like the others. *I* don't begrudge you the ham, and I'll avert my eyes while you eat.'

He really did look away, although with a deep sigh.

And indeed, little of the ham was left for the next day. It had been a long time since any monk of Corvey had earned such a justified claim to a martyr's crown as Father Adelhard von Bruch on this very evening.

But now the massive bone hit the plate as if it were wood. Brother Henricus had had his fill, and the tankard resumed its passage between the two worthy old fellows.

'You should have been at home', said the cellarius. 'You remember what it was like when Herr von Turenne made Höxter his headquarters. But how amiable at the very end Herr von Fougerais was, the commandant whom Turenne left behind, *that* unfortunately you missed. It was life in high style, by day and by night. They never left our side and it would have been stupid of them if they had. Because we regaled them till the tables creaked – oh, you should have seen the brothers. That went on like – our Greek scholar Father Agapetus has translated it for us from Homer – like – in the castle of *King Odixus. And the abbey was Queen Penelope, and the Frenchmen were the *ambitores*, the *proci*, the suitors! *Ebibe*, drink up, my son. *Deposuimus eos vino*, we frequently drank them under the table, but the next morning they always rose again. His Princely Highness of Münster, our administrator, will never forget all we have done to make the stay of his allies with us most comfortable. Of course, whether they'll reimburse our outlays remains to be seen. After all, you don't get such glorious allies for a piece of oat bread and a drink from our Schelpe Creek, which otherwise is supposed to be a cool and very healthy drink!'

'That too was the mocking opinion of the Duke', said Brother Henricus.

'Let's leave that until later. Now let me continue my tale. Look – there lies the ham – bone! We had hundreds of them in the smoke house, one next to the other. It used to be a picture to gladden your eyes, *nunc lugubris et tristis memoria!* They are gone. Aye, my son, *via ad coelum nonnisi lacrymis struitur* – the path to heaven goes through a valley of tears. We had them, *gallos*, that is, on the table and at the table. And now they are gone, *galli et Galli*. The ones in the stomachs of the others. And how the hens of Höxter fared, that the next nine months will show. In that regard they were all the same, those from the Languedoc and those from Bretagne, those from Normandy and those from Picardy, and their chief cock was no better than his people. *Diabolus accipiat animam ejus*, may the Evil One grab him by the collar on his way to Wesel! Well, my son, in your youth you rode with Tilly, so you know what it's like – '

'Please say grace now, Father', sighed Brother Henricus. 'It is because I rode with Tilly that this would not be appropriate for me at this moment. Afterwards let's go to sleep.'

'Certainly not', cried Pater Adelhardus. '*Omnia tempestive*, everything in its own good time. If I talked myself hoarse for your sake, it is now your turn to tell me what good news you are bringing from Duke Rudolfus Augustus.'

'How you take it is up to you', whispered Brother Henricus. 'He has mightily fortified his woods, the Solling. He has put up guns, horsemen and foot soldiers from the *Ith Hills to the river. This far and no further! he said, after having had his preparations shown to me. It would have been a hard march even for Turennius through the wild forest and the Weser Hills.'

'That's why he remained *comfortabiliter* with us and showed the Huxarienses, the citizens of Höxter, and us his might and power and that of our bishop and administrator.'

'Afterwards, today I found the bridge over the Weser pulled down.'

The cellarer of Corvey thoughtfully inclined his head:

'Everything in this world has its reason. This time we are in *trouble in Holland, otherwise our ease here in Corvey would have lasted longer – don't you think, Messieurs? ... *Our* ease? Yes, ours! My dear son Heinrich, we are living in bitter, bewildering times. Since we have had the Duke's pikemen and musketeers here, we may yet see his artillery move across the river, too. Herr von Fougerais was a clever man and kept his eyes behind him as he was marching off. You know, son Heinrich, what solace heaven sends me in these evil days?'

'Well, Father?'

'That I am only the cellarer of Corvey and not Herr Christoph Bernhard von Galen, bishop of Münster, and that after the death of our blessed abbot Arnold he became administrator of our monastery and famous abbey, and not I. And now we can go to bed, my son.'

It is true that they could, but for the time being they did not yet get to it. Because they heard the same bells that had wakened from his slumber the student from Helmstedt, Herr Lambert Tewes, in the tavern of St. Vitus.

'Saint Vitus, what is it?' called Brother Henricus, cupping a hand behind his ear.

'Are you hearing something, Henricus?'

'It sounds like an alarm.'

'A buzzing like this has been in my ears for days – I think it must be in the air of Corvey. *Collusio diaboli*, deception and delusion of the devil! Let's go to sleep.'

'No, no, these are not tricks of the airy spirits. The bells are sounding alarm in Höxter!' called Brother Henricus. He had stepped over to the high window with the small, round glass panes, and had opened one wing.

'Can you hear it, Father?'

'My son Heinrich, once again you are right. Help me up; oh those herringmongers; they will probably have to put out a fire there too! Let's see whether the western sky is turning red.'

Supported by Brother Henricus, good Father Adelhardus tottered through the long corridor to the west wing of the building, and the two old men looked toward the town. But the vault of the sky there was dark. And the night was equally dark in the east and west.

'Then it must be something else, and now the *prior, together with subprior and provost, will have to get out of their warm nests after all', muttered the cellarer, wavering between malicious pleasure and his own discomfort.

'I saw it coming; things looked bad in Höxter when I came from the ferry this evening. I did not like the streets, and what was being spoken and whispered in them I liked even less.'

'Rebellion? Tumult in the town? *Seditio ante portas?*'

'Our precious brothers at Saint Niklas weren't too happy either.'

'Alas – the old game! Trump Luther – trump the Pope! May the Lord protect us. King of diamonds – ace of clubs! A trick for Münster – a trick for Braunschweig! – Pull the alarm bell of Corvey, Frater Henricus; get the abbey-guard into their pants; I'll get the fathers and brothers up. Oh Herr von Zitzewitz, oh Herr von Metternich. The Lord imparts it to His children in their dreams. Ho! Ho! Up with you! Alarm! Alarm! Huxar is in rebellion!!!'

Now it is really amusing to stand at this moment in this hallway of the great Abbey of Corvey and to observe how on the call to arms the sonorous snoring sounds behind the cell doors suddenly ceased – as if the works of a mill had been brought to a halt. But then it rumbled and grumbled behind these doors, then the first of them opened – and then they swarmed out, out of all of them in fact.

'Saint Vitus and Benedictus, what's the matter now?'

Father Adelhardus did not wait to answer; he woke the prior for the second time. But Brother Heinrich von Herstelle on the other hand, though quite indifferent to the discovery in his abbey of the first five books of the *Annals of Tacitus, still knew very well how to pull the alarm bell and get a guard company into armour and to the pikes.

Corvey was running pell mell:

'St. Vitus, the troops from Braunschweig have crossed the river! St. Benedict, Fougerais has returned! They are fighting it out in Höxter! Out of your beds, defend the abbey! Up for Christian Bernhard – up for Corvey!'

The oldest of the old came staggering out. The provost Ferdinand von Metternich came; there came subprior Florentius von dem Felde, and at last there also came the prior, Herr Nikolaus von Zitzewitz.

'That was quite a hard job', Father Adelhardus recounted later. '*Elinguis stabat*, he stood like a statue, like a stick, and was rubbing his eyes. **Vae turbatori*; whoever's fault it was – he won't forgive my disturbing him for the rest of his life.'

Be that as it may – this is how Corvey got to its feet! ... Höxter and Corvey!

VIII

As for us, we have not yet been able to take the weight off our legs. Let us go back to Höxter, and this with a cool head and in a calm mood: we need both, and of the latter we are especially proud. The great author of the *Dassel Chronicle, Master Hans Letzner, maliciously nicknamed Fairy Tale Hans, could not peer into the hubbub of his times, and in particular the tumult of the St. Vitus celebration, in a more calm and objective manner than we in this clamorous Höxterian night after the decampment of Maréchal de Turenne and Monsieur de Fougerais.

In the town, everyone had been on their feet for some time. The anger had to get out, and now the fermentation had blown the cork out of the bunghole: the cloudy flood gushed out and bewildered the senses, and since we come from Corvey and therefore know how things look there, we also know that for the time being there was no one present who could have carried the olive branch across these evil waters or, better yet, poured oil on them himself. Even the women were out in the streets, and that was the worst of all. They had suffered from the French billeting in more than one way, and truly more than the men. Into what hiding places they had had to crawl with their howling and starving children! And they were lucky if they were not pulled out from them to embellish the daily and nightly merriment with their presence. Now they came from their empty cupboards, soiled beds and filthy floors, and for their part were looking for suitable people and situations on which to vent their anger and rage. Catholic and Lutheran women agreed that several things had to be said and done before peace and decorum could reign again in Höxter, and it was they – the dames of Höxter – whom the expelled student from Helmstedt, Herr Lambert Tewes, found most entertaining.

Master Lambert, waking up with a start from his hard resting place in St. Vitus's tavern, as we've already described, put the Horace that had served as his pillow in his pocket and stepped out of the tavern door. We have also already told the reader that this pot-house was located near the gate on the Corvey road and hence at some distance from the centre of town. As a result, it was quiet in that area; the uproar that had started was raging more toward the center of town, and that is where the student now betook himself with long strides.

'What good would the softest featherbed together with dressing gown and slippers have done me now? What does it benefit my uncle that he pulled his nightcap over his tender ears? Doesn't he too have to get up now? He does! Indeed, it has been shown again that in the present circumstances a bench is the only proper resting place. *Paratus sum! and with heart and courage into this merry world's hilarity. A pity only that here one cannot call upon his fellow students as under the jurisdiction of the much-praised Julia Carolina.'

But things moved now without academic assistance. Pulled along by a great rush of the mob, he emerged first from the vile throng – of course with the well-known '*Quo, quo scelesti ruitis', but this time without translating it – in front of the Lutheran vicarage and jumped up on a curbstone – of course only to be able to see better what they were really planning to do with his dear relatives.

'Well, well!' he said, and the scene was indeed rather curious to behold. The Catholic Huxarienses were storming the Lutheran vicarage. They had, of course, first encountered the pastor's wife, who from the front of the door, broom in hand, for the time being was fighting off the rabid crowd with remarkable success. Over the head of his wife, the reverend gentleman, his arms raised high, called for reason, but quite in vain – it was his sexton who was hanging on to the bell rope in the tower of St. Kilian and was ringing for help for the Lutheran faith, while across from St. Nicholas the bells were appealing to the town's regents, the Corvey Abbey, the bishop of Münster and the dark stormy night sky, on behalf of one Emilio Altieri, better known as *Pope Clement the Tenth.

The rioters had brought along torches to make sure not to stumble over any stone on their way. In the flickering light, the student observed everything minutely, but he himself carefully stayed in the shadows as much as possible.

'*Coraggio, chère tante', he shouted joyfully. 'You see, dear *Säuberlich, that's good fencing. Parry that one! ... Swish, this one really hit home, right on the beak. See, my son, there you have your mouthful of the French legacy in the gutters of Höxter. Oh goodness, doesn't that lady wield a mean sword, or rather a deadly broom!'

And that she did. But in the end it was not enough against the overwhelming onslaught. She gave way, and if *Pope Joan had been in her place she too would have given way. The student on his curbstone thought he'd split his sides:

'Why does he interfere? Should words do more good here than the deeds of a heroine? *Retro retrorsum, Domine Pastor, don't waste your time! There, uncle – there!'

That's about the way it was. The worthy gentleman of St. Kilian's had realized that his words were of no more use than his spouse's broom. He had taken the arm of his wife and pulled her backwards up the steps into the door of the house. They were followed by the crowd's screaming and the gloating laughter of the nephew:

'Hey there, this is not the first time today that you slammed the door in someone's face and then bolted it! Now you get what you asked for!'

*Contra aegida Palladis ruere, charging the field of Pallas Athena, he called it when those in front of the angry bunch were pushed by those in the back, with their heads against the barricaded door. Höxter of the year 1673 dropped their clubs and picked up stones.

The first one struck the Lutheran vicarage; it was followed by the next dozen. For a brief moment, Dominus Helmrich Vollbort still showed himself at the window, then he disappeared in the interior of the house. The clerical lady stuck it out a moment longer, but the windows splintered around her. She disappeared likewise while the bombardment – or, as Pater Adelhardus would have expressed it, the *infestatio cum bombardis – continued. And at the very moment when the need was greatest, the frightened call for help from the tower fell silent. A handful of upright inhabitants of Höxter had broken open the door of Saint Kilian's church through which the sexton had slipped in, had found the sexton at work at the rope, and now it was no longer pealing, instead it was pelting on him; he got a beating, a most terrible beating.

Unfortunately, we cannot tear ourselves apart so as to be in two places at once, but we can assure the reader on our word and our honour that the caterwauling which the Lutheran citizens of Huxar arranged for the friars of St. Nicholas in honour of the French departure, in no way fell short of that at St. Kilian's. The Catholic vicarage suffered no less from the friends of our friend Lambert Tewes than the Lutheran one. The spectacle was the same there as here. Nothing was left out in word or deed, and the only consolation for the gentlemen at St. Nicholas in this grim night was that the 'gentlemen on the other side' were faring no better. Even a poor consolation is still a consolation.

But would it not be our duty now to call for the mayor? Not at all; because in the end he always comes on his own, and so also this time, and he is accompanied by the oldest and most respectable members of the community.

Groaning, he arrived, the mayor Thönis Merz, and with him the others: Senator Caspar Albrecht, and Jobs Tielemann and Heinrich Kreckler and Hans Jakob zum Dahle, and Hans Freisen and Hans Sievers and Hans Tropen and Hans Heinrich Wulf and Henrich Vosskuhl and Adam Sievers, the deans of the guilds, and Konrad Kahlfuss, the elected *master of the commoners! They appeared so as to establish order, and that was not normally easily done wherever they appeared.

'The mayor!' croaked a voice in the crowd, and immediately a hesitation came over the surging flood and then it came to a standstill. Head over heels the attackers rushed down from the steps of the vicarage, the mob scattered, and the consul poked his elbow into the side of the senator and said:

'See friend, didn't I tell you?!'

But whether it mattered more what he had said, or what the pastor and his wife were saying now, we shall leave undecided. *Whosoever gives offence to his brother shall be liable to the council. And such calls were being made – let us see what in the meantime has happened to our student from Helmstedt. –

After the angry Catholic crowd at St. Kilian's had dispersed, they did not peacefully go home and to bed but ran through the streets toward St. Nicholas.

Nimbly the student had jumped down from his curbstone. He had carefully observed whatever was of interest to him, but he was yet to reap the best part of the entertainment.

The space in front of the vicarage was empty. In the door, which was open again, stood uncle and aunt vigorously gesticulating, on the steps the mayor with his hand on his chest, at the foot of the stairs the chorus of senators, patricians, tribunes and guild masters. With measured gait, Herr Lambert Tewes now stepped out of the darkness into the light of the lantern that Master of Commoners Konrad Kahlfuss was carrying, politely doffed his hat, made a deep bow and addressed the assembly in terms that eighty years later the *Literaturbriefe, in attacking Herr Dusch and in keeping with the letter-writing fashion of the day, called courtoisie. Then he slowly crossed into the next alley and as soon as he was out of sight of the indignant authorities, ran as fast as his feet would carry him toward the tumult at St. Nicholas:

'*Who fears the Scythians, the Parthian's raid,
Who of Germania's hordes is afraid?
We quietly sit at a merry meal,
Where an honest man safe from the villains can feel!'

Herewith, that is, with this cheerful though not quite fitting quotation from the fifth ode of the fourth book of songs by Quintus Horatius Flaccus, he arrived at the Franciscan church of St. Nicholas by the Pyrmont Gate, and again just at the right moment.

IX

Just in right time. For at this instant the Catholic alarm bell fell silent, and the Catholic sexton also was beaten up. But in all of Höxter, Lambertus Tewes had no closer acquaintance than Jordan Hunger, the Catholic sexton. He even surpassed the ferryman Hans Vogedes, the corporal Polhenne and His Noble Highness Wigand Säuberlich, who had gone to school together with the student and who, like Master Tewes, did not take sides, but from each side only what he liked.

This enjoyment was now in full swing in front of the living quarters of the Franciscans, who had been installed at St. Nicholas by Christoph Bernhard. The Catholic crowd rushing away from St. Kilian's fell into the arms of the Lutheran one at St. Nicholas. In the end, they all had only one purpose: to cause mischief, and that they now undertook without any formality. The stone bombardment of the windows of the Catholic gentlemen was carried out as vigorously as that of Uncle Vollbort's windows.

'Well, well!' the student said happily, as he had done before. But just as he was about to swing himself up onto a curbstone again, a woman grabbed his coat, pulled him back and shrieked:

'For the sake of Jesus Christ, master scholar, they have beaten my husband to death! He is lying under the bells and they are dancing around him!'

'O *mon Dieu!*' exclaimed the student. 'Is it you, cousin? *Mon Dieu*, and he was such a good friend of Fougerais during our recent dispute!'

'That's why they have beaten him to a pulp, and he is lying beneath his rope. Oh Lambert, come and help me, don't let your best companion perish! They say the abbey is on its way here but what good does that do me if by then they have finished my husband off? That's what we have to suffer for the sake of Corvey!'

'Höxter and Corvey!' exulted the student, and then he was only too happy to be pulled by the sexton's wife toward the bells of St. Nicholas. In this night there was fun to be had for him everywhere in Huxar. –

The wretched Monsieur Jordan had not run away from his vault in the tower while his wife had called on the barbaric world for help. He was still lying beneath his dangling rope, just the way his worthless enemies and his good wife had left him, with his nose in the dust. His shoulders were shaking, he was kicking his feet and he was groaning pitifully.

With his nose in the dust! The student immediately knew a quotation from Horace and of course recited it for the unhappy, stricken man first in Latin and then in his own free translation:

'*Thus crashed the fir tree with thundering sound,
Thus the sexton after his fall can be found!
In the field of the Trojans, for his victors a spoil,
Don Bravatscho now has his nose in the soil!'

'Eh?' whimpered the sexton of St. Nicholas. 'Is it you, Lambert? Is my wife here too? Oooh, turn me over – for God's sake, gentle! Careful, gentle! It wasn't the Trojans, or whatever is the name of that village. May the devil repay those villains from Höxter who have mistreated me so horribly on account of the Church. Oh, oh, oh. This is much worse than the last battle over the *Bosseborn Lantern – remember, Lambert, the one three years ago where you also carried a cudgel, although as a Lutheran heretic it really was none of your business.'

The student had taken the poor fellow gently and carefully by the arm while his wife had lifted his feet in order to turn her half-dead husband on his back. But the sexton immediately regretted groaning out his last word.

For when Herr Lambert Tewes heard of the Battle of the Bosseborn Lantern, he instantly let go and, giving vent to a feeling quite different from that for his friend, extended his outspread hands high into the air.

The sexton fell back on his face with a loud cry. But the student shouted jubilantly:

'By the immortal gods, the Battle of the Bosseborn Lantern! Yes indeed, Jordan, from that occasion you are already used to filling your mouth with nourishing soil. You certainly did get your share of the beating in the battle of the sextons.'

'But it really was a battle of the sextons!' whimpered Jordan Hunger. 'A Catholic battle of the sextons! We only fought among ourselves for the glory of God, but this time – '

He was not able to end his sentence, but the student kindly took over for him:

'Just suffer in silence, old friend, your martyrdom thereby becomes that much greater.'

'Eh, you don't need to tell me', moaned the martyr, and while he is being turned again and laboriously brought into a sitting position, we will be able to tell our readers what the Bosseborn Lantern is all about.

Today the story is put about as a myth with which on every possible occasion to annoy the people of Bosseborn from village elder down to the poorest tenant farmer, to annoy them to death as one expression goes, or until they turn black according to another. They, namely the Bosseborners, returning home from a wedding, supposedly could not find their way and instead got lost in swamp and bog. Then the sexton, being the most sober of the group (*Socrates at the symposium of Plato), supposedly provided illumination for them in a rather singular way. He is said to have had an idea, itself an illumination under the circumstances: namely to pull the tail of his shirt out of his pants and let it hang down, and it had shone sufficiently brightly through the night to serve the villagers as a lantern. In this manner the sexton had staggered ahead, after him the alderman, followed by the village councillors, and then the reeling common peasants, all in single file – one after the other – an eternally memorable procession, until they reached the village.

It is a good story; if it only were true! But the matter ended in a different and much more serious way.

> '*When comes in summer Sanctus Veit
> Then change occurs in day and night
> Sleep gains but waking loses ground;
> As old age t'wards the grave is bound,
> Whom then too many pennies pain
> In this direction take your aim
> And wend your way toward St. Veit
> Where they will make your burden light – '

Thus, in Hans Letzner's account, sings a 'much experienced historian', and it is in the great procession to Corvey on *St. Vitus's day that the lantern story has its origin, as does every battle which for that reason was fought on this day, but most particularly that of the year seventy. This was one of the most stubborn and bloody as a result of the Indulgence which His Holiness *Pope Clement the Ninth had granted for the day in that year shortly before his death.

Now there was an old tradition that the youngest parish would open the solemn procession – older and more venerable ones would follow in order. Accordingly, those of Bosseborn were supposed to lead 'with the lantern', and of course wanted to pass it off to those from Ovenhausen who followed them: *hinc illae lacrimae! After those from Ovenhausen came those from Fürstenau, then the Bödexers, after them the Amelunxers, and then those from Wehrden and Jakobsberg. Then marched Ottbergen and Bruchhausen and after them the village of Stahle, followed by those from Albaxen, Brenkhausen, Lüchtringen and Godelheim. Finally, just before the relics of the saint, came the town of Höxter with its municipal band, together with those from Corvey. Behind St. Vitus walked the *chapter, as well as the ambassador from Braunschweig holding a small abbot's staff in his hand covered with a velum (even after the Reformation and being a Protestant!); he was led by the marshal of Corvey. The procession ended with the shrine beneath a canopy carried by Höxter's most eminent citizens. Jordan Hunger, the sexton of St. Nicholas had, in the memorable year of 1670, been sexton of Bosseborn and was supposed to carry the Bosseborn Lantern, that is, the flag of the church of his village –

> '*Many a one starts clever and smart
> But on the way home from wisdom doth part.
> Many a one starts out with good sense
> But then comes back having taken offense.
> Thus many go out both healthy and sound
> But on their return close to death can be found
> Wounded, or beaten, or heavily struck – '

This is how the 'experienced historian' continues his song, and this is how it was. Each time they had a mighty fight over the Bosseborn Lantern and though Bosseborn and Overhausen began the dispute among themselves, no village wanted to be left out, but they all pitched in and into each other. There was no St. Vitus celebration at Corvey without it, and there was nothing the abbey's chapter or the ambassador from Braunschweig could do about it except to ensure that next time Bosseborn would once more carry the 'Bosseborn Lantern'. –

But while we were here, straightening out what was askew and helping truth to prevail, wantonness rages on brutishly in Höxter, the battered Master Jordan Hunger is being dragged to his bed by his wailing wife and his merry friend, and – another procession is slowly approaching. To this latter we now turn and we meet it on the path that a while ago Brother Henricus had taken to the abbey. Brother Henricus now was walking back on this path; he was among those at the head of a column coming from Corvey. In his youth he had been a warrior and his prior, Herr Nikolaus von Zitzewitz, relied on him and would not leave his side. Close behind him walked subprior Florentius von dem Felde and provost Ferdinandus von Metternich. Good Father Adelhard, the cellarer, had been left at home because of his infirmity in these perilous times, and to keep order there.

The Abbey proceeded heroically toward the town to find out for itself what had happened there since '*impie et nefarie*', wickedly and thoughtlessly, no one had come to apprise them of it.

But Corvey could not do otherwise; Corvey had to make an appearance! The abbey, having just been strengthened by its foreign helper, the greatest of the French commanders, in its 'rights' vis-à-vis the rebellious citizenry of Huxar and the protector from Braunschweig, had to make every effort so that the supremacy it had finally regained after a long struggle would not slip from its grasp once again. The challenge was to secure Höxter against any enemy or rebel, and so the abbey moved, under arms, toward the town. At times like this, Herr Christoph Bernhard von Galen knew how to make a singularly angry face; Corvey was aware of that and was familiar with it.

The alarm bell that Brother Heinrich von Herstelle had pulled had been heard. The monastery guards had put on their armour, the Benedictine monks had equipped themselves as well as they could and from Lüchtringen, the nearest village on the other bank of the Weser, the men able to bear arms had crossed the river in boats to come to the aid of the abbey. The prior and other high Benedictine dignitaries of course went only in clerical garb, but many a stout pater or frater had courageously and voluntarily shouldered a musket or half-pike and was ready to carry out heroic deeds which the chronicles of Corvey would recount centuries later. But the most warlike of the whole clerical-secular army was Brother Henricus. Despite his advanced age he went about, confidently and manfully, with a huge sword, which had probably been left in the monastery when the *Hussites had crossed the Weser. The column looked more toward him than to the flag with the image of St. Vitus which was waving in front in the light of the torches. The holy patron saint was *carrying his head under his arm, Brother Heinrich, on the other hand, still carried his proudly on his shoulders.

59

'You take my blessing with you, my son, but be sure to come back healthy and cheerful', Father Adelhardus had said to him in farewell at the gate to the monastery, and had tenderly patted him on the shoulder.

Now they were on the path that had been ripped up and slashed and which we have described earlier, with the slogan: 'St. Vitus!' and the battle cry: '*Abbatia urbi imperat*: Corvey over Höxter!' At one moment they got into swamps, holes and among hard rocks – at another they stopped to catch their breath – and then they groaned on.

'Brother von Metternich, this is a night to *pronounce *anathema!* moaned the prior over and over. 'What do you think?'

'The righteous one looks at the ground before his feet and treads the path on which the Lord sends him.'

'*Bene, bene*! But how dark the night is! If only each of us had taken along a lantern instead of the torches! Now even the alarm from the tower has ceased, Henricus.'

'Perhaps it was just the din from the streets after all, and the rioters have become tired of the fun and are going to bed.'

'And we got up and here we are in the midst of a field? O Corpus Christi, a curse on their heads! – On with it, forward, all of you. Truly, one shan't make fun of Corvey with impunity; *abbatia urbi imperat*, there is the Corvey Gate! Shout: St. Vitus! and let us enter!'

Having marched for more than half an hour, they had finally arrived at this gate of Höxter; alas, entering was not that easy. First of all, the abbey found the door locked, although it had the keys for it – however, the key was in the hands of its courageous Captain Meyer, already mentioned earlier, whom we shall soon meet in person.

'Let us knock', said the subprior.

'Much good that'll do, what with the ditch in between', murmured the provost.

'Then bring up the abbey's cornettist, son Heinrich. Even if it bursts his lungs, he must get the porter onto the wall. What a horrible night!' grumbled the prior.

The old abbey had brought its hornist along, and he blew – he blew and nearly blew out his lungs, until his blowing had the desired effect.

Finally, finally lanterns glimmered on the wall, and then the bridge under the old gate tower came clanking down. Hat in hand, accompanied by his lantern carriers, Captain Meyer eagerly and breathlessly waddled out to greet the prior and the abbey: an amiable elderly gentleman, with a ruddy face, pot-bellied and agreeable, also one of the closest friends of the Pater Cellarius, Adelhardus von Bruch.

This time he was received very sulkily by the other dignitaries of the abbey.

'You are really here with your sword and sash, Monsieur?' shouted the prior. 'Why don't you come in robe and slippers, Captain? After all, you look as if you just got out of bed! By St. Vitus, sir, they are having a merry time in Höxter, the alarm bell brings the whole country into an uproar, and the captain turns onto his other side and sees fit to rest some more. Where have you and your people been, Meyer? Is it for this that the town's protection has been entrusted to you a second time?'

The commanding officer of the bishop of Münster let this and a whole series of similar charges and questions roll over him like a flood over a pile of rubble. Only when the prior came to the end of his breath did he justify himself, or at least began to justify himself.

'I am not coming from my warm bed, Your Reverence, but from the Weser walls at the Bridge Gate where, since the tumult started, I've been on the lookout for Sergeant-Major Noht, according to my oath and my duty.'

'For Noht?!'

'Yes, Your Reverence, Duke Rudolf August's Sergeant-Major Noht!'

'St. Vitus and Corvey, but why just for him?'

'Who else has contrived this riot than he? But by the devil, he took my drums once, he won't get his paws on them a second time, even if he sneaks across the Weser ever so stealthily!'

In the glow of torches and the light of lanterns the prior, Herr Nikolaus von Zitzewitz, looked about him in doubt and desperation at the faces of his retinue. They were all grinning and Brother Heinrich von Herstelle was even laughing. So the prior of Corvey had no choice but to stamp his feet and turn once more to the steadfast captain.

'But for God's sake, why are they ringing alarm? Who pulled the bells and why?'

'Well you see, Mylord Prior', the brave captain said, quite at ease, 'just step closer and look for yourself! As far as we are concerned, since the commotion started we have been armed and on the wall. I sent Corporal Polhenne into the melee, but he cannot do much either. Once again they are all intermingled, rat, cat and heretic, and our people are part of it too. In honour of the august French retreat, they have smashed the windows in all the rectories, and they have beaten all the sextons dead or half dead. But they have finished that, too, and just now they – the heretics and the Catholics – in Christian harmony, are going for the Jews.'

'And meanwhile the fellow stands there, leaning on his elbows and from the Bridge Gate looks out across the Weser for Sergeant-Major Noht!' groaned the prior, wringing his hands above his head. 'His drum?! His drum! Lord and St. Veit, one could wish that for the last ten years the drum had been beaten on him.'

'I would advise that we move into Höxter as fast as possible', suggested Brother Heinrich von Herstelle now, and the prior, not at all like a spiritual shepherd and counselor, commanded very angrily:

'Forward, march!'

Thus the abbey moved into the town and took its captain back in with it. –

X

'Now for the Jews!' Who at St. Nicholas first cast these words into the raging Catholic and Lutheran mob, which made common cause and formed a brotherhood in wickedness, has never been historically clearly established. We suspect our friend, the ferryman Hans Vogedes. To move against the Jews – here, as the young sage who had been expelled from Helmstedt expressed it, the *tertium comparationis had been found. The mob had first surged against the house of Master Samuel, and Lambert Tewes had of course also followed it there.

'I'll write an immortally heroic poem and shall become professor of rhetoric in Helmstedt. By Venus and Mars, my rustication by those ancient wigs there shall not go unpunished. I will be remembered as an Imperial Poet Laureate! This bloody Trojan night has been arranged by the gods just for me. My thanks go out to them!'

This is what he shouted, and as he ran, his Horace thumped against his thighs. We change direction and take a look at how Kröppel-Leah and little Simeath have spent this heroic Trojan night up to now.

Dead tired, both had wanted to crawl into the bed of the sergeant and the hay of the French cavalry shortly before the alarm started, and of course did not get to it. With a cry of fear, the child had drawn back her foot from the edge of the bed:

'Listen, listen! What is that, grandmother?'

It was the Höxterians in front of the vicarage of St. Kilian's. –

'Let them riot. Come, little one, we'll sit down at the table again. Lean your head against me. We'll pull the warm blanket around us, and I will tell you again of the olden times', said the grandmother, and her granddaughter came. They huddled once more in front of the small lamp in the cold, devastated room.

'Our kings were shepherds in the times of honour. But the herds grazed under palm trees – the sun of the Lord shone, the land of our fathers carried the scent of myrrh and incense. They were stout warriors in gleaming armour and fought battles – they feared no one – they were braver than any warring prince today – '

It did not work. They could not help but listen intently to the uproar in front of the broken door, the demolished windows. The old woman too, who during her lifetime had seen so much blaze and blood, had to listen. Even the strongest and most tested heart never ceases to learn in this respect.

'They'll break in on us again', wailed Simeath.

'They won't be able to take anything from us. Be quiet dearest; take courage. Yes, if the door was still bolted and the house wealthy, then there would be cause for fear. If the house was still as in the time of your great-grandfather, my father, plain from the outside but full of goods inside, we might be afraid. But today, what can they take from us when all we have is our misery?'

'They too only have theirs nowadays', the child said wisely. 'They are so fierce because this time they are as badly off as we are. And the less they find, the more cruelly they will treat us.'

'The Lord, the God of our fathers, has been our comfort since the beginning of the world. He will hold his hand over us tonight, as he has held it over his poor people in their affliction for two thousand years. We are still here to honour the Lord, despite all they have done to us with torture and malice. Listen – it is triumph! They are raging against each other! Be quiet, child, tonight they are not after the Yids!'

'But grandmother, they saw you going home with your large bundle. You have talked to them about your inheritance, grandmother', Simeath reminded her in a whisper.

'Those poor rags!' cried the old woman, pulling the bundle under the table closer toward her. 'We are wrapped in the cover from the deathbed of your uncle. That is the most precious piece of the whole inheritance.'

'If they were to believe that, we would be fortunate, grandmother', sighed the girl, and – it was, as she said.

From St. Kilian's to St. Nicholas, and from there first of all to the house of Master Samuel and his pious wife Siphra! They broke in and stole, they knocked the master of the house to the floor and pushed his spouse against the wall. They also beat his young children since no sexton was left to mistreat, and everything went helter-skelter. The municipal guards and Corporal Polhenne resisted in vain – and as we know, in the

63

meantime Captain Meyer watched very carefully that his drums were not taken from him for a second time by the Braunschweigian Sergeant-Major Noht. They were now applying the first incendiary torches, and just as the last man of the column from the abbey moved through the Corvey Gate, flames started out of the windows, the red cock leaped to the roof, stretched, beat his wings and fiercely crowed:

'Fire! Fire-ho!'

Now Father Adelhardus at the high window in the abbey's hallway did see the sky turn red above Höxter.

'Oh the *incendiarii*! Oh those heinous arsonists!' he said. 'Do those idle fellows still have too many roofs over their godforsaken heads? Well, I warned my good friend Heinrich that he should not get his fingers burnt. Mylord the prior and the others will know how to protect themselves and won't get too close.'

Then he ordered a lay brother to push an easy chair and a footstool to the bow window, sent a second lay brother to the cellar for a bottle of something good 'for his anger' and stood this bottle with the glass ready to hand on the window-sill. And there he now sat, his hands folded over his tummy, and did not hear at all how the oldest patres behind his back compared him to the cruel emperor Nero at the burning of Rome. But in the street in front of the house of the Jew Samuel, which was now completely ablaze, our friend, Herr Lambert Tewes, began to feel rather ill at ease.

He was no longer laughing but instead gnashed his teeth. He no longer had any desire to quote from his Horatius.

'Enough is enough!' he groaned. 'And this is inhuman. *Hierosolyma perdita*? Stand up for Jerusalem! Down with these murderous arsonist villains! Monsieur Samuel is the only one in Huxar who can count on my gratitude. And now they are stealing my father's watch from his locker! Heaven, hell and all devils, down with you, you brute!'

The last word was accompanied by a blow of his fist directed at one of the rioters. The fellow immediately fell to the ground, but at the same moment his hat was pulled down over his brow, eyes and ears, and he got a kick in his ribs which for several minutes took his breath away. When he finally had raised his hat again, he found himself for the second time this night eye to eye with Brother Heinrich von Herstelle, and the brother immediately took hold of him, grabbed him around the chest and thundered to Captain Meyer:

'Away with him! Lock him up! If anyone this night has been part of it, it is this one. Into prison with him!'

'Halt!' called the student, laughing. 'If anyone this night has seen to order, manners and virtue in Höxter, it was me. Meyer, you know me, and you have an eye for innocence. Rather, accept my help, *domine* – alone you won't get the better of these rascals.'

Prior, provost and the whole column from Corvey looked somewhat dubious in the red glow of the conflagration. But Captain Meyer, scratching his ear, said:

'I don't know what I should say. But, reverend sirs, I do indeed know him, and the most useful thing to do would be to enlist him in our patrol.'

'All right then, forward and charge!' commanded Brother Henricus, raising his sword. And with left shoulder in front, with pikes, halberds, half-pikes and clubs of hornbeam thrust forward, the armed might of Corvey threw themselves onto the Huxariens, in order to save for the Jews under the abbey's protection whatever was still left of their lives. Lambert Tewes carried two naked children out of the burning house; Siphra was rescued from further iniquity by Brother Henricus; friend Säuberlich was subdued by Captain Meyer with the help of Corporal Polhenne. The honourable knights von Metternich and von Zitzewitz conducted themselves valiantly, and bravely drove any vassal of Corvey who seemed inclined to sneak home, back into battle. And now the first stirrings of good sense appeared in the population, and Höxter began to feel ashamed. On their part, Mayor Thönis Merz and his town council started to take action. The arsonists and looters were overpowered or fled in all directions. The streets emptied and since now, toward midnight, the wind was dying down, Master Samuel's house was burning to the ground quietly and without further danger. It was left to burn.

XI

Wrapped in the woollen cover from the deathbed of her nephew in Gronau in the principality of Hildesheim, Kröppel-Leah and Simeath had in the meantime been listening with fright and horror. The red glow of the conflagration shining into the empty window openings and the doorway, had broken the courage of the old woman.

'See, grandmother, they are coming after us again, they have set fire to father Samuel's house; – shouldn't we leave? We can steal across the courtyard and into the neighbour's garden. Herr Jakob zum Dahle won't be too hard on us if tomorrow morning he finds us in his stable.'

'Yes, yes, my child', moaned the old woman. 'Softly, softly – there is my bundle – help me up again! You are right, we have to get out – they are coming and they show no mercy.'

She tried to get up; alas it was in vain. The journey from Gronau had been too much for the old woman after all. She fell back onto the chair, put her arms on the table and her face on her arms.

'Grandmother, grandmother', wailed the young girl. 'Rouse yourself – wake up, let me carry your pack! Let them have the sack, but let us run – mercy, they are coming – there they are!'

Now the old Jewess screamed even louder than the young one. They came, they tramped noisily up the stairs – they were there – only three of them, but the worst in Höxter – Hans Vogedes, the ferryman, with an axe, ahead of the other two. At the moment at which the abbey was approaching and Lambert Tewes felled his friend Wigand Säuberlich, they had slipped out of the crowd in front of Master Samuel's house, and from the start they made it no secret that they were following the scent of the Gronau inheritance.

Five minutes later, after they had crossed the demolished threshold, such a horrible and shrill howl of wailing cut through the night from the house of Kröppel-Leah that it drowned out all other noise in the street and everyone raised his head and listened with sudden fright. –

But at the site of the conflagration the picture had already changed. In full clerical garb, the Reverend Helmrich Vollbort had come onto the scene among the monks and the town officials and uttered harsh words against the dark night sky as well as against the prior of Corvey, Herrn Nikolaus von Zitzewitz, and against the Münsterian commander, Captain Meyer.

He had called for revenge for the offence committed against his house and his maltreated sexton; hiding behind the shoulder of Brother Henricus, the nephew was ever so proud of his uncle.

'But they beat our sexton to a pulp at St. Nicholas as well, reverend sir', the prior had interjected. 'There really was complete parity – and under those circumstances, what else do you expect from us tonight?'

'It has always been possible to talk sense with the abbey and his Princely Highness of Münster', Herr Florentius von dem Felde had added soothingly, and –

'Suggest to him that you'll have me hanged in front of his door', the wild fellow from Helmstedt had whispered in the ear of Brother Heinrich von Herstelle.

Brother Heinrich did not suggest this because now Herr Ferdinandus von Metternich, the provost of Corvey, had talked reason and had said some really sensible things.

It was an evil night, he had opined. Nobody knew what was going on. Tomorrow was another day – thank God and with St. Veit's help no one had been killed so far – the villains were behind bars in prison, and even the Jews had escaped with their lives, as far as was known. The party that had suffered the most in this horrible turmoil had evidently been Corvey Abbey which now, on top of all that, was still facing the miserable march home. At the end of his speech he – the provost – had advised to go back to bed now and, perhaps just as a precaution, to leave behind a *salve-guardia here on the street, drawn from the Corvey company and the municipal guards.

'That's what we'll do!' the prior had concluded, and ten minutes after its arrival in front of Master Samuel's house, the abbey was about to march back home to bed.

'Let's hope that while we were defeating the Philistines, Father Adelhardus has prepared some good hot ale for us', the subprior whispered to the provost as they passed through the Corvey Gate.

Be that as it may; with anger in his heart, the rector of St. Kilian's was still walking up and down in earnest conversation with Mayor Thönis Merz, and threw black glances at the good Brother Henricus, who, together with several sturdy farm hands from the monastery, had been left behind as an armed detachment in case of further eventualities. And while the Lutheran pastor agitatedly walked back and forth, the old monk stood in the glow of the conflagration, thoughtfully leaning on his sword and remembering earlier days. The student kept close to him, and now pulled at the sleeve of his habit.

'In such deep thoughts, Pater? Earlier I had offered you my Horace volume for the price of a seat at your warm hearth. Now fate has heated an even warmer stove for us. Why, if I may ask, are you so downcast, Pater?'

The old monk looked up and murmured:

'Oh, Just von Burlebecke!'

'You should talk to me, Your Reverence', the student suggested companionably. 'I like you, and I would be happy if you also liked me. Although earlier you made short shrift of me, we have now fought shoulder to shoulder, and – if only for the sake of the grim glances of my uncle over there, you should take my arm and *suaviter chat our watch away with me. By morning I'll be on my way to Wittenberg, where they have long been yearning for me with an aching heart, and you'll never see me again, old cock.'

'You are a dunce, master scholar', said Brother Henricus, laughing at the rascal in spite of himself. 'If it weren't for Just von Burlebecke, I would instantly send you on your way to Wittenberg without my blessing. But that's how Just was in his day, too, and I never stand at this place without sadly thinking of the old times and of Just von Burlebecke.'

'Then tell me who Just von Burlebecke was, and I'll gladly join you in your sorrow over him.'

'There', said the monk, pointing toward the gate. 'In the summer of the year *twenty-two he took Höxter in a charge with twenty horsemen. He was riding under Crazy Christian, I with Tilly. Christian crossed the Weser here with twelve thousand men on foot and nine thousand riders and I, as an ensign in the Baumgarten Regiment, after him and the reckless Just. On the meadow at *Stadtloo, Just von Burlebecke is interred among Christian's soldiers. I saw him among the dead, and he was my very best bosom-friend.'

'That was the big war, and today you are a Benedictine monk at Corvey, Father!' exclaimed the student.

'Yes', the kind old man said quietly, and shook his head once more looking down the street.

'Laughing, he came storming into their gate and pitched into the Philistines like a bolt out of the blue. It still makes me laugh today! Oh, if you had known Crazy Christian and his riders, you would also know what to think of Just von Burlebecke, my dear scholar. They were sitting outside their doors in the sunshine without a care in the world, and then he struck out of nowhere. Before they knew it, he and his twenty companions had Höxter in their hands like a boy with a bird's nest, right under the nose of the abbey and the League's armada. Only for a quarter of an hour, it is true, but that was precisely the joke.'

By now the old man had taken Lambert's arm and slowly walked up the street with him to Kröppel-Leah's house.

'Here, this is the place where it happened: *The Philistines be upon you, Samson! But why am I telling you all this instead of admonishing you to lead a respectable life and send you to your books, as I should?'

'Because I have been sitting over the books for too long and too respectably, Herr Pater. Oh, you will buy my Horace from me yet; by now he is lodged in my head so firmly that it only makes me stupid! The Amsterdam edition, frontispiece by Romyn – '

The monk waved him off. 'No', he said, 'I am talking to you because you are still a foolish boy, and because when one is old it feels good to have youth close by when recalling one's own youthful follies. What was it like? Well, when they came to their senses and realized how small the force was that Just von Burlebecke had brought to subdue them, they sounded the alarm. In those days Höxter still had a sizable population, full of trade and commerce, and there were no ruins and desolate sites within its walls. They gave no thought to Crazy Christian, they only saw Just and his twenty horsemen. So they fetched their spears and muskets. It was a merry fray. But here, on this spot, they shot the horse of my bosom-friend, and he landed on the ground beneath the horse and the fists of Huxar. The same of course happened to his comrades. By the hundreds they swarmed about the patrol and suffered many a bloody head themselves, but they also gave mighty blows and with hooks and poles dragged the conquerors down from their horses. It was quite a struggle until some older and sensible people were able to force their way through the throng and talk sense. Then the town clerk brought a protocol of the case to paper, and once they had it on paper they suddenly saw it in the right light, and they were horrified at their own heroic bravery and what they had got themselves into as a result.'

'They realized that Christian was trotting right behind the good knight Just, and not with a mere twenty men', laughed the student.

'With nine thousand on horse and twelve thousand on foot, as I have already told you. Later, when I rode with the League after the *Administrator, I heard the whole story. Indeed, from then on it was no easy thing for the council and citizenry at this troublesome river-crossing, to manoeuvre through the times and factions.'

'And today it's hardly any better', suggested Herr Lambert, but the monk replied:

'Had you witnessed the *Bloodbath of Höxter, and yourself fought at the wall, you would speak differently. Think about it and take care not to offer your hand to create still more ruins.'

Then he continued with his narrative:

'Even in Tilly's headquarters here in Höxter they were laughing their heads off. *Merode laughed, Piccolomini's belly shook, and Savelli was shaking under his enormous wig. They all liked the way Just von Burlebecke had taken the town. I was then quartered at the town clerk's and had him show me his protocol. It was a wretched scribble and scrawl, just as if dysentery had sat at the table with this nervous wreck for his feat of penmanship. And Just, as a brave cavalier, had also slammed his name down and it sprawled across half a page and through all the signatures of the mayor and the councilmen, heavy and black like a regiment of cuirassiers through a field of peas. For a whole evening the town clerk had to tell me about Captain Just – how they had pulled him out from under the horse, how they brushed off his coat, how one came with the pistol he had thrown at the head of the chief of the borough, how a second brought him his sword which he had lost in the final scuffle, and how the strife and bloodshed had ended with festivities at the town hall. Yes, all day long there was feasting and drinking in honour of Just von Burlebecke and his horsemen – Crazy Christian included! They fraternized and with tears in their eyes fell into each other's arms, the mayor of Höxter and Just von Burlebecke. And in the evening the Jewry of the town had been ordered to pay for provisions for the good knights' journey. And then in triumph, the musicians in the lead, they had brought them to the gate and let them ride on their way with a polite compliment to His Princely Highness of Halberstadt. And not one of them had held on to his horse at this hour as firmly as they had in the morning when storming the gate.'

'I too have taken many a door by storm, but no senate or council has ever rewarded me for it so gallantly', said the student in mock lament. And at that moment the piteous screams of female voices sounded from the house, in front of which Just von Burlebecke in former times had been lain beneath the fists of Huxar on the Weser. We know whose screams they were.

XII

They all halted in the street, but especially the monk and the student.

'Saint Veit!' called Brother Henricus. 'Will this murderous night never end? Here! Here Corvey!'

He hurried toward the house from which the screaming issued, and some of the workers from the monastery also came running from the site of the conflagration.

The refuse left behind by the French lay in a higher pile in front of Kröppel-Leah's house than anywhere else in Höxter, and before the brother studiosus followed Brother Heinrich von Herstelle with a leap over the filth, he of course waved his hat in the air and exulted:

> '*Now Roman youth, unsheathe your sword
> And to your parents' fame accord.
> The sea with Punic blood dye red,
> 'Gainst Pyrrhus' rage with laughter tread;

Vanquish and crush the Syrian king,
Destruction to his kingdom bring;
With cannons and with guns arrive
Dread Hannibal away to drive!'

Not all of these measures were strictly necessary, but haste was required. Herr Lambert jumped and with his jumping passed the wading Benedictine by one step on the stairs. Brother Henricus and the student were the first of all those who at this new cry for help found themselves on the scene of misery, grappling with the evildoers before anyone from the abbey or the town could come to their aid and lend a hand. No barred door slowed them down, and ahead of the monk the studiosus vaulted into the quarters of the sergeant from the regiment Fougerais and the merry Mamsell Génévion from the same regiment.

They came at the right moment – although not for the three Höxterian ruffians. The good ferryman Hans Vogedes was just holding the old woman on the floor, squeezing her throat. One of his comrades in the robbery was pulling the screaming Simeath through the little room by her tresses with rough paws; the other blackguard had already dragged the paltry bundle with the Gronau inheritance from under the table. Kneeling, he was greedily rummaging and cursing while scattering the contents around him on the dirty floor. The lamp of poor Father Samuel and his burning house spread their glow over this ugly scene, the kind which *Callot was fond of drawing and painting in that horrid century to which all those present belonged. Sixteen hundred such pictures Maître Jacques had produced up to the year 1635, and the only consolation for us is that, in the end, his heiress converted all the copper plates of these 'Misères et malheurs de la guerre' into pots and pans for cooking her soups. –

'*Ecce iterum Crispinus!' shouted the student and charged Hans Vogedes, who released his grip on the old woman's throat. Raising his arm in a wide arc he threw the stiff pigskin volume of his Flaccus at the fellow's nose so that blood streamed from it immediately.

'There's some Roman law for you, you mousehead!'

And then, before the ferryman was able to pick up his murderous axe, he had him by the throat and on the floor. But Brother Heinrich von Herstelle lifted his mighty battle-sword with both fists and let its flat side fall on the head of the knave who was assailing Simeath. The third robber cravenly abandoned the old woman's bundle, jumped up, and in one leap across the felled body of his comrade tried to gain the door, the stairs and the street. But on the stairs he fell into the arms of the men from the monastery who were tramping up, and of the brave and wise Captain Meyer, who was panting after them. They caught him tenderly and nearly squeezed the soul out of his body, and quite willingly he let his hands be tied behind his back. Thus this battle was ended nearly before it had begun in earnest, and standing next to the two who had been vanquished and were squirming on the ground, even the two victors, monk and studiosus, looked at each other with some astonishment.

But now Captain Meyer entered and for his part looked around a bit in Kröppel-Leah's chamber. Giving a military salute and pointing to the ferryman and his companion, he asked:

'With permission, Pater, what about the jurisdiction in Höxter? Here we again have the case: should we keep these louts for the abbey, or do we send them to Mayor Merz? In the end they will in any case presumably be hanged by Corvey since his Episcopal Highness has taken the right of capital punishment away from the town.'

Uncertainly, Brother Henricus scratched his head; but the student spoke up instead:

'Give my best regards and warmest compliments to the old donk–, I mean to His Honorable Excellency of Huxar, Herr Thönis Merz, and tell him that I, Lambert Tewes, am hereby sending him something, and in exchange am asking for some travel money and sustenance for tomorrow on my way to Wittenberg in recognition of services rendered to the community. Don't make long speeches, for once keep your wisdom and *sesquipedalia – your half-baked long objections – to yourself. Hans here I recommend to you, *Centurio, and to the mayor in particular. Give him a good whipping also with a compliment from me.'

The captain looked rather annoyed at the speaker who paid so little respect to the dignity of his office, but Brother Henricus remarked with a smile:

'For tonight it might indeed be best to do as this madcap suggests, Captain. Give my regards to the mayor, too. To preserve the rights of the abbey, station two men with the town's guard at the tower.'

The captain martially raised his hat again, and the two bleeding violators of domestic peace were dragged out and down the steps. Now Brother Heinrich and the student could finally look after the two poor females whom they had so bravely saved from the clutches of the Huxarienses rioting in the wake of the French billeting, in the wake of Herr von Turenne and Herr von Fougerais.

The young girl was kneeling on the floor and holding the head of the old woman in her lap.

'Oh grandmother, grandmother', she sobbed, 'say something! Just speak one word! We are still alive! They weren't able to carry out their wishes; these good gentlemen have released us from their grasp, praise be to the Lord — oh grandmother, come to your senses!'

For the time being the old woman only twitched her shoulders and convulsively opened and closed her fingers. The Benedictine monk bent down to her and shone the little lamp into her face.

'The villain has choked her quite badly. Help me, learned friend, we'll carry her to bed. It's a great pity that we don't have Brother Briccius here who is knowledgeable about medications. He would have her upright again in the blink of an eye.'

Herr Lambert Tewes had already taken the head of the old woman out of Simeath's arms; the monk took hold of her feet, and thus the two carried her to the bed of the sergeant, the student stealing a glance at the pretty roughed-up Jewish girl.

'Dry your tears, *Neaera with the black tresses', he said good-naturedly. 'Do it for my sake – this little granny has endured more in her long existence than such cat scratches. – Your patriarchs, male and female, have a deuced tough life, and your grandmother will get over it safely this time, even without Brother Briccius's assistance.'

'I will never forget the help of you noble gentleman', cried Simeath, weeping even more loudly; then she leaned over, took the hand of the unruly scholar and was about to press her lips on it, when Master Lambert quickly withdrew his paw and gave her a resounding kiss on her mouth.

'That's what it says in the statutes of the Julia Carolina, and the chancellor *Mynsinger von Frondeck knew what he was doing when he inserted that paragraph.'

Blushing, the girl stepped back toward the bed of the old woman. The monk had wrinkled his brow a bit, but he was too busy with Kröppel-Leah, who was gradually returning to consciousness, to be able to pay too close attention to what else was going on around him. With the water from Master Samuel's pitcher, he rubbed the temples of the old woman – at that she finally sneezed and uttered a hoarse cry, and then she sat upright on the straw and looked about her with dazed eyes. The red glow of the waning conflagration was still illuminating the chamber.

'*The Bloodbath of Salzkotten! The League in the town!' she moaned and fell back putting her hands over her eyes.

'She is not yet quite herself – the fire confuses her', murmured Brother Henricus, turning toward the student. 'She sees the Maundy Thursday of 1634 again. We gave no quarter because no quarter was given to us in Salzkotten.'

And the old man, too, put one hand on his brow and with the other supported himself against the wall with the lewd drawings of Fougerais's troops:

'Lord, Lord, my God, when will peace come to this poor world of yours?!'

Lambert Tewes was now standing gravely enough with folded arms.

'Höxter and Corvey!' he said grimly. 'My Lutheran ancestors stood for town and abbey. It was the League that demolished Höxter and broke the sarcophagus of St. Vitus. It was your foreign colonels and officers who distributed the bones among themselves which *Emperor Ludwig had brought here to the Weser.'

'True enough', said Heinrich von Herstelle. 'That is the *historia* of Höxter and I – am a monk at Corvey! I marched for the League. And Just von Burlebecke rode for the *Winter King, the beautiful Elisabeth and Crazy Christian; Just grew up with me and was raised by my mother together with me.'

'Just von Burlebecke!' The voice from the bed came like an echo and, supported by her granddaughter, the old woman pointed with trembling, wavering hand toward the floor where her inheritance lay scattered.

XIII

The student was just picking up his Horace, which only a moment ago he had used for the first time in this story as an incontrovertible argument. The book was lying amidst the litter rummaged by thieving hands and Lambert, looking it over, called:

'By *Mercury and Rhadamanthus, is that the bait that attracted the vermin? Mother Leah, that's what you lugged on your old back from the principality of Hildesheim to Höxter? Oh Moses and all your prophets, if *Titus had not brought more than this from Jerusalem, the *spolium*, the loot, would surely not have been worth the trouble.'

That was true enough, and the spectacle that now had been brought about by chance and the paws of robbers did not make a pleasant impression. Paltry pieces of clothing, cheap coins of tin or lead commemorating all kinds of events like Imperial, Swedish and French victories and defeats – a partly burnt Hebrew prayer book with silver clasps, and seven poor spoons! A necklace of Bohemian pearls with a copper cross and a flattened tiny silver cup were the most valuable objects, a copper pan and a small iron pot the most voluminous, except for the cover from the deathbed of the Jewish man from Gronau.

'What do you know of Just von Burlebecke, woman?' asked Brother Henricus agitatedly, taking hold of the woman's hand.

'I held his bloody head in my lap, here in front of my father's door', said old Leah, pushing out her words with difficulty. 'They had shot his horse, and at first no one wanted to lift the wicked enemy. Oh, and yet the war was only beginning then! There – there, look. He gave me a keep-sake which then went from one hand to the other in our family. In Gronau I found it again.'

Kröppel-Leah sank back onto the straw, the student held out his book to the monk once more:

'What do you think, Reverendissimus, I'll throw it in with the rest and we'll start a junk store *in compania. But what do you contribute to the venture?'

The old monk, now noticeably angry, pushed him away. He was already kneeling and searching on the floor. With an unsteady hand, he threw the rags and tatters hither and thither, and made the kitchen dishes and wretched rarities and valuables rattle against each other.

'By St. Veit', he suddenly cried. 'This is the work of my late mother! She gave him the gloves when he left before me. In her heart she was for the new doctrine; I for my father's sake joined the Emperor's side! This is Just's glove with my mother's maxim: Walk straight! ... Oh woman, oh Leah, she stitched these golden threads with her skilled hand!'

Brother Henricus was holding a rider's glove which was embroidered with faded gold and, visibly moved once more, took the feverish hand of the old Jewess:

'He gave you this, Leah?'

The old woman pushed her white hair, which had been loosened in the struggle with the robber, away from her forehead and said:

'I don't understand the gracious Sir Abbot.'

She still had not completely regained her senses, or the numbness had begun to set in again.

'The Crazy Duke's mad horseman, Just von Burlebecke!' cried Brother Heinrich, turning again to the student and young Simeath. 'He had a good and merry year left. Then at Stadtloo he was shot dead in earnest, and no one showed pity and took his bleeding head in her lap, Leah!'

'How was that?' murmured the old woman. 'So much has happened since then – the Fieldmarshal von Tilly and in the year twenty-nine the Swede Baudissin – no, in twenty-nine it was Tilly again and the *Herr von Pappenheim. *General Baudissin conquered the town in thirty-two … Then came the bloody Maundy Thursday of thirty-four. Anno forty his Excellency the Quartermaster Piccolomini attacked Höxter. They got in through negotiations, but in forty-six Quartermaster Wrangel struck. – Who was mentioning Duke Christian and Just von Burlebecke? What year do we have now, Simeath?'

The young girl softly stated the number, and the feverish old woman whispered with closed eyes:

'God of Abraham! The Lord is the Lord of hosts; Zebaoth is his terrible name.'

'That's what my uncle said earlier', opined the student, raising his shoulders in discomfort.

Brother Henricus had moved the stool next to the sad bed of Kröppel-Leah and now sat down on it, his rusty sword at his feet.

'Yes, yes', said the old woman in her confused state, thinking back, 'I remember it well. We were young and the war had just come to us across from Bohemia. My father was the only Jew who was allowed to live in Höxter, and I was a young girl, Simeath. We were still enjoying the summer when the young nobleman laughingly rode into the gate. What made me leave the house? It does not matter – with my little kerchief I dried the blood from his brow. His companions were still fighting with the citizenry. But he looked at me and said: "Merci, mademoiselle!" He of course did not know that I was a Jewish girl. Then the mayor came, and my father pulled me into the house and my mother beat me. They heard in the town about the great force with which Duke Christian was approaching, and then they caroused together at the town hall. Yes, yes, and in the evening before they escorted him to the gate, he came to my father's house on the noble horse that the town had given him. I was sitting at the window and he threw me his glove and a kiss and called: "Remember Just von Burlebecke, Miss; he will always remember you!" And yet by then he already knew that I was a Jewess – but he was a good knight, and I really often did think of him. In the evening my mother beat me once more, and my father too. Because the Council had laid the contribution of travel money, which they presented to the good knight, on the Jews. The glove I secretly hid, otherwise they would have burnt it in front of my nose with a curse. Then my children played with it. It is a miracle that it has survived. My children are dead; three times my house has been razed. Yes, I have brought the brave knight's glove from Gronau, reverend Sir. Do take it, but don't take it out on Simeath that you found it here. Help the innocent child, Simeath, through the night!' …

All this had been more croaked than spoken. Now the old woman fell silent, and breathed heavily in her somnolent state. The old man said:

'So it is, mother, we both remember the times of peace. When my mother handed this glove to Just on his horse, no one could yet imagine that for longer than the span of a lifetime the German people would wade through a sea of blood beneath a red sky filled with smoke from the burning towns.'

'What's that to me?' shrieked Kröppel-Leah suddenly from out of her dream. 'My forebears never had peace since Emperor Titus. What's it to us what you have done with your country? I am fighting for breath; the scoundrel has smashed my chest in, yet I would sing in this night if it weren't for Simeath.'

'Your grandmother is right about good Emperor Titus', the student whispered to the child. 'Now I am a Roman too – *civis Romanus sum* – and I know my Latin, little maid. But for the two of us this should be no reason to scratch each other's faces.'

'Oh, kind sir, don't make fun of me!' cried Simeath, who was just putting the pitcher of water to the old woman's lips again.

Leah drank long and greedily; then she pushed the pitcher back and energetically sat up again. She was now completely awake and looked about her with clear eyes.

'Let him be, child. He does well to launch himself into the world with laughter. The times swing back and forth – the hour too will come for him when he looks at the heavy pendulum with wrinkled brow. Reverend Herr Monk, you used to be a horseman, now you are a brother at Corvey – and you are an old man too; have you found peace in the walls of the great abbey?'

Brother Heinrich von Herstelle, leaning his brow on his hand, had been sitting deep in thought. At the question he looked up startled and repeated:

'Peace?'

As if he were playing, he put on the glove of Just von Burlebecke; then he said:

'Peace? ... Walk straight! ... Peace? Why should I wish to find peace? I am not a learned man like the student here who knows his Horatius by heart, that heathen philosopher. I cannot tell how I feel. In my youth I enjoyed life in all its variety – was I trying to find peace when I became a monk? Yes, yes – by St. Veit, that's probably what it was! Well yes, I guess I found it. Of course, I am an old fellow and so I am content at Corvey, but – walk straight! – the times have left me as I was when I began to become aware of the world. What blood and blazes?! Since God has ordained that for us, then it is also up to Him – may His name be praised – to settle the account. I expect it will balance, for Him as well as for us.'

The old woman gave a harsh laugh:

'So you too have arrived at the solace that has been sung to us since the days of *King Nebuchadnezzar. Those filled with pride shall bow down, and the Lord will laugh at them – '

'And all this because that knave, Monsieur Fougerais, yesterday marched off from Höxter!' the student now interrupted impatiently. 'The devil, we'll only have peace when no one picks up the club in the corner any more after hearing: Vivat, Doctor Luther! and from the other table it croaks: Hurrah Pope Clement the Tenth – or the other way around! Fougerais is gone – –

> *Nunc est bibendum, nunc pede libero
> Pulsanda tellus —

This song of drinking and dancing was sung after the *Battle of Actium and coined for the downfall of Queen Cleopatra of Egypt, but I frequently apply it to something else, and a thousand years after me, someone else will still do so. Likewise, Jerusalem has been rebuilt more than once, Mother Leah.'

'But aliens reside in the homes of the seed of Abraham, young sir. The children of Judah and Israel roam aimlessly, ridiculed and demonized. They no longer have a place in which they are masters of their house and limbs. For you too it is too early to dance a victory dance, young sir. Do you really want to sing and dance after Monsieur de Fougerais and the great Marshal Turenne? They have done enough to make Höxter empty.'

'The glorious allies of my most reverend lord at Münster!' murmured Brother Henricus. 'Leave the dancing for a while yet, Herr student.'

At this moment a violent clamour once more filled the street and was approaching the house of Kröppel-Leah.

XIV

After the flooding has subsided, mud still clings to the bushes and covers meadows and fields for a long time, and it takes more than one cleansing rain and cheerful sunshine to rid the land of its grimy state. And when the flood even reached into people's towns and chambers, then what it carried along and left behind is also not so easily swept away and discarded outside of the gates.

But in these foul and evil days the Lord is partial to those lighthearted, indestructible fellows who laughingly skip over the filth and who gladly and jovially offer a helping hand where many an honourable, sagacious and distinguished person turns away with disgust and displeasure and lets matters take their course. The Lord of Hosts, after the French had left Höxter, was pleased with that expelled Helmstedt student, Herr Lambert Tewes.

'Don't exert yourself unduly, Your Excellency', called the student. 'Say some nice things about me behind my back. I will inquire what new mischief that old tormentor, Master Beelzebub, has now hatched in Huxar. Haven't I said it a dozen times – *neque tectum neque lectum*, that is the only relevant motto for this night!'

He darted out, but the present violators of the peace met him at the open door, his uncle, the Reverend Helmrich Vollbort, rector of St. Kilian's, at their head.

While at Kröppel-Leah's bed the talk was about Just von Burlebecke's glove, in the street the Reverend Helmrich had vigorously continued his conversation with Mayor Thönis Merz, and had found willing listeners in the irate citizenry of Huxar.

'So the gentlemen of Corvey have once again arranged the affairs of the town according to their wishes', he had stated angrily. 'Will the Lutheran citizenry put the muzzle on itself this time too? The office of the Lutheran Church will speak and not let itself be gagged!'

'We too aired our views, Your Reverence – but what good does it do?' pointed out the mayor.

'What good does it do? Oh, you silly people, haven't you heard enough of the conditions which von Galen, who calls himself Bishop of Münster and your sovereign, will pull over your ears like a nightcap? Just keep your words in your mouth and your fists in your pockets according to your lazy way and wait for next year. They'll leave you the fishing rights and a few other shoddy nothings, but your churches and schools they'll close in front of your noses. Then you may see whether you'll be able to catch the keys again in your nets, out of the river.'

'But what should we do?' called the mayor, and 'What should we do, Your Reverence?' the crowd echoed angrily and plaintively.

'The duke – ', Herr Thönis Merz was about to start again meekly, but the ardent old preacher immediately interrupted him:

'Don't talk to me of that fellow from Braunschweig. He won't cross the Weser again to come to your aid. You crawled before him as you crawled before the one from Münster, and behind your back they laughed at you.

Take hold yourselves when and where you can, give only an inch, then advance again, clause by clause; let the least be as the greatest for you. What more do you have to lose?'

'God only knows!' groaned the Lutheran citizenry of Höxter.

'He does know and He does help those who are willing to help themselves', solemnly pronounced the Reverend Helmrich Vollbort. 'Don't let this night go by without moving against Corvey. They have gone home and to bed, but we have stayed awake. Raise your banner against the abbey. State your demands with a strong voice, be they what they may. Don't let the battle go to sleep as the monks have gone to sleep. They swear by St. Veit but we call on Almighty God – onwards against Corvey!'

'They have taken the Jew's levy from us, although we have it on paper', the mayor mentioned timidly.

'Don't let the day dawn without the abbey finding itself confronted by a new *factum, actum et gestum. We are engaged in a war that they started, and the last peace will be made by God the Lord.'

'The Jews out of the town!' a shrill voice yelled from the crowd, followed by a hundred voices crying: 'Away with the Jews from Höxter! Our rights! Our rights! Our rights!'

And now the women furiously pushed to the front:

'They fraternized with the French! Just look at their houses – they remained unharmed while in ours no chair and no bench was left whole! – They paid Turenne! They paid that blackguard Fougerais – they were able to ransom themselves, and the high officers billeted with them and let their vile people do with us as they pleased. The Jews, out of the town with the Jews! Away with the Jews from Höxter!'

Now we, too, are again facing a *factum*: the words that came from the Lutheran citizenry found complete resonance in the Catholic one. For the second time this night all of Höxter fell upon its Jews, and even Captain Meyer went along – although unwillingly, but they amiably pulled him along, one taking each arm – on the right the Catholic, on the left the Protestant church.

They took Master Samuel together with his family from the street in front of his burning house; they gathered the other two or three families; and so they arrived pushing and shoving, the wretched lamenting little pile of half-naked people in their midst, and stopped with an ear-piercing din in front of Kröppel-Leah's house, to collect her too, together with her granddaughter, and to escort them with the others, in defiance of Corvey, outside of the gate.

The monk had risen from his stool and had picked up his Hussite sword from the floor; but in the antechamber the student confronted the Höxterian dignitaries who were pushing into the house. He paid no attention to the mayor and the captain, but instead embraced the pastor of St. Kilian with tender impudence and called:

'*Mon dieu*, my uncle – after two o'clock in the morning still up in the harmful winter air! To what do I owe the honour in these, *my* poor quarters?'

'Get away, you tom fool!' said the old man, and he punched his nephew on the chest and pushed him away.

'What do you gentlemen want?' asked Brother Henricus from the threshold of the sergeant's chamber, and commandant Meyer meekly stepped forward, hat in hand, and stuttered:

'Reverend Pater, the house and street are full of them – of ours and theirs. They are coming and they are all demanding the same thing. They are coming arm in arm against the Jews and want to put them outside the wall before the night is over.'

'We only insist on our rights, Reverend Father', cried the mayor. 'We have had the levy on the Jews both before and after *the year twenty-four, and *the peace settlement quite specifically and totally restored it to us. That is known in Münster as it is in Corvey, and in this regard there is no difference in Höxter between our faiths. We have all come for our rights.'

The pastor of St. Kilian stood with folded arms and grimly looked at the monk, but Brother Henricus looked at him and at him alone.

'You are standing in a bad light, Pastor', said the monk. 'The flames of the conflagration are still licking behind your back; could this not have waited until the ashes and wreckage of this night had cooled?'

'I come with the same people who this very night assaulted my peaceful house and who threw stones at me and my wife – that is what Höxter and Corvey is like!'

During this conversation, more and more people had pushed into the chamber. A woman's shrill voice called out Leah's name, and in the street hundreds repeated it. Brother Henricus had angrily gripped the captain's arm and shook him: 'Where are your men – send a messenger to Corvey – oh St. Veit and – confound it, on my honour as a knight, the first one who takes a step forward will lie on the floor with a bloody pate! Here for Corvey! Münster and Corvey!'

'Höxter and Corvey! Hand over the Jews! Away with the Jews! Höxter and Corvey!' it came back, and now the student jumped up, nearly as high as the blackened ceiling of the room:

'Höxter and Corvey! Can I shout the ocean into silence and should not be able to silence Huxar?! By my honour as a student, who in this hubbub knows me as a good companion and as the only Höxterian with some grey matter in his *cranium? Are you now going to listen to reason or aren't you? Hey, Wigand – Wigand Säuberlich, for my sake bring that screamer there in front of you to reason and escort her home. You want to get hold of Kröppel-Leah? *Et tu Brute, my son Hans Rehkopf?! Thunder and devil, if you are for Höxter and Corvey, then I, Lambert Tewes, am this time for Judah and Israel. Helmstedt gave me *consilium abeundi – Höxter *relegatio in perpetuum, isn't that so, uncle?! But Jerusalem has fed, nourished and clothed me for years – here for Judah and Israel, and whoever has the good of Höxter and Corvey at heart, shout with me: *Vivat Hierosolyma!'

Now he had the laughers on his side and had thereby achieved a lot. He had also turned around among those closest to him and now slapped Brother Henricus on the shoulder:

'Do you understand yet what's going on in Höxter, Pater?'

'Saint Veit!' called the monk, helplessly looking up toward the ceiling. 'You, Mayor?'

'Oh my, oh good heavens!' groaned Herr Thönis Merz.

'You, Herr Captain?'

'Lambert, you knew me before Noht, that pirate from Braunschweig, took away my drum. That is my solace and my reputation. Now I just go where I am pushed.'

'So go on your way, uncle', said the student to the preacher of St. Kilian's, and –

'Yes!' replied the Reverend Helmrich Vollbort, and stepped over the threshold into the old Jewess's little chamber.

Reason? Who, an hour after the great flood, is capable of being reasonable?!

XV

To the preacher's 'Yes', Brother Henricus had shrugged his shoulders, but he had stepped aside and had put no further obstacles in his way. The student said:

'Not even a *citatum* from my Flaccus comes to mind.'

Simeath was sitting at the bed of her grandmother and fearfully looked up to the grim man in his black cassock.

'Grandmother has fallen asleep.'

The Reverend Helmrich Vollbort bent over the straw and the paltry bundle of clothes on it. Then he took Master Samuel's lamp from the table and let its light fall on the bed:

'Arise, woman. Do you want to be the only one in this miserable town who sleeps tonight?'

Indeed that was so: Kröppel-Leah was asleep. Her breath came heavily and gasping, but she slept! At that Brother Heinrich von Herstelle could keep the others out no longer – they pushed into the chamber, as many as it would hold. Lambert Tewes put his arm around the trembling Simeath:

'Don't be afraid. Since the time of the *Maccabees, Judah never had a better cavalier than me. The abbey has gone to bed. Should they keep at it, there are other people besides the Lutheran and Papal sexton who can ring the alarm in Höxter. If they carry it too far, the broom still stands in the corner, and in the end, together with the Jews we'll sweep Höxter as well as Corvey into the Weser!'

That was an insolent remark, but there was truth behind it. There was laughter in the crowd, and a hairy fist raised a substantial knotted stick toward the ceiling:

'You give good advice, brother Lambert! That's our cue, you hellraiser. There are enough of us here who finally want some quiet in this ruckus. Höxter and Corvey into the Weser, and – Hurrah for St. Veit at the Corvey Gate! You take charge, Lambert!'

Reason?! ...

They set up a great clamour and shook the sleeping old Jewess by the shoulder. Once more she raised her arm as if to protect her face from a blow; but then her head fell back heavily and also her arm down again, the body stretched out, and the one who had shaken her shoulder stepped back, startled, and cried out:

'By thunder, no one will wake this one again in Höxter and Corvey!'

At that the child gave forth a cry of distress and threw herself over her grandmother, but the grandmother could no longer respond even to poor Simeath.

'She has indeed left the town now, and it was not necessary for us to come with poles and firearms to fetch her', Brother Henricus said, turning toward Herr Helmrich Vollbort. 'Only minutes ago she asked me whether I had found peace.'

The pastor of St. Kilian's did not answer, but the mayor murmured:

'Even Herr Christoph von Galen would have to let her lie where she is lying. Herr Pastor, let us speak to the citizens and continue our conversation tomorrow at the town hall. You people, who of you will take this corpse outside the gate?'

At that a muttering went through the brutish company in the bedchamber of the sergeant from the Fougerais Regiment, and there came the sulking reply:

'For that, call the masters of the guilds or carry her yourself.'

The room and the stairs began to empty. For some time now Brother Heinrich von Herstelle had looked around in vain for his student, who at the right moment appeared again at the threshold pushing Master Samuel's trembling wife Siphra in front of him:

'Now stop the blubbering, mother. I will get the children for you and if that will complete the consolation, your old man too. There, pick up the poor girl and talk to her. Your house is gone, so make your quarters here and settle in. No one will bother you anymore. Höxter will go to bed at last, and you can keep vigil for the dead.'

Reason! ... if anyone in Höxter had talked reason during this night, it was Death.

Tonight, the good town of Huxar refrained from using its Jews to hook a political barb into the flesh of Corvey Abbey and the Episcopal See of Münster. We would have reached the end of our story now if we did not know from long experience that our well-disposed German reader is not satisfied that easily.

In the large refectory of the famous Benedictine abbey of Corvey, it looked rather strange this early in the morning. After Father Adelhardus von Bruch, from his bow window, had observed and explicated long enough the glow of fire over Höxter, he did not disappoint the confidence of subprior Herr Florentius von dem Felde. Chuckling contentedly, he had thought of his clerical brothers in the rough winter night, and at their return the abbey's armada had indeed found their hot ale served in steaming mugs on the long oaken tables; the stoves, too, were on full glow and the *cellarius* also – ready, modestly but aware of his worth, to receive full praise from prior and provost.

Now the abbey was lying asleep for the second time, but Father Adelhardus had proved himself even greater. He had not climbed into bed like the others; solitary and alone he had persevered in the centre of the hall, directly beneath the great copper lamp, and had waited for his son Heinrich.

'Selfishly they departed after enjoying the good things, but me he shall find when he arrives *labente lingua*, with parched tongue!' And Brother Henricus had found his spiritual father at his post after he and his troop had rung the porter's bell for a second time that night. And now we wish we still had as much blank paper in front of us as at the beginning of this veritable story. Because along with Brother Henricus the brother studiosus now came to Corvey after all, and across the table they shook hands, Pater Cellarer and Master Lambert Tewes.

It was five o'clock in the morning when the cellarer finally sighed:

'*Molliter, molliter!* Gently, oh gently, my child!' And the warning had been necessary because it was no other than the student who brought him to bed. – And at the cellarer's door they embraced, and Father Adelhardus sobbed:

'You want to go to Wittenberg, my boy? Boy, what do you want in Wittenberg? – Stay with me – we also have a lib-ra-ree – I will show it to you tomorrow – stay in Corvey, my good child – I will even show you the cellar.'

'Well, old fellow, let's sleep on it. But you see, Pater Henricus, that the gods in their wisdom – which you so contemtuously challenged – provided this harbour for me after all!'

But Brother Heinrich von Herstelle had shaken his head as he leaned his Hussite sword against the wall in front of the door to his cell:

'There is only one person who reached her harbour in Höxter or in Corvey this night.'

The good old monk was still wearing Just von Burlebecke's glove on his left hand. Now he pulled it off and fitted it into the handle of the Hussite weapon. He did not take this old memento with him into his cell. He directed the student to a bed and ten minutes later Lambert sawed, sang and rasped as if in competition with all of Corvey, vespers and matins at the same time. Then something rustled in a pile of branches in the abbey's courtyard; cautiously a head with a sharp beak and a red comb pushed out: the *one* cock the Gauls had left behind, that is, had avoided the kitchen knife. Half starved, he dared for the first time to leave his hiding place, swung himself atop the branches and crowed. Father Adelhardus heard it in his deep sleep – and a new day had arrived, just as gray, stormy and wintry as the one just passed. – – –

In Höxter, the small group of Hebrews held vigil beside dead Leah's body. The women sang the song of mourning and tried to comfort Simeath. But Master Samuel had something else to attend to as well. With hammer, saw and axe he was busy reinstalling the door of Kröppel-Leah's house. The stove had been more or less repaired and a small fire was already flickering on it, and the water was singing in a little kettle. But the wind was still whistling through the window; if anyone was hard to obtain in Germany in the seventeenth century, it was the glazier.

The Reverend Helmrich Vollbort had locked himself into his study, which looked out onto the garden and still had its panes intact. Very manly, the pastor of St. Kilian's was sitting surrounded by his armaments, sharpening wedges for insertion into the paragraphs and junctures of the imminent edict issued by Christoph Bernhard von Galen, bishop of Münster and administrator of Corvey, who together with the French king Louis was in the middle of waging war against Holland and doing his part in word and deed to make *Colmar French. – But the mayor of Höxter was about to begin to sweep the streets after the French departure. – To set a good example he, Herr Thönis Merz, had himself taken a broom and politely had pressed the second one into the hand of Herr Wigand Säuberlich.

In the afternoon Herr Meyer, commander of Corvey and captain for the bishop of Münster, was once again inspecting the guard at the Bridge Gate and throwing watchful wary glances across the river toward the suspicious foggy bank on the other side. He still did not trust Sergeant-Major Noht, and the treacherous fog made him very uneasy. The old river was roaring and rumbling over the broken bridge as it had done yesterday, but a new ferryman had been installed and was forcing his way, panting as yesterday Hans Vogedes, against the waters.

The ferryboat was swimming across the Weser and in it stood the student Lambert Tewes, with food for the journey from Corvey Abbey in his pocket and his Horace under his arm. He swung his hat toward Brother Henricus, who benevolently waved back to the madcap Latin scholar. The student was going to Wittenberg after all, although he had made the acquaintance of Father Adelhardus and his cellar.

Just then the captain came up to greet Brother Heinrich von Herstelle, and the brother turned to him and said:

'They have talked about you in the monastery, Herr Commandant. At the first suitable occasion you will be proposed to His Highness of Münster for a promotion, for an advancement.'

The captain smiled coyly and suggested:

'What I would like best would be a pension, perhaps with the title of major. Since that cursed business with the drum, I am no more than half a person.'

The brave old monk shrugged his shoulders and again looked after his friend Lambert.

Just then the boat reached the other bank and the ferryman said to him:

'So you want to go back once more into the world of learning, Tewes? Don't do it. Take my advice, stay in Höxter. We all support you and eventually will make you mayor, you are just what we need.'

The student laughed and once more quoted Flaccus, but this time not in bad rhyme but, as he believed, in singularly poetic prose; he himself was surprised at the lofty cadence:

'*Nonsense a long time I practised and wandered astray; avoided
the church, scorning gods both and humans. But now the sail I am
turning and pensively am steering backwards.'

'Well, there is still time', muttered the ferryman. 'Think it over, Lambert. It's no small thing, mayor of Höxter.'

'For now, we'll leave old Merz in peace on his consular chair, Jochen', retorted the student, shaking the boatman's hand. 'Although I would not begrudge my uncle and aunt that pleasure and surprise. Know what? … I'll be back!'

With that he leaped ashore and headed with rapid strides towards Lüchtringen.

'I'll be back!' This is often and easily said. This Helmstedt student of jurisprudence died *two years after the crowning of the first King in Prussia as professor of rhetoric in Halle. His Horatius supposedly turned up again in the seventeen-forties in the library of the first *Professor of Aesthetics, Alexander Gottlieb Baumgarten.

At the Sign of The Wild Man

At the Sign of The Wild Man

Chapter One

Far and wide they were commenting on the weather, and it truly was the kind of weather on which everyone could voice his comments without risk of damage to his reputation. It was, to all appearances, an exceptionally inhospitable day for humankind toward the end of October, a day just now fading into evening, or should we say, night. Farther up in the mountains, a mighty cloudburst had already poured down that morning, and the foothills had received their share as well, albeit not quite so harshly as people, livestock, forest, rock, hill and valley farther up. To the north, below the foothills, they were perfectly satisfied with what they had received and would gladly have done without anything more; but more – the rest of it – came nevertheless, and they had to accept it as it came. They were certainly free to comment on it; no one prevented them.

It rained with gusts into the growing darkness, and gusts of a sharp, biting north wind out of Iceland, or even Spitzbergen, came whistling up off the North German Plain, making the air, the chimneys and the ears resonate and raging mightily against the mountains it had found – quite unexpectedly, so it seemed – barring its way southward. But it had bumped its nose on them, or had perhaps had it shoved into them, and now was howling like a naughty boy having some misdeed pointed out to him and his attention directed to it by that same facial feature. In plain words: the autumn evening came on early, was dark and quite stormy; whoever was still on the road or the sodden paths between the wet fields made haste to reach the inn or his own house; and we – that is, the narrator and those friends he has brought with him *from the German to the North German Confederation and from there into the new Empire – we also make haste to get in under the sheltering roof of this next story.

Evening, generally speaking, turns to night sooner than one had thought possible. So it is this time as well: It has well and truly turned to night. Again and again the rain sweeps in sheets from right to left over the road bordered with bare fruit trees. We stop, catching our breath, one hand shielding our eyes, looking around for some glimmer of light in any direction ahead of us. There must be settlements of almost incalculable length stretched out up ahead there in the direction of the hills, and the slightest gleam of lamplight to the south would give us the comforting assurance that we were approaching one of these settlements. In vain!

Hoof beats, the rumble of wheels, human footsteps behind us? Who knows? We hurry on, and suddenly we have what we were so ardently hoping for, on our left, close to the path: there is a light that was struck by a human hand! A sharp turn in the path around dark bushes brings it into view with surprising abruptness, and we find ourselves standing before the apothecary shop at the sign of The Wild Man.

A two-storey house, to all appearances quite solid, with steps leading up to it, stands there at the roadside, drenched, wind-lashed trees all around it. Opposite, on the right-hand side of the road, another house; a bit farther, announcing their presence with fainter light, more human habitations: the beginning of a village street extending for three-quarters of an hour into the hills. The village, we might add, has only this one street, but one is quite sufficient for anyone who has it to walk; and whoever has walked the length of it usually stops for a few minutes at the end of the street, looks around (especially back the way they've come), and expresses some opinion or other according to their character, age or sex. But since we are just now arriving at the end, or beginning, we are not obliged to do that yet. We are simply seeking, as we have said, to find shelter for the moment and we hurry quickly up the six front steps, the narrator with opened umbrella from the left, the reader, likewise with umbrella open, from the right. The narrator has made haste to open the door, pulls the breathless reader in behind him, and already the wind has wrenched the handle out of the narrator's hand and slammed the door shut behind him and the reader, making the whole house reverberate. We are in – in the house, and in the story of *The Wild Man*! We find ourselves standing in an apothecary shop, a fact at once confirmed for us by the smell.

The two lighted windows we caught sight of from the sodden, rain- and wind-lashed road were the windows of the shop itself, and the lamp hanging from its ceiling was also sending its light through the wide sliding windows into the entrance hall. The pharmaceutical workshop was marked not only by that familiar odour but also by the proverbial orderliness and cleanliness of German apothecaries. The white canisters and jars in cases along the walls, labeled in blue letters and marked here and there with black skulls and two crossed bones, the green-black stone mortars and gleaming pestles, the scales and all the other utensils looked thoroughly pleasant and inviting. If only that terrible bench hadn't been there (the one where most of us, at one time or another, have sat waiting, feverish, tense and fearful), the tools and instruments of that noble art would have inspired enormous trust in anyone.

But the evil bench! The nasty chair rubbed smooth with sitting. There upon it we sat, perhaps on a bright, frosty winter afternoon, or worse yet in the quiet warmth of a summer night – horrifying night, no matter how lovely it might have been! We put small trust in the canisters and jars, the bottles, scales and mortars; we remember only the way we watched, uncouth and ignorant back then, as the man behind the counter went about his calmly measured, mysterious work.

There was no one in the shop just now, but the light of another lamp shone from an adjoining little room whose door stood half open. And with the light there emanated a different odour that conspicuously altered and diluted the *pharmacopoeial air of the place, though, admittedly, *herba nicotiana* is one of the plants normally found in a druggist's shop. We will follow *that* smell and step into the adjoining chamber.

The cramped room made a rather cosy first impression. From one corner, an iron stove radiated comfortable warmth; in the other one, drawn over to an enormous upholstered easy chair (unoccupied and about which we will have more to say later), stood a round table at which the regular guests, likewise seated on upholstered high-backed chairs, pipe in mouth and a medicinal or non-medicinal, warm or cold drink in front of them, could surely make their visit quite relaxed and comfortable. At this moment, however, only the master of the house, the proprietor of The Wild Man, had taken up his post on his chair, and if he was actually expecting any other visitors on this stormy evening, and if anyone was actually meeting his expectation, we cannot yet say. We are not yet finished with the description of our stage setting, so let us continue with that.

The little parlour behind the shop was done, as far as one could tell, in a yellowish-grey wallpaper with a grey-black floral pattern. On the windowsill, next to several potted plants, stood a birdcage with a sleeping canary that huddled more comfortably into a tight feathered ball, secure in its place of safety, each time the wind caught hold of a twig in the yard and hurled it scratching against the glass pane, or a gust of rain drummed harder on the window.

A corner buffet with all kinds of cups, painted china pots and glasses, and, standing on top, a stuffed wildcat in a glass case, should not be omitted from the inventory. A once rather flowery but now long since faded and threadbare rug covered the floor. From the ceiling hung a woven wreath of artificial grass – a dust and fly catcher. And now, once we have devoted a few words to the pictures on the walls, there will be nothing more to prevent us from moving on to more interesting things.

The pictures on the walls were certainly interesting enough by themselves. The sheer number of them must have utterly astonished anyone who entered the room and left him gaping open-mouthed at all four walls, in all four points of the compass, for quite some time. Having once recovered from his surprise, he could begin to count, or at least to make an approximate guess at the number of them. But either one was difficult, for the pictures and miniatures framed and under glass covered the walls from top to bottom in nearly incalculable array – and we mean, as far down as physically possible. All kinds and formats in copper and steel engraving, lithograph and woodcut; all the subjects and situations in heaven and hell, on earth, in water, in fire and in the air, in black and white or colored.

Many artistic works by *Ramberg and Chodowiecki; countless scenes from the lives of *Frederick II and *Napoleon I; the three monarchs of the *Alliance in three different views on the battlefield at Leipzig; the giant snake hanging from the palm tree with the familiar negro climbing up to skin it; *scenes from The Corsair: A Poem by Lord Byron; fashion pictures; a portrait of *Washington; a portrait of *Queen Mathilde of Denmark and Count Struensee; and, lost amid all the curious, variegated uselessness, in between two street scenes from the year 1848, a genuine old *Dürer copper engraving: Melancholia!

So much, then, for our catalogue. Thirty years it had taken the apothecary Philipp Kristeller, tied down to his shop for all those thirty years, to assemble his collection, so he could certainly not be blamed if he set store by his picture gallery and took pride in his fondness for art and his good taste. His little back room was well decorated, and he had a few more things besides on which he could pride himself.

Let us turn our attention now to the man at the table. He could have been in his fifties or sixties; in physical appearance he was more lank than fat, in complexion more yellow and grey than red and brown, and in stature of medium height. He was wearing a grey dressing gown, down-at-the-heels dark-red slippers, and on his smooth, silver-grey hair a dark-green house cap with worn gold embroidery depicting a wreath of acorns and oak leaves. He was smoking a long-stemmed pipe with the design of a beetle painted on its bowl, pensively resting his forehead in his hand, his gaze directed at the great, empty, comfortable armchair across from him.

He looked up only when the door was gently opened – not the one leading into the shop but into the hallway – and the head of an old woman poked in.

'Goodness, brother, such weather!'

'Indeed it is stormy weather, dear sister.'

Whether the old lady actually heard his answer must remain in doubt, for she pulled the door closed again just as rapidly and quietly as she had opened it.

'Weather stormy enough to make itself heard, indeed it is', murmured the druggist of The Wild Man, smiling and listening to the storm that battered the window. At that same moment the bell at the entrance door rang and someone knocked at the sliding window of the shop. Herr Philipp Kristeller arose from his seat, set his pipe down against the chair and walked with a stoop into his workshop. He emerged again, shaking his head, a quarter-hour's work later, the bell at the door sounded a second time, and someone went hurriedly splashing off, heedless of where he was stepping, through the puddles of water on the road back into the village.

Still shaking his head, the old man returned to his seat, lighted his pipe again, and said: 'An unhealthy season – an apothecary's autumn! – Good income, but a bad business all the same.' He heaved a sigh, and his words and his sigh alike bore indisputable witness to good-heartedness.

Now he sat a few minutes longer before suddenly giving a start:

'Good heavens – yes, but – is it really?!'

He got up again hastily, walked quickly this time into the shop, unlocked the lid of a desk at the window, took out a book and began paging through it. His fingers trembled, his lips twitched, he looked around several times in the aromatically suffused room as if doubting something. There was no doubt: every canister and every glass jar, with or without skull and crossbones, was still in its place. Apothecary Kristeller closed the book, laid his hand on it, and exclaimed:

'It really and truly is! Sure enough: today is the day, or rather the evening. It's been thirty years to the hour – an anniversary – and I'd completely, completely forgotten. Dorothea! Dorothea!'

'Brother dear?' replied the shrill voice outside.

The old man paced up and down for another five minutes in his excitement; then his patience was gone. He opened the door:

'Doretta! Doretta!'

'What is it, Philipp?' he heard the distant response. 'I hear the wind, all right, but what can you do about it? Doors and windows are all secured, and all the rest is in God's hands.'

'No, no', muttered Herr Philipp, and he called back: 'It isn't about the wind and weather. Just come in here for a moment, would you, Dorothea?'

It took another several moments until that was possible; but finally it did happen. There was the old spinster's face again, and now the rest of her, including a back that was, beyond all polite doubt, hunched.

'We're just a bit rushed in the kitchen for the moment, dear Philipp. Did you wish something, brother dear?'

'No; but thirty years ago today, in this house, at this very hour, I received our first *groschen for a bottle of wound disinfectant. Old Herr Timmermann – God rest his soul! – had been kicked in the hip by his horse. I made the notation thirty years ago, and I'd completely forgotten it – in spite of the armchair over there!'

'Oh, for heaven's sake!' the old woman exclaimed and left the room again after some, as it appeared, perplexed hesitation; but then slammed the door all the harder behind her. In the hallway Fräulein Doretta Kristeller already knew precisely what she had to do, and for the remainder of the evening they were considerably more rushed in the kitchen of the shop at the sign of The Wild Man.

Chapter Two

Despite his excited state of mind, the apothecary Philipp Kristeller could not help glancing in astonishment at the doorway through which his sister had so suddenly disappeared.

'Lord Jesus!' he said, and then tried once again to sit down calmly, but he simply could not. The ominous date burned as if in fiery letters and numerals before his eyes, so he pushed the chair back under the table and shuffled back and forth in his picture gallery, all the while shaking his head; and more and more clearly, vividly, the world as it had been thirty years ago, a generation ago, rose up before his mind's eye. Indeed, all at once, everything from his earliest childhood onward lay before him in sharpest outline, and only his parents, taken from him much too soon by death, traversed the bright landscape like spirits. In contrast, his guardian stood with rough, cheerless clarity in the magical light and centre stage in that small provincial town beyond the mountains, over towards Thuringia, with the *Kyffhäuser nearby and the Kickelhahn in the blue, enchanted distance.

'The most common, ordinary person can say he's seen a thing or two in life when he can remember back a generation, even more than a generation', murmured the old man. 'How it all comes right back to life, everything lying dead and forgotten inside of me just a moment ago. There stands that worthy old fellow, firm as bedrock, my old master, and his whole house and household. What a curious, obstinate character he was. And then the old fellow's wife! – I mean, my employer's wife! Dear Lord, how You in Your goodness and wisdom provide so that those whom You give a little spoon for their journey in life also receive their gruel in proper measure! It seems even now that I can feel my stomach growling beneath my ribs just as it did in those good old days. And it was indeed a happy, hearty time! And you surely learned your stuff under the old bedrock's tutelage. You have to give him that. He knew the business, knew the art, and he knew how to fit us out for it. Everything that came along after that – '

The bell in the shop rang once again, and once again the pharmacist went in to go about his work, which this time required a bit longer than with his last customer. While he went about mixing and boiling his potion he carried on a conversation in the local dialect – a conversation that we will not deprive the reader of hearing, though of course not in its original idiom.

'You have bad weather to be coming out tonight, neighbour. Things must not be well at home?'

'Bad as the weather out there', the ruddy, very robust farm wife replied crossly. 'A body's hard put not to wish she could say her own last goodnight on account of it all. He can't stay alive and he don't want to die. I think he's holding on just by the nuisance he's causin' us. Not a blessed thing you can do to his satisfaction any more, and he just lives off that annoyance from one day to the next.'

'Mm-hm', rumbled Herr Philipp.

'Yes, well it's true! and the doctor makes out the best of all. This one here he prescribed last night and told us it's very urgent. But I think you know better than anybody, Herr Kristeller: not a day goes by that you don't see me sittin' on this bench. So then I thought it can wait till tomorrow, and anyway, we're just wastin' our money.'

'Mm-hm', rumbled Herr Philipp, but this time he added: 'I imagine nobody likes to pay doctors' and apothecaries' bills – but we make it as cheap as we can, neighbour.'

'Like it should be for a poor, miserable widow', sobbed the jolly woman into the corner of her apron.

'There, there now', said the druggist. 'Confound it, he's not dead yet! Poor widow? Young woman! Yes indeed! – and in my opinion, he'll see many a good, long year to come. The doctor and I stand ready to do our part.'

The inconsolable wife there on the bench uttered a sound that could have signified anything and everything: gratitude, hope, joy, fear, displeasure, anger and scorn. The apothecary had his mixture finished, passed it across the counter, and the grief-afflicted young widow-to-be departed, stepping out – to his heartfelt satisfaction – just into a renewed raging and lashing of the autumn storm.

'Riffraff!' grumbled the old man and returned to his picture gallery, perturbed by this last exchange and dropping heavily into his chair again once he had thrown fresh wood into the stove with more than usual force. 'That woman very nearly destroyed my sweetest memories just now', he muttered. 'I'd barely got into them when she rang the bell; but I suppose that's always been my lot in the world, and I imagine others don't fare much better. And besides, it all came to nothing anyway, Johanna! It was just not to be for the two of us. Each one had to go his own way: I, under such strange circumstances, to this godforsaken corner of the earth, and you, my poor child and dear heart, to your grave. *Nunc cinis, ante rosa*, twenty-one years old – ah, Johanna, dear, dear Johanna! – Ah yes, how lovely it would have been if we had found our way together and if I had you here with me today, a generation later, as my old, good, beautiful wife!'

It wasn't possible, on this strange night, for the worthy man to stay seated long. Now he went to get a packet of yellowed letters from the above-mentioned writing desk and untied the cord from them.

'Dried flowers and leaves', he sighed. 'Everything I have here in my boxes and tins was fresh and blooming once, just like each word on this paper. Apothecary's wares, or drugs perhaps? No, no, no! Those things are dead and remain so; but these here are still alive and go on blooming and know no time or changing years. These have taken root within me: how could they ever wilt and fade away? In the sunshine, in fleeting shadows of clouds, in the light of the moon, in drifting mists, in grey days of rain, in merry squalls of snow – the valley, the hills alive as ever they were. There's the old town – aye, there it is, just as it was when we were young, each house like an old acquaintance! There is the corner window, the one I always go past when the old man sends me out hunting for plants. There sits the dear child with her sewing box, and it takes a long time, so long, before she notices me, and even longer before I come to believe that she really is looking at me and following me with her eyes. For a long, long time it's an unspoken love, until the heavens at last are so kind as to send a rain shower at just the right time during an outing, having first given me the brilliant, inspired idea to take an umbrella along despite the most beautiful sunshine and the bluest skies. And so we met up close – from heart to heart, from soul to soul! From that moment on, life was heaven on earth. She had little and I had nothing, but God had untold riches in store and heaped them all on us for a brief, brief time. It was not until the second summer after our secret engagement, when we'd lived an entire year like millionaires in our joy and our hope, that it occurred to us to stop and think about what might, what could eventually come of all this – '

Once again the bell rang and interrupted the memory-laden dream. But this time it was not customers disturbing the master of The Wild Man. The ever-distinct voice of his sister Doretta could be heard outside:

'There you are, gentlemen! Thank goodness you've come. This is lovely, this is very kind of you. I just knew you wouldn't disappoint me in my request. My brother only just now remembered the grand anniversary, and I took it very much to heart myself, and then I sent Fritz off posthaste. I know him only too well, my brother. Without good company he would've patched together a mournful night for himself, his melancholy fantasies would've made us all quite miserable enough. But now all's well, for we do belong together this evening, and my brother will be very pleased indeed – a fine good evening to you, gentlemen!'

Chapter Three

The two gentlemen to whom his sister Doretta had immediately sent word, on account of her brother's proclamation of the evening's significance and the melancholy fantasies that followed it, were the village pastor, Herr Schönlank, and the forestry inspector, Ulebeule. The former arrived with overcoat wrapped tight around him, carrying lantern and umbrella; the latter, defying any kind of weather, in a short, green-collared jacket of pilot-cloth, his stout, iron-hooked staff tucked under his arm. They both stopped first in the entry hall to shake themselves thoroughly and exclaim, like everyone far and wide this evening:

'Brr, what weather!'

And the forester added:

'This is what I'd call coming up against the wind, but I can't exactly say it was a pleasure. Well, Pastor, here we're on the leeward side, and Fräulein Doretta will see to everything else, I'm sure.'

The old fellow in the back room, who had been listening somewhat bewildered at first, soon figured out what was happening. The smile on his good-natured face grew wider and sunnier, and now he was the one throwing open the door leading from his hideaway into the hall, calling out in sheer delight:

'Come in, come in, and praise be to every melancholy fantasy that brings a man such welcome company! That was a splendid idea – well done indeed, Doretta! Come in, dear friends! This is surely an evening for making a night of it, and that's just what we'll do, as befits the occasion! Come in, each one take his place, and a cheer for the old apothecary shop!'

'We'll get to that later, once we have the Chinese bowl on the table', said the forester, standing his staff in the corner. 'First though, old boy, our best, most sincere congratulations on this glorious and noteworthy anniversary. If the pastor wants to proclaim it again, with more ceremony, I have nothing against that. Now if we had that coward of a medicine-man here, he'd outclass all of us – we won't find a more highly ranked hunter to present our greetings and propose a toast – but he's out on a house call.'

'And he'll find my message at home when he gets back', said Fräulein Doretta Kristeller.

'Good', said the forester, 'in that case, I'm sure he'll turn up, then. Besides, it's in his nature, and he's probably already caught wind that the pack's gathering here. We'll be here enjoying each other's company till midnight at least, don't you think?'

'Of course! Three cheers!' cried the apothecary. And now, in anticipation of the Chinese bowl, that is to say, the punchbowl, the pastor did indeed deliver – gracefully, elegantly and fittingly – his own congratulations.

By this time, the entire house was so filled with appetizingly pleasant aromas that they overcame even the smell of the druggist's chemicals. In the kitchen there was a downright bustle of activity; all sorts of utensils clattered and rang in merry confusion. At nine o'clock precisely, the first steaming bowl was on the table, and not just the bowl, but all the trimmings as well. For five minutes now the apothecary's sister had time to sit down with the men herself and receive their initial words of praise.

Praises were uttered at the proper time, but then there ensued a moment of that silence which always occurs when a drink worthy of quiet reflection is placed on the table. That this silence is soon overcome and each one comes to terms with the solemnity of the moment remarkably quickly, is well known.

'So it's really one full human generation already?!' exclaimed the clergyman. 'I thought it nearly impossible at first; but now that I've quietly added it up, I find, and I admit, that it is indeed so. I had only just entered into the state of holy matrimony with my good Friederike that year, and my eldest son, the actuary, has in very fact already turned twenty-eight.'

'True indeed, Pastor, and when I think in what poor condition you arrived here, and then look at you sitting here now, I don't need to count on my fingers to believe it's been thirty years. Matter of fact, I was here and did the official honours when all of you arrived. You were the first to move in, Pastor, and married your predecessor's daughter; and after you came our – likewise still resident – man of the hour, to make this healthy place even more healthy with his pills and compounds. The doctor I don't even count, for a person who's been lodging among us a mere dozen years isn't to be counted at all.'

'The good Lord did truly bless you in your coming here, dear old friend', the pastor said to the master of the house. 'Your two predecessors had very speedily gone bankrupt in this house; but you were fortunate –'

'And astute', the forester Ulebeule broke in. 'You saw right off how things stood; because in a healthy place like this one, for example, the wise apothecary puts his eggs in more than one basket – a new digestive bitters, shall we say, one like *Kristeller*. He invests in wholesale fruit juices, in the wine business and – let's not forget – in the herbal extract business, all across Germany and beyond. And so this evening, in the natural course of events, the old fellow there in his dressing gown is the only one of us who's amounted to something. The doctor will never amount to anything.'

The man of the cloth sighed, but the master of The Wild Man, Herr Philipp Kristeller, sighed too; and now, just as wind and storm drove stronger and more angrily, with rain and hail, across the land, he looked up startled from the tranquil group around the table at the rain-lashed, clattering windowpanes. His kind old sister moved closer beside him, whispering:

'Now, gentlemen, we must never anticipate a person's good fortune. It serves no good purpose and has often done ill; that's my opinion. And whether my brother's fortune has been all that good, is really still in some doubt. We've accepted our lot in life as it was given us, and that's all there is to it. But I'll still drink to the anniversary, and now I'll give you my toast and say: Long live The Wild Man Shop!'

She had, as she was speaking, filled the glasses all around, and everyone clinked them, though with earnest reflection as the occasion demanded. Philipp, however, shifting restlessly back and forth on his chair, said softly and more to himself than to the others:

'It's just the night for it! – just the perfect night. There's more than a generation gone by since what I should call my greatest good fortune came to me. Just listen to the storm out there throwing a tantrum; you'd hardly believe that tomorrow there might not be a breath of air to take the last leaf off a tree! They say everything fades away in time, but it isn't true. Everything comes back to us again, the gale and the times gone by. You, dear friends, if you will listen to me, I'll tell you a story – a curious, truly curious tale. I'll tell you how, more than thirty years ago, I became the proprietor of the apothecary's shop at the sign of The Wild Man.'

The pastor said nothing at all, but he too moved closer to Herr Philipp, touched his elbow encouragingly and offered him, as even greater encouragement, his bright-rubbed silver snuffbox.

'I love to hear a good story, even a hunting story if need be!' exclaimed the forester eagerly. 'We've flushed him out at last! The chase is on – '

'Just a minute!' Fräulein Doretta asked. 'I just have to go to the kitchen for one minute, then I'll be right back here with you, Philipp. If the two gentlemen will excuse me?'

They did of course excuse her and, while waiting, made a few more comments on the season and the weather. But once his sister had returned, the brother did indeed tell a story – a curious tale.

Chapter Four

'Dear, good, loyal friends and neighbours', began the man who, in the forester Ulebeule's opinion, had amounted to something in life, that is to say, had the portion of his reward in the village, 'before you arrived this evening, and irresistibly drawn by times gone by, I twice opened my strongbox there in the shop and blew the dust off the past; now I shall have to pull out one more document. Despite all the peculiar secrets, my destiny is written with absolute clarity on that paper; not that I kept anything like a diary, but in actual, official papers that I'll show you later for your own expert opinion.

My father had left me several thousand thalers, but my guardian, a good-natured, well-intentioned, but terribly absent-minded and irresponsible man, had paid little attention to the money. When I could have used it, it had dwindled to almost nothing, and the trustee made the sobbing confession that he was the last person who could know where it had all gone. He went on to say, as consolation, that exactly the same thing had happened to his own fortune. He was an older gentleman with three older, unmarried daughters, and all of them were best friends of mine; so what else could I do but mourn along with them and thus help to soften with tears the hard, dry fact of it in mutual love and affection. The three daughters kindly took care of my laundry and other personal effects, packed my valise for me, and so, once my apprenticeship was completed,

I set out expecting to spend the rest of my life as some kind of laboratory assistant, knocked about for five or six years that way, through good times and bad, from one epidemic to the next, one urgent middle-of-the-night call to the next, one doctor's illegible scrawl to the next, until I arrived in ***, where I met my Johanna. And there, friend Ulebeule, I truly did have the portion of my reward, namely, the only good, the only happy days in my life!'

'My congratulations on that, too, then', rumbled the forester.

'Yes, I had stepped into the happy period of my life, and everything came together perfectly – for one whole year!

I was well off in every respect. My employer at the time was a comical old bird, and I must tell you a bit more about him; I really owe him that, for both my sake and his, in every regard. He was an apothecary for the love of it, but also, in a certain manic way, a devotee of the lofty science of botany, and he was in fact a plant expert of some note. For as long as he was able, he would leave his dispensers and assistants in charge of the shop while he pursued his favorite studies in forest and field. But by the time I joined the business, that had just changed. He was past sixty years old, his eyes had gradually grown weak and his back stiff; and when he bent down for a plant out there in the wilds, he couldn't straighten up again without groaning and clutching angrily at his lower back. I arrived on the scene, and he administered a test of my botanical knowledge that covered every last detail but which, thank heaven, I passed satisfactorily and which marked the beginning of all my subsequent well-being in his house. After this examination, as a sign of his satisfaction, he presented me with a copy of *Stöver's *Life of Carl von Linné* and a lecture on the *martyrs of our 'goddess', commending most emphatically to me the example of the greatest botanical genius of the sixteenth century, *Master Charles de l'Ecluse – Carolus Clusius of Arras in the Netherlands – who in the service of science and in his twenty-fourth year contracted dropsy; in Spain, in his thirty-ninth year, fell with his horse and broke his arm, and as soon as it was mended, his right femur; who in Vienna, in his fifty-fifth year, broke his left foot, and eight years later dislocated his right hip and from that time on had to walk on crutches; had a hernia and pain from stones; and despite all that, wrote his marvellous book, *Rariorum plantarum historia*, and shone like a glorious, bright light out of the dark century in which he lived and worked, and across the ages yet to come. After that, he sent me out hunting *in re herbaria* while he heaved a sigh and stayed at home, managed the shop and leafed through his plant books – which were truly remarkable for their kind and were no doubt thrown on the rubbish-heap after his death. In nearly every season I had to scour the countryside for him, for he was also known for his knowledge of mosses, and in the months when the other flora was at its peak I walked almost daily for miles into the fields or hills searching for some particular plant that he'd set his heart on having and studying just then. – That was a wonderful time! Those were days as I hadn't lived them in such uninterrupted, happy sequence for years; and since, as I've said, I could soon carry the name and image of my fiancée with me to the heights and the sunlit slopes and into the shaded valleys, there is nothing that can compare with the brightness that lay over the earth and in my heart. But I don't mean to say that I was turning cartwheels through the sunshine on the hills. Quite the opposite! There was always an apprehensive feeling that accompanied my joy of living. When I came back from the woods to the little provincial town, back to the entanglements and the bickering confusion of even such a small place as that, it often gave me an uneasy, ominous feeling.'

'That happens to everyone whose work keeps them outdoors a lot, it happens to me, too!' said the forester Ulebeule.

'But for a long time', the storyteller went on, paying no attention to the interruption, 'for a long time everything outdoors existed in present time for me, and only little by little, everything down below in the town became the future – a worrisome, anxious, hazy future: Whatever will eventually become of you and your girl?

As I've already said, the real apathy didn't overcome me until the second year of my stay there. At first, the morose, anxious thoughts stayed behind, inside the walls of the town, whenever I set out on my searches. Then gradually they started going along with me and following me farther and farther, till at last, in the spring of the third year, the dark finger threatened wherever my path led. My employer observed that I was growing noticeably thinner and, well-meaning and concerned, recommended various drugs from our stock for nervous and digestive disorders.

Alas, no medicine could restore me to fuller contours! Tossed back and forth between hypochondria and a healthy outlook on life, I drifted aimlessly until I found the man who could help me!

Gentlemen, my dear friends, it was in precisely that summer that I made an acquaintance, a strange, mysterious and in fact, as Johanna said, weird acquaintance. I have it to thank for the fact that today I am the proprietor of The Wild Man, and to this day – this very day, for more than thirty years – it has remained the unsolved riddle, the great mystery in my life.'

'Go on, please go on!' the pastor cried breathlessly, on the edge of his chair and interrupting in the story's most exciting, suspenseful moment, and Herr Philipp Kristeller took the opportunity to catch his breath before going on. It seemed very important indeed that he unburden himself of this great secret in his life, and so he continued:

'Quite simply, I found a fellow wayfarer and colleague, so to speak, on my walks, a young, well-dressed man who also worked as a botanist, appeared to be just a bit younger than I, and proved to be a nature lover and plant specialist exceeding even my employer's expert knowledge of our beloved science. He wasn't from that region and we never quite learned his name; we called him Herr August, and later on just August. That was not his family name in any case.

It was by sheer chance that we literally bumped into each other one hot July afternoon on a scorching, deforested hillside, both of us stooping down amid the jumbled granite boulders and foxglove spikes as tall as a man. We exchanged respectful greetings as fellow tradesmen would do; but first, of course, we politely introduced ourselves and then stood there looking each other over. What the stranger observed of me, I don't know; but he stands before me as clearly and sharply today as when I first saw him back then. He was a young man, as I said, about my age, tall, well built, with black hair and a serious, determined face of somewhat waxy but by no means sickly complexion. He carried his head slightly lowered and his voice was pleasant, but he too seldom used it. During the whole time we were around each other, he would leave it entirely up to me to carry on a conversation. And as you know, dear neighbours, I've always been one for a lively conversation – perhaps too much so at times.'

At this point, his sister had a word to interject, exclaiming somewhat indignantly:

'Now dear brother, there's enough stupid talk about you in the village as it is!'

The reverend gentleman just smiled; but the forester laughed out loud:

'Yes, Fräulein Doretta, it's certainly not in his nature to hold back. I've had that experience twice now and I won't have it a third time if I have any choice in the matter. It's like this: he'll deliver a full oration to the fox crossing his path before he gets his shot off for a clean miss. Now on the other hand, if you're flushing game, he'd be just the man to have along, for a noisemaker's a right useful thing for that.'

'I thank you kindly for your comments, Ulebeule!' the old spinster replied tartly, and Herr Philipp Kristeller smiled and permitted no further delay in his narrative.

'And so I gave in to my nature – how could it have been otherwise? – and gradually told this new acquaintance about everything that seemed to me important concerning myself, my life and circumstances. Before long, he knew everything from my birth onward. What I learned about him, on the other hand, was as little as possible – in other words, nothing! But he was good company and became even better company the more time we spent together. We started planning the locations where we would meet and he, as the more independent one, would always be there waiting. Sometimes he accompanied me as far as the hillside the town was situated on, but as many times as I invited him to come down there with me he would firmly decline, though without ever giving a reason for his refusal. At the edge of the woods above the north gate he would take leave of me, shake my hand and turn back. No one in the town or the surrounding area knew him, no matter how much and how often I asked people about him. A number of them had seen him, and some had also noticed his particular manner and doings, but no one could give any more information about him than that. In one village up in the mountains he stabled a horse and had a buggy, but there, too, he was known simply as Herr August and they took him for a student from the university town down on the plain who, "like many of them", come into the mountains to "study about all these plants".'

'Sounds to me like a trail that's gone cold', said the forester, and the pastor was of the same opinion.

'I thought nothing of it either', Philipp went on. 'I simply continued the association as the occasion presented itself, and after I'd met with Herr August a half-dozen times, it chanced that he also made the acquaintance of my fiancée. She and some of her relatives and friends had gone on an outing in the woods one beautiful Sunday, and there, as Johanna and I had gone off away from the merry group and were walking by ourselves along an overgrown path, we happened upon my mysterious friend. We were going along arm in arm and he was walking alone, and his face looked more solemn and gloomy than ever. When he caught sight of us, he did brighten up, but not for long. He wanted to be lighthearted and cheerful with us, but he couldn't manage it very well. He spoke very politely and pleasantly to my darling, but the longer he walked with us and the more we tried to converse with him, the quieter he became. And then, when the others rejoined us singing, laughing and shouting, he suddenly just vanished and we saw nothing more of him the rest of that glorious day.

"Philipp, he must have experienced some great misfortune, or he's still struggling with one", Johanna said to me later. And she said, "Philipp, I feel terribly sorry for that man; has it never put you in a troubled, apprehensive mood when you're around him?"

Women have a sharp eye and a keen sense for such things and they're good at pointing out to us men folk a lot of things you've felt without being exactly conscious of it. I had to stop and think; and now for the first time it occurred to me that on several occasions I'd also felt very sorry for my silent friend. I must say, I'd never felt apprehensive when I was with him, but even now, on our merry way back into town, I clearly realized that I, too, could very well be overcome with anxiety now and then. From that day on I watched my friend August more and more closely, and then one day I asked him, summoning up all my eloquence and persuasiveness, what could possibly be troubling him and if there wasn't something I could do to help him. I implored him most urgently to take heart and tell me everything that was weighing on him. I told him I would give my own heart's blood to help him, and went on to tell him all the other sincere, heartfelt things you could say to a cherished, admired and respected person in a situation that seems so ominous it makes you tremble. Of course he tried to laugh and assured me he was feeling physically and mentally just fine, and that his conscience was not burdened by some unspeakably horrible deed, but that there was nothing he could do about his temperament, that it was in fact what you might call a rather unpleasant one, and that a number of other people had noticed it too. He said he'd inherited ill-fated blood from his ancestors, and the truth was that it required effort and vigilance all the time to keep it in check, otherwise each day of his life would end in violent anger. He thanked me sincerely for my kindness, as he called it, and I almost thought I saw a tear in his eye, though I'm sure I must have been mistaken, for a face like his, like the profile on a Roman coin, was not cast in a form suited for such tenderness.'

'A face like the emperors *Nero, Caracalla or Caligula on their ducats!' explained the pastor. The pharmacist of The Wild Man shook his head but felt no desire to reply and continued with his story:

'He quite approved of my fiancée, in fact had the highest praise for her – her appearance and everything she had said during our brief time together. He called her a dear, sweet girl – which she truly was – and with deep sighs he expressed the wish that he might have had a sister like her. At that, I naturally asked once again about his family, but he assured me that he was all alone in the world, father and mother both had died, and that he'd never had a brother or sister. Then, as if wishing to change the subject quickly, he asked if we had already set our wedding day.

When I told him how things stood concerning that, he sighed and said: 'Oh, if I could help you, Philipp, I would do it today!' – – How he helped me, and the reason why the seat of honour there has stood empty for thirty years waiting for him, I will tell you now.'

Chapter Five

The little group in the picture-gallery back parlour of the shop at the sign of The Wild Man had drawn close together around the table. They knew their old friend was not bad at telling a story, but this evening his gift was on display as they had never heard it before. Forester Ulebeule's pipe had gone out, Doretta had a tight grip on her brother's hand, and the village pastor tapped his snuffbox lightly on the table and said:

'Well, finally! – You'd never think it possible for such a normal piece of furniture as an upholstered armchair to keep a person on pins and needles for all of thirty years. My dear Kristeller, this chair right here has indeed kept me on pins and needles for thirty years!'

They laughed despite their excitement, and Herr Philipp laughed along with them and then went on with his story.

'Summer passed and autumn arrived. It was September and then October, and the splendour and fullness of nature were starting to fade once more. My employer, who always began to suffer from headaches during the autumn storm season, was now obliged to keep me in the shop most of the time. A good month must have passed before he sent me back outdoors, but on the fifteenth of October he sent me *three miles away to that famous rock formation that you all know by the name of *Blood Rock, in search of a variety of moss that bloomed there, and only there, around this time of year.

I was up on Blood Rock that day, but never again since. I've had a fear of that savage place, despite the fact that what I was given then brought this house into my possession and made possible the life that I've led. There's a riddle still unsolved. If you, my friends, would like to test your wits on it later, you are welcome to do so. I have given up after racking my brains over it these thirty-odd years, and by now it hardly matters any more whether any of us sitting here now finds the key at last. But that day, that fifteenth of October, filled with meaning for me, is what I mean to describe to you now in all its circumstances and as much detail as possible, and now you're obliged to hear it.'

'Curiosity has me sitting up straighter than a hare on the alert!' exclaimed the forester.

'Good Lord, what a night!' said the reverend gentleman. 'Just listen to that storm! Oh, tell us – do tell!'

Indeed it was a stormy night! The longer the night wore on, the more wildly it raged out of the north and up against the mountains, and The Wild Man received its full share.

'It wasn't weather like this on that day', said Herr Philipp in his accustomed tone, calm and relaxed, like someone who has had a full generation to reflect on an experience. But he was interrupted yet again, for a customer came in for a groschen's worth of epsom salts and spent a quarter of an hour explaining to the druggist what he needed it for – while the purchase and the explanation both could have waited till morning, as Ulebeule remarked grumpily. But Doretta took advantage of the pause to refill the Chinese bowl on the table, and at last the friends did learn what apothecary Kristeller experienced on that fifteenth of October.

'At nine in the morning, with my assignment, lunch in my bag, specimen canister on my back, I left the house – which, by the way, was called The King David – with calm winds and thick fog, and this time completely crushed and demoralized. I had good reason to gaze melancholy at even the most beautiful weather! Just the evening before, Johanna's uncle had sent word asking me to be so good as to visit him for a few minutes, and I had visited him, and he had kept me there for two hours. For two hours he had urged me very earnestly to be reasonable and for once take a clear view of my prospects in life and – not to make his niece unhappy! To put it briefly: he had asked me to break off my engagement to her and thus be assured of his – her uncle's – eternal friendship and favour. And the man had been correct in everything he said, and he had spoken both reasonably and amiably. Without the least agitation or anger he had presented his and the world's opinion to me: He found nothing to complain of in me – indeed, I was very close and dear to him – and yet! So I had simply gone, or rather staggered, home and had sat all night on the chair beside my bed, holding my head in my hands, now – thanks to that reasonable talking-to – incapable of any reflection and rational thought whatsoever. That Johanna, my poor, dear Johanna, had wept all through this very same night, I knew as well. In a daze, I could barely comprehend my employer, who was also suffering from sleeplessness, when he came to my door with night lamp in hand at five in the morning to tell me his latest heart's desire and to give me my assignment for the day. He left, out of humour and shaking his bandaged head, once I had finally understood him, and I could hear him clearly enough in the doorway, muttering:

"He'll end up a madman, too, before my very eyes!"

"Write the girl a nice, friendly, straightforward letter in which you say what's necessary; add a bit of poetry, if you like. I will deliver it and append my own remarks (without the poetry, of course). And then, just give the whole unfortunate business – and your poor, miserable self too for that matter – the time everything needs to resolve itself satisfactorily", Johanna's uncle had advised me in concluding his eloquent address of the previous evening. And that should not be enough to make a madman of me? The flowering moss three miles away from The King David and from the house of my fiancée and her uncle was, under these circumstances, truly the only consolation springing up for me in the world out there. The walking and the harvesting would gain at least one day for me and my poor darling; and the way a person in dire need clings to the *one* day, the *one* hour, the *one* minute – who has not once experienced this in some form or other?

It goes without saying that I slipped past beneath Johanna's window. I did not catch sight of my girl, but her uncle I did see. He was standing with his pipe behind the window and seemed to be checking the thermometer. His own temperature had not changed since yesterday evening, for he politely removed his nightcap, raising his index finger. The gesture could have meant only one thing: 'Remember, my good lad, what I told you. I insist upon it, and I know what's best for all of us – I am an old, experienced fellow, and I know the world just a bit better than you fine, young, scatterbrained, inexperienced folks!' And I returned his greeting as courteously and respectfully as I had never before acknowledged anyone. And sighing feebly, I dragged myself on through the grey mists of that autumn morning.

"*O, how full of briers is this working-day world!" as the English poet Shakespeare has one of his characters in one of his dramas say. I have always taken pleasure in reading this poet, and I own a translation of his works with many parts underlined in it. The line about the briers and the working-day world is one that spoke profoundly to me this time, and I repeated it over and over to myself all the way up into the mountains. Surely the world around me now was overgrown on every side with the densest brier thicket, and that it was a wretched working-day world, awash in the tears of ordinariness – the ground under my feet and the vault of the sky above me bore witness to that.

The fog may have been left behind me in the valleys, but in my breast I carried a clouded spirit up to the sunniest peaks. I stepped along briskly and several times dipped my handkerchief in a cold forest brook to soothe my burning, sleepless forehead and feverish temples. I didn't look around as I went, and it is an error, perhaps even a lie, to claim that a beautiful place or a supremely magnificent view can give healing and wholeness to the unhappy man, or one beset by need and care. It simply is not true!

Quite the opposite: there is nothing worse for one so wounded, so burdened with pain, than a broad, sunlit panorama, aglow in all the lovely colours of the earth, seen from high on a mountain peak. It's harsh – terrible in fact – but that's the way it is: the storm, the rain can be accepted in that foul mood; but nature's beauty strikes you as a mockery, an insult, and you begin to hate all seven days of the Creation.'

At that, the pastor shook his head doubtfully; Fräulein Doretta Kristeller nodded, though with a rather doubtful expression herself; but the forester Ulebeule tapped his pipe on the table and exclaimed:

'Sure enough, there is something to that! In fact, on second thought there's quite a lot to it. Any one that's been wounded – I mean, any deer in decline because of an old bullet wound or disease has no more interest either in the splendour of creation that gave it pleasure and well-being in its days of good health. And anybody who's had much to do with animals knows how little the distinction between them and the human race matters in anything having to do with earth, water, light and air. You were a real wounded animal that day, Kristeller. The uncle had hit you with a pretty good shot, and fate has brought many a one in your condition to bay in short order.'

'Now let us hear further!' spoke the clergyman; and they heard further.

'I experienced something that day that had rarely happened to me in the region I knew so well: I lost my way several times and each time had great difficulty finding it again. The confusions of life and the terrible loss of direction were all around me as well as within; but my path was always upwards, and fortunately I also carried a compass on my watch chain. Thus I wound my way through the beech woods, then into the conifer stands, angling upward along steep slopes from which those strange prehistoric granite boulders had once rolled down in absolutely eerie formations. Then I crossed bare plateaus similarly strewn with wild, fantastically tumbled rocky debris – out of the fog and into the sunlight. The autumn sun was shining brightly at midday and I stopped to catch my breath, looking back over the way I'd come and the valleys I'd crossed.

There in the valleys the fog remained all day long, and when I started off again after an hour's rest, it crept up quietly behind me again and caught up with me that afternoon just as the famous place my employer had sent me to this time came into view; although it was no longer the thick fog of the lower elevations, but a light haze wrapping everything in a magic garment. At a bend in the path, there before me loomed the indescribably, grotesquely fissured mass of stone: Blood Rock. Coming out from a stand of fir trees, I caught sight of its highest surface sixty to eighty feet above me, and now, slowly and wearily, I walked across the stretch of grass-covered ground into the shelter of its lowermost boulders, where I could gather strength for the search and discovery of my rare lichen.

You, Ulebeule, you know Blood Rock. It's a labyrinth of stone blocks covering quite a large area on the upland flats. Many of the formations have been given strange mythical names. The highest one can be climbed by a series of eroded steps, and the entire massif is named after it. In the ancient heathen prehistory of our people it bore that same name, as a sacrificial site – and perhaps with good reason.

First of all, despite my troubled state of mind, I'd worked up an appetite and so consumed the victuals I'd brought along; then I set about completing my assigned task, which was no easy matter. The tiny creeping plant that the old fellow wanted a fresh specimen of was certainly not to be found growing in just any one of Blood Rock's crevices. And with the events of the previous evening, the images from a sleepless night and the uncle in his nightcap this morning all floating before my eyes, it made searching all the more difficult.

So I crawled and clambered around in between the rocks. A lichen I didn't find, but I found something else: I found a fortune!'

'Ah!' said the little group of listeners in the back room of The Wild Man.

'Laboriously, in my fruitless effort, I had worked my way up nearly to the foot of the flat-topped stone pinnacle, the actual sacrificial cliff, when suddenly a person appeared up there, in a hurried climb from the other side, so it seemed, and let out a scream that made me jump back in alarm. The figure, lightly veiled by the haze, like everything else, threw its arms up, clutched its head with both hands, let out another cry and dropped first to its knees, then full-length on the ground. I stood trembling, supporting myself on the nearest boulder, and it took some time before I'd pulled myself together enough to pose the question: What is that?

Yes – what was that? What could that be? A drunk? A madman? An epileptic? An unfortunate soul weary of life who had sought out this place to put an end to it, here and now? All of these possibilities raced with lightning speed, one after another, through my brain; but from the heights of the sacrificial cliff there came no answer to my question.

'It is your duty to go and see what, or who, it is!' a voice inside me cried out. So, clenching my teeth and pressing my lips tight, I summoned up my courage, grabbed my walking stick more securely so as to fend off an attack if need be, and began slowly and cautiously climbing the stone steps leading to the holy sacrificial site of our ancestors. Cautiously, warily I raised my chin over the edge: there he was! – stretched out full-length, unmoving, his face pressed against the stone, the unfortunate fellow lay there. And now I leaped up onto the plateau, went over to him, took him by the shoulder, spoke to him, and after a while he did raise up his face and stare at me.

This time, I nearly screamed the way he had earlier. It was my companion, my mysterious friend, my comrade in botanical studies, and with features so stricken, so ravaged by pain, fear and rage that I truly can't describe for you what he was like.

Slowly, really as if coming out of an epileptic seizure, he got up, looked at me unseeing and expressionless, until little by little his consciousness of place, time and situation came back to him.

"Philipp!" he said in a monotone.

"Oh, August!" I cried.

"Is it you that found me here?"

"Oh, and you – what's wrong with you? What happened to you? What can I do to help you?"

"There's no way you can help. You'd better go and leave me here the way you found me. I'm no longer fit for human company."

He said all of this so reasonably, so evenly and calmly, that his distracted state only moved me more heartbreakingly. I wanted to take him by the hand, but he pulled it back quickly, almost angrily, and cried out:

"No, no! No more of that, sir – Herr Kristeller! I have sealed my fate with this hand today and will never again offer it as a sign of friendship, affection or love. Do not think me a fool – ah, I wish I were a fool; but I am not! Three days ago it would have been a blessing if the final thread still binding my spirit to your world – your everyday world – had torn, and I were found as otherwise poor, lost, deranged souls have no doubt been found in the wilderness. No face I could have wished to see today as much as yours, Philipp. But my hand I will not give you. Look all around you, see how the towns and villages are strewn here and there; and see – all these hundred thousand human dwellings are closed to me from now on.

I have no more contact with any of you, I am alone; there is not another person on the earth who's so alone as I!"

"But I'm here, fate led me to you at just this very hour, for me to stay with you! My bride, my fiancée, I've lost her – or she's going to be taken from me. The world will be closed to me as well. Let us rely on each other then!"

Now it seemed that he must be struggling in the depths of his soul with a mighty adversary, and then it was as if he had defeated his enemy, and then as if he were standing triumphantly with one foot on the chest of his downed opponent. He ground his teeth and rubbed his right hand as if it were wet and he had to dry it. Finally he looked sharply and coolly at me and said in a low voice:

"Good sir, you can be of no use to me. I ask you not to trouble yourself. You see, Kristeller, I have never in my life spoken anything but what I believed. And this day, too, *there was method in my madness; I did not cast myself down on this cold and hard stone without a certain intent. My heart's blood has flowed down this gutter as once the blood of *Frankish prisoners from the emperor Charlemagne's army ran down it. As for the rest, I am alone and I intend to be alone. Go now, good sir, I understand completely your feelings, your good intentions toward me, and I am sure we will remain true to each other in memory – Fare you well, Philipp Kristeller."

That was cool and aloof as could be, but I was also psychologist enough to know what a differently motivated reason there was for that tone of voice. It would just not do to drag this unhappy man before the court of egoism and, with a "Farewell to you, sir", turn on my heel and walk angrily home.

"It may be that today we must say good-bye to each other forever", I said. "But why should we be doing it this way?"

At that, tears sprang from the man's eyes.

"No, no", he sobbed, "you are right, it really isn't the right way!"

He flung his arms around my neck and kissed me and now seemed unable to let go of me.

"Farewell then, my good fellow. Only think of my misery and nothing more about me! Don't look back after me. You shall hear from me again, Philipp! Farewell, farewell!"

So we held on to each other for a long time, and then we did part ways. I never saw him again; but hear from him once more I did indeed: he wrote me a letter, and for thirty years I've been the proprietor of the apothecary at the sign of The Wild Man!'

Chapter Six

The pastor and the forester had leaned back in their chairs and were looking up at the ceiling. The sister, hands folded in her lap, was looking at her brother. They could hear the storming wind quite clearly again, and when the silence had lasted long enough, the forestry inspector spoke, apparently just to say something:

'I'll bet it's howling and whistling up there around Blood Rock right now, too.' Then, oddly enough, he added: 'Thirty-one years is a long time!'

'It surely is!' said the reverend gentleman, then turned to the pensive master of the house and asked: 'And you have absolutely no idea what he was by trade or profession and what his real name was?'

'Excuse me, gentlemen', replied Philipp Kristeller, and he went one last time this night to open the file cabinet in his shop. He returned with a large envelope containing only a single letter, handed Ulebeule the envelope covered with several postmarks and five crumbling seals, gave Pastor Schönlank the letter, sat back down slowly, placed his hand over his eyes, lighted his pipe again and waited calmly to see what effect these papers would have on his guests.

'Contents – nine thousand five hundred thalers in government securities!' murmured the gamekeeper. 'Free! – to Herr Philipp Kristeller! – '

'Most wondrous!' exclaimed the pastor, scanning the cover letter. 'Indeed a curious letter! A puzzling, mysterious missive!'

'Well, hang it all then, read it aloud!' cried the forester, and the pastor read aloud:

'A man desiring to start his life over again herewith releases himself from his heaviest and most vexing burden and sends his friend the enclosed money. A man vanishes and leaves no trace behind; it is useless and unnecessary to seek him or call after him. Ah, Philipp and Johanna, take for yourselves what would only drag him down to the depths. Build a house to stand firm and see happy, joyful children grow up within its walls. Fare well, dear friends – fare well! – Philipp Kristeller, this greeting comes – on my way back to humanity,

the Fool of Blood Rock
Hamburg, 30 October 183– '

115

The pastor laid the letter down without a word. Ulebeule struck the table with his fist, making everything on it jump and the glasses clatter alarmingly:

'By thunder! Can you imagine! Well, if *that* doesn't bring down the stag!'

'And you, even with this letter in your hand, didn't think at the time that you were dreaming all of this, old friend?' asked the pastor.

'For days, even weeks, I walked around like one in a dream, not just with the letter, with the money in my hand as well. And they were the most conservative government bonds and promissory notes from various countries! They didn't change overnight into fallen autumn leaves – they didn't go up in ghostly smoke right before my eyes – they were genuine and worth the amounts they claimed, and the bankers were more than ready to trade or cash them in for me. But I took them, and the letter as well, to my fiancée and asked her what I should do in the face of all this. (I did not seek her dear uncle's wise counsel for the time being.)

Johanna of course also had to overcome a kind of initial shock; but then she told me her opinion clearly and calmly, and I did as she suggested:

"I felt sorry for your friend and his behaviour worried me, but I didn't fear him as I would an evil or malicious person. I felt great sympathy for him and should have liked to help him in his misfortune. But you see, Philipp, he also always gave me the impression that he thought things over carefully and knew what he was saying and doing. He has a clear, intelligent mind for all his melancholy, and what now seems so strange to us and might look like insanity to the rest of the world, he thought about and made his plan, and I'm sure he found what was best for him to do. I think you may take the money and use it to establish your fortune. Let us treat it as a loan, Philipp. We'll always save a chair for the donor at our table and always reserve the best place for him. We'll expect him from one day to the next and – I'll tell my uncle it's an inheritance, and you can do the same. I don't mind having that little white lie on my conscience."

So you see, friends, that's the reason why the armchair here is always vacant, why there's always been a place reserved at my table through all these last thirty-one years. But to this day, our friend still hasn't come back! You've known me since I arrived here among you – you know how I took over this shop when it had already failed twice and how my hard work enabled me to secure the ground that had proved so treacherous for my predecessors. But you also know – '

'What great pain you had to suffer, dear brother?' exclaimed his old sister. It was an impassioned interjection. 'No, no, they've heard about it of course, but they don't truly know it.'

'It was very sad, Fräulein Kristeller', said the pastor, and Ulebeule heaved a sigh and muttered:

'Yes, yes. But you're not the first one to have the cup knocked out of your hand that way just as you were about to drink, Philipp.'

'The house was built, but the bride, the young woman, was not destined to take her place in it. She died on the day that had been set for the wedding, and it's in her place that I've managed the household for my poor brother all these thirty years, this full generation we've been talking so much about on this stormy night.'

'And we've lived our days well enough in quiet', said the apothecary of The Wild Man with a melancholy smile. 'In peace we've grown old and grey, and the storm roaring outside the window there doesn't bother us much anymore. The chair I've saved is still empty, and the one for whom the seat was reserved has likely found his rest, too, in some distant, foreign place – let's hope it was after he'd found his way back to humanity, as he says in that reckless letter of his. As for us, grown old together here, let us stick together in friendship and good faith, never bearing ill will toward one another beyond the next meeting.'

'That we will!' the other two men spoke with one voice.

'Indeed, indeed', said his sister.

Chapter Seven

The rain had stopped momentarily, but the wind had become a good bit stronger. After all that had just now been said, it was not easy to pass to a casual conversation; yet each one of them keenly felt the need to do so.

When Ulebeule finally gathered his wits and remarked dolefully, 'That's a proper wind, all right!' Fräulein Kristeller did offer the fitting reply: 'Oh yes – and the poor people at sea in all this!' But that was the end of that conversation, too, and again the pall of silence fell. Philipp had returned his fateful letter to the yellowed envelope and was just entering the doorway to his shop with it when he stopped and cried out:

'Here's the doctor now!'

'The doctor!' they all repeated after him, with a sigh of relief and a brightened look spreading over their faces. 'The doctor! Of course, that must be him now.'

And he it was. From outside the windows – of the shop, not those of the back room – came the sound of carriage wheels creaking, a horse stamping, the snap of a whip, and calling out over it all a loud, jovial voice:

'Hallo! Ahoy! Poison vendor! A lamp to the window! Are you there, Frederick? Open that door to the stable and light the way so we can get ourselves and the buggy inside and out of this biblical tempest and flood!'

The old woman ran out quickly to meet their always welcome third friend of the household. The forester and the pastor leaned back more comfortably in their chairs. The apothecary stood there smiling, with his yellowed letter in his hand, and listened along with the others. Now they could already hear the doctor's jolly voice in the hallway and Dorothea's voice, too, and then a third voice joined in, strong and cheerful like the others.

'He didn't come alone. He's brought us a guest, or one of his patients is with him', said the apothecary of The Wild Man, and in the next instant they could see that the former was the case. The door leading from the entry hall into the picture-bedecked parlour was flung wide, and along with the local physician, Dr. Eberhard Hanff, came the guest, politely deferring on the threshold to Fräulein Dorothea to precede him into the room.

'No need for ceremony, Colonel', boomed the doctor as he pushed the broad-shouldered, distinguished-looking old gentleman with snow-white hair, keen black eyes and cheerful, suntanned face ahead of him through the doorway. And without any further ceremony, he introduced:

'Colonel Dom Agostin Agonista – in the service of His Majesty, the *Emperor of Brazil – plucked him up on my way – oh, dear me! Punch?! – There, Colonel, didn't I tell you so? Fräulein Doretta, you unfailingly sense my emotions and my frame of mind at a distance of three miles – Punch!! You gentlemen can best introduce yourselves to the colonel. Ah, Fräulein Doretta, the nastier the weather, the more sensitive your prescience – permit me to kiss your hand.'

'Stop that foolishness now and hang your coat up on the hook there', said the apothecary's sister. 'The colonel is most welcome here, and may I invite you all to be seated.'

The doctor was in the habit of 'plucking people up as guests' now and then as he made his professional rounds and bringing them along to one house or another, where he would always introduce them in somewhat this same manner, usually causing them no little embarrassment. The Brazilian colonel, however, was not so easily embarrassed. He turned his cheery, scarred, old soldier's face with a bright, friendly expression from one to another in the little group and said, with just the least trace of a foreign accent:

'For my part, I would call this a surprise attack, dear lady and gentlemen, and I sincerely beg your pardon for this nighttime invasion. The good doctor did find me, stranded on my way by storm and darkness and sitting at a table in the most wretched little tavern, and ever so kindly played the good Samaritan. He showed me to his carriage and offered me much better quarters for the night in this village. I went with him gladly, and then he stopped in front of this house – to have a *Kristeller*, as he said – for just a moment, as he said, and I came inside with him to have a *Kristeller* myself, and my name is indeed Agonista, and I am a colonel in the Brazilian service.'

'My name is Kristeller; but my good friend the doctor calls a liqueur by that name, the recipe for which was my accomplishment, Colonel', said the druggist. 'In any case, your arrival here in our little circle is an honour and a great pleasure for us all.'

The pastor and the forestry inspector now likewise expressed their satisfaction at the timely arrival of this interesting foreigner. There were handshakes all around and the chairs were pulled up to the table again.

'Oh, Fräulein Doretta, once again I must pay you my usual compliments!' exclaimed Dr. Eberhard Hanff ecstatically, raising his head after a long inhalation of the steam rising from the evening's punchbowl. 'Now, Colonel, don't you agree that we are in much better hands here than at The Uncorked Jug, or whatever the name of that bandits' hideout might be? Eh? And to think how you resisted and protested against the better advice of a man who knows the territory!'

'It surely is better here', said the soldier, bowing to the master of the house's sister. 'We often protest and resist our good fortune, Senhora – and one should not do that.'

The others of course agreed that the colonel was right, and then of course they spent some time talking about the weather again; but then, too, about the roads, the roadside tavern where the doctor had found the stranger, about the region in general and in particular, about this year's early departure of migratory birds, and about one thing and another. Only the pharmacist of The Wild Man did not take much part in the conversation.

He, Philipp Kristeller, was seated across from his Brazilian guest. He had not locked the old letter up in his desk again; he'd been prevented from doing that by the sudden arrival of the doctor and this stranger, and he'd brought it back and laid it down again on the table in front of him.

Now he was resting his elbow on it and smiling at the others' conversation, though somewhat absently, as if lost in the web of his own thoughts. One could not say that the foreign gentleman who had turned up so suddenly and unexpectedly in his quiet household heightened the agitation he felt; but he – the master of the house, that is – glanced inquisitively now and then at his guest, and the replies that he gave to questions asked of him then were a bit less coherent than usual.

The doctor was the first to inquire jokingly about the reason for it, and Ulebeule answered for the apothecary:

'Leave him alone, sawbones. If the bear's down on all fours, he'll soon rear up again all the higher. What do you think he has those hind legs for? — as they say in Poland. If you'd got here a quarter of an hour earlier, you'd have found all of us here in a much stranger mood. Like hares moving through a field of grain, we've been chewing our path through a pleasant conversation here tonight. Oh, we've heard strange stories!'

'Ulebeule!' cried the apothecary. But the forester in his enthusiasm was in no state to heed the cry.

'I tell you, Doctor, it's a downright shame that Fräulein Doretta's punch didn't lure you and the colonel this way a bit earlier. Like flushed birds, the strangest stories have been flying up all around us here. We know now why none of us has been allowed to sit in that armchair for the last thirty years. We know how it was that our friend Philipp ended up here in our village. We've heard a lot about love and death, wild men and old letters of credit of the kind most people don't get by mail. Were you ever in your life up on Blood Rock, Doctor?'

'Ulebeule?!' the reverend called out this time, and this time the forester heard.

'Well then – yes, yes. You're right', grumbled the chastened huntsman. 'Don't take it amiss, Kristeller. Since you were so open about it your-self – '

Herr Philipp amiably refilled his worthy friend's glass and gave him his hand. But now it was Dr. Hanff who said:

'It seems that we who might have experienced something like that ourselves now and then got here too late for the curious tales this time. But permit me to ask one question: Have you perhaps concocted this splendid beverage here in connection with those same stories?'

The Brazilian colonel, Dom Agostin Agonista, who had been gazing pensively all this while at the unoccupied seat of honour, now glanced up sharply and looked keenly, clearly at each one in the circle, but last of all and most keenly at the master of the house. Meanwhile, the pastor answered both the doctor's question and the colonel's searching gaze:

'You've arrived just in time for a commemorative celebration as serious as it is happy, my dear Doctor. Our friend Kristeller has been situated here in this house at the sign of The Wild Man for exactly thirty years today, Colonel. For us and for all the inhabitants of the area far and wide, he has been a true helper and friend for an entire generation. The punch was concocted by Fräulein Dorothea, and you, dear Doctor, would have found your own invitation waiting for you at home.'

'Well then, it seems I've spared myself the detour', laughed the doctor. 'My own father marvelled at my discerning nose the first time the midwife laid me in his arms.'

Adding one more remark, something about the key to his house, the village humorist looked around from one to the other, but this time they just smiled, no one was really laughing or holding on to the table to keep from collapsing with laughter. The colonel appeared to be enjoying himself the most, and he now raised his steaming glass and spoke:

'Then may I also permit myself, a foreigner dropped as if from the heavens into this congenial gathering, to drink to this lovely and significant anniversary evening. Thirty years are indeed a long time; many things change – faces and opinions. And, my dear lady, gentlemen – I, too, have an anniversary to celebrate today, one that is very noteworthy and momentous for me. Exactly thirty years have passed for me, too, since the first time I came under fire, aboard the Chilean frigate *Juan Fernandez* against the *Diablo blanco*, the *White Devil*, a vessel from the *Republic of Haiti; to awaken from unconsciousness the following morning, with a splinter of wood in my hip and an axe blow to my shoulder, in the lower deck of the black pirate ship!'

'For which you're certainly to be congratulated even today', growled the doctor, while the others indicated their empathy and interest in different ways.

'For which I can surely thank my lucky stars even today', said the doughty old warrior, 'for in that goddamned ship's bilge, the blackest, foulest-smelling hole that ever floated on water, I made the acquaintance of a doctor who performed a cure on me that no European doctor of medicine could have done – '

'That would be the Devil!' exclaimed the European physician.

'And, in a manner of speaking, he was', the Brazilian colonel replied calmly. 'And he clapped me on the shoulder and said: "Senhor, for a certain length of time everyone on earth has the right to play the fool, but he must not go on playing beyond the allotted time or he will make himself ridiculous. I like you, Senhor, and I mean well with you – this time you have escaped with your life. Remember me and call on me when you need me; I am always standing at your left elbow." – And that, dear lady and gentlemen, is precisely how it has turned out, and every time I've had need of him, I have called upon the black man, and it has always been to my benefit. Before that, things had truly gone badly for me in this world, and I had been quite miserable.'

The reverend gentleman moved a bit farther away from this strange guest. Fräulein Dorothea Kristeller murmured:

'Dear me! Hm-hm.' The apothecary still said nothing at all. But Ulebeule cried out with delight:

'Well now, if this just isn't like a chapter out of that *Arabian Nights* book! We're all telling our stories, and as far as I'm concerned, we could go on like this till morning. Now Colonel, our old friend Philipp here never intended from the start to confess all that he's told us, either; he just sort of gradually picked up the scent, and we just kept him on the trail with friendly encouragement. So, Colonel, if we could ask you to follow his example and tell us more about the blackamoors. It's a perfect evening for it – What do you think, Pastor?'

The pastor had drawn closer again and offered the foreign veteran his snuffbox.

Dom Agostin Agonista looked pleased; he smiled kindly and said:

'I don't know what sort of wild stories our good host has told about himself. My own life, like a garden, surely grew wild and produced fruits that would cause amazement in any market place. At first, it produced luxuriant growth, and more than one botanist waited expectantly for its unearthly flowers and fruits. Oh yes! Then came the great "hurricane", the wind and storm over land and sea – the foliage was torn away, the blossoms – or what appeared to be – likewise. Finally there appeared, three or four feet down in the earth, something that bore a resemblance to a potato – all sorts of tubers connected by filaments – inedible, tough, an unappetizing product of old Mother Earth. So that's what it all came to, lady and gentlemen, and the only consolation is realizing that not everyone can become an orange or a palm tree by his own choice. But the sooner a person discovers where he fits into *Linnæus' or Buffon's classification, the better it is for him, and the sooner he will find peace and contentment with his condition. Until he's figured that out, he rages at the loveliest sunshine and declares allegiance to snowstorm and winter winds. I consider this, too, a philosophy of life, Herr Kristeller.'

'And so it is, Colonel', said Herr Philipp. 'But as long as the person is young he rarely discovers the great truth. Indeed, many – most people – never discover it and go on believing in their destiny as palm trees up to the very end.'

'And that's their good fortune', exclaimed the weathered, philosophical old warrior. 'For without that happy illusion, all humankind would be nothing more than a miserable tangle of scrub growth and vines creeping over the ground. And by the way, potatoes and truffles are nothing to turn up your nose at.'

'But that story about the pirate ship and the black Satan that clapped the good colonel so cordially on the shoulder – this hasn't the least thing to do with all that, does it?' asked Ulebeule.

'Bravo, woodsman!' cried the doctor. 'You are indeed a master of the hunt. Tally-ho! Tally-ho! They can't throw you off the scent, can they? Just resign yourself now, Colonel, and tell us about the black pirate ship and your other serious and entertaining experiences. The night's black enough for it, and we're all ears.'

That seemed to set the proper tone for the conversation to follow now; but in that very moment, Colonel Agonista brought all of them – all but the master of the house – to their feet in sudden, astonished trepidation. He had raised his glass and now he spoke, slowly and calmly:

'Let us toast the health and wellbeing of all stalwart hearts, no matter whether they fight their battles within their own four walls or are tossed about through blood and fire over half the earth. Do you no longer know me, Philipp? Do you truly no longer know me, Philipp Kristeller?'

—— —— —— —— —— —— —— —— —— ——

The apothecary of The Wild Man had grasped the old letter which had lain there under his elbow up to now and crumpled it in his trembling hand. For the last five minutes he had known who his guest was, and Colonel Dom Agostin Agonista had known it, too. But now his sister reached over to support her brother, the colonel took hold of him from the other side, and so he struggled to his feet like the others, placed both arms on the guest's shoulders, rested his face against his chest and groaned:

'After one whole generation, then!'

The doctor, the pastor and the forester were left wondering, each in his own way, and it was quite a while before they had all taken their places again.

Finally they were seated once more, the colonel, however, not in the cushioned place of honour reserved so long a time for him. Dom Agostin, after finally almost rudely declining the honour, had sat Fräulein Doretta Kristeller down in the armchair with elegant, courteous insistence, and she remained there, once having registered her protest:

'I cannot prevail against force, Colonel, but I assure you I do not sit comfortably here, and I shall need to return to the kitchen any minute now.'

This was true. The punchbowl needed to be filled twice more in the course of the night and the guest room prepared, too, for the mysterious, venturesome friend. Meanwhile, without resisting in the least, the old soldier told *his* story to the company at The Wild Man. What came to light there would – under other circumstances – have prompted any gathering of townsfolk to back slightly away from their cheery storyteller, then, with their pipes and punch glasses, begin to look around for another seat, and then – until time to go home – to stare furtively, fearfully and dumbfounded over their shoulders from their new vantage point at this uncanny, jolly old South American fellow.

Chapter Eight

The bare tree branches were no longer scratching as hard as before at the window panes of the little back room in The Wild Man. Ulebeule the forester had stuck his head out into the night air, pulled it back in and given the others in the room the comforting assurance:

'It's clearing right up. You can see the stars through the breaks in the clouds. The wind's done a proper cleanup there over our heads and chimney caps. I know how this goes, and I'll bet we have a beautiful clear day tomorrow.'

This was spoken in the pause that ensued after the wondrous reunion in The Wild Man.

Philipp Kristeller, up to now, had not let go of his benefactor's hand. The two old friends sat there next to each other, and in his left hand the colonel toyed with the letter he had written in mortal desperation thirty-one years ago and had laden with 9,500 thalers in government securities for his botany-student comrade. Now for the first time he withdrew his right hand from his friend from Blood Rock, tossed away the last stub of his cigar and pulled out a short pipe, which he then filled from a very exotic, very Indian-looking tobacco pouch, and quickly – before the apothecary's hasty grasp and outcry could stop him – lighted it. Before he could stop him: for Dom Agostin Agonista had torn off a sizeable piece of his superannuated, wildly fantastic letter, twisted it up tight and applied it to the very purpose for which one uses that kind of spill. At the same moment, calmly and contentedly, he began telling his story; and it started well, namely with the words:

'Wouldn't you say, Doctor, that anyone who has never killed a man will find it difficult to know the feelings of one who *has* accomplished that deed? Please don't be too shocked, lady and gentlemen; I did eventually come to know those feelings. Anything in the world can be learned eventually and one can become accustomed to, hanging and shooting as well as – beheading. I come from one of the most disreputable families in Germany, and three days before that meeting with my friend Philipp Kristeller on Blood Rock, I had done what I had to do. To put it bluntly, I had, with the consent and support of state and church, on the open field and before ten thousand spectators, struck off the head of a good-for-nothing fellow man in this hurly-burly world. Do not be shocked, dear lady – that, too, is a story of things long past.'

Ah, but what good did it do to say: Do not be shocked! – ? They all gave a start, even Herr Philipp Kristeller.

'The office that my ancestors had held – and held with distinction – for more than two hundred years in unbroken succession had been passed on to me, and I exercised it – one time! – as I've said, three days before that attack of *St. Vitus dance when this man here discovered me on Blood Rock. You see, Philipp, *that's what it was!* and your Johanna was surely right if, long before that last encounter, she pointed out to you certain things about me that disturbed her. Dear God, I wish I could tell the poor, dear child this very evening how much I always liked her. And now she is dead – dead a whole generation? Ah, Philipp, Philipp, you can hardly have known how much sunlight she radiated, wherever she went or rested, and how black and repulsive the world appeared to me in that beautiful light. That's long past, too! Since we're still alive and doing well, let's talk about us. –

I'd had a curious upbringing. My grandfather, August Gottfried *Mördling, had exercised the terrible hereditary office with sinister zeal and in fullest measure; my father, on the other hand, had had the good fortune that not once in his entire, albeit not very long, lifetime did the unpleasant necessity arise of unlocking the chamber in the upper story of the house and running his eye and his finger up and down the blade of the broad sword engraved with the year 1650. Of my mother, there is little I can tell you. She was a sickly, peevish woman and I have just one particular memory of her, namely that she raised various kinds of poultry and always did the slaughtering of chickens, turkeys, ducks, pigeons and geese by herself, and with great skill and a certain wild energy. My father, a gentle, educated man who revered *Schiller, understood Goethe, was crazy about Uhland, and raised me, would always leave the courtyard or kitchen with rapid steps and muttering 'O good and gracious Heaven!' whenever these executions took place. – My father, Alexander Franz Mördling, a lover of both art and nature, had also travelled; he'd been in France, England and Holland, spoke English and French quite well, and raised me very well. He made an educated person out of me, one who could discuss the rising and setting of sun and moon and, above all, knew how to lay out an herbarium. As true, genuine, self-taught men, both of us fashioned our own world – a world from which neither of us could be called away on business without going half mad and completely to ruin.

Our entailed estate lay outside the town limits, of course, hidden away in the countryside, shaded by ancient linden trees, protected by high walls and an enormous gate – a house dating from the end of the sixteenth century, warm in winter, cool in summer – fit for a bishop to live in and compose his Sunday sermons. The noise and the hubbub of the outside world was hardly perceptible inside our walls, and even though my father certainly didn't hide our true circumstances from me, what I did know about them never preyed on my mind. For a young boy, it even had a certain allure – you were alone, but you were also something that the others weren't. – Dear lady, you could sit up on that wall like an enigmatic ape, grinning eerily, aristocratically at the youngsters on the other side of the moat, who didn't dare to grin back. You may not believe me, Fräulein Doretta, but that really is how it was. And since my reclusive father spent his days in relative comfort and contentment, I had all the less reason to complain of my fate. We had our small pleasures through summer and winter – *Matthias Claudius would surely have felt at ease with our various pursuits, our dreamy musings and fancies.

Yes, come to think of it: the old *Messenger of Wandsbek was the one that my old man most resembled by nature. He could surely never have guessed what a well-travelled devil lurked in his own little son. But at last there came one winter when the snow lay deep and the ground was frozen hard, in which my father departed this life; and I – a grown, adult man confronting everything that existed or transpired outside our walls like a callow, immature youth – watched him die.'

At this point, the storyteller, Colonel Dom Agostin Agonista, got up and went to the window to check the weather.

'It's the only thing that helps in such emotional turmoil', he said, returning to his seat. 'The forester is right, by the way: it is clearing up, and it looks like we'll have a beautiful day tomorrow. Well, where was I now? Ah yes, my father's death and all that went along with that. And so I must presume upon you gentlemen and lady for a while longer.'

All of them but the apothecary had been staring with eyebrows raised at the back he'd turned toward them to peer out the window. Now, as he turned round again, each of them – all but the apothecary – looked away here or there, behaving as naturally as they could.

'You call this presuming upon us, August?' asked Philipp Kristeller in gentle reproach.

'Augustine – Agostin – Agostin Agonista, if it's all the same to you, old fellow', laughed the Brazilian colonel, and – went on with his story.

'We were alone in the house, my father and I and an old witch of a maid who'd cunningly kept the two of us in subjection ever since my mother's death. My father had been ailing for some time, doctoring himself, and had now reached the limit of his medical skills. My dear Doctor, even the town physician we finally called in could do no more than shrug his shoulders. And Philipp, my friend, the night before he passed away, my father gave over to me the keys to the archives of our house! Three days after he was buried, I opened the black oak cabinet in which the chronicle of our family, carefully recorded for almost two hundred years, was kept; and thus I made my entry into the time of crisis during which old Philipp here and his Johanna, so young and beautiful, made my acquaintance and had such good reason to wonder about me. I found in that cabinet a thick manuscript compiled by my forebears and bound in black leather with brass corners and hasps. They'd kept strict account and made quite a nice ledger out of it, with all the numbers and other documentation. And I read and checked the calculations all the way down to my grandpapa – I read it from beginning to end, word for word, date by date, number by number; and the third night, around two in the morning, when I went to get up from my gruesome reading, I found that I could not. I was stuck in the chair, scourged from head to toe, and outside it was bitter cold – the dog in the frozen yard was howling and whining from it, and I, too, felt frozen to the bone and, what's more, half insane, my life, my feeling, thinking and believing – broken, like a staff broken over the knee. My fearsome witch of a housekeeper had to thaw me out by the stove like a stiff-frozen towel, and more than a week passed before I could feel the very least animal warmth once again. I lay in bed for more than a week with my teeth chattering, mentally and physically; but then I ran outside, ran myself warm through the wintry countryside – stayed away from the house for two weeks this time, trying to run my way to sleep along with the warmth, but the only thing I got with my running were dreams of the most terrible kind. It's a wonder that no one can tell by looking at me today what a madman I was at the time! After coming back home I sat by the hearth, an idiot, until springtime, and if spring hadn't come, I would surely have ended my days a pitiful, miserable idiot in the county madhouse. And, dear Philipp, concerning that period in my existence I have nothing more to say. I drove my wagon *over the border, took a room in one of the villages in your province and went up into the hills. That's where we met, and you thought me a crackpot scholar whose friends had advised him, for reasons of health, to take up a little botany.'

'I've already told my friends what great respect I had for your expertise', exclaimed the apothecary of The Wild Man, and all around the table they nodded and said: 'Yes indeed! That he did!'

But now, for the first time this night, the expression on Colonel Dom Agostin Agonista's face grew earnest, dark, almost angry, and he said:

'I would have explained my condition more clearly to you in due course, Philipp. I would have told you everything about myself and my life, but your gentle nature prevented me and made me keep my silence. And, dear boy, if there was anything that made me despise the world even more, it was your fiancée. By God, so many times I hated you for your happiness – oh, Philipp Kristeller, more than once I would gladly have dug a pitfall for the two of you and your tender affections. Had it been a matter of jealousy, that would have been bad enough; but it was worse than that, it was envy – vile, wrathful envy. Ah, friend, friend, back then I certainly had no intention of helping you get a start in life nor, as far as I was able, to find a bride! It required a frightful turn of events to change my mind about that, and the frightful turn of events came to pass – today I can say, thank God! Returning home from one of my ostensible botanical rampages, I found a letter waiting for me, a document bearing the seal of the chief state prosecutor's office. I was ordered to report at once to the county seat, and what the authorities there required of me, as they were fully entitled to require, you gentlemen and gracious Senhora can very well imagine; I'm sure I needn't demonstrate it with a gesture. I was presented with a death warrant already signed by the governor, and I had three weeks' time to prepare myself and my patient for the operation I was charged to perform. During those three weeks, you did not see me, Philipp Kristeller; but you found me three days after the completion of my official duty, up there on the sacrificial rock. Oh yes, gentlemen, a man is entitled to rest when work is done, and that, too, was a holiday excursion! – I had done my job well and been praised by the authorities, the newspapers and the mob of spectators; but the honour was a burden to me – quite literally: on my own back I carried my silent patient, now made shorter by a head, and I had just dragged him up onto Blood Rock as my friend Philipp climbed up from the other side. You see, we always wonder what the poor sinner standing before the high court is feeling, but this time one might also wonder what his executioner felt; well – let's not speak of that. As I was saying, I carried the poor devil's carcass down from the scaffold; he hung there on my back, his hands dragging behind along the ground, with me gripping one foot in blue woollen stocking on each shoulder! That's the way I dragged him up onto Blood Rock where you, Philipp Kristeller, found me lying, my face pressed to the ground, that headless blackguard riding my back – one claw caught in my hair, and singing his diabolical song of triumph over me – an incomparable ventriloquist; but absolutely loathsome, even now, after thirty-one years of calm reflection and more settled thought!'

Chapter Nine

The colonel fell silent and wiped his handkerchief across his forehead. The others around the table cleared their throats. The forester and the pastor enveloped their uneasiness in exceptionally thick clouds of tobacco smoke, the doctor seemed about to drown his internally, and all three of them – by no means bad people – looked remarkably stupid just now. Fräulein Doretta Kristeller, in the chair of honour, had drawn back as far as she could out of the lamplight and into the shadows. You could hear her groaning and sighing softly, in fact it even sounded like sobbing now and then behind her handkerchief. A story like this one could not be told with impunity, whatever one might say – not even in the circle of one's very best friends.

The old soldier certainly did not fail to notice the impression he'd made, but once he had brushed the repulsive memory aside, as it were, with a sweep of his hand, he placed both elbows on the table and glanced around more cheerfully than ever. He had, as it was soon revealed, experienced even more extraordinary things than that in his later life. He had not sat in a safe corner like the others, he'd turned his face into winds that most people would have called gale-force but that he considered just wind. It was not for nothing that he'd risen to Colonel of the Imperial Brazilian Gendarmerie.

'Dear, good August – Augustine', whispered the apothecary, 'you set off into the world as a penniless beggar in your confusion; – you turned over the inheritance of your fathers to me – '

'So I did! Never has a person turned his back on old Europe with pockets as empty as mine were!'

'Oh, my Johanna – my dear, poor Johanna!' sighed the druggist softly. But there the soldier of fortune very considerately broke in on his old acquaintance's line of thought.

'No, no, Philipp, by all the powers that be, no! That's not how it was! That's not the way Heaven deals with us here on earth! You would have lost her in any case – Fate did not cause her to die on account of my bequest! What did her life and destiny have to do with all that that money signified, those thalers I cast away when I fled back then, and hung around your neck because you happened to be standing closest to me? The child did not die because of that, Philipp! The two of you would have built a wonderful life on the legacy of my forefathers if the good and beautiful young woman had not had to leave you. And besides – – who here among us has actually drawn a better lot than she?'

The question called for an answer, and each one did answer in his or her own way, but no one affirmed or denied it aloud. The proprietor of The Wild Man shook Colonel Agonista's hand for the hundredth time, and the colonel returned his handshake heartily, exclaiming:

'What can we do, after all? – Each one lives his own life, and whoever can tell his story with a sense of humour is a blessing in any gathering, and even the wisest, most honourable and revered will do well to hear him out. Now I would like to make a wise observation: namely, that people's greatest individual discontent comes from the fact that they consider the world at large as too peaceful. My friends, the world is not a peaceful place, and one needs only a proper acquaintance with its confusion in order to put into perspective all that befalls him from his first breath to his last. The devil take those fools who think their four walls are caving in on them. Climb up on the rooftop when fear overcomes you and see for yourselves that the firmament has no intention of collapsing just yet! So there I stood, not a penny in my pocket, on the dock in New Orleans, feeling rather like someone waking from a drunken stupor, holding his throbbing head but feeling the cool morning breeze on his temples with a sense of relief. What was to become of me now, I really didn't care. I was ready for anything, to live or to die, but since I was hungry and so as to meet at least my most urgent needs, I sold my neck-cloth and my handkerchief to a traveling peddler. After that, I treated the first good fellow I met on American soil, the one-armed mulatto Aaron Toothache, in a bar patronized by the sort of people we here at this table can scarcely imagine. There I met a ragtag bunch from the aforementioned frigate of the *Republic of Chile, the good old *Juan Fernandez*, and we took a liking to each other. The way that acquaintance finally played out below decks on the *White Satan* is a story I've already told you.'

They had all drawn close around him by this time. They seemed, after these last revelations of his, to have overcome completely their reticence and aversion to him! They had pressed in so tightly that it seemed he had almost no room to breathe. Puffing, he spread his arms as if to push them back a little, and we – we'll do exactly the opposite of those rapt listeners in the back room at The Wild Man: we'll move away from the Imperial Brazilian Gendarmerie Colonel Dom Agostin Agonista.

What this wondrous storyteller had to tell now was exciting enough, filled with fireworks and crackling flames at sea and on land; but that sort of thing had been experienced by others a hundred thousand times before, and the stories told aloud or written down, even published in books every so often. We'll let him, Colonel Agonista, brush his hand over the table one more time, sometime around one in the morning, and summarize his present view of life and the world with just a few more words:

'So, in the second year after I shipped out from Hamburg, I was serving as private in a unit with orders to report as a firing squad outside the fortress wall. The lieutenant raised his sword and we fired – I, like the others, without a second thought. From that moment on, I was completely free of the burden of my past life in Europe. I gave not the slightest thought to the day that had been yesterday nor the one that might be tomorrow – Hurrah! In the words of the poet, *I placed my trust in nothing now! Thus I was always at home, at home and alone: whether on the march or in the sentry box, by the fire in an Indian hut or in the salons of garrison towns. Yes, my friends, I've seen many a president in many a republic over there come and go, I've had a hand myself in pulling up a chair for their excellencies or pulling the seat out from under them, whatever was called for at the moment. Venezuela makes me a lieutenant, Paraguay makes me a major; but *His Majesty Dom Pedro of Brazil was the most beneficent of all to me and also the one who pleased me the most. The two of us have kept law and order among the multicoloured rabble of Rio de Janeiro for a good many years now – he with normal, proper constitutional kindness, I with a whack of the saber blade and, if need be, a quick gallop, three squadrons one after the other, right through the mob. Gentlemen, and you, dear lady, you will no doubt be startled once again and look at me askance, but this is how it is, and a man must stick to the truth: while I did give up beheadings, I changed over all the more vigorously to hanging, and I found that it's much cleaner work and serves the purpose just as well. As for *being* hanged, I've felt the noose around my own neck more than once, but thank God, I've always slipped back out of it up to now. Oh yes, I can get along pretty well with anybody now – have my place at court and ride alongside their Imperial Majesties' coach in formal parades. If I get back home to Rio I shall marry; it's getting a bit late for the bachelor's life of drifting and roving. But more about that tomorrow. And now for a final glass of this most excellent drink, and with it – advice, a wish and a toast: Esteemed friends, as long as we are here, let us live as best we can; and since whatever it is that will finally push us out of existence is always at work, let us push back without scruples; but most important of all, long may *he* live – my friend, my dear, old, good friend Philipp Kristeller, and together with him may there grow, flourish and prosper, on and on, his apothecary shop at the sign of The Wild Man!'

At that, they all joined in, clinking their glasses one with another, and they rose from their seats and stood there dazed, uncertain of all the fantastic things brought forth and revealed this evening. The guests themselves could hardly recall afterwards exactly how they had taken their leave of the master of the house, his sister and Colonel Agostin Agonista.

But the colonel said:

'Philipp, a dressing gown and a pair of slippers, if I may. I intend to be comfortable at least one time more in the German fatherland.'

The two friends from Blood Rock embraced once again. We, for our part, will accompany the forester Ulebeule and the pastor a few steps on the way to their abodes.

Chapter Ten

Now the forestry inspector, the pastor and the good Dr. Hanff – had wished their kindly hosts a good night, or rather a good morning, that much is certain.

Kristeller had escorted them to the door with the lamp, and now they stood at the roadside where the doctor had found his buggy already waiting. They heard the master of the house turn the key in the lock, and nothing more kept them from throwing wide the doors of their own sentiments, feelings and points of view.

The first to speak his word was of course the doctor, who exclaimed as he stood there on the footboard:

'Well, wouldn't you say that once again I hauled a pretty first-rate fellow into town for you? I doubt you had the slightest notion there could even be someone like that in the world, eh? I've taken a tremendous liking to the old chap and I can't wait to become better acquainted with him –

I'm sure he'll give someone else the chance to talk, in good time. We can all take our turns inviting him to dinner, can't we?'

'We certainly can, and that way he can marvel at us, too', cried Ulebeule. And the doctor drove off down the road to the right; he had quite a distance to go before reaching his house.

The other two turned left, the reverend gentleman carefully leading the way with his lantern. But when their ways parted they stopped once again and looked back in the direction of The Wild Man. The house stood there in darkness now beneath the dark, scudding clouds. Although the wind had subsided a bit and the stars were visible, there was still enough threatening vapour swirling in the dome of the sky, and the poplars near the pharmacy swayed like drunken phantoms.

'That house there will never again look the same to me as I've known it up until this evening', said the pastor. 'What do you say, dear friend?'

'The devil only knows!'

The reverend drew his shoulders in. 'You should use that evil word more carefully, old chap', he said. 'Of course, of course, after what we've just heard – who can tell which one had a hand in that business? I prefer a situation that rests on better, more solid ground than – – Well, anyway, what do you think of our friend Kristeller's situation from this point on, after this evening?'

'I like the old fellow more than ever now!' the forester exclaimed, brimming with enthusiasm. 'I call him an upright man and a good person! If anybody deserved to cross paths with that top-notch hangman and Brazilian field marshal general at just the right time, it was our Philipp. It's true, he wouldn't have conquered the world, or even a little piece of it, but what you give him he takes with modesty and gratitude, and for us in these parts he's truly been a blessing these thirty years long.'

'And the other one – that other – that Dom – Dom – Agonista?!'

'Well, you know, Pastor, I'd have to see him in the light of day before I could make a decision about him; by lamplight there's none better in the whole wide world! He's a splendid chap, sure enough, and you won't find yourself every day of the week sitting elbow to elbow with a fellow made of such stout timber. What shall I – ? I suppose it bothered me more than anything in a long time that he didn't offer me a toast to our friendship right then and there.'

'Well, there I really must say I'm a little more hesitant than you, my dear Ulebeule', said the pastor, shuddering just a bit. 'I think this person suddenly sprung up out of the ground is absolutely frightful! The cold-blooded way he makes no secret of anything at all in his life touched every nerve in my body. If I've had too much punch to drink, I'm not to blame; it's that – that – that strange storyteller's fault. Just try passing up one glass after the other when you're having hot and cold shivers one after the other! Is it really true you had no idea that people can lead such hair-raising lives on God's green earth?'

'I've read more fantabulous things in books, but here we had the genuine article, in the flesh, for once. His story didn't give me the hot and cold shivers, but I did let my pipe go out quite a few times listening to him. If you had a visit from a fellow like him every night, you could quit smoking with no trouble at all. Aside from the fact that I'd never before laid eyes on a Brazilian colonel, this colonel could tell a story better than any Brazilian, I'll wager, and what's more, without using a single word of hunting lingo. That's my field, and I'd have spotted his first mistake and let him know it – with a smart whack of the hunting knife on the seat of the pants: "*Hoho, here's once for our good prince and master! Hoho, here's twice for the good knights and men! And here's for the law of the noble hunt!" '

'Ulebeule?!' came the pastor's despairing reproach.

'Yes, yes, you're right, it's late and the wind is up', said the forester. 'But that story of the black ship alone would make a good picture on any street singer's barrel organ. By George, it makes us look completely outclassed, outdated and out of touch in our burrow here, when you stop to think what kind of experiences we were having while *he* was spitting out his casts around all those other nests.'

'I just thank heaven that I was allowed to turn grey in peace here. Such an existence would not have suited my nature.'

'You needn't tell me that', laughed the gamekeeper. 'But hasn't this very person, this odd, renegade fellow just shown us that nobody knows what he has in him and what he can pull out of himself when the time comes? Good Lord, how many times, when I was young, out of fear or distress, did I plan to run off into the wide world! After an evening of storytelling like this, you understand less than ever why you never did it, never slipped through the fingers of your schoolmasters, parents and all the other authorities in your life.'

'We are all led rightly on our way, and we are in good hands', spoke the shepherd of souls, stepping at precisely this inopportune moment into one of the deeper puddles in which he would have perished without mercy had his stalwart companion not caught him just in time.

'You can return the favour another time', said Ulebeule solemnly.

But this little incident now brought their conversation about the House of Kristeller and the Imperial Brazilian Colonel of the Gendarmerie, Dom Agostin Agonista, to a close.

One or two other things were discussed before the pastor went on straight ahead to his parsonage and the forester turned left into the dark path leading to his lodge.

'Shall we see each other tomorrow? With all that's happened, we surely must see and hear a bit more, and then have our say about it all.'

'We do feel that need, to be sure', agreed the pastor. 'And I expect we shall meet somewhere. We owe it to our good apothecary to inquire about his health.'

'And no less to the colonel.'

'Of course, of course. Well, we shall see. And now, good night – or rather good morning, my dear friend. We've rarely sat around together so long as we did this evening.'

'And yet, it was always too early to call it a night, and I'd have been ready any time to follow that wild Indian's tracks through the early-morning dew. But he's snoring away by now – I'm as sure as can be, he's lying there in his den and snoring louder than anybody with a clear conscience in a twenty-mile radius. Confound it all, as soon as my head hits the pillow I'll be dreaming of Blood Rock and that Brazilian dragoons general, and tomorrow – tomorrow I *will* drink a toast to our friendship!'

——— ——— ——— ——— ——— ——— ——— ——— ——— ———

Thus spoke the world! — And if a million people had been listening to old Philipp Kristeller and Colonel Agonista there in the picture-filled back parlour at the sign of The Wild Man, those million thinking, speaking beings would have heard little more nor much different than what the pastor and the forestry inspector have just said. The exchange of views in their words was quite sufficient. Let us turn now to the aged brother and sister at The Wild Man, and to their strange guest.

Chapter Eleven

Brother and sister sat alone in the back parlour, which was growing rather chilly now in the settling fumes of strong punch and tobacco smoke. Their guest had gone to bed.

The master of the house had shown his friend upstairs to the guest room with his lamp and had tried to sum up once again all his overflowing feelings in word and emotional tone. The colonel had gently tried to calm him and then, with his good Philipp still standing there before him, had yawned broadly and taken off his jacket. But then he had affectionately called him back once more from the landing and, laying his hand on his shoulder, had said:

'Philipp, old chap, my dear boy, it is indeed a sincere pleasure to take my rest under your roof. Truly, in many a difficult, uncomfortable hour on land and on sea, I would imagine setting up most luxurious quarters here, under this roof, and now I have them in reality, and this is wonderfully comforting!'

To this reassuring expression of his feelings we should also note that he appended the very practical request for a bootjack.

While her brother lighted the way to their guest's bedroom, Fräulein Doretta had remained sitting in the picture gallery, but she had given up the seat of honour and taken back her usual chair. There she sat, both elbows propped on the table and looking blankly through the smoke that the men had left behind, over the empty punchbowl and the empty glasses, at the array of pictures on the opposite wall. There she sat and listened to the footsteps overhead and then to the footsteps of her brother coming back down the stairs.

'What a thing to have happen!' she murmured. 'What does this mean for our life now? – So late in our lives! – And what will come of it all? – Oh, oh, oh!'

Now her brother came back in to join his sister. Now he was the one to lay a hand on her shoulder.

'Are you still having trouble, too, puzzling out the good fortune this evening has brought us? Oh, Doretta, dear Doretta, how beautifully everything has now come together and closed the circle – and precisely on this day, this evening! Who could think this a coincidence? Has anyone ever seen more clearly at work in his own destiny than we the hand of Providence that makes all things right?'

'Oh!' groaned his sister. 'Ah, brother, brother, what's to become of our life now? Oh, if only he'd come sooner! But so late in the day – so late in the day – what are we to do?'

Herr Philipp Kristeller had sat down on his chair and looked at his sister in wide-eyed amazement.

'What – what do you mean, Dorothea?'

'Don't ask me anything more just now', the old woman answered sharply. 'We'll see soon enough – tomorrow, the day after! Yes, tomorrow is another day! – But you just can't help thinking – good brother, what if he were to stay? What if he intended to stay here with us? One has to consider every possibility, you know.'

'What if he were to stay? What if he intended to stay here with us? But that would be marvellous!' exclaimed the apothecary, rubbing his hands with delight. 'How cosy and pleasant we would make his life for him!'

Baffled, he watched his sister shake her head doubtfully and sadly.

'You don't believe we could manage to do that, Dorothea?'

'No', she replied bluntly, and with a deep sigh she said, more to herself than to her brother:

'And then there's the other possibility – what if he plans to leave tomorrow, and on top of that – '

She broke off her sentence and didn't finish it, even when her brother asked tensely, urgently:

'And on top of that? – What do you mean? what are you trying to say?'

'We must simply wait and see', said Fräulein Dorothea Kristeller, getting up from her chair. 'We can't really discuss anything more this night; and now let us go to bed, too, and try to sleep.' After that, they remained sitting there a while, a good half-hour, but in silence. Once they did go to bed neither brother nor sister slept a peaceful sleep.

The most peaceful sleep, of all those whose acquaintance we've made this time, was the sleep of the Brazilian colonel, Dom Agostin Agonista. He lay contentedly on his back, smiling in his slumber, even while snoring. He could be heard throughout most of the house, and if he dreamed, his dreams lasted, contrary to all soldierly custom and habit, well into the new day.

That new day came fresh, clean-washed, gleaming and sunny – a perfectly clear, chill October day. The hills in their brown autumn garb stood out sharply against the light-blue dome of the sky; the bare fields below stretched distinctly into the farthest distance; and the villages, the individual farmyards, the adjoining houses and sheds appeared to the eye in sharp outline, as if lifted from the *mirror of a *camera obscura* and set into the morning landscape.

But in this clear, sunny, autumn-morning landscape, the apothecary shop at the sign of The Wild Man, more than anything else in the scene, looked handsomely washed down and cleaned up. The gilt lettering on the sign over the doorway gleamed far down the road to the right and the left. And whatever else belonged to the house, the garden fence, stables and stone walls – they were all in the best of condition. One could see that a devoted and caring spirit had charge of each item on this property and took pleasure and satisfaction in the task and did his utmost, day in and day out, to keep everything in house, yard and garden in good shape. Except for the sunflowers, tattered and torn by the storm of the past night and now hanging their wilted remains over the garden fence, everything about The Wild Man Shop was, in the fullest sense of that lovely word – presentable. And brother and sister waited with the coffee for their guest. He had just now sent down word: for the moment, he was shaving and would make his appearance in ten minutes. The vapours of last night were dispelled, the back parlour swept and spread with white sand. The house cat was washing itself under the table and the canary twittering gaily in its cage. It was a pleasure to see Herr and Fräulein Kristeller sitting at their breakfast table and to be invited to take one's place there with them.

The colonel made them wait for him only a bit past the indicated ten minutes. Now they could hear his heavy military footstep on the stair. Apothecary Philipp Kristeller threw open the door of his favourite room –

'A very good morning to you!' boomed Colonel Dom Agostin Agonista from the threshold, and now the hosts and their guest got their first quick look at each other by the clear light of day. Keenest of the three was the sister's eye; the Brazilian warrior would inspect his men somewhat less carefully than that; and the pharmacist of The Wild Man saw nothing at all – his friend and guest was a blur before his eyes, at least for the first few minutes.

'Gotten pretty old', thought the colonel to himself, and he was right.

'Under other circumstances I'd have nothing at all against him', said the sister in the depths of her soul. 'A respectable, easy-going gentleman!'

The apothecary Philipp Kristeller said nothing; again he shook the hand of his old, rediscovered friend, his benefactor and guest, and this time insisted, despite all protests, that he sit down in the place of honour. Only when the colonel was seated did Philipp say something, and not to himself or in the depths of his soul, but calling out joyfully:

'August, I'm incredibly happy – you've stayed remarkably young!'

'By all the gods of waters and dry land, I should hope so', laughed Colonel Dom Agostin, and there was truth in what he said: in spite of his snow-white hair and the number of his years, he had remained very young; but the youngest thing about him was his voice.

That alone could be considered a remarkable thing. With an engaging resonance it filled the house, passed round and full through the ear and to the heart, and fitted itself in comfortably, one might say jovially, reassuringly, with anything and everything, good or bad, that the moment might bring. Anyone hearing it from a distance, and especially accompanied by its owner's hearty laughter, would have to say: 'There's a good fellow who enjoys life.'

Now the colonel shook the sister's hand again and said to the apothecary:

'This morning I have given you the right to consider me a late sleeper, but you'll probably learn better tomorrow morning. Usually it's my custom to be on the march three hours before sunrise. You learn that, even if you're not so disposed, south of the equator; and if some morning you should find the nest entirely empty, you needn't be all too surprised.'

'Oh, friend', cried the apothecary, 'I'm sure we can hold on to you! We certainly won't let go of you that quickly! You are ours! You mustn't go the way you came – you would be taking away all our joy, our comfort, for a long, long time!'

'Hm!' said the colonel, and then they had a leisurely breakfast – the old soldier with an exceptionally hearty appetite. He also displayed enviably well-preserved teeth and made admirable use of them.

When breakfast was finished he leaned back with a satisfied sigh and lighted his pipe. Doretta went to tend to her household, and the two men were alone. They chatted now – now was a time when they could chat – having overcome, for the moment at least, the serious side of their mutual connections. They had found the calm they needed simply to chew the fat, and so they did now – two comfortable elderly gentlemen, one of whom had seen somewhat more of the world and preserved himself considerably better than the other had been permitted to do.

The Brazilian was pleased with the German houseflies that buzzed around his nose, and we could certainly not blame him; but this matter deserves to be treated in a chapter of its own.

Chapter Twelve

'You lucky people have no idea how many things the likes of us have to envy you for', said the colonel. 'Here you sit in your everyday cosiness, and if you didn't really need to get upset now and then over the fly on the wall, you would actually have it *too* good. Just look how daintily that one there on the sugar bowl wipes its nose and cleans its wings! How is it possible that even the most even-tempered one of you here in Germany will fly into a rage if it should walk across his forehead during his afternoon nap? One of our bivouacs on the Rio Grande without a mosquito net, that would be something for you, to teach you patience in adversity.'

The apothecary smiled and said:

'We have adversities enough of our own without that, dear August.'

'Dear Agostin, if you please', exclaimed his guest. 'You cannot imagine how I detest that former name. When someone discards his coat by the side of the road as decisively as I did, he takes all the more pride in his new uniform. The one I wear now fits me like a glove, as I would remind you – Dom Agostin Agonista, Colonel of the Gendarmerie in the Imperial Brazilian Service – everything in order, commission and passport – '

'Don't get all worked up, dear fellow', said old Philipp soothingly.

'I'm not getting worked up, it just angers me', insisted the colonel.

'Yes, like a true German angry about the fly on the wall, my dear Augustine', said the pharmacist of The Wild Man, and then they changed the subject. That is, the colonel began inquiring in great detail concerning the circumstances and careers of the gentlemen with whom he'd become acquainted the evening before. Then he told more precisely how it was that he had met Dr. Hanff along the way, and that led to his remarking that it was not purely by chance that he had happened into this place, but that in fact he had come there with the intention of looking up the old woodlands-and-botany comrade of his youth, his loyal friend from Blood Rock.

'I had no idea where you could have got to and if you were even still alive, Filippo!' exclaimed the Brazilian. 'But I had set out to find you, dead or alive, and that is what I've done. It wasn't like hunting down a rebellious black slave, old boy. But I have learned how to follow the trail of animals and humans – in the jungle, over the plantation fields or in the maze of streets and alleys above and below ground – until I caught them. I picked up your trail, or the trail of your name, or rather some kind of schnapps or liqueur by your name, in the newspapers. I went off in search of *Kristeller*, and here I am; and I'm sure you won't take it amiss if I express the desire, in the course of this morning, to taste this drink at the source. It was entirely unnecessary for your good doctor to tell me about *Kristeller.*'

Old Philipp had been rubbing his hands with delight throughout this entire account; now he leapt up, slapped his friend on the shoulder and cried out:

'So it's my *Kristeller* that put you on my trail! O dear August–ine, yes, I think I really did create a beneficial formula there; give me just a second – '

'Later!' said Colonel Agonista. 'See how gloriously the sun is shining, how blue the sky is! Now first of all, show me all around your property, inside and out – ah, such a pity that you have no wife or children and grandchildren to show me! – the garden, the shop, your laboratory, supply room, kitchen and cellar, stables and livestock – I want to see all of it!'

Since the master of the house was now back sitting next to his guest, he slapped him on the knee this time:

'O Augustine, how kind of you it is! How happy you make me now! Shall we go then?'

'Certainly', said Colonel Dom Agostin Agonista, jumped to his feet, tamped down the tobacco in his pipe and took the arm of his friend.

The two men set out on their tour of house and yard, garden and stables, and it was both a curious thing and a pleasure to see how knowledgeable and informed the military man was in discussing it all and – how carefully he inspected each little thing.

The delighted master of the house repeated his amazement at this several times, but Dom Agostin laughed and said:

'You go knocking around half your life over there among the citizenry and the tribal peoples, the monkeys and other animal life included – of course I mean, as a thoughtful and practical man by breeding and inclination – and see if you don't hark back to the way things were in the old homeland, but also acquire new experiences daily. If it was my fate to become an adventurer, Philipp, at least I became a respectable one. My plans to marry in the near future I believe I already told you about last evening.'

'If you really meant that in earnest, Augustine – '

'Deadly earnest. You all seemed to take it for a joke, I did notice that. Actually, I should have taken it amiss and I'm not sure even now why I didn't ask right away for some explanation of your smiles. It even looked to me as if that doctor – Dr. Hanff – shrugged his shoulders. Well, we'll blame it all on your sister's excellent punch. But I repeat: I am head over heels in love and carry the picture of my beloved over my heart in a locket under my waistcoat. You shall see her portrait, and your sister shall see it too, later on, and then you shall tell me what you think! She is a splendid woman and not without means: Senhora Julia Fuentalacunas – rather a melodious name, wouldn't you say? She came to Rio as a young girl, Julchen Brandes, from Stettin and married Senhor Fuentalacunas of the customs office. You know, dear friend, the uniform of His Imperial Majesty's forces may be handsome and honourable garb, but once the freshness of youth is past you start to care less for honours and to prefer life's comforts to serving other masters. I will purchase a hacienda and hope to end my days in peace as a well-to-do patriarch surrounded by my family. You – you and Fräulein Doretta – are of course part of that family, and we'll have a wonderful life together.'

'What?' – – asked the apothecary of The Wild Man, Herr Philipp Kristeller, staring at his guest with eyes wider than ever.

'Just as I said', the Imperial Brazilian Gendarmerie colonel went on, disregarding completely his old friend's astonished look, standing instead in the middle of the property and gazing about at the surrounding buildings. Once again he really seemed to mean what he said in deadly earnest.

'I hope it won't be too difficult to convince your sister', he added, as if just incidentally.

The pharmacist laughed, but the colonel was by no means laughing with him; he was in the stall walking with critical eye around the two cows, tapping them on their flanks and remarking:

'Several years ago I was in *Fray Bentos and had a look at the meat-extract facility there. Amazing! – Right before your eyes they send a steer into the processor and give it back to you ten minutes later, concentrated, in a tin you can stick in your trouser pocket. If there was no ocean nearby to hear your cry of amazement, you wouldn't know how to express it. Philipp, two weeks ago I was at *Liebig's plant in Munich – pretty much the same atmosphere and smells as here at your place, just a bit more metallic. Kristeller, we can help each other out the same way: I provide you the animals and you provide me the extract. Philipp, I give you my word of honour, in three years we'll be so competitive with the gentlemen in Fray Bentos that it'll bring them to tears.'

'Oh, Augustine, what a great sense of humour you've brought back out of your new fatherland!' cried the apothecary; but –

'Humour?' The colonel was quite serious, and he added, almost screaming: 'Numbers! Numbers! The most exhaustive, irrefutable calculations: Here! – and here! – '

He had already pulled out his notebook and was rapidly reading off to his friend some very detailed lists indeed of figures relating to the manufacture of meat extract. Herr Philipp Kristeller was rubbing his increasingly numb forehead:

'My sister – my sister ought to hear this', he mumbled, and now the gendarmerie colonel was finally smiling as well and said:

'I shall of course acquaint your good sister with our plans at the midday meal and try to win her support for them. I'm confident she won't sit there as rigid and surprised as you and do nothing more than praise my sense of humour.'

'O dear God!' sighed Herr Philipp.

The goat next to the two cows in the stable, an animal that owed its pampered existence to the special care of Fräulein Doretta Kristeller, was passed over without further comment by the colonel; but in the chicken yard he remarked, shaking his head:

'These beasts are always a strangely vivid reminder of my dear departed mother.'

He still had the notebook in his hand and made notes in it from time to time. They spent almost two hours on their inspection tour and when they returned to the house they found the doctor waiting for them in the shop with a little glass of the famed *Kristeller* digestive liqueur on the table in front of him.

The physician greeted the two men with his accustomed joviality. They shook hands heartily all around and inquired most cordially whether the others had slept well and how they were feeling in general.

'What day of the week is it, anyway?' asked the colonel, with his notebook still in hand.

'The barber hurrying by there's the best one to tell you that', laughed Dr. Hanff. 'The farmers are getting their week's stubble ploughed under; it's Saturday – '

'And tomorrow I'll attend a German church service for the first time in a generation!' cried Colonel Dom Agostin Agonista with delight. 'And the day after tomorrow I leave.'

'August? – Augustine?!' cried Herr Philipp Kristeller, stunned.

'Colonel?' said Fräulein Doretta Kristeller, astounded.

But the local physician, brusquely pushing his glass away, exclaimed:

'Impossible under any circumstances, Colonel! I ran into forester Ulebeule; he's on his way here with an invitation to dinner on Monday. For Tuesday I am requesting the honour, on Wednesday it's the pastor's turn, on Thursday – but let's not presume to speak for the other gentlemen. In any case, under no conditions will we release you that quickly, Colonel. Anyone with such a rare bird as you in hand will hold on to him as long as possible. Give me another *Kristeller*, won't you, Kristeller, and you have one too, my dear Colonel; it seems you still don't have a proper idea of what a good and agreeable drink this little spot on the planet produces.'

Chapter Thirteen

The forestry inspector, who was just coming through the door at that moment, heard what was being talked about and immediately joined the others in trying fervently and urgently to persuade the dauntless old South American warrior. But he resisted in silence and with gestures only, all the while holding his glass of Kristeller's herbal bitters to the light and eyeing it critically.

Now he raised the glass to his lips – sipped it – paused – tasted a second time more reverently – poured the rest of it down his throat with almost wild abandon – held out his glass at once to be refilled from the squat, round, green bottle, and exclaimed:

'Bless my soul, now this is truly – truly what I'd call a *drink!*'

'Isn't it though?' said the forester and the doctor solemnly, while the apothecary of The Wild Man smiled with modest satisfaction over his sister's shoulder.

'By the gods, this *is* a drink, Philipp! And you really are the one who created it? And you have the recipe under lock and key? – And you're still sitting here in this forgotten corner of the world grinding out pills for the doctor there and mixing potions for him? – Fräulein Kristeller, may I ask to speak with you privately directly after dinner! Gentlemen, this may change everything; my dear Master of Forests, in the course of the afternoon it will be my pleasure to give you word whether or not I am able to accept your invitation.'

'Bravo!' cried the physician and the forester; the pharmacist said:

'You shall absolutely stay, dear fellow; and it was certainly not necessary to give us all such a fright. It was not kind and brotherly of you, Augustine.'

'I should like another *Kristeller*', replied the colonel. 'Philipp, here's to you! I assure you, I've always liked you, but now I add my respect to my affection – gentlemen, for all these thirty years you have had a great man in your midst without knowing it. Philipp, your schnapps is wonderful, but as far as my departure is concerned, our kind is always shoulder arms and forward march, and a man has to take a wife and run an ordinary business if he's to learn how to sit still. By the gods above, what we have here could be more profitable than Fray Bentos! Kristeller, we're going to bring fiery seventh heaven down to earth with a distilling column over there. Fräulein Doretta, we're going to bottle sunshine and lightning and set our prices accordingly. Kristeller & Agonista – São Paradiso – *Province of Minas Gerais, Empire of Brazil! With this drink we'll make our name in every nation on the face of the earth. We'll make a name for ourselves, Senhora, and as I said, after dinner I should like a friendly little chat with you in the little back parlour, Senhora Dorothea.'

They all laughed, with the exception of Fräulein Dorothea. As for the laughter of the ingenious master of the house, it made a decidedly bewildered and helpless impression. But a person like Colonel Agonista, who had already lived one life, was able to see the world with different eyes and take hold of it with different hands than the members of this household and the friends of the apothecary shop at the sign of The Wild Man, and could also, as innocently as you please and without ever being called to accounts for it, demand that others agree with his viewpoint. Colonel Dom Agostin Agonista could truly present his firm, incontestable decision to reverse once again, even after the passage of thirty years, the good fortune and the fate of his friend Philipp Kristeller, and without listening to any objection or counter-proposal whatever.

Since the entryway was now filling with customers, the sturdy old soldier accompanied the forester and the doctor on their way back to the village by himself. He walked between them, linking arms with both, and anyone meeting the three of them, stopping and looking after them, had to admit that each one of the three was, in his way, 'right'. But the men's conversation remained on the subject of old Philipp and his *Kristeller*; and even over this short distance, the Brazilian gendarmerie colonel obtained several more rather useful notes on The Wild Man and returned, whistling merrily and inhaling the clean, fresh autumn air – just in time for dinner.

They dined; they had their siesta – the colonel took his this time in his seat of honour in the picture-plastered back parlour.

At three o'clock sharp he strode, refreshed, back into the shop to have another *Kristeller*. From there he knew precisely his way to the kitchen and had no need for a guide.

'Fräulein Doretta', he said, 'this would probably be an appropriate time. I have just now accompanied our good Philipp to his supply room, and we two, dear lady, have the realm down here to ourselves. Children, children, I am as happy as a little child to be together with all of you in such familial friendship! And we'll remain a family – won't we, we'll remain *one* family? – It is so magnificent! Outside, the German autumn sky, in here, the warmth of the German stove, and – fair Brazil like the land of promise in the distance! Senhora, I beg to offer you my arm.'

He unerringly directed the old lady, who kept anxiously looking back over her shoulder, to her own sitting room, the formal parlour of the house, and remained there with her a good half-hour in most urgent negotiations, while her brother, in order to keep at least some control of his agitation, stacked and unstacked all the herb packets, and opened and closed again all the drawers in his supply room.

Under certain circumstances, half an hour can seem very long even to the most phlegmatic person; this is a well-known fact, but must be repeated here nonetheless. For the apothecary of The Wild Man, that short span of time seemed *very* long. For Fräulein Doretta, on the other hand, it passed uncommonly quickly.

Already the colonel was very politely opening the door to her sitting room for her and – letting her out. He stayed inside! – She held on to the door frame as if to keep from fainting; she had meant to make a curtsy to the kind soldier, but that hadn't been possible. But while she leaned against the wall out there, struggling to look around as if with eyes suddenly blinded, the colonel inside, whistling to himself, had gone to the window, opened it and leaned on the sill.

There he stood, resting on his elbows, and heaved a deep sigh, then looked up and down the road, first to the right, then to the left.

The lady standing outside now put both hands to her temples and also heaved a sigh, and she groaned:

'Great God, it's just as I thought! O dear God, my poor, poor brother!'

From his place at the window, the colonel called to a boy from the village, who was just running past:

'I say there, my boy, d'you know Herr Ulebeule the forester and d'you know where he lives?'

'Sure?' retorted the lad, looking up at the side of the house, indignant over such an obvious question.

'All right then, son. I'm waiting here with five groschen in my hand for you. Run to the forestry inspector's lodge and give him best regards from the foreign gentleman at the apothecary's, and tell him the apothecary and the foreign gentleman will be pleased to eat at his house on Monday.'

The boy ran, and as he ran he looked back several times to see if the white-haired gent with the brown face at the window would really keep his word and stay at the window with the promised payment. Downstairs in the back room, in the Brazilian colonel's seat of honour, sat Fräulein Doretta Kristeller, her elbows on the table and her face in her hands, and moaned softly:

'My brother, my poor brother!'

Chapter Fourteen

The following day was Sunday, a German village Sunday. The bell was ringing for church, and Pastor Schönlank had his sermon finished and ready. Carrying his friend Philipp's hymnal and grandly escorting his friend's sister, the Brazilian Colonel Dom Agostin Agonista went to church, too, and he went in uniform. He had completely unpacked his portmanteau and his small traveling bag and adorned himself in full dress. He was wearing all of his decorations and looked not just martial, but truly magnificent and aristocratic, and he thoroughly disrupted the village congregation's devotions by his appearance. And he sang with them. The pastor in the sacristy could hear him over the organ, the cantor and the congregation; such a resounding bass had not shaken the vault of the little house of worship in a long time. After church, the foreign officer, again escorting Fräulein Doretta Kristeller on his arm, had to take the salute, so to speak, from the entire congregation. They formed a lane along his way. And smiling good-naturedly and touching his cap again and again, the colonel strode through the hedgerow of staring, open-mouthed peasant faces.

He was the talk of the village today. Fräulein Dorothea, however, came back home from church feeling very unwell and obliged to lie down in bed and remain there for the rest of the day.

On the following day, the colonel went with his friend Philipp to the forester Ulebeule's to dine on boar's head. Fräulein Doretta sat down with the household account books. The men at the forestry inspector's lodge had a jolly time at table; the colonel told them once again of the glories of his new homeland and drove the people from this sleepy little place nearly wild with his eloquence and the colourful splendour of his descriptions. This time he invited the doctor to travel there with him and become a millionaire and privy imperial court physician, and by the time they were on the fourth bottle, the medical man had definitely promised the colonel to do that and given him his hand on it.

'As for you, dear Pastor, we wouldn't be so sure what use to make of you over there', boomed Dom Agostin, 'but perhaps we could send for you once we've built our own private chapels.'

The reverend gentleman had smiled at that but said, somewhat dolefully:

'I imagine we are a little too old to emigrate that way, Colonel. And besides, you'd certainly have to discuss it with my good wife first, dear sir.'

'And why should I not, if all the other conditions are met?' asked the Brazilian.

They had an exceptionally good time at forester Ulebeule's, and night was already falling when Philipp and August came back home to the apothecary shop, arm in arm and shoulder to shoulder, very lively and animated.

'A *flacon* of *Kristeller* for the bedside table, if you please, old chap', said the colonel. 'It enchants me each time anew, even after a *dîner*. *Pereat* Fray Bentos – this is what I call a real concentrated bouillon! The devil take every bovine in the Pampas; if we can cook up liquid fire this good here at home, just imagine how it will turn out over there in the *Land of Fire, Fi-lip-po!*'

'Ex-qui-site!' replied Herr Philipp Kristeller, whereupon the two friends hugged and bussed each other three times heartily on the cheek.

It happened that they were sitting by themselves in the back parlour this evening, the colonel and the apothecary of The Wild Man. Fräulein Doretta sent word by the maid excusing herself and saying she had a terrible headache.

The two men sent word back upstairs at once saying they were very sorry to hear that and sending heartfelt wishes for a speedy recovery. After that, they sat there in the picture gallery until sometime around midnight talking, enveloped in tobacco smoke, about the years of their youth.

When the clock struck twelve, the colonel rose and said affectionately:

'You don't really know what a good feeling I have here, Philipp. But from now on we won't be separated any more, old fellow! From now on we'll have *one* destiny and *one* good fortune, won't we? We will, won't we? That's agreed, eh, Philipp?'

'That's agreed', stammered Herr Philipp Kristeller, and then the colonel went to bed. He knew the way to his chamber by now and needed no one to go with him. The *flacon* of *Kristeller* he carried with him as he had carried his friend's hymnal on Sunday. But before doing that he had obliged his friend to sit in the seat of honour; and in that seat of honour Herr Philipp remained a while longer in the nighttime quiet and tried to think it all over before going to bed himself.

The night was quiet, the house was quiet. It was just striking one when a door creaked upstairs and soft, slow footsteps came down the stairs. The master of the house's intention of thinking it all over in the colonel's special chair had by now turned into a rather sound slumber. Waking with a start from that slumber, Herr Philipp listened: there were the ghostly footsteps just outside the door –

'Who's there?' he called, struggling to rise and clumsily supporting himself with both hands on the armrests.

'It's me, Philipp', said Fräulein Doretta Kristeller, tottering into the room in a long, white nightdress like a veritable Lady Macbeth. 'It's me, Philipp; I can't get any rest in bed, no rest anywhere in the house. I thought I might still find the stove warm in here, but now I'm glad that you're still awake, too, dear brother – oh, brother, brother Philipp, he really and truly is serious!'

'Serious? Who is serious?'

'Deadly serious! Oh, I thought so from the very beginning, when he first slapped you so familiarly on the shoulder and all of you laughed about his fantastic plans. It's possible that he does mean well with us, but he's going to make us miserable. Philipp, he needs money! He needs his money, and he's come to get it!'

The apothecary of The Wild Man suddenly saw this disconsolate old maid with shining, sympathetic eyes.

'He needs his money, and he's come to get it? But Doretta, that would be wonderful!'

'Wonderful?! – '

Herr Philipp Kristeller, his hand trembling with excitement, unbuttoned his vest in spite of the cool night:

'Doretta, if you were right! – Why, that would be splendid, splendid! But – if it were true, I rather think he would have told me first?!'

'And hasn't he done that? And in every way possible – directly and indirectly!'

The apothecary made no reply to that. He strode quickly back and forth in the small space of his picture gallery, rubbing his hands in that way he had, and murmuring to himself:

'The good man – gallant fellow – my God, what a joyous night! – And I completely misunderstood him! Oh, these women, these wise women! Doretta, supposing that you were right!'

'I am right!' groaned the old woman, almost angrily. 'So sit down and listen to reason. What's going to become of us, brother? You've pursued your hobbies and the business these past thirty years; but I've kept the books and know how we stand. Oh, it's enough, but it's only just enough. And Philipp, I'm absolutely convinced he won't just take the principal, he's going to want the interest as well – thirty years' interest!'

'I can't forgive him all that easily for not telling me his wishes right away, clearly and directly', muttered Herr Philipp, who was in no condition to sit down but could only go on walking, back and forth, utterly disregarding his sister's words. 'Oh August, August, at last the hour has come when I am able to help you on your path to happiness!'

Overcome by the magnitude of this prospect, he stopped in his tracks, and something he had not done for as long as he could remember, he did now: he gave his sister a kiss – a long, affectionate kiss – and then he took his lamp and retired to his room. He felt a need to be alone and, in the stillness and dark of the night, to envision the joyful morning that approached and his first words of greeting to his friend, Colonel Dom Agostin Agonista.

Fräulein Doretta stood there in the glow of her night light with arms hanging limply and hands folded, watched him as he went and groaned:

'Well, there we are then! – Oh, these men! What's to become of us? Dear Lord God, what's to become of us? Going to live among the *Pottakuds, those new people of his, is not for me! Of course, with all his flattery and sweet-talking, he'd be capable of carting us over there with house and home, plunking us down in the middle of the wilderness and starting up a schnapps factory on the good name of my brother and his liqueur. But just let him try, that cut-throat, that executioner, that man-skinner, that devil's hangman! Not for all the free passages in the world would I go to his America with him. He'll roast us on a spit once he has us over there, I don't care how cleverly he plays the friendly, contented fellow and loyal, trustworthy soldier over here with us.'

Colonel Dom Agostin Agonista's slumber was not disturbed in the least by what transpired downstairs at The Wild Man. Once again he slept long into the bright morning sunshine of Tuesday. The bottle of *Kristeller* stood on his night table, and the old soldier had also placed the matching cordial glass close at hand. But on the chair by the bed, at half past eight, listening quietly for the last quarter of an hour, sat Herr Philipp Kristeller waiting for his guest, friend and benefactor to awaken.

'As soon as the good fellow wakes up, we'll decide which is the most satisfactory and advantageous way to arrange it for him', the apothecary had whispered as he stole into the chamber on tiptoe. And he had a good hour to wait until the Brazilian opened his eyes, stretched fearsomely, gave an enormous yawn and then, sitting up in surprise, cried out:

'*Diablo!* Is that you, Filippo? Aye, and a fine good morning! Well, this is really very thoughtful of you!'

'Good morning, August. I hope you won't mind my calling you August again just now; for I've been sitting here waiting for you to wake up so that I can give you a piece of my mind.'

'A piece of your mind? How so? Why? What for? Concerning what?'

'Because you have placed greater trust in my good sister than in me, August.'

'Ah, – – – yes!' The Brazilian gendarmerie colonel's response was very drawn out, and he lay back down with his head resting on the pillow. There was a pause, after which he added, somewhat subdued:

'And you agree, don't you? Your decision stands; together we're crossing the ocean to pile up mountains of gold for ourselves and our descendants?!'

Herr Philipp shook his head sadly.

'My sister Dorothea and I – I'm afraid not; but for you it's certainly a different matter. No, my dear August, you shall have to go alone this time, too.'

'Well, that really upsets all my calculations', grumbled the old warrior testily.

'You'll return with our very best wishes; we'll always have you in our thoughts.'

'Thanks!' said the colonel, if anything even more out of humour.

'I've already set up the table in front of your chair, my dear August. My account books lie open for your inspection. You will be pleased with my sister, for she has prepared the balance sheet. I hope you will find that we – my sister and I – have managed our – my – your fortune to the best of our ability.'

'I'll be downstairs in an instant, old boy!' cried the colonel, shaking off all his ill humour in a flash. And smiling brightly, he thrust his right leg out from under the covers and fished around on the floor with one foot for the apothecary's spare luxury bedroom-slippers. 'Just a moment – I'll be down there with you in ten minutes. Philipp, you're a top-notch fellow! And you shall see that I know the world and know how to seize the most advantageous thing for you, too.'

'We have the coffee waiting for you, dear August!'

'My very best compliments in advance to your sister! Be with you in just one moment! And as you said, Philipp, you'll give me your recipe for the *Kristeller* to take along, isn't that right, old chap?'

The inventor of *Kristeller* promised, and a quarter of an hour later Colonel Dom Agostin Agonista was seated comfortably, without all his earlier protestations, in the chair of honour in the brother and sister's back parlour with the household and business account books spread out before him. Fräulein Doretta Kristeller's job was to ask him from time to time if he would like another cup of coffee.

Chapter Fifteen

Just try to hide a man like the colonel under a bushel when he turns up in a locale like the one we have been describing, that is, when he drops from the sky. For miles around, the most fantastic rumours about him were soon spreading. Once again, as thirty years earlier, respect mixed with a little fear accompanied him in every glance sent his way and could be heard in every polite word addressed to him; but no one felt sorry for him any more. The soon so familiar foreigner corresponded in every way to the popular mind's images of a 'mythical beast', and the joviality of his nature and behaviour did nothing to lessen the effects of the personal shyness he inspired in people. He himself felt well indeed among the people of the area, enjoyed the excitement he caused among them and – innocuously ate his way through the village.

That is to say, it had turned out that for the first few weeks there could be no thought of his leaving the area, of traveling on from the apothecary at the sign of The Wild Man. The colonel stayed, and all of them invited him to their tables. After the village dignitaries, the estate owners and wealthy crown-land tenants of the region all took their turns. Colonel Dom Agostin Agonista felt more and more comfortable in his comfortable quarters in the house at the sign of The Wild Man.

But while he was frequently absent from the apothecary shop, old Philipp Kristeller remained all the more sedentary within his four walls, writing a lot, receiving many letters from bankers and other business people, and making all kinds of business deals himself. He began to speculate in real estate – his own, in fact.

And while the colonel lost not the least bit of his considerable girth, Fräulein Doretta Kristeller, who already had little to lose, grew thinner from day to day; and the apothecary, too, lost weight, as much as was still possible. The brother and sister looked more and more sallow. As for Dom Agostin, people were starting to say to him:

'Colonel, the air here seems to agree very well with you, thank goodness.'

The local air did indeed agree with him, and word of what he had done thirty-one years before for the owner of The Wild Man also hovered in the air above him and around his cheerful white head and transfigured him with a rosy glow. Women called him a splendid old gentleman, and the men called him a splendid fellow and added: 'We wouldn't mind finding a lad like that out in the woods and the shrubbery and trying to make his close acquaintance. In a case like that, you could even enjoy going in for botany.'

The colonel also received letters in the course of the following week. A package from Rio de Janeiro arrived containing a large number of documents. This package was sent by Senhor Joaquimo Pamparente, his legal adviser, and Dom Agonista thought it well to discuss its contents in detail with his friend Philipp Kristeller. He, the colonel, wrote Senhora Julia Fuentalacunas an affectionate letter which was, however, also a business letter; unfortunately there would no longer be sufficient time for a reply from the lady.

'No matter', said the affectionate warrior. 'Everything can be settled quite satisfactorily once I'm back over there myself.'

The company Dom Agonista kept most often in these days of serious business matters was that of the jocular local physician, Dr. Hanff. These two carefree cronies had toasted their friendship and were now on informal terms, and Colonel Agonista rode out with him to the doctor's rural practice now and then for enjoyment. No matter what the weather, it did not deter the intrepid old soldier, and the doctor, who could weather a fair storm himself, had to marvel at his companion as something of a miracle in this regard, too.

'By the gods of both hemispheres, you at least will come back there with me', exclaimed the colonel on one of these trips around the end of November, as he looked from the window of a village tavern at the year's first snow falling across the distant fields. 'I've already guaranteed you a hundred times the most brilliant good fortune of a lifetime, and I give you my word on it again today. Just look at that weather. Is this any climate for sensible, respectable people, and on top of that, ones blessed with reason and wife and child? Is this any place to spend seventy years growing old?'

'My wife – my boys', mumbled the doctor.

'Will acclimatize themselves very well there; that's just what I'm telling you: the climate! You leave them behind for a year, giving you the chance to get comfortably situated over there. In the fall of next year I shall take my wife to Paris for our honeymoon and you'll accompany me; that is, you make a detour back here and collect your household. Well – what do you say? Damn, look at the churchyard there in all that rain and blowing snow and tell me if it'll be your joy and hope some day to have a sandstone marker there with the inscription: "Here Lies *Doctor Eisenbart"?!'

'The devil take it, brother', groaned the doctor. 'You know what I wish?'

'Well?'

'I wish you'd stayed where you felt so at home. My sound sleep at night is gone since you've been in this country and the majority of my acquaintances are having the same trouble sleeping. You could say you've spoiled the healthy optimism of the whole place. I don't know anyone in a three-mile radius who can sit quietly on his chair. There's not a one of them who doesn't shift back and forth, calculating and thinking of all the things he's missed so far in life.'

'That may be true for the others, but someone your age hasn't missed a thing yet – you need only look at me. But permit me to say one thing: *I'm* not talking anyone into anything! *Diablo*, why should I with my white hair take it into my head to start all over again, to repeat all the foolishness of my youth, just to assume a fresh burden of remorse? In three weeks I am definitely leaving – definitely, I tell you! By then I will have settled things again with my old fatherland and how it relates to me and be on my way and off to sea, helping to plunder the good ship *Fortuna* of the Spanish silver fleet, for my old friends at the apothecary shop, too. Oh, they shall stay here, cosy beneath their sign of The Wild Man. I will handle their affairs, and the next post you receive from me will tell the rest of the story.'

'He's leaving in three weeks!' sighed the doctor, quickly downing his glass.

Chapter Sixteen

He had, as they say, always been on the point of doing it, the Imperial Brazilian Colonel Dom Agostin Agonista, but this time he really did leave – in fact, at the very hour and day he had announced, at noon on the 23rd of December. Of course everyone had urged him strongly to stay at least over the Christmas holiday, but all their asking and pleading had been in vain.

'Don't torment me any longer', he had told them. 'I know my nature and what's good for it. This lovely celebration in the kindly old fatherland, this charming festival in dreamy, sentimental Germany would put me in too gentle a mood, and it's absolutely necessary for me to remain a bit tough for a little longer. I owe that not only to myself but also to my dear good friends at the apothecary shop. My obligations demand it, no matter what my heart might have to say in protest.'

With that, he vanished, vanished without a trace as everyone stood ready to shake his hand one more time and say goodbye. The departure was as strange as everything else that had marked the man's arrival and sojourn in the village. They all got there too late: Herr Philipp from his laboratory, Fräulein Doretta from the kitchen, Dr. Hanff from his nearest patient's.

The colonel had called for the carriage at the back door, had simply got in and driven off. He had sent his bags on ahead, and the whole neighbourhood – watched him go.

Those from the apothecary shop said nothing, but only sighed. The doctor slapped his forehead and exclaimed, a little angry and disappointed:

'I really would have liked to tell him a bit about my projects! You don't just turn a man's thoughts upside down and make his blood boil for ten times nothing. Damn it all, that Brazil!'

The rest of their friends and acquaintances, bewildered and astonished, gradually came by the shop window.

'Perhaps he wanted to avoid any unnecessary fuss', said Fräulein Doretta Kristeller in a curt monotone. Her brother was not available, even for the pastor and the forestry inspector. The apothecary of The Wild Man felt very affected by the separation from the friend of his youth and wished to remain completely by himself for a few days. Their good acquaintances could certainly understand that and did indeed leave the brother and sister alone over the holiday.

Alone over the holiday!

——— ——— ——— ——— ——— ——— ——— ——— ——— ———

Here we sit once again beneath the pictures in the back parlour of the apothecary at the sign of The Wild Man, and it is evening on the twenty-fourth of December. A dim tallow light in a plain brass candlestick that Fräulein Doretta brought with her into the room burns on the table. The old man was sitting in the dark until his old sister brought this light. In its dim glow he sits in the seat of honour, and the old sister has sat down across from him. They both look exhausted, full of worries; they are both celebrating a troubled Christmas.

After a long silence, Fräulein Doretta said:

'Plagmann from Borgfelde will come right after the holiday to take the cows.'

She said this with a deep sigh, for Bless and Muhtz were the joy of her heart and her pride, and she had to part with both of them.

Her brother merely nodded and said, after another pause:

'I think maybe around the fifteenth of January would be the best time for the auction.'

And his sister nodded, too, and groaned:

'Yes, yes, that's fine with me! It's all fine with me! O God!'

Now the old man, as if to make at least something of the holiday, tried to put on a calm, serene face and said:

'Cheer up, old girl! We mustn't be so despondent. Now you'll be amazed to see how much useless junk we've gradually loaded ourselves down with in our lifetime. Getting rid of the cropland, the bother and worry over meadows and fields, is not so bad when you come right down to it; at least it's not the worst thing. To tell the truth, lately my bones haven't been doing any more what they used to do gladly.'

The encouragement was well intended but of little help. Suddenly, his sister broke into high-pitched, convulsive sobbing:

'O merciful Saviour, it wouldn't really matter, it would be all right with me, but this all comes so very late! Brother, it's too late for this, this misery! If that – man had come twenty years earlier, I would gladly have given up my own bedcovers and the pillow from under your head; but honestly, it's too late in life for us now! The mortgage on the house is like a mountain weighing on me! And besides all that, not one person – not one – that we can tell our troubles to, that we may, yes, *may* tell our troubles to!'

'No', cried Herr Philipp Kristeller, putting all the emphasis he had on the word. 'No, what we have to bear here we bear for ourselves alone! We surely can't have strange noses poking into our present situation, Dorothea! We could not do that to a friend – my friend – my friend from Blood Rock! Oh, just take heart, dear Doretta, and above all, don't put on such a despairing face; you'll see, we'll still keep our heads up and go on leading a good, peaceful life, even under these present circumstances. What would my Johanna say if she had shared my lot with me until this day? Look, people can think and say what they like, for all we care.'

'And I can just see them now, sticking their heads together, the pastor and Ulebeule, the men from the stud farm, the magistrate and the doctor. They'll concoct some lovely, fantastic stories and paint a picture of us in vivid colours!'

'Let them! Just so everything goes well for my marvellous friend and his new-found happiness! I tell you, dear sister, it would be a consolation for me simply knowing that no one means as well with us as he does, however miserable I might be feeling. Right now he believes he's on his way full sail to find his happiness and ours. And look, old girl, his money has at least helped someone out a bit for the second time, which you certainly can't say about all money, even if it were twelve thousand thalers as in our case.'

His sister made no reply but only shrugged her shoulders, which then again caused her pangs of conscience. She got up, went to the window and looked out into the dark, wintry and also heavily mortgaged garden for a good three minutes before turning back to the room:

'It's snowing hard, brother. Do you remember, Philipp, what enjoyment and what mysterious contentment we used to feel when it snowed on this very day?'

'I do indeed', said her brother. 'How else could we have gotten along so well with each other all this lifetime? Doretta, today we were really fools not to have decorated a fir tree with candles for the first time in our lives. In spite of everything, we should have done that! Well – next time! Next year – '

'When your friend from Blood Rock has sent the ship with chests of gold and jewels, in repayment – at least for the recipe for *Kristeller*! And to have kept his armchair there waiting for thirty years – for that!'

That was a typical woman's reaction, so nothing to be done about it. Herr Philipp kept his own manly, unperturbed disposition, and would not have his thought cut off in mid-sentence, which he then completed:

' – we'll make up all the more sincerely and heartily for what we've missed this time.' But in response to the woman's interruption, he added, under his breath: 'However it turns out.'

As for their friends in the surrounding area, they were indeed very surprised when, through the winter and spring, many changes took place at the apothecary's shop at the sign of The Wild Man – when the furnishings disappeared from rooms, the livestock vanished from the stables, when the flower garden was transformed into a vegetable plot, the young servant girl went looking for employment in some other good house, the stable boy was let go, and there was a notice in the local paper that the apothecary Herr Philipp Kristeller had sold so-and-so-many acres of meadow and crop land to one and another of the farmers from the village and the district. But when the auction in the house itself was held, they were all present and bidding. And at this auction, the forester came away with the apothecary's picture gallery, the doctor took the Chinese punchbowl and the pastor bought the armchair of the colonel in Brazilian military service, Dom Agostin Agonista.

A more barren house was not to be found in the town after that. Only the contents of tins and jars in the shop were spared. But friends and acquaintances pondered and conjectured all kinds of things, and finally all came to the not entirely improbable supposition that their friend, Herr Philipp Kristeller, had secretly speculated in bad securities and lost his investments.

Naturally, they strongly advised him to turn without delay to his friend, the Brazilian colonel, and did not understand what reason he could have for refusing so stubbornly.

*

Explanatory Notes

German Moonlight

p. 3 The Brunswick Succession] Without an heir to the Duchy of Brunswick (Raabe's homeland), the House of Hanover had legitimate claim to the throne but could exercise it only if it surrendered its claim to Hanoverian territories annexed by Prussia in 1866. The dispute was not finally resolved until 1913.

p. 4 The Red Cliff] A tall bluff, about one hundred feet high and one of the North Sea island Sylt's distinguishing landmarks.

p. 4 washerwoman of both genders] The German 'Waschweib', though grammatically feminine, can serve as a gender-neutral metaphor for 'gossip'.

p. 5 Luna, Selene] In Greek and Roman mythology respectively the personification of the moon as a goddess. Both are daughters of Hyperion, in Greek legend one of the titans, father also of Helios/Sol and Eos/Aurora.

p. 5 bathing machine] A small wooden cabin on wheels rolled down to the water's edge, often by a horse team; used almost exclusively for upper-class women to ensure bathing privacy and safety in the spirit of Victorian-era etiquette.

p. 10 waters, sour or bitter] Mineral waters were widely prescribed at spas for the treatment of digestive and circulatory ailments.

p. 10 Heinrich Clauren] Pseudonym of Karl Heun (1771–1854), the author of many popular stories and novels of mostly romantic or lewd subject matter.

p. 10 You are mistaken] It is suggested here that the narrator supposes that Löhnefinke was swept out of his prosaic family environment by the revolutionary fervour of 1848, just as he would have assumed earlier that the sins of his youth were wine and women.

p. 10 old-liberal] Member of the branch of the German liberal movement that pursued a moderate and constitutional course after the revolution of 1848/49. After 1858, 58% of the deputies in the Prussian parliament belonged to the old- liberal faction. After 1866 largely absorbed into the National Liberal Party.

p. 10 Chinese pagoda] Here: a small, sitting porcelain figure with a moving head.

p. 11 court intern] German 'Auskultator' or, more commonly, 'Referendar': entry-grade of higher civil servants; phase of professional training after graduating from university.

p. 12 Schiller and Goethe, Voltaire and Rousseau, Börne and Stahl, Ranke and Raumer] The pairings here are interesting: Friedrich Schiller (1759–1805) represents the more idealistic, Johann Wolfgang von Goethe (1749–1831) the more restrained side of German classicism; Voltaire and Rousseau are representative of similar directions in French Enlightenment; Ludwig Börne (1786–1837), German democratic writer, was closely associated with the radical Young German movement, while Friedrich Julius Stahl (1802–1861) espoused a more religious-conservative trend of social theory and served reactionary political forces in a variety of capacities; Leopold von Ranke (1795–1886), the main protagonist of the school of Historicism and towering historian of the nineteenth century, represented moderate conservative political attitudes, while Friedrich von Raumer (1781–1873), politician turned historian, represents a more idealistic tendency in historiography (both taught at the University of Berlin during Raabe's time there).

p. 12 Kommersch] The name of a festival held by university students, which takes place at the beginning and end of each semester to honour the graduating students and welcome new arrivals.

p. 14 Battle of Königgrätz] 3 July 1866 in Bohemia, the most decisive battle of the Austro- Prussian War, which paved the way for German unification in the aftermath of the Franco-Prussian war of 1870/71, was called by Prince Friedrich Karl of Prussia a 'victory of intelligence over stupidity'.

p. 15 ottava rima] Rhyming stanza of Italian origin consisting of eight iambic lines, usually following the rhyming pattern a-b-a-b-a-b-c-c.

p. 17 beneficium inventarium] A right, specified by law, by which beneficiaries receive protection from potential claims of creditors on inventoried inheritance.

p. 17 Jean Paul Friedrich Richter] German Romantic writer (1763–1825), composed humorous and imaginative novels and short stories. His works are characterized not only by a meandering and frequently digressing form, but also by scepticism and irreverence.

Höxter and Corvey

Raabe's main source for his narrative, for the conflicts between the confessions inside the town of Höxter and between town and abbey, for the names he uses, even for the wordings of complaints, accusations and decrees, was Heinrich Kampschulte, *Chronik der Stadt Höxter* (Höxter 1872).

The English prose translations of Horace's works are taken from Horace, *Odes and Epodes*, ed. and transl. by Niall Rudd (Cambridge, MA: Harvard University Press, 2004) and Horace, *Satires, Epistles and*

Ars Poetica, transl. by H. Rushton Fairclough (London: Heinemann and Cambridge, MA: Harvard University Press, 1926). Page references in the notes refer to these editions.

p. 21 Höxter] Town on the bank of the Weser river at the crossroads of the old east- western (salt) trading route ('Hellweg') and the north-southern route downriver towards the North Sea port of Bremen. Formally under the rule of the Benedictine abbey of Corvey, in the Middle Ages de facto able to govern itself with some degree of independence; but coming under ever more direct rule during the period described in the story.

p. 21 St. Peter, St. Kilian, St. Nicholas, Brothers] Churches in Höxter; the latter, originally built by the Minorite Brothers, became a Protestant parish church after the Reformation, in 1674 re-catholicised.

p. 21 Corvey] Benedictine abbey on the Weser north of Höxter. The territory ruled by the Abbey became an imperial fiefdom in the thirteenth century. After the devastation during and after the Thirty Years War, the chapter elected not one of their own ranks, but the prince-bishop of Münster, Christoph Bernhard von Galen, as prince-abbot (under the title of 'administrator').

p. 21 Solling] The Solling is a wooded ridge on the eastern side of the River Weser, opposite Höxter and Corvey. Raabe knew many of the places on or near this part of the Weser, such as the ones named in the text (Fürstenberg, Godelheim, Meigadessen) from his youth and several vacations and family visits (his brother-in-law lived nearby) in later years.

p. 22 Drusus, Tiberius, Chlotar, Charlemagne] According to Heinrich Kamp-schulte, *Chronik der Stadt Höxter* (Höxter 1872), the Roman generals Drusus and Tiberius on their campaign against Germanic tribes crossed the Weser at this point in 9 BC and 4 AD respectively, and so did the Franconian kings Chlotar in the 550s and Charlemagne in the 770s.

p. 22 Fougerais] According to Kampschulte, *Chronik der Stadt Höxter*, commander of the French forces in Höxter. Nothing else is known about him.

p. 22 Turenne] Henri de La Tour d'Auvergne, Vicomte de Turenne (1611–1675), French general, fought many battles during the Thirty Years War and during Louis XIV's campaigns thereafter; made a marshal of France in 1643. According to Kampschulte, *Chronik der Stadt Höxter*, he had his headquarters in Höxter for a few weeks during November 1673.

p. 22 Christoph Bernhard von Galen] (1606–1678), prince-bishop of Münster since 1650, 'administrator' (prince-abbot) of Corvey since 1661. In an absolutist spirit, he strengthened his rule against the regional estates (including municipalities like Höxter), pursued alliances with foreign powers (such as Louis XIV of France against Prussia and its allies) and aimed at a recatholicisation of his territories.

p. 22 the French card against the Emperor and the Republic of Holland] Galen's alliance with France was also an attempt to gain more independence from the Holy Roman Empire; later he changed coalition and sided with Emperor Leopold I against the French.

p. 22 Wars of Reunion / Seizure of Strasbourg] Campaign by Louis XIV of France to bring the Alsace region under French control ('reunite' it with France) which culminated in the seizure of Strasbourg in 1681.

p. 22 Wars of the Spanish Succession] 1701–1714. Series of wars between France and a Grand Alliance of England and Austria over the succession to the Spanish throne after the death of the last Spanish Habsburg, Charles II, in 1700.

p. 22 Huxar] Together with Höxar, spelling of the name of the city found in sources before the eighteenth century. Only then superseded by the form now common, namely Höxter.

p. 22 Herr von Herstelle, Herr von Zitzewitz] Herstelle is the name of a village, castle and Benedictine nunnery south of Höxter; the character named after this place, however, is fictitious. Nicolas von Zitzewitz is a historical figure; he had been a candidate for abbot in 1661 when Galen was elected; he was made prior instead and in this capacity acted as official governor of Höxter.

p. 22 Wickensen] Seat of a Ducal Braunschweigian district administration; close to Raabe's birth place Eschershausen north-west of the Solling mountains.

p. 23 Duke Rudolf August von Braunschweig] (1627–1704), reigning duke of Braunschweig-Wolfenbüttel since 1666.

p. 23 Inasmuch ...] Reference to the victory in 1671 of the ducal house over the city and corporation of Braunschweig. Here the dukes pursued the same policies of curbing municipal autonomy as Christoph Bernhard von Galen attempted vis-à-vis Höxter.

p. 24 Herr von Bruch] Raabe used many of the names signed under the *Gnaden-und Segen-Receß* of 1674, a kind of capitulation with which prince-abbot Galen imposed his rule over Höxter. Adelhard von Bruch was sub-dean and, as cellarer, in charge of the abbey's economic interests and tithes (cf. Kampschulte, p. 152).

p. 24 Lüchtringen] Village on the right bank of the Weser, opposite Corvey, in direct tribute to the abbey.

p. 25 Master of the Ordinance Wrangel] Count Carl Gustav Wrangel (1613–1676), commander of the Swedish forces during the Thirty Years War; achieved many of his military successes through close coordination with Turenne. In 1646 he besieged the Austrian garrison of Höxter.

p. 25 Kasper Pflugk] Bohemian nobleman (d. 1576), military leader of the Protestant Bohemian estates during the Schmalkaldic War (1546–47); not known to have visited Höxter during his campaigns.

p. 25 League] Federation of Catholic princes and estates against the Protestant Union; forces of the League occupied Höxter numerous times during the Thirty Years War, alternating with their Protestant counterparts.

p. 25 Christian von Braunschweig] (1599–1626), duke of Braunschweig and 'administrator' of the bishopric of Halberstadt, led bands of mercenaries against the Catholic League; his armies crossed over the Weser at Höxter in 1622; nicknamed 'der Tolle' (the mad or crazy one) for his wild and daring military campaigns.

p. 25 Gronau] City on the River Leine, about 100 kilometres north of Höxter.

p. 26 tempora et mores] Lat., times and customs.

p. 27 Quintus Horatius Flaccus] Latin poet and satirist (65 BC-8 BC). Raabe owned and always cherished Horace's works for their unsentimental view of the chaos and temporality of human existence and the attempt to defend intellectual freedom and a contemplative enjoyment of life.

p. 27 Now reigns in my heart ...] Horace, Odes III, 9, lines 9–12: 'Thracian Chloe now rules me; she can sing sweet songs and play the lyre delightfully. I shan't be afraid to die for her, if the fates spare my darling and let her live.' (p. 171)

p. 27 Julia Carolina at Helmstedt] University founded in 1576 by Julius duke of Braunschweig, one of the chief seats of Protestant learning in Germany; the name Julia Carolina, though, only came into use after its enlargement by duke Karl I in 1745. The university was closed by Jérôme, king of Westphalia, in 1810 and incorporated into the University of Göttingen.

p. 28 O nata mecum consule Manlio] Horace, Odes III, 21, 1: 'O born with me in Manlius' consulship' (p. 193).

p. 28 Corvinus adjures us] Horace, Odes III, 21, 7–12: 'so come down, for Corvinus urges me to bring down an especially mellow wine. Although he is steeped in the Socratic dialogues he will not neglect you like an uncouth ascetic; they say that even Cato, with all his moral rigour, often thawed out with unmixed wine.' (p. 193) Marcus Valerius Corvinus (64 BC – 8 AD) was a Roman general and patron of the arts. For his first novel, Raabe used Corvinus (Lat. raven, Germ. Rabe) as a pseudonym.

p. 29 ultimo scabies] Horace, Ars Poetica V, 417: 'the devil take the hindmost!' (p. 485). Literally: the last shall contract scabies.

p. 29 avunculus divinus ac singularis] Lat., divine and singular uncle.

p. 29 Serenely take whate'er you may] Horace, Odes III, 29, 33–45: 'Everything else flows away like a river that now glides peacefully in the middle of its channel down to the Etruscan Sea, now rolls along eroded boulders, uprooted trees, livestock and houses all mixed together amid the roar of the mountains and neighbouring woods, when a wild flood enrages its quiet streams. That man will be master of himself and live a happy life who as each day ends can say "I have lived." Tomorrow let our Father cover the sky in dark cloud or bright sunshine, he will not cancel whatever is past' (p. 215).

p. 30/31 ab ostio ad Ostiam] Pun on Lat. ostium (front door) and Ostia (port near Rome) – from house to port.

p. 31 Aelius Lamia] Friend of Horace, the following poem was dedicated to him.

p. 31 Musis amicus, tristiam et metus / Tradam protervis in mare Creticum] Horace Odes I, 26, 1–5: 'As friend of the Muses, I shall fling gloom and fear to the turbulent winds to carry them into the Cretan sea; I am singularly indifferent about what the king of the frozen region under the Bear is causing alarm, what it is that's frightening Tiridates.' (p. 73)

p. 32 Evoë, Evoë] Jubilant call at Bacchanalia.

p. 32 Bacchus and Venus] Bacchus: Roman name for Dionysos, the Greek god of wine and intoxication; Venus: Roman name for Aphrodite, the Greek goddess of love.

p. 32 1618] First year of the Thirty Years War; Höxter was occupied by Protestant troops from Hesse and Brunswick.

p. 32 To whom should our people groan] Horace, Odes I, 2, 25–32: 'What divinity are the people to call upon to restore the fortunes of their crumbling power? With what prayers are the holy Virgins to weary Vesta who at present pays no heed to their chants? To whom will Jupiter assign the task of expiating our crime? Come now, we beg you, Augur Apollo, with your bright shoulders clothed in cloud' (p. 27).

p. 33 alma mater] Lat., kind mother; reference to the nurturing received by one's university.

p. 33 Maecenas, Glycene, Varus] Horace dedicated odes to Caius Maecenas, confidant of Emperor Augustus and patron of artists like Horace, Vergil and Propertius, to a fictitious beloved called Glycene and to his friend Quinctilius Varus.

p. 34 Phoebus] Epithet of Greek god Apollo, equating him to Helios, the sun.

p. 34 Amstelodami, ex officina Henrici et Theodori Boom] Lat., Printed in Amsterdam by the publishers Henry and Theodor Boom, in the late seventeenth century well-known for both scholarly and erotic works.

p. 34 Romeyn de Hooghe] Dutch painter and sculptor (1645–1708); illustrator of a manual of the art of wrestling (Amsterdam 1674).

p. 34 Palsambleu! Mille millions tonnerres] French curses; English equivalents would be 'zounds', 'a thousand thunders'.

p. 34 fleshpots of the alma mater Julia] Allusion to the fleshpots of Egypt (cf. Exodus, 16, 3).

p. 34 Bœotian] Here: philistine, barbarian. In ancient Greece, Bœotians (inhabitants of a region in central Greece) were ridiculed for their alleged lack of education.

p. 34 Tilly and Marshal von Gleen] Generals of the Catholic League during the Thirty Years War. Johann Tserclaes Count Tilly (1559–1632) 'visited' Höxter several times between 1623 and 1630; Gottfried Count Gleen conquered Höxter in 1634 from Swedish, Braunschweigian and Hessian forces that had occupied the city the year before. On this occasion he committed the infamous Bloodbath of Höxter.

p. 35 United Dutch Estates] Term for the assembly of the provincial estates of the Dutch Republic, adopted to designate the portion of the Spanish Netherlands that had declared their independence in the union of Utrecht in 1580.

p. 35 Per vulnera Christi] Lat., by the wounds of Christ. Phrase contained in a letter by Duke Rudolf August to Christoph Bernhard von Galen to indicate how dearly the Protestant citizens of Höxter begged him for support against the alleged oppressor of their religious liberties.

p. 36 levy on the Jews] The so-called 'Judengeleit' was a temporary head-tax on Jewish residents in a certain jurisdiction; the right to impose such a levy traditionally rested with the ruler, in Höxter's case the abbey of Corvey. After the town council had exercised this taxation right in the early seventeenth century, Christoph Bernhard von Galen claimed the lucrative privilege for himself as administrator of Corvey, sparking a series of conflicts with the citizenry. Often payable on entry to a town or district like an excise duty on goods, the German word 'Geleit' denotes free passage.

p. 36 judex, pars et advocatus] Lat., judge, party and advocate in one person.

p. 40 the Duchess of Hessen, Field-Marshal Holzappel] Count Peter Melander von Holzappel (1589–1648) was a mercenary in the service of the Protestant Landgraves of Hesse-Kassel; he later changed sides and in 1642 became imperial field marshal. After the death of her husband Landgrave William V in 1637, Amalie Elisabeth von Hessen-Kassel (1602–1651) served as regent of the principality on behalf of her son William VI.

p. 40 Basolamano] Corrupted Ital., baciare la mano – hand kiss.

p. 41 Signor Strillone] Ital., Mister Bawler.

p. 41 Scabies capiat] Lat., may he contract the scab.

p. 41 Merxhausen] Village on the eastern slopes of the Solling Mountains on the right bank of the Weser.

p. 42 I hated you since time began] Horace, Epodes 4, 1–4: 'Great is the enmity assigned by Nature to wolves and lambs; no less is that between me and you – you with your flanks scarred by Spanish ropes and your legs by iron fetters.' (p. 279) What follows is the Latin original.

p. 42 Apage] Gr., Be gone! Temptation of Christ; see Matthew 4, 10: 'Then Jesus said to him: "Be gone, Satan! For it is written: 'You shall worship the Lord your God and him only shall you serve.'"'

p. 43 en avant] Fr., let's go.

p. 44 What din assaults this quiet hearth?] Horace, Epodes 5, 3: 'what does this uproar mean' (p. 281).

p. 48 King Odixus, Queen Penelope, ambitores, proci, suitors] Reference to the end of the first book and beginning of second book of Homer's *Odyssey* when Penelope, wife of the missing king Odysseus (Odixus), manages to fend off the suitors (or candidates for marriage, ambitores) but has to stand by while they plunder her larder.

p. 48 nunc lugubris et tristis memoria] Lat., now, the woeful and sorrowful memory.

p. 48 galli et Galli] Pun on the homonymity of Lat. gallus – cock and Lat. Gallus – Gaul (i.e. French).

p. 48 Diabolus accipiat animam ejus] Lat., May the devil take his soul.

p. 49 Ith] Ridge between the rivers Weser and Leine north of Höxter.

p. 49 trouble in Holland] Germ. 'Holland in Not', Dutch 'Holland in last', proverbial comments on the distress experienced in 1672 when the United Netherlands came under attack by French armies and their British and German auxiliaries. The phrase particularly refers to the measure of last resort to break the dykes and flood the low-lying polders.

p. 50 prior, subprior, provost] Ecclesiastical titles, prior and provost are different names for the same position, namely the rank immediately below the abbot. Here, in the absence of the abbot-administrator, all the governors of the abbey are listed.

p. 50 Annals of Tacitus] Roman historian (56–ca. 120). The only extant manuscript of the first five books of the *Annals* was produced in the ninth century in Corvey and re-discovered there at the beginning of the sixteenth century. Pope Leo X ordered the codex to be brought to Florence where it survived the devastations of the Thirty Years War.

p. 51 Vae turbatori] Lat., woe to the troublemaker.

p. 51 Dassel Chronicle, Master Hans Letzner] Johannes Letzner (1531–1613) inserted invented stories into his chronicles of Corvey (1590) and the cities of Dassel and Einbeck (1596), hence his epithet.

p. 52 Paratus sum!] Lat., I am ready.

p. 52 Quo, quo scelesti ruitis] Opening of Horace, Epode 7, 1: 'Where, where are you rushing to in this evil madness?' (p. 289) Reference to the conditions in Rome after the internal turbulences following the murder of Julius Caesar had left the republic vulnerable.

p. 52 Clement the Tenth] Emilio Altieri (1590–1676), pope from 1670–1676. Continued the policies of his predecessor Clement IX (see note on p. 58 below) towards France.

p. 52 Coraggio, chère tante] Ital. / Fr., Courage, dear aunt.

p. 52 Säuberlich] The name plays on the meaning of the German adjective 'sauber', clean.

p. 53 Pope Joan] Legendary female pontiff, originating from Mainz, who supposedly reigned from 855 to 856 under the name of John VIII. According to later legends, her sex was revealed when she gave birth during a procession and died in childbirth, or was stoned to death.

p. 53 Retro retrorsum, Domine Pastor] Lat., Retreat, go back, lord shepherd.

p. 53 Contra aegida Palladis ruere] Horace, Odes III, 4, 57: 'charging against the ringing breastplate of Pallas' (p. 157) Pallas Athena here evoked as the goddess of wisdom.

p. 53 infestatio cum bombardis] Lat., attack with cannon.

p. 54 master of the commoners] Germ. 'Der Gemeinheit Meister', elected head of the citizenry that was not organised in guilds (mainly manual labourers).

p. 54 Whosoever gives offence to his brother shall be liable to the council] Cf. Matthew 5, 22: 'Whosoever shall say to his brother, Raca, shall be in danger of the council.'

p. 54 Literaturbriefe] Abbreviated title of the literary weekly Briefe, die neueste Litteratur betreffend [Letters Concerning the Most Recent Literature] (1759–65), edited at first by Gotthold Ephraim Lessing (1729–81). In the second 'letter', Lessing criticized the work of Johann Jakob Dusch (1725– 87) with mocking 'politeness' (Fr. courtoisie).

p. 55 Who fears the Scythians, the Parthian's raid] Horace, Odes IV, 5, 25–27: 'Who would fear the Parthian, who the frozen Scythian, who the rough brood Germany breeds, as long as Caesar is safe? (p. 235)

p. 56 Thus crashed the fir tree with thundering sound] Horace, Odes IV, 6, 9–12: 'Like a pine tree struck with the biting steel or a cypress blown over by the East Wind, he fell on his face, covering much ground, and laid his neck in the dust of Troy.' (p. 237)

p. 56 Bosseborn Lantern] Bosseborn is a village near Höxter belonging to the abbey of Corvey; the motif of leading the way in the dark of night by using a white shirt sticking out of trousers was common in the region of Lower Saxony; also attributed to other places.

p. 57 Socrates at the symposium of Plato] In Platon's *Symposion*, Socrates's ability to hold his drink, and to remain lucid, is praised by Alcibiades.

p. 57 When comes in summer Sanctus Veit] Popular song warning against pickpockets and brawlers at Vitus Fairs (Kampschulte, pp. 147–48)

p. 57 St. Vitus's day] 15 June. Vitus's relics were donated to Corvey in the ninth century, hence revered in this Westphalian region.

p. 58 Pope Clement the Ninth] Giulio Rospigliosi (1600–1669), pope from 1667–1669. Clashed with Louis XIV of France over revenue and Christian nations' help for the island of Crete against Turkish aggression. In Kampschulte, *Chronik der Stadt Höxter*, p. 145, Raabe found the information that Pope Clement IX had granted the abbey the right to issue indulgences on St. Vitus's day and benefit from the revenue thus raised.

p. 58 hinc illae lacrimae] Lat., hence those tears.

p. 58 chapter] Corporation of canons in a church or monastery.

p. 58 Many a one starts clever and smart ...] Second excerpt from the Vitus Fair song.

p. 59 Hussites] Disciples of Czech religious reformer Jan Hus (1372/73–1415). Hussite armies went deep into Thuringia and Saxony during the Hussite Wars (1419–34), but are not known to have raided Höxter. The reference here might relate to the incursion into Westphalia in 1447 of an army largely consisting of Hussite mercenaries aiding archbishop Dietrich of Cologne in his conflict with duke John I of Cleve over the possession of the town of Soest (the so-called Soester Fehde, 1444–49).

p. 59 carrying his head under his arm] Normally Vitus is depicted in a cauldron as reference to the torture in burning oil he had to endure. Raabe's change of the iconography is not accidental; St. Vitus died through beheading, and this 'losing one's head' provides a commentary on the events and the mood.

p. 60 Abbatia urbi imperat] Lat., the abbey rules the city.

p. 60 pronounce anathema] Gr., to curse or ban.

p. 62 tertium comparationis] Lat., the third (part) of a comparison, common ground between two extremes.

p. 64 Hierosolyma [est] perdita] Lat., Jerusalem is lost; anti-Semitic slogan, the anagram of which ('Hep! Hep!') provided the battle cry in pogroms as late as the early nineteenth century.

p. 67 salve-guardia] Guard of Honour.

p. 67 suaviter] Lat., sweetly, amiably.

p. 68 the year twenty-two] 1622 Christian of Braunschweig crossed the Weser near Höxter. The (fictitious) story of Just von Burlebecke is based on Kampschulte, *Chronik der Stadt Höxter*, p. 124, who relates that an unnamed captain from Christian's army entered the city, but was captured and later released. The municipal Jewry was ordered to supply the provisions for his return to his corps.

p. 68 Stadtloo] Town in western Westphalia where Tilly defeated Duke Christian von Braunschweig on 6 August 1623. The narrative suggests that Heinrich von Herstelle took part in that battle on the side of the Leaguists and afterwards found Just amongst the fallen enemy soldiers.

p. 68 Samson, the Philistines upon you] In Book of Judges 16, 9 Delilah's warning call. In Germany, the term 'Philister' was used to decry bourgeois narrow- mindedness and bigotry.

p. 69 Administrator] Title of non-hereditary rulers of religious territories in Germany after the Reformation (normally elected by the chapter). Christian von Braunschweig served as administrator of the diocese of Halberstadt 1616–1623.

p. 69 Bloodbath of Höxter] The bloodiest of the many attacks on Höxter during the Thirty Years War. On the Thursday after Easter 1634 the troops of Leaguist general Gottfried von Gleen entered the city after a long siege, destroyed most of it including the Weser bridge and killed many inhabitants irrespective of their creed; the relics of St. Vitus were also desecrated and the prince-abbot of Corvey was almost slain.

p. 69 Merode, Piccolomini, Savelli] Leaguist generals, only Octavio Piccolomini, Duke of Amalfi (1599–1656) is known to have conquered and occupied Höxter in 1640/41.

p. 70 Now Roman youth, unsheathe your sword] Cf. Horace, Odes III, 6, 33–36: 'Not from parents like these came the young men who stained the sea with Punic blood, and cut down Pyrrhus and the mighty Antiochus and Hannibal the terrible. No, they were the manly children of peasant soldiers' (p. 165).

p. 71 Callot] Jacques Callot (1592–1632), French copper engraver, created series of engravings on the brutality of war.

p. 71 Ecce iterum Crispinus] Lat., behold again Crispinus; invective used by Horace to ridicule a contemporary Roman poet whom Horace loathed, adapted by Lessing in his polemics against Dusch (see above, note on p. 54, *Literaturbriefe*). Raabe could have intended a dual reference to St. Crispin, a Christian martyr, in his capacity as champion of the downtrodden.

p. 72 sesquipedalia] Lat., a foot and a half; allusions to Horace's *Ars poetica* V, 97, where he dismisses words with one and a half metres (or beats).

p. 72 Centurio] Lat., officer in charge of a hundred soldiers; here: captain.

p. 73 Neaera] In Horace's *Odes* III, 14, 21 name of a singer with flowing hair.

p. 73 Mynsinger von Frondeck] Joachim Mynsinger von Frondeck (1517–1588) was chancellor of the duchy of Braunschweig and for a time vice-chancellor of the university of Helmstedt.

p. 73 The Bloodbath of Salzkotten] Reference to the Bloodbath of Höxter in 1634 that was preceded by a bloody defeat of the Leaguist troops at Salzkotten.

p. 74 Emperor Ludwig] Louis the Pious (778–840), son and heir of Charlemagne, emperor since 813. Under his reign the Benedictine abbey of Corvey, at that time standing at the border to a Slavonic East, received the relics of St. Vitus which were damaged during the events of 1634.

p. 74 Winter King, the beautiful Elisabeth] The Elector Palatine Frederick V (1596– 1632) was elected King of Bohemia by the Protestant estates in November 1619, but defeated and forced to abdicate only a few months later (hence his nickname). This provocation of the Catholic emperor triggered the Thirty Years War. His wife was Elizabeth Stuart (1596–1662), daughter of James I of England; she was famed for her beauty.

p. 74 Mercury and Rhadamanthus] According to Greek mythology, the god with the winged sandals was assigned to escort the nymph Larunda to the underworld where Rhadamanthus served as a judge of the dead.

p. 74 Titus] (39–81), son of the Roman emperor Vespasian, commander of the Roman army that, in 70, defeated the Jewish uprising and conquered Jerusalem. The destruction of the Herodean Temple marks the beginning of the dispersal of the Jews and hence the period of exile. Ruled as emperor 79–81.

p. 75 in compania] Lat., together.

p. 75 Herr von Pappenheim] Gottfried Heinrich Count Pappenheim (1594–1632), in Höxter 1629/30 and 1633.

p. 76 General Baudissin] Wolf Dietrich Count Baudissin (1597–1646), commander of the Swedish troups, in Höxter 1632.

p. 78 King Nebuchadnezzar] King of the Neo-Babylonian Empire (ca. 634–562 BC).

p. 78 Nunc est bibendum, nunc pede libero / Pulsanda tellus] Horace, Odes I, 37, 1–2: 'Now let the drinking begin! Now let us thump the ground with unfettered feet.' (p. 93)

p. 78 Battle of Actium, Queen Cleopatra of Egypt] In the naval battle in 31 BC the forces of Octavian defeated the combined navies of Mark Antony and Cleopatra, thus enabling Octavian to declare himself Princeps and later Augustus. The battle thus marks the end of the Roman Republic.

p. 79 neque tectum neque lectum] Lat., neither roof nor bed.

p. 80 factum, actum et gestum] Lat., legal formula meaning 'done, deliberated and passed'; used with reference to precedents creating legal fact.

p. 81 the year twenty-four, the peace settlement] 1624 was enshrined in the Peace of Westphalia as the so-called 'Normaljahr'. The settlement ending the Thirty Years War in 1648 thus declared that conditions should be restored as they had pertained in that year.

p. 82 cranium] Lat., skull.

p. 82 Et tu Brute] Shakespeare, *Julius Caesar*, III, 1 expressing Caesar's disappointment on finding the once-trusted Brutus amongst his murderers.

p. 82 consilium abeundi, relegatio in perpetuum] Lat., legal terms for the temporary and permanent relegation from a school or university.

p. 82 Vivat Hierosolyma] Jerusalem shall live; response to the anti-Semitic battle-cry 'Hierosolyma est perdita'.

p. 83 Maccabees] Dynasty of high priests that resisted Syrian rule over the Israelites, asserting Jewish independence throughout the second and first centuries BC.

p. 86 Colmar] The Alsatian city had been occupied by French troops from 1635 to 1649; in 1673 Louis XIV conquered it again and incorporated it into the French kingdom where it remained until 1871.

p. 87 Nonsense a long time I practised and wandered astray] Horace, Odes I, 34, 1–5: 'I was a stingy and infrequent worshipper of the gods all the time that I went astray, expert that I was in mad philosophy. Now I am forced to sail back and repeat my course in the reverse direction.' (p. 85)

p. 87 two years after the crowning of the first King in Prussia] In 1701, Prince-Elector Frederick III of Brandenburg crowned himself King *in* Prussia (after the large parts of his dominion lying outside the Holy Roman Empire) to distinguish his title from royal titles in use within the Empire (King *of* Bohemia, King *of* the Romans – a title used by the incumbent emperors' heirs).

p. 87 Professor of Aesthetics, Alexander Gottlieb Baumgarten] (1714–1762) Enlightenment philosopher who established Aesthetics as an independent academic discipline, held an extraordinary professorship at Halle before being appointed to a chair at the university of Frankfurt an der Oder. In his major work *Aesthetica* (2 vols, 1750 and 1758) Baumgarten drew heavily on Horace as an example of the beauty of vivid description.

At the Sign of The Wild Man

p. 91 from the German to the North German Confederation and from there into the new Empire] The German Confederation was established at the Congress of Vienna in 1815 instead of the Holy Roman Empire that had been abolished by Napoleon in the Final Recess of the *Reichsdeputation* in 1803. The formation of the North German Confederation in 1866 after Austria's defeat in the Austro-Prussian War (The Seven Weeks' War) replaced the German Confederation and provided the nucleus for the German Empire established in January 1871.

p. 93 pharmacopoeial] Relating to drugs, esp. the description and classification of pharmaceutical agents.

p. 93 herba nicoteana] Herbs of the nightshade family including tobacco.

p. 94 Ramberg and Chodowiecki] Johann Heinrich Ramberg (1763–1840), German painter, illustrator and caricaturist, after 1793 court painter in Hanover, in the early nineteenth century one of the most sought-after illustrators of popular books; Daniel Nikolaus Chodowiecki (1726–1801), the most important German copperplate engraver of the eighteenth century, also famous for his drawings and book illustrations.

p. 94 Frederick II and Napoleon I] Frederick II (Frederick the Great, 1712–1786), King of Prussia since 1740; Napoleon Bonaparte (1769–1821), Emperor of the French 1804–1815.

p. 94 Alliance / battlefield at Leipzig] The armies of King Frederick William III of Prussia, Tsar Alexander I of Russia and Emperor Francis I of Austria defeated Napoleon near Leipzig in October 1813.

p. 94 The Corsair: A Poem by Lord Byron] Popular verse narrative (1814) by the English Romantic poet (1788–1824).

p. 94 Washington] George W. (1732–1799), commander-in-chief of the colonial armies during the American Revolution (1775–1783), subsequently first president of the United States (1789–1797).

p. 94 Queen Mathilde of Denmark and Count Struensee] The German physician Johann Friedrich Struensee (1737–1772) became a confidant of the mentally unstable Danish King Christian VII, court physician, privy Cabinet minister and count. In 1771 and early 1772 he introduced a number of progressive reforms, but was tortured to death after his arrest for his liaison with the queen.

p. 94 a genuine old Dürer copper engraving: *Melancholia*] One of Albrecht Dürer's (1471–1528) most famous engravings, probably dating from 1514–15. The pensive allegorical figure contemplates the futility, unpredicatability and contingency of human endeavour. The figure is surrounded by astrological and mathematical instruments, tools, scales, magic signs, hieroglyphs and other objects symbolizing various fields of human achievement and ways of making sense of the world and finding meaning in it. The heavenly bodies are reminders, however, of forces determining human life that are beyond human understanding. While conveying a Christian sentiment, the picture is infused with the symbols and icons of Renaissance Humanism.

p. 96   groschen] currency unit.

p. 96   Kyffhäuser, Kickelhahn] Kyffhäuser: Mountain range straddling Sachsen-Anhalt and Thuringia. According to legend, Emperor Frederick I (Barbarossa, 1122–1190, ruled from 1155) lies sleeping here in a cave and will rise when the Empire is in particular danger. Kickelhahn: Wooded mountain near Ilmenau in Thuringia.

p. 98   Nunc cinis, ante rosa] Lat., Ashes now that once were roses.

p. 103   Stöver's *Life of Carl von Linné*] Dietrich Johann Heinrich Stöver (1767–1822), historian; biographer of Swedish botanist Carl von Linné (Linnæus): *Leben des Ritters Carl von Linné* (Hamburg 1792). The work was quickly translated into English: *The Life of Sir Charles Linnæus*, transl. by Joseph Trapp (London 1794).

p. 103   the martyrs of our 'goddess'] Part of the motto for Carl Ludwig Willenow's *Grundriß der Kräuterkunde* [Outline of Herbalism, 1805], taken from Stöver's book.

p. 103   Master Charles de l'Ecluse – Carolus Clusius of Arras in the Netherlands *Rariorum plantarum historia*] Charles de l'Ecluse's book on rare plants appeared in Antwerp in 1601; the title is cited in Willenow's volume.

p. 103   in re herbaria] Lat., in pursuit of herbs.

p. 107   Nero, Caracalla or Caligula] Raabe here lists Roman emperors with a reputation for madness, brutality and self-aggrandizement.

p. 108   three miles] German 'geographische Meile' = approx. 4.6 English statute miles; three miles then would thus be about fourteen modern miles – quite a distance in mountainous terrain.

p. 108   Blood Rock] Germ. original 'Blutstuhl' (chair of blood), a name meant to evoke the executioner's scaffold or a gynecological chair.

p. 110   'O, how full of briers is this working-day world!'] Shakespeare, *As You Like It*, I, 3.

p. 114   method in my madness] Cf. Shakespeare, *Hamlet*, 2, 2.

p. 114   Frankish prisoners from the emperor Charlemagne's army] Assumes that Germanic tribes used the place to execute enemies, in this case the soldiers of King of the Franks and later Emperor Charlemagne (742–814) who, from the 770s to the 790s, incorporated Saxony and Westphalia into his realm and converted the inhabitants to Christianity.

p. 118   Emperor of Brazil] Pedro II (1825–1891), son of Brazil's first emperor, Pedro I; inherited the throne in 1831 when his father unexpectedly abdicated, reigned until 1889.

p. 121 Juan Fernandez] Archipelago in the South Pacific, ca. 600 kilometres off the Chilean coast. The main island, originally Isla Mós a Tierra, was renamed Isla Robinsón Crusoe in 1970 in recognition of the fact that Daniel Defoe based his famous character on the fate of the Scottish sailor Alexander Selkirk who lived alone on the island from 1704 to 1709.

p. 121 Republic of Haiti] In 1804, an uprising by the descendants of plantation slaves ended over a century of French colonial rule on the island of Saint- Dominique and erected the first independent republic in the Americas after the United States.

p. 122 Linnæus' or Buffon's] Swedish botanist Carl von Linné or Linnæus (1707–1778) was the first to propose coherent principles for classifying and naming genera and species of organisms. The magisterial opus *Histoire naturelle, générale et particulère* (1749–1804) by Georges-Louis Leclerc, Comte de Buffon (1707–1788), was the first modern attempt to systematically present the totality of geological, natural historical and anthropological knowledge.

p. 125 St. Vitus dance] Fit of paroxysm. Legend has it that St. Vitus healed the Emperor Diocletian's son of his convulsive condition. St. Vitus since has become the patron saint of epileptics.

p. 125 Mördling] August's family name is revealed here for the first time. 'Mördling' is, of course, etymologically related to 'murderer'.

p. 126 Schiller, Goethe, Uhland] German writers particularly admired by educated middle-class readers of the nineteenth century: Friedrich von Schiller (1759–1805), Johann Wolfgang von Goethe (1749–1831), Ludwig Uhland (1787–1862).

p. 126 Matthias Claudius / Messenger of Wandsbek] Matthias Claudius (1740–1815), Enlightenment poet and writer of simple, folksy and devout poetry; the name of his journal *Wandsbecker Bote* was frequently applied to the man himself.

p. 128 over the border] Reference to the intra-German borders between different states and jurisdictions. Before the establishment of the North German Confederation, the Harz region was surrounded by the duchies of Brunswick and Anhalt, the principality of Sondershausen and the kingdoms of Prussia and Hanover.

p. 131 Republic of Chile, Venezuela, Paraguay] Venezuela and Paraguay were the first Spanish colonies to declare independence in 1811, Chile followed in 1818. With the reference to American independence by mentioning George Washington and the Republic of Haiti, Raabe evokes the process of decolonization in the New World.

p. 131 I placed my trust in nothing now] Line from Goethe's poem *Vanitas!*: 'Ich hab mein Sach auf Nichts gestellt. Juchhe!'

p. 131 Dom Pedro of Brazil] Pedro II (1825–1891), Emperor of Brazil 1831–1889. Under his father, Pedro I, the Empire of Brazil was established in 1822. He had originally promised constitutionality, yet the political reality, as perceived in continental Europe, was one of abject slavery for the population of African origin and debt-bondage for many European immigrants – Raabe's 'multicoloured rabble'.

p. 134 'Hoho, here's once [...]! Hoho here's twice'] According to Hanns Friedrich von Fleming, *Der vollkommene teutsche Jäger* (Leipzig, 1719), p. 281, chants accompanying mock blows against people who have violated rules of a princely hunt.

p. 137 mirror of a *camera obscura*] Ancestor of the photographic camera, consisting of a small darkened compartment with a tiny hole through which an outside scene was projected onto the opposing wall upside down. In the nineteenth century, angled mirrors ensured the projection of the image right side up.

p. 142 Fray Bentos and had a look at the meat-extract facility] City in western Uruguay, became the centre of the meat-packing industry in the 1860s. The German chemist Georg Christian Giebert mass-produced the famous meat extract here under license from Justus Liebig.

p. 142 Liebig's plant in Munich] Justus Liebig (1803–1873), pioneer in the fields of organic chemistry, biochemistry and chemical education, inventor of condensation of meat extract. Professor at the universities of Giessen (1826–1852) and Munich (1852–1873) where he also set up an agri-chemical company.

p. 142 Minas Gerais] Province in south-eastern Brazil, economic heartland5of the empire; name derived from the mining industry (esp. gold and diamonds).

p. 148 Pereat] Lat., perish, here: step aside.

p. 148 Land of Fire] Tierra del Fuego (Patagonia), word play with the German for spirits in the language ascribed to native Americans: 'Feuerwasser' – fire water / liquid fire.

p. 150 Pottakuds] Corrupted form of 'Botocudo', one of Brazil's indiginous ethnic groups. named after plugs worn in lips and ears (Portuguese 'botoque'). Settlement area in the nineteenth century partly in the province of Minas Gerais.

p. 154 Doctor Eisenbart] Johnn Andreas Eysenbarth (1661–1727), German physician, infamous for his radical treatments, in folklore synonymous with quackery.

Notes on Translators and Translations

German Moonlight

Translated by Alison E. Martin and Michael Ritterson.
The translation is based on Wilhelm Raabe, *Sämtliche Werke* [Braunschweiger Ausgabe], ed. by Karl Hoppe. vol. 9/2: *Erzählungen*, ed. by Karl Hoppe, Hans Oppermann, Constantin Bauer and Hans Plischke (Göttingen: Vandenhoeck & Ruprecht, 1963), pp. 379–402.
The translation emerged from a collaborative project between the English Department at the Martin Luther-Universität Halle-Wittenberg (Germany) and the German Department at Gettysburg College (Pennsylvania, USA) in 2007/08. The contributing students were John Capasso, Calynn Dowler, Alexander T. Englert, Christopher Martin and Jonathan Neu. See Alison E. Martin and Michael Ritterson, 'Reading Raabe, Writing Raabe: *Deutscher Mondschein* as Collaborative Translation Project', in *Germanistik in Ireland* 4 (2009), pp. 33–37. The translation was first published in *Germanistik in Ireland* 4 (2009), pp. 39–51. Reproduced here with permission of the translators.

Höxter and Corvey

Translated by Erich Lehmann, revised by Michael Ritterson and Florian Krobb.
Translation based on the following edition, which follows Raabe's original manuscript much more closely than the text of the *Braunschweiger Ausgabe*: Wilhelm Raabe, *Höxter und Corvey*, nach der Handschrift von 1873/74 herausgegeben von Hans-Jürgen Schrader (Stuttgart: Reclam, 1981) (= Reclams Universal Bibliothek, 7729 [3]). With the editor's permission, the explanatory notes provided in this edition were drawn on here extensively.
Erich Lehmann was born in Strasbourg in 1917 and raised in Frankfurt am Main. Of Jewish descent, his family had to flee from Nazi Germany in 1933. He attended high school in Switzerland and then the University of Cambridge. He enrolled at Berkeley in 1940 and essentially he never left. He received his PhD from Berkeley in 1946 and embarked on a teaching career in statistics. His books *Testing Statistical Hypotheses* (1959) and *Theory of Point Estimation* (1983) are considered milestones in their field. In his retirement he translated into English texts by some of his favourite German authors like Adalbert Stifter and Wilhelm Raabe. His translation of *Höxter und Corvey* was completed shortly before his death on 12 September 2009.

At the Sign of The Wild Man

Translated by Michael Ritterson.
The translation is based on Wilhelm Raabe, *Sämtliche Werke* [Braunschweiger Ausgabe], ed. by Karl Hoppe. vol. 11: *Meister Autor, Zum wilden Mann, Höxter*

und Corvey, *Eulenpfingsten*, ed. by Gerhart Mayer and Hans Butzmann (Freiburg i. Br. and Braunschweig: Hermann Klemm, 1956), pp. 159–256.

A time-worn image of translation is that of physical transfer across some obstacle, often a river or other body of water, from one realm to another. And we tend to imagine the original work of literature being transported thus into new territory, where it arrives refashioned and comfortably accessible to a new audience. But bringing a literary work wholly into the idiom of the receiving language can rob it of its distinctive linguistic character and authorial voice. Conversely, a strict adherence to the source language's patterns and idiom is likely to yield a text so foreign-sounding as to puzzle and alienate readers. The translator's truth lies somewhere between these undesirable extremes. A better image would be a kind of neutral territory on dry land where the original-language author and the target-language reader can meet. We have attempted in this spirit to make Wilhelm Raabe readable in English but still distinctively himself – neither a dutiful replication nor a domesticated reflection of his work.

Raabe presents us with several challenges: German and English editors alike find it necessary to provide pages of explanatory notes for his many historical, geographical, cultural and various other references; that rich, interwoven layer of his narratives would otherwise be lost to today's readers in any language. At times, he exploits structural patterns available to him in the more grammatically inflected German in ways, and to effects, that are hard to reproduce in English. Only occasionally can such a pattern be transferred without a disabling breach of English syntactical form to reveal the distinctive rhythms and contours of his writing. But more important still for us is to offer insight into his narrative temperament, for it is with his narrators and in their techniques that the reader will find Raabe's views on human history, society and behaviour, and his implicit and explicit critiques of his readers and of himself. As the introduction points out, Raabe's narrators bring both themselves and their narrative activities into the foreground, but in ways that subvert the claim to veracity implicit in conventional authorial narration. In order to appreciate both the content and the force of Raabe's project, we must be willing to enter into the spirit of his writing and meet the challenge of his deceptive, subversive narrative forms, assuming that initial judgments of character or situation are not necessarily final; prepared for breaches of the fiction by direct allusion to the narrator's own experience; aware that reader and narrator stand in a relationship of mutual mistrust, that the narrator inclines to disguised and critical self-portraiture, raises false issues, and offers us misleading information.

The need for attentiveness on the reader's part applies at the level of word, phrase and sentence, too, as when the narrator of *At the Sign of The Wild Man* urges that we hurry into the shelter of 'this next *story*'. The German *Geschichte* can equally well mean 'story' or 'history'; and the narrator sounds a historical note in that same sentence with his reference to the young German Empire of the early 1870s. The double meaning will not elude the alert reader in English, given the close aural and semantic relation of 'story' and 'history'. But other features of Raabe's usage can be impossible to represent in the translation – and impossibly cumbersome to explain outside of it. Only the German reader will note that August addresses Philipp at the end of chapter five with three different, successive forms of the pronoun 'you', for which English does not have separate forms: the archaic, courtly *Ihr*, the familiar *du*, and the more formal *Sie*. We can probably attribute August's erratic usage to his delirious state of mind, but in the English translation the leaps are invisible, and the reader must infer his condition from Kristeller's account of the action and dialogue.

Nearly every step on the translators' way through each of these narratives, nearly every word, called for choices of sense, form, sound, register, placement and implied meanings. Add to that the fact that the three stories, all written within the space of just over two years, nevertheless differ significantly one from another in their settings, their casts of characters and in their narrative forms. Readers familiar with Raabe in German will not have much trouble recognizing his voice in each of them, but new readers of him in English must rely on his translators to provide not just the content but also a 'feel' for Raabe on which to base their recognition of him in future encounters. We therefore hope that we've struck a balance with texts that sound distinctively Raabe-like, but only as strange to us as the original German creations will sound to German readers.

Michael Ritterson

The editor would like to thank Nora Maguire, Michael Ritterson, Gabriele Henkel, Mark Opalka, Ritchie Robertson, Hans-Jürgen Schrader and Stephen Lehmann for their support.

Further Reading

German Editions of Raabe's Works

Sämtliche Werke. 3 series with 6 vols. each (Berlin: Klemm, 1913, 1915, 1916; 2nd edn. 1920; 3rd edn. 1923).

Sämtliche Werke [Braunschweiger Ausgabe], ed. by Karl Hoppe and Jost Schillemeit. 20 vols. and 5 supplementary vols. (Freiburg i. Br. and Braunschweig: Klemm, 1951–1959; Göttingen: Vandenhoeck & Ruprecht, 1960–1994; and more recent editions).

Werke in Einzelausgaben, ed. by Hans-Jürgen Schrader. 10 vols. (Frankfurt a. M.: Insel, 1985).

Höxter und Corvey. Eine Erzählung, ed. by Hans-Jürgen Schrader (Stuttgart: Reclam, 1981).

Zum wilden Mann. Eine Erzählung, ed. by Axel Dunker (Stuttgart: Reclam, 2006).

English Translations of Raabe's Works

Abu Telfan; or, The Return from the Mountains of the Moon, transl. by Sofie Delffs, 3 vols. (London: Chapman and Hall, 1882).

The Hunger-Pastor, transl. by [Gilbert] Arnold [Congdon] (London: Chapman and Hall, 1885).

'How the *Black Galley* Took the *Andrea Doria*', transl. by R. G. L. Barrett, in *Great Sea Stories of All Nations*, ed. by H. M. Tomlinson (London: Harrap; Garden City, NY: Doubleday, Doran, 1930), pp. 947–953.

Else von der Tanne (*Elsa of the Forest*), transl. by James C. O'Flaherty, introd. by Janet K. King (University, AL: University of Alabama Press, 1972).

'Horacker', transl. by John E. Woods, in Wilhelm Raabe, *Novels*, ed. by Volkmar Sander. The German Library, 45 (New York: Continuum, 1983), pp. 1–153.

'Tubby Schaumann', transl. by Barker Fairley, rev. by John E. Woods, in Wilhelm Raabe, *Novels*, ed. by Volkmar Sander. The German Library, 45 (New York: Continuum, 1983), pp. 155–311.

'Celtic Bones', transl. by John E. Woods, in *German Novellas of Realism II*, ed. by Jeffrey L. Sammons. The German Library, 38 (New York: Continuum, 1989), pp. 74–108.

'St. Thomas', transl. by John E. Woods, in *German Novellas of Realism II*, ed. by Jeffrey L. Sammons. The German Library, 38 (New York: Continuum, 1989), pp. 29–73.

The Odin Field: A Story, transl. by Michael Ritterson (Rochester, NY: Camden House, 2001).

Studies

Barker Fairley, *Wilhelm Raabe: An Introduction to His Novels* (London: Oxford University Press, 1961).

Jeffrey L. Sammons, *Wilhelm Raabe: The Fiction of the Alternative Community* (Princeton, NJ: Princeton University Press, 1987).

Jeffrey L. Sammons, *The Shifting Fortunes of Wilhelm Raabe. A History of Criticism as a Cautionary Tale* (Columbia, SC: Camden House, 1992).

John Pizer, 'Wilhelm Raabe and the German Colonial Experience', in *A Companion to German Realism 1848–1900*, ed. by Todd Kontje (Rochester, NY: Camden House, 2002), pp. 159–181.

Wilhelm Raabe: Global Themes — International Perspectives, ed. by Dirk Göttsche and Florian Krobb (London: Legenda / Modern Humanities Research Association, 2008).

German Moonlight

Olaf Schwarz, '"… das Entsetzliche im ganzen und vollen": Zur "Modernität" von Raabes "Deutscher Mondschein"', in *Jahrbuch der Raabe-Gesellschaft* 1998, pp. 32–49.

Christian Stadler, 'Unterdrückte Poesie: Der kranke Bürger in Wilhelm Raabes Erzählung "Deutscher Mondschein"', in *Signaturen realistischen Erzählens im Werk Wilhelm Raabes*, ed. by Dirk Göttsche and Ulf-Michael Schneider (Würzburg: Königshausen & Neumann, 2010), pp. 125–135.

Höxter and Corvey

Dieter Arendt, ' "Nun auf die Juden!" Figurationen des Judentums im Werk Wilhelm Raabes', in *Tribüne. Zeitschrift zum Verständnis des Judentums* 19 (1980), pp. 108–140.

Martin Loew Cadonna, 'Schichtungen des Geschichtlichen. Zum Erzählverfahren in Raabes "Höxter und Corvey"', in *Jahrbuch der Raabe-Gesellschaft* 1985, pp. 63–91.

Jeffrey L. Sammons, 'Wilhelm Raabe and His Reputation among Jews and Anti-Semites', in *Identity and Ethos. A Festschrift for Sol Liptzin on the Occasion of His 85th Birthday*, ed. by Mark H. Gelber (New York: Lang, 1986), pp. 169–191.

At the Sign of The Wild Man

Michael Schmidt, 'Nichts als Vettern? Anspielungsstrukturen in Wilhelm Raabes Erzählung "Zum wilden Mann"', in *Jahrbuch der Raabe-Gesellschaft* 1992, pp. 109–138.

Adolf Muschg, 'Der leere Blutstuhl. Einige Bemerkungen über Wilhelm Raabe's Erzählung "Zum wilden Mann"', in *Jahrbuch der Raabe-Gesellschaft* 1994, pp. 85–93.

Jennifer Cizik Marshall, 'Wilhelm Raabe's Apothecary: Two Texts Tracing the Pharmako-logy of the Wild Man', in *Colloquia Germanica* 34 (2001), pp. 27–40.

Axel Dunker, 'First Contact and Déjà Vu: The Return of Agostin Agonista in Raabe's *Zum wilden Mann*', in *Wilhelm Raabe: Global Themes – International Perspectives*, ed. by Dirk Göttsche and Florian Krobb (London: Legenda / Modern Humanities Research Association, 2008), pp. 52–60.

Florian Krobb, ' "Die Ordnungen der alten Heimat": Historisches Erzählen aus der Zeitgeschichte in Wilhelm Raabes "Zum wilden Mann"', in *Jahrbuch der Raabe-Gesellschaft* 2009, pp. 100–112.

Lynne Tatlock, 'Communion at the Sign of the Wild Man', in *Contemplating Violence: Critical Studies in Modern German Culture*, ed. by Stefani Engelstein and Carl Niekerk (Amsterdam and New York: Rodopi, 2011), pp. 115–137.

MHRA New Translations

The guiding principle of this series is to publish new translations into English of important works that have been hitherto imperfectly translated or that are entirely untranslated. The work to be translated or re-translated should be aesthetically or intellectually important. The proposal should cover such issues as copyright and, where relevant, an account of the faults of the previous translation/s; it should be accompanied by independent statements from two experts in the field attesting to the significance of the original work (in cases where this is not obvious) and to the desirability of a new or renewed translation.

Translations should be accompanied by a fairly substantial introduction and other, briefer, apparatus: a note on the translation; a select bibliography; a chronology of the author's life and works; and notes to the text.

Titles will be selected by members of the Editorial Board and edited by leading academics.

Alison Finch
General Editor

Editorial Board

Published titles

1. *Memoirs of Mademoiselle de Montpensier (La Grande Mademoiselle)* (P. J. Yarrow. Edited by William Brooks. 2010)

2. Júlio Ribeiro, *Flesh* (Translated by William Barne. 2011)

3. Wilhelm Raabe, *German Moonlight; Höxter and Corvey; At the Sign of The Wild Man* (Translated by Alison E. Martin, Erich Lehmann and Michael Ritterson. Edited by Florian Krobb. 2012)

For details of how to order please visit our website at:
www.translations.mhra.org.uk

Lightning Source UK Ltd.
Milton Keynes UK
UKHW021933240519
343286UK00004B/788/P